Blonde Eskimo

Blonde Eskimo

a novel

KRISTEN HUNT

SparkPress, a BookSparks imprint
A division of SparkPoint Studio, LLC

Published by SparkPress, a BookSparks imprint,
A division of SparkPoint Studio, LLC
Tempe, Arizona, USA, 85281
www.gosparkpress.com

Published 2015
Printed in the United States of America
ISBN: 978-1-940716-62-6 (pbk)
ISBN: 978-1-940716-61-9 (e-bk)

Library of Congress Control Number: [LOCCN]

Cover design © Julie Metz, Ltd./metzdesign.com
Author photo © Dave Kelley
Interior Illustration © Kristen Hunt

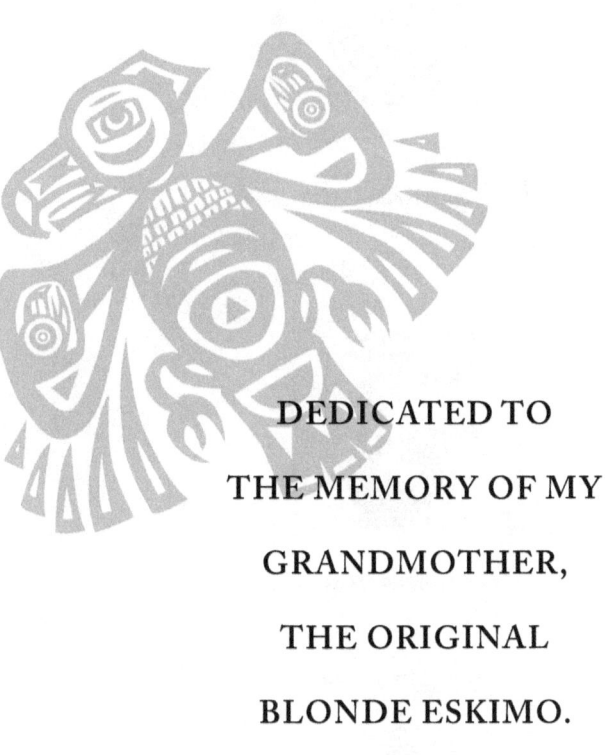

DEDICATED TO
THE MEMORY OF MY
GRANDMOTHER,
THE ORIGINAL
BLONDE ESKIMO.

The Raven: trickster and truth seeker

~~~~~~~

The Fox: swift and cunning

~~~~~~~

The Bear: strength and courage

~~~~~~~

The Eagle: leader and protector

"You never really know your friends from your enemies until the ice breaks."

— ESKIMO PROVERB

〰〰〰

Prologue

August 11:

I'm almost there. I can see the island just on the horizon. It looks ominous with the heavy mist surrounding it. I can feel the sweat trickling down my back and my heart accelerating at the thought of stepping foot on its pebbled beaches. I don't want to go there, I don't want to stay there, but I have to. There's no other choice.

My grandmother lives on this island and I'm staying with her for my senior year while my parents travel throughout Europe. It wasn't originally planned this way. My parents were going to wait until I finished my senior year of high school and take me with them, but something changed their minds. Something they felt they couldn't share with me.

There's no arguing with them. Believe me, I tried! I gave them several examples of why I needed to stay with my friends but they wouldn't listen. They didn't care how devastated I was about spending my senior year on the island. I can still hear their steely voices bouncing around in my head, telling me there was no other option. I had to live with it because I was the child and they were the adults. Really? Like I needed to be reminded I don't have control of, or even a say in, my own life until I turn eighteen. My father says twenty-one, but he is joking, right? Right???

Eventually, I had to deal with their decision and the drastic changes that were in store for me. I played along with my parents by letting them think I was excited to stay with my grandmother; when in reality, just the thought of staying longer than a week at that place makes my stomach turn. It terrifies me. Oh, don't get me wrong, I love my grandmother with all my heart and I would love to see my friends again, but it's the island and the town itself. There is something off about it, something strange and disturbing.

What island am I talking about? Well, it's one you've never heard of. You won't find it on any map or on the Internet. Most people forget once they're told. I tried to tell my friends several times about my visits, but once the name passes through my lips, my friends' eyes glaze over. They start mumbling about Nome, Alaska, and how that's a great place to visit. Really, how can you not know a place exists? It's like it's been obliterated from existence and no one believes me. It makes me feel crazy. Anyone reading this journal entry probably thinks I am. Well, I'm not, and I'll prove it!

All right, here goes nothing. The island is called Spirit. It's about seventy-five miles off the coast of Nome, Alaska, resting in the Arctic Ocean. One town is located at the heart of the island. I can't explain it, but the town seems off, like it's hiding a secret.

The townspeople are nice, but they stare a lot and keep their distance, as if I have a virus and they don't want to catch it. Maybe it has to do with feeling like an outsider or maybe it has to do with my appearance. My father and mother are full Inuit. I, on the other hand, don't even look native. I was born with white-blonde hair, fair skin, and gray eyes. Most of the people in Spirit call me the Blonde Eskimo. My parents named me Neiva after the river outside of Nome. It also means snow in Latin, and I think it fits perfectly with my fair skin and light hair. It has a fairy-tale ring to it—kind of like Snow White? Yay, something right in my life.

Sometimes I ask my parents if I was adopted at birth or the product of the milkman. They insist that I'm biologically theirs, that somewhere down the Ellis line we had Swedish descendants and I must have inherited their looks. Sounds believable, right? I still ask my doctor every year if I'm adopted. He laughs and I frown every visit.

Anyway, back to the real focus, Spirit. I feel it's a mystery waiting to be solved. I heard my history teacher talk about the Alaskan Triangle, also known as the Devil's Graveyard. This triangle is similar to the Bermuda Triangle, where planes, ships, and people disappear. My teacher said the triangle is located between Juneau, Anchorage, and Barrow, Alaska. That's where strange things happen and people vanish. The tribal elders believe it's the doorway to the spirit world. But I know they're wrong. I believe the island of Spirit is at the center of the triangle and the doorway lies there.

I've been frustrated and misguided for the longest time. Now, spending my senior year at another school and being excluded from the trip to Europe is the final straw. I've decided I'm going to find out Spirit's secret. I'm going to prove to my friends and family I'm not just a teenager with a vivid imagination. I'll prove my history teacher's wrong and I'm right. That this triangle, this Devil's Graveyard, lies in Spirit. Once I uncover the truth, everyone will listen.

Watch out, Spirit. Secrets are going to be revealed and I'm telling the world.

THE BOAT LURCHED FORWARD, causing the journal to fly out of Neiva Ellis's hands. It dropped onto the deck with a smack, quickly sliding toward the side railing. To Neiva's dismay, the journal stopped at the very edge of the ship and now was teetering like a seesaw over the edge. One wrong move would cause it to fall into the icy waters below.

She bought the journal to chronicle her experiences on the island. Thinking photos and firsthand accounts might persuade her family and friends to see the truth, she thought a journal was a good start, but apparently the island didn't agree.

Could this be the beginning of her discoveries or was she just being paranoid?

Grunting loudly, Neiva sprinted from her chair. It only took her three long strides to reach the journal before she snatched it up, her long fingers wrapping around its black leather cover. A loud sigh escaped her lips as relief washed over her. The journal was safe. Her work could continue and she could write another entry before the boat entered port.

Clutching the journal to her chest, she cradled it like an infant, as if that would keep it safe. She quickly glanced over the railing toward land and narrowed her eyes.

"You're not getting this journal," she whispered.

A piercing scream broke the silence, causing Neiva to whip her head up to the skies. Circling above her was a giant bird unlike anything she had ever seen. Black, oily feathers blanketed its body with lethal talons anchoring below, gleaming like obsidian knives in the sunlight. She could feel its eyes upon her, a hard gaze that made her feel like its next meal.

Doom seeped into her chest, making her breathing labored and her heart torpedo into overdrive. The hairs on the back of her neck tingled with anticipation while sweat trickled down her back. Something horrific was about to happen, and she needed to take cover.

Creeping across the deck, Neiva kept her eyes on the bird as it continued to circle the ship. The door leading to safety was almost within reach, but before she could grab the copper handle, the bird let out another ear-piercing scream. Folding its wings, it dove straight for Neiva with its talons exposed.

Fear cracked through Neiva like a whip, pushing her forward. She scrambled for the door, shoving the journal over her head and into the path of the oncoming bullet. Unbeknownst to her, that was exactly what the bird wanted.

Within seconds, the bird was on top of Neiva. Its massive talons shredded the leather case as it tried to rip the journal free from her grasp. She screamed for help, to no avail. Not a soul was around. It was just her and the bird, fighting over the journal.

This can't be happening, Neiva thought as the bird finally wrapped a talon around the shredded leather. It was too late. The bird's claws had so much strength behind them; there was no way she was going to get her journal back.

With renewed determination, she clutched the bird's tail feathers with her free hand and pulled. A wail of pain erupted from the bird's chest causing it to beat its wings frantically. Its talon pierced Neiva's hand, causing a sharp pain to lace up her arm. Crimson blood trickled between her fingers, loosening her grip. With a final tug from the bird, the journal broke free from the safety of her hands and became airborne. She fell to the ground, cradling her injured hand. She could only watch in defeat as the bird took flight with her journal, straight toward the island.

Very carefully, she sat up and glanced around the deck. There wasn't a soul in sight. She was the only person on her way to Spirit, which meant no witness to the strange attack. No one to tell her she wasn't crazy and a bird did in fact steal her journal.

How could she have predicted this? She thought she would uncover a secret society similar to the Illuminati or maybe buried treasure, but this encounter had left her mind reeling. She had to wonder what she was getting herself into.

It was scary, but she wasn't going to give up. What happened today just added fuel to the fire and made her more determined to unearth the truth. A teenager's revenge can be lethal. If you hide something, they will find the truth. A small devious smirk spread across her lips as the island drew closer.

"Bring it," she whispered.

Chapter 1

PEERING OUT THE WINDOW, Neiva nervously tapped her fingers against the glass. Storms raged outside and gloomy clouds hovered overhead. The wind and rain distorted Neiva's view, making the town look like something out of a Picasso painting. Pressing her face against the window, she searched for her friend's black truck, but there was no sign of him—only darkness.

She peeked down at her hand. The wound was slowly healing. The bird had broken the skin and the cut was deep enough to leave a little scar, almost in the shape of a heart. *Thank goodness the scar wasn't any bigger,* she thought. How would she explain the attack? Her story would sound unbelievable, and everyone would laugh at her. In fact, she still couldn't believe what had transpired on the boat. Did it really happen?

With a deep sigh, Neiva got up from her perch by the window and walked toward her bathroom. Halfway across the room, she noticed the stack of postcards littering the top of her desk. They looked like leaves covering the ground on a fall day, reminding everyone that the warmth of summer was over and winter was on its way. A sudden rush of sadness briefly washed away the nervousness and excitement burning deep in her stomach.

The postcards were from her parents, wishing her good luck on her new adventures and encouraging her to have a great time at her new school. She loved receiving the postcards, but they did not fill the gaps of loneliness or the anger she felt about being left behind. They only reminded her of what she was missing out on—an adventure—and how she would rather be in Europe exploring the sights than living on this island.

Her eyes flashed over to the object next to the postcards. It was a new journal. Once her grandmother learned of the demise of Neiva's old journal, she bought Neiva a new one. Three weeks had passed since the attack and nothing strange had happened. It almost seemed like it was a dream. Sometimes she wished it was a dream and everything would be normal.

Neiva rushed into her bathroom before the tears started to form in her eyes. Usually when she got angry, she cried. Her mother said it was just hormones, but Neiva knew she was holding back a ferocious temper, one similar to a volcano waiting for the right elements to explode. Wanting answers and missing her parents more than she thought made her even more sensitive than normal. And who wants to go to a new school during their senior year?

With a deep breath, she peered into the mirror to reassure herself that she was ready for the day. Her platinum-blonde hair lay in thick waves down her back, landing just above her waist. Her eyes were lined with black liner and mascara, emphasizing the intensity of her gray eyes. It was the only makeup she allowed herself to wear. She believed in focusing on her strongest features, and to Neiva, they were her eyes, the windows to the soul. She could tell a lot about someone just by catching a glimpse of the emotions burning within their eyes. She could even catch someone in a lie just by the way the person's eyes flickered off to the side, avoiding eye contact.

Neiva's eyes were not a normal gray color but rather a

grayish blue similar to the freezing Arctic Ocean. The strange thing about her eyes, other than the color, was that they seemed to change color when she was moody. She considered them a curse because her parents could easily tell what mood she was in by the color of her eyes. If Neiva was angry, her eyes would turn the color of storm clouds; if she was sad, the blue in her eyes became more prominent. So, when her parents asked if she was okay, she couldn't use the typical teenagers' response of "I'm fine." Her parents would call her bluff, and she would have to tell them the truth. Like most teenagers, Neiva didn't like talking about her feeling with her parents.

With one final look at herself, she headed for her closet. Quickly reaching in, she grabbed a heavy black sweater, which was fitting for the mood she was in, and a pair of ripped jeans. She pulled the jeans over her black leggings, tucking them into her knee-high combat boots. Laced all the way to the top, the boots landed just below her knees, making her legs feel like they were encased in armor.

"Neiva! Neiva!" Her grandmother shouted from downstairs. "Nate is here! You better hurry or you're going to be late!"

Neiva was about to dash out of the closet, but froze. Out of the corner of her eye she could see a strange shadow floating near the ceiling. Long tentacles spread out from its center, like octopus arms moving from an unseen current. Whatever the thing was, it was alive and moving toward her.

Paralyzed by shock, she shut her eyes. This might be her second encounter with the island's sinister secrets. She shouldn't be afraid. She had to be brave. As if a switch turned on inside her, Neiva relaxed. This is what she wanted, what she needed to prove her first encounter was real. Taking a deep breath and readying herself for what she might see, she opened her eyes.

Dumbfounded, Neiva stared at the wall. Her eyebrows furled in puzzlement. Nothing was there. The sudden excitement of another discovery evaporated and the doubt seeped back into her thoughts. Maybe she was getting her hopes up.

"Damn," she hissed.

"Neiva! Hurry up!" Her grandmother's stern voice echoed throughout her room.

Snatching up her pink backpack and brown bomber jacket from the bed, she flew out of her room. She stumbled down the stairs, taking two steps at a time. In a last attempt to pull her jacket on, she ended up bumping into the couch and knocking a lamp over.

"No!" Neiva exclaimed as she dove to the floor. She caught the lamp just before it hit the ground.

"Are you okay, Neiva? I thought I heard a noise?" Her grandmother asked from the kitchen.

"Oh! Everything's fine. I'm just lacing up my boots!" Neiva lied as she hastily got up.

Fumbling with the lamp for several seconds, Neiva finally placed it back on the side table. She examined it doubtfully, expecting the lamp to fall over. There was something mysterious about the lamp. It was an antique with faded pictures of polar bears and hunters etched onto its glass. It was supposed to be the story of her family and how they came to Alaska. The story told of her family's clan battling polar bears and Vikings before settling in the town of Spirit. Neiva didn't know whether she believed the story or not. Stories tend to be exaggerated as they're passed down from generation to generation. But the lamp was her grandmother's favorite and she would've been devastated if anything had happened to it.

Feeling satisfied the lamp was secure, Neiva's eyes scanned the room. The living room was sparsely furnished. Two brown leather couches formed an L shape with an ivory coffee table sitting in the center. The walls were decorated with photos of the Alaskan wilderness and her family. It made the room homey and inviting. On the far wall rested a huge fireplace with a fifty-six-inch flat-screen TV hanging above the mantel. Her grandmother's pride and joy. Every Friday night Neiva would pick a movie to watch with her grandmother. It was their girls' night together, and Neiva enjoyed the time with her grandmother.

With one last look at the lamp, Neiva bolted for the kitchen. She found her grandmother by the oven, keenly watching the timer. Quickly giving her a kiss on the cheek, Neiva ran for the front door. She was almost down the hallway when her grandmother called out her name.

"I'm going to be late," Neiva huffed. Turning around, she saw her grandmother standing at the end of the kitchen. A huge smile lit her face as she held a single chocolate cupcake in her hand.

"Happy birthday," she sang sweetly.

Neiva's eyes grew large. It was her birthday. With all her thoughts focused on finding the island's secrets, she had forgotten her own birthday. She wondered if she would have eventually remembered—probably not. Her mind was too preoccupied. Starting a new school didn't help the situation either. Just the thought of school made her want to throw up all over the kitchen floor.

Walking over to her grandmother, Neiva watched her light the candle with a single match. Once lit, Grams quickly threw the match into a glass of water, killing the flame. She lifted the cupcake up to Neiva's five-ten frame. Her grandmother was petite and shorter than Neiva by six inches. Her skin was lined with age and her black hair was dusted gray. She looked every bit of her seventy-two years, but it was her eyes that made her young. They sparkled all the time, like she knew a secret the rest of the world didn't know.

"Make a wish," Grams whispered.

That was easy. Neiva only ever had one wish: to know the island's secret. She exhaled, lightly blowing out the candle. "Thanks, Grams."

"You've had a lot of things on your mind lately." She stared at Neiva intently, as if she knew what her granddaughter was thinking. Placing a hand on Neiva's shoulder, she continued.

"It was a last-minute decision for your parents to go to Europe and leave you here for the school year, but they needed too. Your parents had a great opportunity." She gave Neiva a comforting squeeze, then turned to pack the cupcake up in a plastic bag and handed it over.

Yeah, Neiva thought. Usually she visited her grandmother every other summer and then headed back to Anchorage to be with her parents. This year, her mother and father were five to six thousand miles away, and she wouldn't see them till the end of the school year. It was her first birthday without her parents, and she was stuck in Spirit.

Neiva gently placed the cupcake in her backpack and gave her grandmother another kiss on the cheek. "Thanks. I just miss them and it's hard to start a new school without them."

"I know, Tanaraq. It will get easier as time passes. You'll adjust. And remember, you're a very special girl," she replied, winking at Neiva.

Neiva's heart melted and pride swelled throughout her chest. Given to her on her sixteenth birthday by her grandmother, Tanaraq meant granddaughter of the tundra, free-spirited, and at one with nature. A wild child. The name made her feel more connected to her Eskimo heritage, making her feel less of an outsider and more a part of her family's culture.

Grams took something out of her pocket and handed it to Neiva. "This is a birthday gift for you. You will need it for tonight."

Her grandmother didn't give Neiva time to ask questions before she rushed Neiva to the door. "Well, you better get going. Nate is waiting, and you don't want to be late for school!" Grams gave her a soft push out the door. "Have a great first day!"

The door slammed shut, and Neiva was suddenly outside, promptly getting drenched. As the rain poured down, her hair started to curl. Grimacing, Neiva ducked as she ran toward Nate's truck. She bounded awkwardly through the yard, trying to avoid the mud puddles. Even with the obstacles in her way, Neiva was practically flying across the yard. She had one mission and that was to save her hair, because starting the first day of school with a fro would be devastating. Warm air greeted her as she entered the truck. The air felt wonderful against her cold, wet skin and was a small comfort on a dreary morning. She directed the vents to blow against her face and hair. Once satisfied, she put her backpack down on the floor and turned to look at her friend, who was looking right at her with the biggest smile on his face.

Long black hair fell to his shoulders, slightly blowing in the vent breeze. His white teeth glimmered against his tanned skin, while his caramel-colored eyes gleamed at Neiva. Looking like he just jumped out of a romance novel, the sight of Nate made Neiva's heart skip several beats, and she tried to keep her mouth from dropping to the floor. When did Nate get so cute?

"Happy birthday, Neiva!" he exclaimed. His smile slowly faded when he saw the look on her face. "What? Do I have something stuck in my teeth?"

While Nate was checking his teeth in the rearview mirror, he didn't notice the blush creeping across Neiva's face. She couldn't help but stare at Nate's lips. They looked luscious and sensuous, making her wonder what it would be like to kiss them. Would his kiss be gentle and passionate, or would he be rough and demanding? Shocked at her new feelings, Neiva bit her cheek trying to kill the enchantment.

"You're fine, Nate. I was just noticing your braces are gone, and thanks. I'll let you know how happy my birthday is once school's over," she grumbled. Just saying the word "school" brought back the excitement and nervousness she felt when she first woke up. Pointing to his jeans, she asked, "Are those new? They look nice."

Nate slyly brushed the jeans with his hands. "Yeah, they look good on me, don't they?"

"Yeah, they look really comfy," Neiva gawked.

Tight and very form-fitting, the jeans showed the muscle

definition in his legs. Did Nate recently take some extra testosterone or growth hormone? When Neiva last saw him, he was a scrawny little boy with braces and acne. Now he looked like a Greek god.

Neiva bit her cheek again.

"What's that in your hand?" Nate asked, backing the truck out of the driveway.

"Oh, Grams gave it to me. She said it was a birthday gift for tonight!" Neiva exclaimed. She unrolled the item from the cloth. In her hand was a piece of wood, about two inches long and one inch wide. It had a thin strip of leather looped through the top, and by the way it caught the light, it reminded her of a tiger's-eye.

"Is this supposed to be a necklace or something?" Neiva asked, turning the wood over in her hand. She lifted it up to get a closer look. It was unlike any other kind of wood she had ever seen before. When she ran her index finger against the edges, it was soft to the touch. The wood looked ancient, almost magical.

"Oh yeah," Nate replied, shifting the truck's gears. "That's for your birthday tonight. Every Native gets one when they turn seventeen. It's sort of a ritual of passing into adulthood."

Nate paused briefly, seeing the confusion in Neiva's eyes.

"You give it to Old Lady Gertrude, and she'll carve out your totem. Every person in Spirit receives one on their seventeenth birthday," Nate patiently explained.

Neiva didn't know the town's customs. Her father didn't want her to be a part of any traditions related to the island. No one could comprehend his reasoning, but at least her grandmother refused to keep Neiva completely in the dark.

Still confused, Neiva stared hard at the wood. "Why does everyone receive a totem? I thought totems were usually in front of a house or placed in town squares."

Nate let out a long exasperated breath as he drove the truck forward onto the road. "Totems are considered guardians. Each person receives a totem for protection. It's known as their spirit guide. It connects the owner to nature, and some people believe it helps them control the spirit of the totem when it's needed the most. The legend is when you turn seventeen, you will need the spirit guide for guidance into adulthood."

"So what's your totem, Nate? You turned seventeen a couple months ago."

"Mine is a fox," Nate replied proudly as he lifted his necklace to show her. It was carved from the same kind of wood that Neiva held in her hand. "It's a small animal. But it's swift and cunning. Old Lady Gertrude carved it for me on my birthday. Once you receive one, you should never stop wearing it."

"How come I've never seen anyone in town wearing them?" Neiva asked as she rolled the wood back and forth in her hand.

"We must always keep them hidden underneath our clothes, so the totem lies close to our hearts," Nate replied.

It sounded like a cool ritual, different from anything she had ever heard of, and maybe this was one of the secrets linked to the island. She wrapped the piece of wood back up and put it into her backpack. Once it was nestled inside, she stared out the window and watched the houses quickly pass by.

Unease filled her stomach, then anxiousness, and finally she became sick with dismay. They were almost at the school. Spirit was a small place, and by car it took only ten minutes to get from one end of town to the other.

"Well . . . we're here," Nate whispered as he pulled into a parking space directly in front of school. He shut the engine off and turned to Neiva. "Ready?"

"Yes . . . no," her voice quivered as they grabbed their backpacks and jumped out of the truck. Following Nate as he led her toward school, Neiva couldn't help but notice how his backside equally matched his front side. Tight and well-defined. Oh dear, she was in trouble.

Neiva shook her head several times before glancing up

at the school. Raven Heights was nothing extraordinary. The building was gray with no windows, and cameras were stationed at every corner and at every angle. Great, my new school is a prison, Neiva thought.

It had stopped raining by the time Neiva and Nate reached the front doors. There was a flurry of movement as a group of students rushed to get into the building. Nate grabbed the door before it closed and ushered Neiva inside. The inside was as dull as the outside, with black lockers lining the beige walls and dark brown tile covering the floor. A pair of double doors at the end of the hallway led to more hallways. There were no posters up and no color or liveliness except for the students themselves mingling in the hallway.

The setting made Neiva think of her old school, Ridge Manor, and how different things were there. Bright and cheerful, Ridge Manor could bring a smile to anyone's face as they walked down its corridors. The landscaping around the school was lush and beautiful. Its grassy knolls were a rich green and soft to the touch. When the weather permitted it, she ate outside and enjoyed sitting in the sun laughing with her friends. She was going to miss that. But she felt grateful to at least have Nate.

"C'mon, relax," he said, breaking her reverie. "Our lockers are over here."

Neiva glanced back at him uneasily but followed him down the hall toward a row of lockers.

Nate pointed to the locker at the very end. "That's yours. Be careful," he said as he swiftly played with the combination to his own locker. "Those hallway doors swing inward and you could get hit by students coming in."

Too late. One of the doors slammed into Neiva's shoulder as a student rushed into the hallway. Dark honey-colored eyes grew large as the student caught sight of Neiva. He briefly muttered an apology, and then scurried away to join a group of friends down the hall. Neiva didn't get a good look at the boy's face. The encounter was quick, but she thought it was Nate's buddy Chad. She had briefly met him once and remembered the scar over his upper lip.

"Come on, Neiva. The bell is going to ring soon." Nate slammed the door to his locker shut, spun around, and whisked her through a sea of students.

"Your first class is with me. English . . . it's over here. Room 3-B," Nate quickly said as they entered the classroom. Rushing toward the back of the room, Nate grabbed two chairs near the corner and slammed his body into the chair, causing it to squeak in protest. A look of relief washed over his face.

Casually scanning the room, Neiva noticed it was a stark contrast to the hallway. The room was full of color and personality, with posters of Shakespeare, Mark Twain, and other authors lining the green walls. An old blue recliner sat in the corner by a shelf stacked with a variety of books. At the front of the room was a large dark desk with a fishbowl on top of it. Behind the desk, the chalkboard had a quote written on it by William Shakespeare: "And since you know you cannot see yourself, so well as by reflection, I, your glass, will modestly discover to yourself, that of yourself which you yet know not of."

"What's the hurry, Nate?" Neiva asked as she slid into the desk beside him.

She turned to face him, but he wasn't paying attention to her. His eyes were clearly focused at the front of the room. His neck was at a slight angle and he looked hypnotized with his mouth slightly open. A strange noise gurgled out of his mouth.

Looking to the front of the room, Neiva instantly saw the source of the problem. The girl was five-eight with beautiful long black hair. Her face was molded like an angel and she moved with such grace she reminded Neiva of a ballerina on stage.

Icy-blue eyes locked onto Neiva's stare, sending tingles down her back. Goose bumps started to form on her arms causing her body to shiver. The temperature felt like it had dropped ten degrees.

"So, you're the new girl?" she asked. Her voice was smooth and carried like the wind rushing over the housetops on a cold winter's day. The girl reminded Neiva of a gorgeous block of ice.

Glancing at Nate from the corner of her eye, Neiva could see she wasn't going to get any help from him. He was in a trance, unable to speak. Suddenly feeling jealous, she had the urge to tell this girl to mind her own business, but she promised Grams she would try to be nice and make friends. Her temper wasn't going to get the best of her, yet.

"Well, I'm not really new to the area. I've visited my grandmother a bunch of times over the years." Neiva answered, inspecting her nails. "I'm just attending school here until my parents get back from Europe."

"Oh, yes. The Blonde Eskimo," she paused to look Neiva up and down, "Well, my name is Miranda. I look forward to getting to know you this semester." She abruptly ended the conversation with a turn of her head, sending her hair flying around her like a cape.

"My name is Neiva. Nice to meet you too . . . not," Neiva watched sourly as Miranda took a seat in the front row. She could already see Miranda was going to be trouble, and the fact she had Nate's attention made Neiva's insides flare with anger.

"Hey, Neiva!" a musical voice chirped.

A small figure bounded down the aisle and sat in front of Neiva. She was Nate's friend Brie, aka Breezy. Long brown hair fell over her shoulder blades with messy waves angling around her face, showcasing her high cheekbones. Her eyes were emerald green with specks of yellow floating around the irises. She was very petite, only coming up to Neiva's armpits.

Neiva had gotten to know Breezy over all the summers she had spent in Spirit. She was sweet-tempered and very patient. They instantly hit it off from the very beginning and became great friends.

"Oh, no. Nate's in his robot mode," Breezy snapped her fingers in front of Nate's face.

Pointing to Miranda at the front of the class, Neiva hissed, "I met the lovely girl at the front of the class. Such a charmer. And she apparently has some kind of effect on Nate."

A deep laugh erupted from behind Neiva. Spinning around in her seat, she locked eyes with Vivian, who was casually leaning against the back wall. She was just as tall as Neiva, with long, black hair down to her waist that was always kept in a single braid. Black tribal tattoos graced both arms from her wrists to her shoulders. Always silent and secretive, Viv was a complete mystery to Neiva.

"Nate is enamored with the Ice Queen," Viv said, full of disdain. "He's been crazy about her since preschool. Kind of sad really. She treats him like dirt on the bottom of her shoe, and he would still do anything for her."

Neiva's lip curled. She didn't like Miranda at all, and to hear how Miranda has been treating Nate made Neiva's temper rise to the surface. Suddenly, she felt like she had some competition.

Viv peeled her back off the wall and sat to the right of Neiva. Stretching her long legs into the aisles and leaning back with her arms crossed over her chest, she turned to Neiva, her amber eyes sparkling with playfulness. "So, your birthday ceremony is tonight. You excited?"

What was so big about turning seventeen? Neiva didn't understand. Wasn't sixteen the big celebration because that's when teens get their licenses? That's when she received her Eskimo name. And eighteen was when teens officially became adults. Seventeen was just stuck in the middle, just another birthday. But Neiva liked the idea of getting a totem made just for her.

"I don't know what to be excited for. And there's a whole ceremony? What's the big deal about turning seventeen?" Neiva leaned forward, hoping to get some answers out of Viv.

Feeling the excitement emanating from Neiva, Viv's voice deepened. "Well, it's a turning point in your development. Seventeen is a critical age because that's when—"

In the blink of an eye, Nate appeared in front of Viv, clamping a hand over her mouth. His eyes blazed with both fear and anger. "Neiva, stop asking questions. You will eventually learn the answers. Viv, shut up and mind your own business. You know the rules."

"What?" Neiva opened her mouth, but was abruptly quieted when Nate waved his finger in front of her face.

Knowing not to push the issue further, Neiva kept her mouth shut and didn't ask any more questions. She wasn't going to get any answers from him. She would be patient. The truth always revealed itself in the end. She figured if there was nothing she could do about it, why push the issue? Plus, this could lead to unraveling the truth about the island and its secret. She needed to be patient.

Glaring at both Viv and Neiva, Nate slowly removed his hand from Viv's mouth. He threw his hands up in frustration as he stomped back to his desk.

Neiva wanted to apologize to Viv for Nate's behavior, but their English teacher walked in. He was pleasantly plump and balding on top, with thick, wire-rimmed glasses and a smile that lit up the entire classroom. "Welcome to English. My name is Mr. Perry and I have many journeys to take you on during this semester. Let's get started."

Viv sat silently for the rest of the class with her arms crossed. Not once did she glance in Nate's direction. Miranda, on the other hand, kept glancing back at Neiva, as if she too were sizing up the competition.

Chapter 2

THE REST OF THE SCHOOL DAY went by in a blur and before Neiva knew it, it was 2:15 p.m. and the final bell was ringing. Gathering her books and backpack from her locker, Neiva slowly headed outside. She was surprised to see the sun out and shining very brightly. Its warm rays felt inviting upon her cold cheeks.

Neiva tilted her head back to the sun and closed her eyes. She tried to concentrate on the warmth of the sun, but her mind kept reverting back to the day's events. She had a strange feeling something significant was about to happen, that some of her questions were about to be answered. A flutter of excitement blossomed within her chest, and her fingers began to tingle with anticipation.

"See, it wasn't that bad, was it?"

The soft musical voice startled Neiva. She quickly opened her eyes to see Breezy standing in front of her. Breezy's green eyes glowed in the sunlight, and for a split second Neiva could have sworn they looked wild, almost catlike. But the illusion was fleeting and gone before Neiva could interpret the meaning.

"It was okay," Neiva began, guiding Breezy to Nate's truck.

"I just couldn't concentrate. I have too many questions running through my head about what's going to happen later and why Nate won't tell me anything."

Nate was waiting in the truck with his music blaring. For the whole day, he would not speak to Viv or Neiva. In response, Viv wasn't talking to anyone and stormed out of school when the final bell rang.

"Everything works out in the end," Breezy replied with a wink. "You'll know what you want to know soon enough. And you're going to have a lot of fun tonight. Enjoy your birthday with your family! Viv and I will take you camping this weekend. We can have a great girls' night. And complain about Nate and boys the whole time."

Breezy's eyes were large and full of mischief. She blinked once then contorted her face, crossing her eyes while sticking out her tongue. Neiva couldn't contain herself and burst out laughing. Dropping her books to the ground, she held her stomach and laughed so hard she felt like she was going to pee her pants. It felt great, a release from the day's events. The weight on her chest slowly began to feel lighter.

She could hear Breezy's high-pitched laugh alongside her own, and when Neiva looked up, Nate was standing in front of them with a confused look on his face. This caused both Breezy and Neiva to fall to the ground laughing even harder.

"Girls, you're all *crazy*," muttered Nate as he jumped back into the truck, slamming the door shut.

When Neiva couldn't laugh anymore, she slowly got to her feet.

"Don't let Mr. Grumpy-Pants ruin your day," Breezy giggled. "We'll see you tomorrow. Have a great night! You're in for some surprises!"

Neiva waved good-bye and hopped into Nate's truck. She watched Breezy bounce away, her bag swinging at her hip. Suddenly Neiva had another glimpse of Brie with wings and a tail, but then it faded as quickly as it came.

Great, Neiva thought. She could add hallucinations and

vision problems to her ever-growing list of how the island is making her crazy.

Neiva turned to Nate. He was slouched in the driver's seat with a big scowl on his face. His lower lip protruded out, making him look like he was scowling and pouting at the same time. Spinning to Neiva, he narrowed his eyes at her.

"No more talk about your birthday," he said firmly, staring at Neiva intently.

Feeling as if Nate was looking into her soul, Neiva could only nod in agreement.

"So, that wasn't bad, was it?" he began again. Nate's eyes veered casually back to the road as he eased the truck out of the parking lot.

Regaining her voice, Neiva replied, "It was a pretty good day except for what happened with Viv."

Nate cut Neiva off before she could continue, "She almost ruined everything, but that's beside the point. I think it went well today. No homework, plus we're in all the same classes. We can help each other with our homework and school projects!" A smile lit up his face as he winked at Neiva, causing her to lose the feeling in her legs.

She loved the idea of being in all of Nate's classes. It just meant more time together at school and after school, with homework and projects. Just the thought of all the time they would be spending together made Neiva giddy with excitement. Would this bring them closer together? Could their friendship blossom into something more? Does he do his homework shirtless?

"Yeah, I guess so," she smiled to herself and looked out the window. An old, blue pickup truck was pulling out of her grandmother's driveway. Catching a glimpse of an old man with white hair and a scar over his left eye, Neiva gasped. The old man looked like her grandfather, but it couldn't be. He died in a boating accident long ago, when Neiva was only six. His ashes were scattered around the island as a way of protecting his family and friends.

Her mind was reeling. First, the black thing in the closet,

then Breezy, and now this? Was the island playing with her mind? Could she now see ghosts? Another crazy item she could add to her list.

Ignoring Nate's ramblings about their English teacher, Neiva quickly got out of the truck. Something was wrong. "I see dead people," Neiva whispered to herself, her eyes searching for answers as the Ford drove away.

Rushing into the house, she dropped her bag off by the door and ran into the kitchen.

"Grams, I'm home!"

Her grandmother was sitting at the kitchen table, her head slightly bowed with her hands clasped together. Tears streamed down her checks.

"Oh, Grams!" Neiva exhaled. Fear gripped her chest as she dashed over to her grandmother.

Dropping to her knees so she could be at eye level with her grandmother, Neiva wiped away her tears. Concern killed any other thoughts of the day, even possibly seeing her grandfather's ghost. Nothing mattered right now. Just her grandmother, because she meant the world to Neiva, and whatever was ailing her needed to be fixed.

"What's wrong?"

"Oh, Neiva, you're home. I'm fine. I just had a visit from an old friend," Grams replied.

Hearing the words "old friend" made Neiva's anxiety about possibly seeing her grandfather's ghost slowly dissipate. The man's features were similar, but it just couldn't be him. Believing the hallucinations were brought on by the island, Neiva vowed she would protect her grandmother from its evilness. If this old friend had anything to do with the island's secret then Neiva was going to get answers. She was about to confront her grandmother for a more truthful answer, but Nate ruined the chance.

"What the heck, Neiva? Just leave without saying good-bye!" Nate dramatically exclaimed as he rounded the corner into the kitchen. He jolted to a stop as soon as he saw the scene before him. Wanting no part of the girl drama, Nate slowly backed out of the room.

"OH! I can see you're both busy. I'll be upstairs," he explained as he ran up the stairs, seeking the safety of Neiva's room.

Turning her attention back to her grandmother, Neiva placed a hand on her Grams's leg. Neiva was shocked by her grandmother's willowy slimness and the dark circles under her eyes. "Grams, what's wrong? I can tell you're keeping something from me."

"It's nothing, Neiva. Just an unexpected visit and news from an old friend. Don't worry. I'm fine. I just don't like surprises." She paused and looked at her granddaughter with love. Cupping Neiva's face within her hands, she placed a kiss on Neiva's forehead, "Just know that no matter what happens in life, I love you with all my heart. You are a very special girl. You're my Tanaraq."

Neiva searched her grandmother's face for answers. Whatever was really ailing her grandmother was hidden behind a forced smile.

"So, how was your first day of school? Was it fun?" Grams said with a chuckle. She allowed Neiva to help her up.

Neiva was glad her grandmother was feeling better, but knew something was wrong. For the time being, she wasn't going to push it any further, so she decided to go along with her grandmother's distraction. A fake smile was far better than tears of pain.

"It was a great day and I love all of my classes. It's great that Nate's in all of them," Neiva replied, blushing slightly.

"Ah, he has changed a lot since the last time you saw him. Turned into a big strapping boy," Grams winked back.

"Umm . . . yeah," Neiva blushed.

"Speaking of Nate, you better go upstairs and check on him. I'm sure he is going through your journal right now. You don't want him to know all of your secrets now, do you?"

"Haha. I love you, Grams." Laughing and shaking her head at her grandmother, Neiva left the kitchen. She picked up her backpack and headed upstairs to her room. Once in her room she threw her backpack onto the floor on her way to the closet.

"What are you doing?" she asked Nate, poking her head in.

"Ah!" Nate choked. Gripping his chest, Nate took a deep breath and smiled innocently at Neiva.

He hadn't anticipated Neiva's arrival. Girl drama usually takes hours to de-escalate and he thought he would have plenty of time to find Neiva's journal. He knew she was keeping one somewhere and he eagerly wanted to read all of her deepest, darkest secrets. Searching through her closet was his first choice; he thought he might find her journal in there. However, he never expected it to be out in the open.

"Nate, my journal is on my desk. I haven't really written anything in it yet, so there's nothing for you to read," she pointed out.

"Very funny, Neiva. I was just looking for a jacket that I lost. I thought maybe it was in here," Nate replied, slowly batting his eyelashes, trying to make her believe him. Clasping his hands together, he flexed his biceps for Neiva. Occasionally, his pecs would pulsate in unison, almost like they were dancing for her.

Neiva giggled. Nate was trying to go for the whole punk rocker look, but whenever he gave her the innocent eyes it made him seem like a small boy in his big brother's clothes. It made her want to pinch his cheeks and kiss him at the same time. On the other hand, when he flexed and played with his muscles like he just did, then she thought he was a Greek god and wanted to sacrifice herself at his feet.

"Yeah, yeah. I'm sure you had your eyes on something else," she jokingly said, raising an eyebrow at him.

"No, I swear!" Nate exclaimed.

"Sure, whatever you say, Nate!" Neiva walked out of the closet toward her desk. She sat down and opened her journal. Staring at its blank pages, Neiva grabbed a black pen and prepared to write. Nate's voice slowly faded into the background and the excitement from the day's events quickly dissolved as the pen hit the paper and her thoughts flowed through her hand.

September 3:

I am in trouble. The island is up to something. I think it's messing with my head, making me question my sanity. What's real and what's not real? I'm seeing black spots, hallucinations, and now possibly ghosts?

In a million years I would've never thought I would see my grandfather again. I swear it was him driving the old rusted truck down Grams's driveway. He gave me the same stern stare I always received when I was in trouble. And what about the distinctive scar over his eye? It's exactly like my grandfather's scar, in the exact same spot. What are the odds of someone else having the same scar? Very slim.

And what about the visit to Grams's? Something made her cry. She won't tell me the truth, but I will find out. I don't want to push her because she seems so fragile and pale. I love her so much and just the thought of losing her would crush my world. Seriously, I would be lost without her. She's been my rock, my mentor, one of the few sources of happiness I have on this island. But I need answers. In order to get answers I have to push her. She knows more than she is letting on. Just like the island, she's hiding something.

This brings me to a big question. Why do adults keep secrets from their children? I know they think they're protecting us, but they're really not. What they don't realize about teenagers is that we're human lie detectors. We see right through their lies, because we are the masters of deception. Just like my parents' lies, I can see through my grandmother's lie.

There is one obstacle I didn't see coming. One that

blew my mind and nearly knocked me off my feet. One that could change everything. Nate. What in the world happened to him? I mean, did he take a special concoction? Something similar to what happened to Captain America? I don't know what happened, but he is a BIG distraction. I want to throw myself at his feet, wrap my body around his leg, and beg for his attention. (Really? Is this why people call it puppy love? No thank you.)

I never thought a boy could make me feel so weird. I've had boyfriends before but we were more like best friends. Hanging out all the time, sharing our lunches, and holding hands. Truth is, I've never kissed a boy before. I know, it sounds sad, but I've never felt the attraction or had the urge to kiss a boy until now. Could this be the island trying to distract me from my main goal? Throwing Nate's sudden changes in my face? If this is true, then I will have to control my hormones and fight back. Do they make pills for this?

I shake my fist at you, island. How dare you mess with my hormones? That's so unfair. I'm only searching for the truth. What's so wrong with that?!

SEVERAL HOURS LATER Neiva woke up with a slight headache. She opened her eyes slowly, letting them adjust to her surroundings. The sun had already set, leaving her room dark and cold. The only source of light was coming from her closet.

"I must have fallen asleep at my desk," she muttered to herself.

Stretching her arms up over her head, she let out a long sigh. The stretch felt good and helped release some of the tension in her back. Looking down at her journal, Neiva was glad to see her entry was drool-free and intact. This was a good sign.

As she stood up, the pounding in her head increased, the dull ache intensifying to a roar. Bright spots danced around her vision and her head felt full of lead. Bringing her hand to her temples, she tried to massage some of the pain away. It helped relieve some of the pressure, but what she needed was a Coke, two Tylenols, and a cupcake—her grandmother's cure for all aliments, sugar and pain relievers.

"Ugh, I can't catch a break," she said absently, throwing her hands down at her side in frustration. She marched into her bathroom to brush her teeth. At least she won't have dragon breath before going downstairs, she thought. Grabbing her pink toothbrush, she squirted a bunch of toothpaste onto it, probably more than she needed.

Neiva glanced at her reflection in the mirror. There was something on her face. Leaning closer, she could see a red spot was forming right in the middle of her forehead. She held her breath and leaned in closer. Slightly swollen and red as a cherry, the spot looked like a giant zit.

"Great! I have a third eye now," Neiva snarled as she poked the bump.

A shock wave of searing pain laced throughout her head. She dropped her toothbrush and brought both of her hands to her head. The pain was too much, almost crippling. Grinding her teeth together, she waited for her head to explode. The pain ignited into a thunderstorm then dramatically vanished.

Neiva blinked a couple of times, trying to focus through the tears pooling in her eyes. The spot looked worse. Now, it looked like a giant bug bite. Suddenly, images of tiny spiders bursting though the bump and crawling all over her face caused Neiva to gasp. Slamming her hand onto the mirror, she blocked her view of the massive bump. She hated spiders.

"Wow, too many scary movies," Neiva whispered as she slowly brought down her hand.

"Holy zit!" exclaimed Nate as he walked up behind her.

He tried to touch her forehead, but Neiva swatted his hand away, giving him a ferocious look.

"Tread lightly, Nate!"

"I was just coming up here to make sure you were awake!" Nate said defensively. "I'm sorry. It was the first thing that I noticed when I walked in." Nate paused and glanced at Neiva's forehead. "Are you PMSing? You didn't have that thing on your forehead earlier."

Giving Nate a venomous stare, she picked up her toothbrush and tossed it into the sink. He was right. The bump magically appeared out of nowhere. Her birthday celebration was in less than an hour, and she would have to conceal it.

"Hey, Nate? I'll meet you downstairs. Tell Grams I'll only be five minutes," Neiva said as she stared hard at herself in the mirror.

"Okay. I have a beanie if you need it!" Nate replied as she quickly pushed him out of the bathroom, slamming the door shut behind him. Turning back to the mirror, Neiva assessed the damage.

Five minutes later, Neiva walked down the stairs to greet her family. She fumbled with her freshly cut bangs, making sure the bump on her forehead was covered.

"There's the birthday girl." A loud booming voice welcomed Neiva as she stepped into the family room. It was Mike, Nate's father and her father's best friend. He was a big burly man with giant hands and kind brown eyes.

"Hey, Mike. How's the coffee shop doing?" Neiva asked, plopping down next to him on the couch.

Mike owned the only coffee shop in Spirit. It was called The Magic Pot and it made the best coffee on earth—well, the best coffee Neiva had ever tasted anyway. It was also a great place to work. Neiva worked there whenever she stayed with her grandmother and since she was staying in Spirit for the school year, Mike offered to let her work a few hours a week. It would help keep her occupied during the winter months and put a little money in her pocket, and it meant that she would get free coffee whenever she wanted.

"Oh, same old stuff. Busy all the time and, judging by the numbers, you would think no one in this town owned a coffee maker!" He smiled and winked at Neiva.

"Well, you're lucky that you have such a great staff, especially my help!" Nate piped in, walking out of the kitchen with his chest puffed out.

He was carrying a tray full of cupcakes and five steamy mugs filled with hot chocolate. Placing the tray on the coffee table, Nate whirled around and sat in the chair across from Neiva. Once he saw her, his mouth dropped open.

"I have to admit, Nate, you're doing a great job. I'm proud of you, son," Mike said. Then he shot a stern look at Nate. "And no, you are not ready for a management position. Eventually you will be. But not yet. Hopefully, you won't burn the place down in the meantime."

A dark crimson color slowly crept into Nate's face. Neiva swore she saw steam blowing out his ears.

"By the way, I have your schedule and uniform for you, Neiva. Are you sure you don't want a break from the shop to get accustomed to school?" Mike crossed his arms over his chest.

"Yes, I'm sure," Neiva said confidently. She liked working. It was fun, and it might lead to some answers regarding the island.

"Well, Neiva. I like your new haircut," Grams entered the room and passed out the four mugs, leaving the last one on the coffee table. Sitting in a chair to the right of Nate, her grandmother slowly sipped her hot chocolate while staring intensely at Neiva.

"I just wanted to do something different for my birthday. Kind of like a gift to myself," Neiva replied self-consciously.

"Good for you. It's always nice to do something for yourself." She paused, glancing at Neiva's attire. "You might want to change into something warmer. There is a storm brewing outside. Mike will be taking you out in a few minutes, and I don't want you to get sick."

Neiva gave her grandmother a puzzled look. In response, her grandmother nodded toward the closet by the front door. Shrugging in defeat, Neiva set her mug down and walked toward the closet. She could hear the rest of the family putting their mugs onto the tray and moving around the family room.

A rustling sounded behind her followed by an exasperated grunt. Cologne insulted her nostrils, making the small hairs on the back of her neck rise. She knew it was Nate. She could feel his eyes upon her, an intense gaze. Ever since he had entered the living room, his eyes never strayed from her, watching her every move. Maybe he liked her new look. The thought made Neiva's face turn into a tomato.

Wrapping her scarf around her neck, Neiva peeked at Nate. "Why is there an extra hot chocolate on the table?"

Nate reached into the closet and grabbed a raincoat for Neiva to put on over her jacket. "I know you don't know much about our customs, but this is a great tradition. The extra cup is for our ancestors who have passed on. It's tradition to always make one extra setting for them on a birthday. It's a celebration of life and passing. It's a way for us to tell them that we will never forget them, that we will always cherish them within our hearts, and that they always will be with us."

Tears threaten to spill out of Neiva's eyes. It was the most wonderful thing she had ever heard of and made her heart full of love. She knew the extra cup was for her grandfather.

"Okay. Are you ready for your rite of passage?" Nate asked as he pushed open the front door.

Lightning streaked across the sky. The wind howled like a banshee, sending tree limbs flying in all directions. It looked like hell was unleashed upon the earth, and they were heading right into it.

"Yes," Neiva lied, fighting back the fear threatening to kill her courage.

Why were they going out in this? What was she getting herself into? Whatever it was, it couldn't be good. She knew the island was waiting for her next move.

Chapter 3

MIKE'S WHITE BRONCO SWERVED across the road like a toy, its four wheels barely staying on the ground as it shuddered against the wind. There's no way they were going to make it through the storm.

Tension began to build in her body, starting at the nape of her neck and spreading down her arms and then to her fingertips, where she clutched the seat belt for dear life. And to keep her hands from strangling Mike. He was crazy. Why were they out in this? The storm looked like it was going to eat them alive.

Neiva turned to Mike, who was whistling without a care in the world as his head bobbed from side to side. One gloved hand was fiddling with the radio, while the other barely touched the wheel.

"Uh, Mike? I think you should have both hands on the wheel. The storm looks like it's getting worse." Neiva's voice shook as she tried to talk some sense into the man.

"No worries. This storm is nothing compared to our usual winter storms. Those are practically hurricanes. Now *that's* when you have to pay extra attention to your surroundings," he said with an encouraging smile.

Great, Neiva thought. Storms weren't her favorite part of nature. She was deathly afraid of them. Ever since she was a little girl, she felt uneasy around them. They were unpredictable and a force to be reckoned with.

"No one should be driving in a heavy downpour like this," Neiva squeaked.

Unseen and powerful, the wind slammed into the side of their truck. The Bronco groaned in protest against the wind's might. A quick stab of fear pierced Neiva's soul like a knife in her belly. They were going to die.

"We're going to make a little stop before we head down to the beach. Neiva, do you have the necklace your grandmother gave you?" Mike asked as he turned the Bronco into the driveway of a small house.

The Bronco's lights illuminated the house, revealing its beaten exterior. It looked more like a shack than a house. It was only one story and leaned slightly to the side, as if it no longer wanted to fight the wind. The chimney was crumbling and looked unstable. The entire roof looked like it was going to cave in. Overgrown weeds and bushes encased the front yard, reminding Neiva of a small jungle. The gray paint was peeling off in strips revealing the old, rusted wood below. Diamond-shaped windows were sporadically placed throughout the house. Light escaped one of the windows, casting shadows onto the lawn.

"Yeah, I do," Neiva replied. Reaching into her pocket, Neiva pulled out the necklace, still wrapped in her grandmother's tissue.

Mike stopped the car as Neiva handed him the necklace. He opened the driver's side door. "Stay here. I'll be right back."

He shut the door and headed to the front of the house. He knocked twice before the wooden door opened to reveal an old woman wearing a black robe. Mike greeted her warmly and handed the necklace over. Nodding once, the old woman took the necklace, and then quickly shut the door.

As Mike headed back to the Bronco, Neiva turned to Nate in the backseat. "Who was that?"

Nate glanced at his father who was about to reach the truck. His eyes turned back to Neiva.

"That's Old Lady Gertrude. She's the one I mentioned earlier. I guess you can say she is the town's seer. She warns us about upcoming storms and whiteouts, and does future readings. Anyway, Dad just dropped your necklace off so that Old Lady Gertrude can carve your totem. She should have it done by morning." Nate stopped talking when his father opened the door.

"Wow! It's starting to get bad out here. We better get going," Mike hopped back into the Bronco. He put the car into reverse and pulled out of the driveway.

"I'll pick your necklace up tomorrow, Neiva. It will be interesting to see what totem you get." He pulled onto the street and headed north.

After several minutes, the road opened up and like magic, the beach appeared before them. Mike eased the Bronco onto the soft ground, feeling the pull and give from the tires.

"Well, this is close enough. Let's hop out and get going. Nate, grab the bucket while I get the ax," Mike instructed. He quickly got out and went to the back of the Bronco to open it up.

What in the world do they need an ax for? Neiva cautiously jumped out, pulling her coat tightly around her. She walked to the back of the Bronco and watched Mike and Nate unload their supplies: flashlights, a white bucket, rubber gloves, and the ax.

Nate's attention turned to Neiva. Sensing her curiosity, he smiled slyly, "You will see. Should have a lot of bodies tonight!"

With his fist in the air, Nate ran off ahead, disappearing into the night with his flashlight leading the way.

Neiva laughed nervously. She bet Nate was trying to scare her again. Probably trying to make her believe he was a part of some Eskimo mafia or an underground crime circuit. It would be the perfect prank for her birthday.

Pulling her beanie down over her eyebrows, Neiva marched

over to Mike. She was tired of the secrecy and diversions. She wanted answers and was going to get them. But before the first question could leave her lips, Nate shouted something against the wind. She strained to see him in the darkness, but she could only see the slight glow from his flashlight.

"It looks like we have our first body," Mike stated as he handed her a flashlight and pushed her ahead, "Go on, Neiva. It's your time."

Taking slow, measured steps Neiva pointed the flashlight in Nate's direction. She couldn't see anything past her nose. Rain pounded against her face, restricting her vision. As she got closer she could vaguely see her friend's form and noticed he was not alone. There was a large shape next to him. It was huge, almost the size of a small car.

What is that?" Neiva's voice shook as she asked him, pointing her flashlight at the creature.

"A walrus," Nate stepped out of the way, allowing her flashlight to illuminate the figure. The thing was huge. Its massive head was the size of a coffee table, covered in long whiskers. One long tusk protruded out of its mouth and gashes marked its body.

"Ah, an old one," Mike whispered when he came up beside Neiva. He placed a hand on Neiva's shoulder. "See the scars on its hide. Those are from old battles, maybe from an orca or even a whaling ship. But that one toward his middle is something different, something fresh."

Noticing the wound, courage sprouted within Neiva's chest, giving her the power to creep closer. She could tell the wound was deep and fatal. A large knife or spear could have been the murder weapon. She had watched plenty of shows on the Discovery Channel to know what they looked like.

"It's a spear wound," Mike said, confirming Neiva's suspicion. He knelt down to inspect the wound. "It looks like it was done really recently."

Sadness washed over Neiva. "What happened to it?"

Nate slowly looked at Neiva, his eyes becoming glassy.

"When a storm hits Spirit, it brings with it the bodies of the dead animals at sea. Mostly walruses wash up onto shore because Walrus Island is nearby. It's tradition for the townsfolk to go out in these storms to find the walrus bodies and cut the tusks off. Ivory is a major trade good here. It's worth more than gold. But sometimes we come across bodies that are freshly killed that have no tusks. Hunters illegally killed these walruses, while the tusks we harvest are from mammals dead of old age, sickness, or because of an accident or a fight. Eskimos only believe in hunting for food or to control the population of a species such as bears, so they don't overpopulate an area. That's why there are hunting seasons and licenses. We don't believe in killing for sport. We simply wait for the earth to provide us with what is needed."

"What happened to the other tusk then?" Neiva questioned.

"Well, I bet these hunters lost this walrus when the storm hit. They must have been extracting the right tusk and the storm suddenly surged inland causing the waves to swell in size. I bet these hunters had the walrus in a net on the side of their small finishing boat and just couldn't hold on to it." Mike stood to brush the sand off his pants. He turned to look at Neiva and pointed at the walrus. "This tusk is still in good condition. We might as well take it."

Nate grabbed his father's ax and knelt beside Neiva. "Spirits of the outer world, we thank you for the blessing of this creature's tusks. We accept this offer and ask you to take the creature's spirit into your house. We will treasure this gift and we give our thanks to the creature's spirit. May it rest in peace."

Grabbing a handful of sand, Nate sprinkled it onto the walrus's back. Turning to Neiva, he held the ax out to her. "Go ahead, Neiva. Put the walrus's spirit to rest and claim the tusk as your own."

Shocked frozen, Neiva gawked at Nate like he had suddenly grown three heads. "What are you talking about? Claim what?"

Nate began to twirl the ax in his hand. "That's why we're

here, Neiva. When you turn seventeen, you claim a tusk as your own. It's an old tradition that started back hundreds of years ago. A young lone hunter was sent out on his first scouting mission when he turned seventeen. During his trek, he came across an injured walrus. The walrus was deeply wounded and soon would die, but the pain was too much for the walrus to bear. He asked the young hunter to end his misery, and in return the hunter could take his tusks as a token of the walrus's gratitude. The hunter did as the walrus asked and ended his life with a swift cut to the head. The young hunter brought the head back to the village and told his story. Ever since that day, villagers have sent their seventeen-year-old sons and daughters out to scout for bodies. It became a rite of passage."

"So, you want me to cut its head off?" Neiva gulped and slowly backed away, shaking her head from side to side. There are too many traditions in this town and even if the walrus was dead, she didn't like the idea of chopping its head off.

"I'm not doing it," she hissed.

"You have to, Neiva. We all did it!" Nate exclaimed as he tried to force the ax into Neiva's hands.

"Actually no, she doesn't," Mike said gingerly. "There's no rule book that says someone else can't do it for her. So I think, just this once, we will let it slide." He took the ax from Nate's hands. "Okay, stand back, Neiva. Hopefully this will only take one blow."

As Mike brought the ax up, Neiva started to feel dizzy and the world started to spin. Her focus on Mike began to wane as he brought the ax down. There was a sickening crunch and suddenly everything went dark as Neiva's head hit the sand.

"WHAT HAPPENED?" NEIVA CROAKED.

Her head was slightly spinning and there was a faint buzzing sound in her ear. As she slowly sat up, she noticed something was different. She was on the same beach, but the weather was clear. She could see the stars twinkling in the night sky, the sand sparkled like diamonds, and the ocean was as smooth as silk. The storm was gone. She scanned the horizon. There were no traces of Mike or Nate anywhere.

Neiva stood up. The air was warm and thick with humidity. She no longer felt the cold chill that had settled in her bones; instead she felt the warm breeze gently caressing her skin. The temperature had risen to a comfortable degree, a degree not normally found in Alaska.

Goose bumps of uncertainty spread down her arm. She was no longer wearing her rain gear. Black as the shadows and smooth as silk, a cocktail dress draped her like a second skin. It shimmered in the moonlight falling down to her ankles. She could feel her hair loose and curled, flowing down her back, a black ribbon neatly wrapped around several strands to frame her face.

"Nate?! Mike?!" Neiva shouted, fidgeting with the ribbon in her hair. She strained her ears for any response or sound.

She had no clue what was going on. Where was she and what was going on? The last thing she remembered was the pain that coursed through her head and then everything going black. Was she losing her mind? Was this the island's doing?

Neiva could feel a strange heat along the back of her neck, something she hadn't felt in a while. It was almost foreign, like an alien seeping its way into her chest. Panic was setting in.

"Hello!" Neiva screamed.

Was this a dream? *Please be a dream*, she thought whirling around in a panic. Her hand knocked into something standing in her path. Veering back with her arms out in front of her, Neiva prepared to fight. But to her shock, a large mirror stood before her. Silver markings and gargoyle heads decorated its black frame. It was very unusual, especially since it was floating several feet off the ground.

Her panic dissolved, slowly turning into curiosity. The mirror didn't cast her reflection. Instead, there was a long, dark hallway lit by floating balls of silver fire. The place looked medieval. A slight movement caught Neiva's eye. She swore she saw something moving toward her, a figure at the very end of the hallway. Squinting her eyes, Neiva pressed her face against the glass.

"Shit!" Neiva gasped, pushing herself off the mirror.

There was someone in the mirror and he was walking toward her. Trying to get a better footing in the sand, Neiva backpedalled away from the mirror. The only thing she managed to do was trip over her own feet and fall flat on her butt.

Dazed from the pain, she looked up as the figure reached the mirror. Mist swirled behind him, making him look exotic and supernatural, but it was more than that. He was huge! Well over six feet with broad shoulders and a massive chest. Long black hair fell past his shoulders, disappearing down his back. The color was dark as a shadow cast on a sunny day but occasionally his hair would sparkle, like someone stole the stars from the sky and sprinkled them in his hair.

He was dressed all in black, from his head to his toes. His black shirt with long sleeves flared out at the cuff to reveal black leather gloves. His pants were shiny leather that wrapped around his muscular legs. Neiva could see every curve and definition of his muscles until they disappeared into his knee-high combat boots. Covering his face was a silver mask with human features. Black stars decorated each side of the mask, which covered even his neck and disappeared down into his collared shirt. There were small shadowy slits where his eyes should have been.

Before Neiva could blink, he was in front of her with his leathered hand reaching out to help her up. Glancing at his hand in shock, Neiva bit her cheek to make sure this was real. Her mind could not comprehend what was happening. Was she dreaming or was she just going crazy?

"Don't worry, Neiva. You're not going crazy." His voice was deep and musical, soothing to Neiva's soul. "Just take my hand. I won't hurt you."

For some reason, Neiva believed him, but it didn't stop her

hand from shaking as she reached for his. Warmth emanated through his glove, assuring her that he was alive and not a figment of her imagination. Maybe she didn't see ghosts.

The feeling of comfort disappeared as electricity shot through her hand from their contact. Energy traveled up her arm and straight into her heart. Somewhere deep within her, a door opened spilling out the memories and feelings from past lives. Images flashed before her eyes like an old movie. She saw herself as a hunter, wrapped in thick fur, chasing a herd of reindeer with a long spear. Then another image flashed to her covered in tribal paint, kneeling over a sick child while blowing white smoke around his body. As each image passed, the fear and panic evaporated leaving her full of wonder and knowledge.

As if a TV had turned off, the images disappeared and she was suddenly looking up at the stranger, his face cast down toward her. A beautiful white light wrapped itself around them, linking them together. It felt as though the rest of the world ceased to exist.

A gasp escaped the stranger.

Neiva blinked and shook her head, trying to get her mind back together. She quickly let go of his hand. Like a rubber band snapping in half, the energy disappeared, leaving emptiness in its wake. Sadness washed over her. She wanted to hold his hand forever. She didn't understand any of this. She should push him away, but she didn't want to.

Who is this stranger?

Neiva didn't realize how tall he was until she was standing right in front of him. He had to be way taller than she initially thought because even with her five-ten frame, she had to crane her neck up to meet his gaze. She was used to looking down at the boys in her school, so for once it was nice to be on the reverse side, even if this was just a dream.

"Who are you?" Neiva whispered, playing nervously with the ribbon in her hair.

The tall stranger cocked his head to one side as if pondering

Neiva's question. "I guess you could say a guardian angel."

His voice sent chords of happiness throughout her body. Different from how she felt toward Nate. This was an irresistible feeling of peace and safety. Not a teenager's infatuation. This was something old, something written in history.

"There is not much time. I brought you here to give you a warning," he said as he stepped closer, leaving Neiva's face inches from his chest. He smelled of lavender and the forest, reminding Neiva of something wild and free.

Gently grabbing Neiva's chin, he raised her face to meet his gaze. That one simple touch went through Neiva like fire. It reached deep into her soul, awakening new feelings she had never felt before—feelings that made her body ache for his touch. The desire to have his hands explore her body took her breath away.

"After tonight, everything will change. Trust your friends and no one else," he whispered rubbing his thumb across her chin. He pulled Neiva even closer in, wrapping his left arm around her waist. He brought his forehead down to meet hers. The mask was cold to the touch, but smooth on her forehead.

"Just remember this: The shadows will protect you." He quickly let her go and turned to enter the mirror.

"Wait!" Neiva reached out to grab him. Her fingers brushed the back of his long hair. It felt smooth and soft.

He slowly glanced over his shoulder.

"All your questions will be answered in time," he replied as he entered the mirror. The lights extinguished as his figure walked farther away, leaving Neiva alone.

Dropping her hand to her side, she stared at him dazed and unbelieving. She couldn't think, only stand there and feel. He had stirred something deep inside of her. He had awakened feelings and things from her past. Was she an old soul? Would she see him again?

It was then she realized she never asked him his name.

A breeze gently lifted her hair, bringing the smell of lavender and pine trees to her senses. Music surrounded her mind in a tight embrace as a voice filled her head. It caressed her like a hand would stroke a cheek, making Neiva shut her eyes. It was the stranger's voice. He was whispering to her, one single word. But that single word filled Neiva's heart.

DARIUS COULD STILL FEEL the touch of her hand as he walked away from the mirror. He brought his hand up, turning it back and forth. All of his doubts about Neiva not being the one he was looking for had quickly faded; that one touch had changed everything. His dead heart had awakened, and with every beat he felt more alive. His need to protect her, care for her, and love her was so strong that he would already do anything for her, even give his life. He had to prepare. There was a powerful evil coming, an ancient magic that would change the world, and it was heading straight for Spirit. Its target was Neiva.

Chapter 4

IT WAS MORNING. Neiva was lying in her twin bed, and sunlight leaked through her bedroom window. It made the room look cheerful and bright, full of promises of a good day—a stark contrast from last night's inclement weather.

Neiva groaned as she pulled the covers over her head. She felt lightheaded and spacey. Her head still hurt, a slight ache that was just barely there. But it intensified whenever she tried to remember the previous night's events. She had a confused memory of a strange dream, but it was foggy and vague.

Movement caught her attention. The bed caved in as another body plopped down next to her. She held her breath as the person slowly slithered closer. Just as the covers were ripped back, Neiva screamed right into Nate's face.

"Ah!" Nate screamed. The shock of seeing Neiva awake sent him flying off the bed and onto the floor, landing on his back with his shoes sticking straight up in the air.

"Holy cow, Neiva. You scared the crap out of me." Nate grumbled as he sat up, shaking his head.

"Well, what were you doing creeping on my bed?" Neiva asked flatly, jerking the covers up to her chin.

Nate gave her a sweet smile, "I wanted to wake you up gently. After last night, I wasn't sure how you were feeling." He stood up and walked next to the bed. Placing a hand on Neiva's forehead, he checked her temperature, worry clouding his eyes.

"Oh, I'm feeling better. Just a headache." Neiva gulped as Nate let his hand drop. "What happened last night, Nate?"

"Well, as soon as my dad brought the ax down, you passed out. I didn't know you were squeamish. Anyway, we took you back home to Grams and she took care of you all night." Nate scratched his head in confusion.

Neiva didn't think she was squeamish either but maybe she was becoming sensitive to certain things, like cutting a dead walrus's head off. The dream was the strangest part, though. Bits and pieces were starting to reemerge. It almost felt real, like it really did happen. Just the thought of the masked stranger caused Neiva's chest to tighten.

"Do most people pass out?" Neiva gave Nate a curious look.

"Nope! You're the first one." Nate shrugged his shoulders as a sly smile started to form on his face.

Neiva frowned.

"Dad said it was a combination of the weather and walrus that got you lightheaded. It could happen to anyone." Nate threw his hands up in the air. "I don't know. You're a girl and you fainted. It happens.

The explanations sounded convincing, but why would she have a dream so real that she couldn't tell what was reality and what wasn't? How hard did she hit her head?

She glanced at the clock beside her bed and let out a yelp. It was almost 9:00 a.m. School was already in session and they were late. She ran to the closet to grab some clothes. Fumbling with her pajamas, she rushed to the bathroom. Sometime during the night her grandmother had put her in a pair of cotton pajamas.

Nate tried to catch Neiva as she ran toward her bathroom.

"Whoa there. Grams said we didn't have to go to school today. I already talked to Breezy and she'll get our homework for the day. It's only the second day, Neiva. Relax. Breakfast is ready downstairs."

"I don't want to miss any school, Nate. I hate being behind," Neiva whined, feeling defeated. She let Nate pull her to the bed and sit her down. The pounding in her head started to magnify. She dropped her clothes and started to massage her temples again.

Nate shot her a worried look as he reached into his pocket and pulled out a small bottle of aspirin. He handed the bottle to Neiva, while he grabbed a glass of water on her nightstand. She opened the bottle and poured two pills onto her palm. She accepted the water and downed both pills in one swallow. She sat quietly holding the glass of water.

"Does your head really hurt?" Nate asked carefully, afraid of igniting her temper.

"It's slowly getting better. I'm sure the aspirin will help."

"Okay. Well, everyone was worried about you. You hit your head pretty hard. I'm glad you're feeling better." Nate punched her in the arm. "C'mon, get dressed and meet me downstairs. We can go to school if you really want to go. Let's get some breakfast before we leave. Grams will be happy that you're feeling okay."

Nate walked out of Neiva's room with heavy shoulders. She knew he didn't want to go to school but would go because Neiva wanted to. She had perfect attendance and didn't want to start this school year with a bad start.

Neiva grabbed her clothes off the floor and headed to the bathroom. Just as she was about to reach the bathroom's door, she saw something gleaming in her hair. Reaching up, she grabbed the silk material between her fingers.

Shuddering uncontrollably, she gasped. *It can't be! How was this real? It couldn't be real*, Neiva thought wildly. But in her hands was the black ribbon from the dream.

September 4
OMG!

The dream was real. I can remember everything now. Somehow, touching the ribbon cleared the fogginess and unlocked the events from last night. But it's not just the dream I remember. When our hands touched, electricity shot deep into my soul, awakening feelings and memories I can only vaguely recall. Images of hunting and gathering flashed before my eyes. It was me, but not in this time. It was in the past, before cars and airplanes, when it was just the land and its people.

Does this mean I'm an old soul? I know Eskimos believe the soul never dies. It's not reincarnation but a passing of our souls. We learn from our past mistakes and continue to experience what life has to offer, to make improvements and teach others what we've learned until our journey ends. You can have five to twenty-five different lives, but the old soul is the last leg of the journey. It's the last time to fix things and not screw anything up. Am I on the last leg of my journey? Because if I am, then I'm already screwed.

I'm not sure if the island's a part of this. But I know the masked stranger has the answers. I need to find him. I have a feeling he's the secret I've been searching for.

AN INTENSE AROMA attacked Neiva's senses, causing her mouth to water and her stomach to growl like thunder. She closed her eyes and inhaled deeply. *It smells like heaven,* Neiva thought as she opened her eyes, eagerly taking in the sight before her.

The kitchen was a masterpiece with towers of pancakes drowning in hot maple syrup and crispy bacon piled high next to plates of steaming eggs. Pumpkin bread, blueberry muffins, and waffles littered the table in a colorful assortment. Sitting at the center was a giant bowl of blueberries. It was September—blueberry season—and Spirit was known for its wonderfully large blueberries.

Her grandmother cooked when she was upset, and from the display that morning, Neiva could tell her grandmother was really worked up.

"I'm all right, Grams. I'm fine. Just fainted. No big deal," Neiva urged, giving her grandmother a reassuring smile. "I feel great this morning, just a little headache. But nothing more."

Distress and doubt filled her grandmother's eyes. "Well, take it easy today. You don't have to go to school. I called the secretary and told her you would not be in today."

"Grams, I hate missing school. In all the years that I've gone to school, I've never missed a day. I don't intend to miss one now because of a little fainting spell," Neiva defended.

She was a straight-A student and planned on staying that way. Plus, there wasn't anything she could do at home. If she was at school, she might be able to find out something about her dream.

"Oh, all right. Just eat your breakfast then and I'll take you to school. By the way, I like the ribbon in your hair. Adds a little character," her grandmother said as she placed a large plate in front of Neiva.

Neiva played with the ribbon as she ate her breakfast. She didn't want to take it out. She liked how it looked and it reminded her of Darius, assuring her the encounter was real. But so many questions plagued her mind. What did Darius want with her? When would she see him again? Excitement blossomed at the thought of seeing him again, and this puzzled her. Neiva could not understand how she suddenly had feelings for a total stranger. But then there was Nate, who she was attracted to and suddenly saw in a different light. It wasn't there before, but had suddenly manifested. Was her attraction to Darius the same?

"Oh, gosh. I am in heaven," Nate said as he wolfed down a forkful of pancakes with blueberries on top. Golden syrup drizzled down his chin leaving a shiny goatee in its wake.

Nate about choked on his food. Neiva hit Nate between the shoulders as he was trying to clear his throat. "Nate, if you don't slow down and chew your food, you're going to choke!"

Her remark did nothing to stop Nate from gorging on everything in sight. Soon Neiva found herself doing the same. It was something about her grandmother's cooking. She could make anything taste like it came from a five-star restaurant. And to Neiva, it seemed such a shame to waste any of the food.

"Whoa, guys. Slow down or you will get a stomach ache," Grams said as she took the plates away from them. "I think you've both had enough. Go finish getting ready for school. We leave in five minutes."

Nate tried to grab a biscuit before Grams pushed him out of the kitchen. He managed to grumble a thank you before heading toward the front door.

Helping clear the table, Neiva packaged all the leftovers and placed the dirty dishes in the sink. Giving her grandmother a kiss on the cheek, Neiva encircled her grandmother with her arms, showing her appreciation, "Thanks, Grams. It was delicious. I feel a hundred percent better already."

Her grandmother smiled at her, patting Neiva on the hand. "Go get your coat. We need to get going."

Running upstairs, Neiva gathered her schools supplies, backpack, and jacket. She quickly brushed her hair, making sure the ribbon wouldn't come lose. Buttoning up her flannel shirt, she grabbed her journal on the desk, and then sprinted downstairs. She glanced in the hallway mirror to make sure her eyeliner wasn't smeared.

"Let's go," Grams said as she thrust them out the front door and ushered them to her Toyota truck.

On the way to school, Grams made a short stop, pulling into Old Lady Gertrude's house.

She put the truck into park and turned to Neiva in the passenger's seat. "Go on and get your totem. Do it quickly. Mike didn't have time to pick it up this morning for you. He had to cover a shift at The Magic Pot."

Nate gave a little laugh. "I bet it was Pete. He always calls in."

Pete was Mike's best employee. He helped Mike open The Magic Pot and always pulled extra shifts when needed. But he tended to call in on the early shifts, probably because of the long nights of drinking. This was common among the locals, especially during the long, dark winter season.

Neiva slowly exited the truck and stared nervously at the house. It looked even more menacing during the day. The sky was partly cloudy, casting shadows upon the house, making it seem bleak and wicked. Green, slimy moss grew out of the uneven marble walkway, threatening to trip anyone who crossed its path.

Gathering the courage to knock, Neiva took a deep breath and stepped closer to the door. The dark wood looked weathered and warped, like it could split in half at any moment. Before she could raise her hand, the door opened to reveal an old, haggard woman. She was hunched over making her short and stumpy, barely coming up to Neiva's chest. Her gray hair covered her face like a shawl, hiding her features. An ancient hand placed the totem into Neiva's palm.

"Thank you," Neiva smiled at the old woman.

Jerking Neiva down, the old woman twisted her face up to meet Neiva's gaze. Gray hair parted to reveal a dried up prune face with white, vacant eyes. Thin cracked lips moved as the woman's raspy voice warned, "Take care, child. Darkness surrounds you. Your totem is just the start."

Bam! The door slammed in Neiva's face.

"Uh, did that just happen?" Shocked, Neiva stared at the door for several seconds before slowly shuffling back to her grandmother's truck.

"Well, what totem did she give you?" Nate asked excitedly.

Shaking and feeling disoriented, Neiva unwrapped the cloth. Resting in her palm was a bird. Its details were sharp and strong, almost like it would come alive in her hands.

"Wow, Grams!" Neiva exclaimed excitedly as she looked up at her grandmother and Nate. "It's a raven. That's my favorite animal!" Her excitement slowly dwindled when she saw the looks on their faces.

"Are you sure, Neiva? Could it be a crow?" Grams asked.

"No, Grams. I know the difference between a raven and a crow. A raven's larger. Its beak is curved and bigger than a crow's." Neiva passed her totem to her grandmother.

"It is a raven," she replied quietly, handing it back.

"Wow!" Nate exclaimed, grabbing Neiva's totem. "That's a powerful one. The raven signifies death and rebirth. Eskimo stories say he is the trickster who stole the sun from the eagle. The eagle guarded the sun and would not share his light with the people of earth, leaving them to live in a cold and dark world. The raven was ashamed of the eagle, so he stole the sun from the eagle's home. He flew as high as he could fly and hung the sun in the sky, bringing light into the dark world. Without the raven there would be no sun, only darkness."

"Cool," Neiva replied.

As Neiva's grandmother eased the truck back onto the road and headed toward school, Nate handed the totem back to Neiva. "Yeah, originally the raven's feathers were white but the sun was so hot that it burned and blackened his feathers. That's why the raven is black. It's a cool story. So, what did the old lady say to you?"

"She just said something about darkness surrounding me and that my totem was just the start. I didn't know she was blind, Nate. Does she have the second sight? Is that why you call her a seer?" The questions poured out of her mouth before she could restrain herself.

"She may not have her vision, but she sees many things. It isn't a mistake that she gave you this totem. She always knows what she is doing."

"That's good ... not to be mean but she reminded me of a scary witch from a fairy tale—the kind that eats children for breakfast. I hope I don't ever have to go back there," Neiva muttered.

"Enough talk of totems," her grandmother said, cutting Nate off. "Just put yours on, Neiva, and wear it with pride." She pulled into the school's parking lot. "Can you guys get a ride home from school? I need to stop by The Magic Pot and help out with some of the accounting and office work."

"I'm sure Breezy can give us a lift home. No worries, Grams," Neiva said as she opened the door, anxious to get to class. She waved to her grandmother while she waited for Nate to catch up.

"What's the rush, Neiva? It's break time. We arrived at school between classes. Our class doesn't start for another ten minutes," Nate panted as he tried to match Neiva's pace.

Ignoring Nate's rambling, Neiva walked into the school toward the cafeteria. She walked through the double doors and looked for Breezy and Viv, who both sat in the far corner whispering in each other's ears. A smile slowly formed across Neiva's face. She knew whom they were talking about.

Glancing at the table several rows down, she found their target.

Yup, she thought. They were talking about Austin Brooks, a good-looking boy with blond hair spiked in all directions and piercing golden eyes. He was one of the few tall guys at school, and Neiva thought he was cute. But she did not feel anything for him in the way that Breezy and Viv did. To her, he was just a painting on a wall, something to admire from afar but nothing she would invest in.

"Hey, girls. I see we are gossiping over a certain someone again," Neiva magnified her voice as she sat across from the two of them. She threw her backpack onto the ground and leaned back with a giant smile on her face.

Both Breezy and Viv squeaked in unison as they turned to Neiva.

"So, tell us what happened last night! I got a call from Nate this morning saying you fainted!" Breezy babbled as she grabbed Neiva's arm.

"Whoa. I'm fine. Just a lot happened yesterday and it was all too much. Just a combination of weather and nerves. Plus, my head has been hurting lately. That just added onto everything." Neiva sighed, trying to wiggle her arm loose from Breezy's grip.

"I like your bangs, Neiva." Viv winked at her.

"You should check out her new totem. It's pretty unusual," Nate suggested. He sat down in a vacant chair next to Neiva.

Breezy and Viv both looked at Neiva expectantly.

Excitement coursed through Neiva's hands as she dramatically tossed the necklace to Viv. Swift as a cat, Viv caught the totem, and turning it over in her hand, she whistled.

"This is a powerful totem," Viv stated, her deep voice mixed with shock.

"What do you—" Neiva was cut off when the bell rang, signaling the five-minute mark before class started. Both Viv and Breezy grabbed their backpacks and quickly headed toward the north doors leading to their lockers in the next hallway. They both were leaning into each other and whispering, trying to keep a step ahead of Neiva.

"Hey, guys. Wait up!" Neiva huffed. She kicked back the chair, grabbed her backpack, and ran after them.

A sudden chill emanated throughout Neiva's body. The atmosphere around her became cool and crisp, with the temperature dropping drastically. Her movement slowed, each limb growing heavier and heavier until she couldn't move. Only her eyes were free to move. The rest of her body was frozen.

Rolling her eyes around the hallway, she saw Miranda striding toward her. A dangerous and challenging look crossed her face as she locked eyes with Neiva. Smiling like a jaguar, Miranda's hand flew up in a swift, fluid motion.

A blast of cold air slammed into Neiva, knocking her off her feet. Icy fingers squeezed her chest, restricting the oxygen in her lungs. The warmth in her body began to drain away, leaving her skin cold and her body shaking uncontrollably. Pain pushed tears down her cheeks, freezing around her eyes and nose.

Neiva's mind spun. How did she do that? She had never felt or seen anything like it.

A flare of light ignited within Neiva. Like a match starting a bonfire, adrenaline empowered her muscles to move and gave her the strength to sit up. Irritation skipped through her veins, making her temper boil. Blood rushed to her face, causing the bump on her forehead to pulsate. With every heartbeat, the rhythm became faster and harder until her skin couldn't hold the pressure and split open.

Warmth cascaded from her forehead, spreading down her fingers and hands, as if tiny needles poked her skin. The cold engulfing her melted away like snow on a hot day. Her body relaxed and her head cleared. She felt stronger than ever. Electricity crackled through the air as power rushed out of her like a nuclear bomb, destroying everything in its path. It hammered into Miranda, sending her flying down the hallway.

"Neiva!" Viv and Breezy yelled as they came to Neiva's aid. They dropped down beside her to make sure she was okay.

Peeling her eyes away from Miranda's still form, Neiva's storm-cloud eyes widened in surprise. Everything had changed. It was like a veil had been lifted and she could see clearly.

"Oh!" she wheezed out of her oxygen-deprived lungs.

Gone was the tough biker chick she had come to know as Viv. Instead, a magnificent creature stood before her. A crown of polished black horns rested on her forehead and her eyes glowed an eerie yellow against her red marbled skin. The brilliance of her tribal tattoos radiated down her arms as if lava coursed through them. Jutting out of her hands were sharp black claws, which curved slightly at the tips. Neiva could see a long tail with a sharp stinger at its tip protruding out of Viv's leather jeans.

"Ah, she's okay. Just a little shocked." Viv smiled reassuringly at Neiva, showing sharp incisors behind her black lips.

"You're, you're . . . you're not human," Neiva stammered.

Viv stopped smiling, looking to Breezy for help.

"Neiva, look at me," Breezy demanded, turning Neiva's face to look at her directly.

Her heart beating quickly, Neiva swallowed and gawked at her friend. She was ravishingly beautiful. Emerald-green cat eyes glowed brightly against sun-kissed, golden-brown skin. Long pointed ears poked out of a mane of curly pink hair. Two antennas protruding from the top of her head twitched back and forth, and soft butterfly wings flapped slowly behind her. Her wings were a light golden color with pink spots that sparkled in the light. She had a tail like Viv, except Brie's resembled a lion's.

"What do you see, Neiva?" Breezy asked as her delicate hand grabbed Neiva's chin, moving her head back and forth so she could see the entire hallway.

Confusion and wonder filled her mind. The hallway was not the same boring one as before. Instead it had transformed into something Neiva had never seen before. The black lockers transformed into wooden compartments jutting out of thick, brown walls. On closer inspection, the walls were giant tree roots wrapping around each other forming a solid mass. The floor was made of grass, a bright green color cut short to the ground with flowers sporadically bursting through.

"What's happening to me?" Neiva swallowed, looking horrified. "Why are we in a tree?"

"She can see through the spirit shields," Viv growled, sitting back on her heels.

"Is she okay?!" Nate flung himself beside Neiva. He began to look around like a paranoid rabbit. When he turned his head to look back at Miranda, Neiva could see a tattoo on the back of his neck. It was black and very tribal-looking. Its sleek design formed a fox about three inches long and two inches wide.

"We better get Neiva out of here," Breezy said urgently.

"Viv, grab her backpack while Nate and I help her up."

Breezy helped Neiva stand on her wobbly feet while Nate placed his arm around her waist for support. Viv picked up Neiva's backpack, then whipped her head around to glance behind Neiva.

"Oh, no. Here comes the Ice Queen. Just ignore her and don't answer any of her questions," Viv hissed at Nate.

Neiva wasn't surprised to see Miranda had changed forms too. She did resemble an Ice Queen. Gliding like she was skating on ice, Miranda's white dress flowed around her like snow in a winter storm. Her long hair was a dark indigo blue with frosted white tips, and her skin was the palest blue, similar to the cold September skies. Her blue lips formed into a snarl.

"How the hell did she do that?" Miranda demanded, pointing a frosted nail at Neiva. "She's not one of us."

Breezy opened her mouth to reply, but Nate beat her to it. "It's none of your business, Miranda."

Miranda's jaw dropped. She could make no sense of this. Nate had never talked to her like that before. Ever since they were in grade school, he had treated her like a princess and did whatever she asked. He was enamored of her and whenever he looked at her, he gave her a look of deep admiration. Miranda liked it.

Feeling bitter, she looked over to Viv who gave her a defiant stare. A crooked smile formed at the corner of Viv's mouth as she turned to follow Nate and Breezy, who were guiding Neiva down the hallway. At the last minute, Viv's tail swept past Miranda's face, missing her nose by less than an inch. Miranda knew it was a warning not to follow them.

She stared after them as they ushered Neiva out of the building. Her ice-cold eyes glowed with fury as her temper rose. Blue frost crawled up her arms from her fingertips all the way to her elbows. The room quickly dropped in temperature and ice started to spread across the floor.

Snarling very loudly, Miranda turned and hurried away in the opposite direction. A violent shiver coursed through her.

She was full of determination. She was not going to let this incident go ignored. No, she was going to get to the bottom of it no matter what. Neiva was way more than she seemed and Miranda was going to find out what they were hiding.

Chapter 5

"THAT'S IT—I must have Alice in Wonderland syndrome," Neiva explained while Breezy buckled her into the passenger's seat.

Breezy glanced at Neiva, gave her a reassuring smile, and patted her shoulder before shutting the door. She walked over to Nate and Viv, who were standing in front of her yellow Volkswagen Beetle.

"Is she okay?" Nate asked, peeking at Neiva nervously.

"Yeah, but she is trying to find any excuse not to believe what she's seeing. That's pretty understandable, all things considered. Everyone has kept her in the dark about Spirit and what happens here," Breezy poked Nate in the chest.

"Hold on. We didn't know she would be part spirit. Before her grandfather died, he mentioned that it could be possible, but he wasn't totally sure. She was just different from everyone, as if she was born to be something more than just a guardian. He said something about a prophecy foreseeing a native child blessed by magic. Something about a savior," Nate replied defensively, heat rising in his cheeks.

He took another look at Neiva sitting in the car. Her grandmother and grandfather had said Neiva was special and different from them but they never let on just how different.

"Okay, Nate, but now we need to explain everything to her," Breezy headed to the driver's side of her car. "Why don't you go get Neiva's stuff and tell her grandmother what happened? She will know what to do. Viv will drop you off."

"Oh, and make sure we are excused from school. I already informed the security guard we all had an emergency and needed to get Neiva home. That she just received her powers. Also, tell our parents what happened so they can call the school . . . and the tribal elders; they need to be informed," Breezy instructed.

The school security had a system and protocol when a student suddenly manifested their powers. Get them home right away.

"What are you going to do?" Nate asked Breezy.

"Take Neiva to camp and tell her everything about Spirit."

Neiva's breath caught. She could hear their voices through the cracked window. Their conversation did not reassure her one bit. The world she knew just came crashing to a halt and some new one had magically appeared—literally.

With an aggravated sigh, Neiva pulled the passenger visor down to look at herself in the mirror. She was a mess. Her eyes were wide with fright and her hair looked like a rat's nest. Black mascara streaked her face like a warrior after battle.

Her eyes slid cautiously to her forehead. Weird, she thought. There was dried blood on her bangs. She remembered the pain in her head, but it had abruptly disappeared. Brushing her bangs away to get a closer look, Neiva stared at her reflection with both wonder and horror.

A diamond-shaped crystal, a half-inch wide and an inch long, was protruding out of the middle of her forehead. Bright colors emanated from its center, shining like a rainbow inside the car. The edges were caked in dried blood. It was both beautiful and scary at the same time.

Neiva began to feel distressed. Her body shook and her breathing became labored. She felt like she was going to have a heart attack. Franticly searching the car, Neiva's vision began to darken and time slowed to a stop. Breezy was frozen in place, her hand still on the door handle while both Nate and Viv stood frozen in mid-conversation.

Suddenly, the smell of lavender and forest engulfed the car. It brought a calmness and peace to her heart. Turning back to the mirror, she could see Darius sitting behind her. His mask casting a silver glow within the darkness reminded Neiva of a lighthouse guiding a lost ship safely to shore.

"I don't have much time. I can't keep the sun blocked for long," he said as he leaned forward and put a hand on her shoulder. "I know things may seem crazy and you feel like you're losing your mind, but stay strong. I will guide you along the way."

Neiva tried to ask him what was going on, but she couldn't move her mouth. She could only manage a small squeak to escape between her lips. With some bravery, she gently brushed her hand over his. She wanted to feel his skin against hers, to make sure he was real, but his leather glove prevented the contact. She started to bring her hand down, but Darius grabbed it and intertwined his fingers with hers.

The electricity that had shocked them during their first encounter was back. Darius could feel it spill into his hand from hers. The white light appeared, wrapping itself around their conjoined hands. It sparkled like diamonds and grew brighter as it matched their heartbeats.

He looked up and his breath caught in his chest. Like icebergs drifting in the Arctic Ocean, Neiva's eyes were wide and glazed, and he felt like he was falling into them. He couldn't look away.

Neiva was trembling. It was as if her heart was directly connected to his. She felt she knew him. That he wasn't a stranger or ghost but someone she's known her whole life. He made her feel safe. Nothing would happen to her. The fear and anxiety all evaporated, leaving only desire and courage in her heart.

She stared up at him mesmerized. He was unlike any other guy she had ever known. Who was this masked person that had stolen her heart with only one touch?

"Do you feel that Neiva? That's our energy merging together," he said in a thick voice, slowly letting go.

The connection disappeared, making Darius regret the briefness of his visit. But he had to ensure that his plans were ready. "I will see you soon. Listen to your friends and family. They will help you, Neiva."

He gave Neiva another reassuring squeeze on her shoulder before dissolving into a dark mist. Her shoulder was still tingling where he had touched her, leaving her body singing with a calming sensation.

The sun magnified to its normal brightness and the world seemed to start up again. Breezy climbed into the car, and Neiva was surprised to see her back in her human form. She didn't know how it happened but she had a feeling Darius had something to do with it.

"Well, we are set to go to camp. Nate and Viv will pick your stuff up. Are you doing okay?" Breezy asked, turning her human eyes upon Neiva.

"I'm better now that I know I am not losing my mind. My vision somehow is back to normal. Actually, you're back to normal, too. What's going on? Why are you suddenly human? Why do we go to school in a tree and does my family know about this? I feel like I am going crazy!" Neiva exclaimed. Like a floodgate opening, she couldn't keep the questions back. The only thing she didn't mention was Darius. He was her secret, and she didn't feel any reason to tell anyone about him . . . not yet anyway.

"Wow, okay. I know you have a lot of questions. I will explain everything at camp. And yes, you're family does know, Neiva. Your parents didn't want you to be a part of this world. That's why they moved to Anchorage and kept you in the dark about Spirit's traditions. But your grandmother always believed you were special and different. She believed you deserved to know your true heritage," Breezy paused briefly when she saw the dried blood in Neiva's hair. "How's your forehead?"

"Oh fine, except for this crystal sticking out of the middle it," Neiva dramatically brushed the bangs away from her forehead.

Breezy's mouth dropped open. "I have never seen anything like it. It's so beautiful. It's like a rainbow's trapped somewhere inside and is trying to break out of the crystal."

"I just want to know everything," Neiva said sternly.

Breezy leaned back. She blinked a couple of times trying to gather the right words. "When we get to camp, I promise I will explain everything. You should have been told about this earlier, but I think your family thought it was safer for you to stay in the dark."

"Well, it's too late for that now."

"Right," Breezy said with a small smile. "To sum it up, there is a world parallel to the one you've known your whole life. And obviously, you are now a part of it."

"Obviously," Neiva said as she touched the object on her forehead. Breezy was back to normal, so why did she still have this thing on her forehead? "Why are you back to normal and I'm not? I feel like a unicorn with this thing sticking out of my forehead."

"I don't know, Neiva. Like I said, I have never seen anything like it before. I can hide my image when I want to. But maybe this is happening to you now because you're coming into adulthood and you're new to your powers. It's like learning to ride a bike," Breezy said starting the car.

"When we get to camp, everything will be better," Neiva muttered to herself. She loved going to camp. It was her favorite pastime in Spirit. Her grandmother allowed her to stay with her friends unchaperoned because she trusted them and she knew they wouldn't get into trouble. In Alaska, kids had to grow up fast to deal with wildlife and the elements. It was a tough environment and you had to be ready at all times.

Neiva glanced out the window to see a giant raven flying high in the sky. Chills quaked throughout her body causing her to shake uncontrollably. Could it be the same raven that attacked her on the boat? The one that stole her journal? In school, she had learned ravens were a bad omen and the tribal elders called them the tricksters. They were known for bringing bad luck to anyone who double-crossed them. You did not want to mess with a raven. But Nate's story about the raven stealing the sun and giving it to the people of the earth made her believe all ravens weren't bad. Only some.

It took Breezy about forty-five minutes to reach Neiva's grandparents' cabin. There were several cabins spread throughout the tundra, about ten to fifteen miles apart. It was the kind of place where you never saw your neighbors unless you wanted too.

Climbing out of the car, Neiva took in her surroundings. Deep-green trees and rolling hills lined the valley. Flowers sprang out of the ground giving a splash of yellow, purple, and red to brighten the ubiquitously green surroundings. The air was crisp and fresh, so much better than the polluted air of Anchorage, Alaska. There weren't any noises except the sound of nature—the birds chirping, a river flowing nearby, and the rattling of leaves as the wind blew through the treetops. It was so refreshing and relaxing compared to busy city life.

Everything looked the same as the previous summer. The cabin was still a light blue trimmed in white. Hardy flowers edged the bushes in front of the house. Alaska's famous forget-me-not flowers lined the path that led up to the dark red door. The cabin still looked cozy and comfortable, as it always had to Neiva.

Neiva stretched out and let loose a long sigh. There was a small kink in her back from the drive, or it could be from her bad posture. She had tried to watch the raven the whole trip, but she lost sight of it ten minutes into the drive.

She headed to the back of the cabin to use the outhouse. None of the houses at the camp had indoor plumbing. Nowhere on the tundra was there indoor plumbing. At a certain depth, the ground is permanently frozen. Known as permafrost, it prevents any pipes from being dug into the ground.

The outhouse was about twenty-five feet away from the cabin, a sufficient distance to keep the smell away, but making for a scary jaunt at night. Neiva had to admit, the outhouse was kind of cute from the outside. It looked like a miniature version of the cabin, painted in the same light blue and white trim.

A strange noise made her head jerk around, and sheer terror sent her leaping off the trail for the safety of the cabin. Heart pounding, she stood and gawked at the creature before her. Shiny obsidian-black eyes stared at her, casting her reflection back at her. It was the raven—the same raven that had stolen her journal. Neiva knew this because the raven was missing the tail feathers where she had plucked them during their last encounter. A small chill crept through her body.

"What the hell!" Neiva screamed and ran toward the outhouse. The huge bird cawed at her as she sped by. It took flight, circling around the house until gracefully landing on the back porch.

Neiva made it to the outhouse in record time. As she closed the door behind her, she could still feel the raven's eyes on the back of her neck. Once she was finished, she prayed that the bird would be gone, but when she opened the door to step outside, the raven was still there.

"Neiva! Where did you go?" Breezy shouted from the front of the house. "I opened up the cabin to air it out and heard you scream!"

Staring at the bird, Neiva pondered what to do. This was her favorite animal. She loved seeing them in the wild but this bird was very different from the others. It was huge, which is probably why she felt so intimidated by it. Plus, the fact that it had attacked her and stolen her journal, which meant there was intelligence behind the scary exterior. She found it both fascinating and horrifying at the same time.

Taking a deep breath, Neiva stepped outside. She could

stare at the raven and hope it would disappear. Maybe if she tried hard enough it might work. She did have some magical abilities, but it was the thought of finally learning the truth about Spirit that gave Neiva the final push. She ran to the back porch without taking her eyes off the giant bird. Before she entered the cabin, she gave the bird an evil look and shook her finger at it.

"If I had my way, I would pluck all those beautiful feathers out of you and make them into a headpiece," she hissed as she ran through the back door.

The kitchen was small with an island and some cabinets for storage. There was a tiny fridge and a stove on one wall, and a table with room for four next to a large window with great views of the tundra. Next to the kitchen was an archway leading into the main room, which was both the living room and bedroom. Straight across from the kitchen, two couches sat parallel to a fireplace on the far wall. In between the couches sat a large trunk that served as a coffee table, on top of which was a chess set. On the wall dividing the kitchen from the living room, opposite from the fireplace, was a cabinet full of books and games. Two chairs sat on each side of the cabinet. There was only one picture in the cabin and it was hanging above the fireplace. A giant elk stood in the center of the image surrounded by green and red colors in the grass. The mountains looked almost purple in the faded sunlight. The sky was a dark blue with sunset colors on the horizon. It was a beautiful picture of Denali, Alaska, and one of Neiva's favorite images.

Breezy was sitting on the couch closest to the picture. She was twirling a hairbrush in her hand.

"Come sit, Neiva. I know you're anxious to find out what's going on," she patted the spot in front of her.

Neiva slowly walked to the couch and sat in front of Breezy, leaning her back against Breezy's legs. Anticipation and relief washed over her. This was it. She finally would get her answers about the island and its mysterious inhabitants.

"Well, I guess I should start at the beginning," Breezy said as she grabbed a small section of Neiva's hair to brush.

"A long time ago, there was a small tribe of Eskimos who lived on the outskirts of Nome, Alaska. They were a poor tribe and their hunters had a hard time providing food because of the lack of animals. It was as if the animals had suddenly vanished, leaving no trace or evidence of where they had migrated to. The chief of the tribe decided to send out his most skilled hunters to find a new source of food. He thought that the islands neighboring the coastline might provide food for the tribe. But on the day he sent his men out, a storm rolled in out of nowhere, as if it targeted the small boats. The storm became ruthless and overpowered the boats. The hunters believed they surely would never reach land again and would perish in the sea. When all hope was lost, the storm suddenly passed and the hunters found themselves ashore on a large island, one they never knew existed. It was like it appeared out of nowhere.

"The hunters jumped out of the boat to explore this island, but they soon realized it was inhabited. When they were about to give up, a figure appeared out of the shadows. He was taller than any of the hunters. No one could see his face because he had a strange mask on. He pointed at the hunters and told them that if they brought their tribe to live on the island, they would never go hungry again; that the island would provide for them and their every need. In return, the hunters had to agree to guard the gateway to the Spirit World and never, ever leave the island."

"I knew it!" Neiva yelled, pounding her fist on the table. Breezy paused for a second before she continued on with the story, ignoring Neiva's outburst.

"The hunters agreed to the masked man's demands and returned to their village. They told their chief of their findings. With nothing to lose, the chief agreed to move the tribe to this miraculous island. So, they packed their village up and moved. Everything promised to them was provided, and in return, the tribe's hunters guarded the unseen door to the tall stranger's realm. They became known as the Guardians," Breezy paused. "Neiva, the locals that you see today, including your family, are the descendants of the tribe."

"But what about the conditions? My parents were allowed to leave the island with me. How was that possible?" Neiva asked, jumping up from the floor. Breezy had finished braiding her hair halfway through the story.

"Times have vastly changed since the tribe first inhabited this island. In order to keep up with the modern age and what's going on in the world around us, Guardians are allowed to go out into the world to explore or to go to college." Breezy explained, watching Neiva intently.

"Why wasn't the island protected before? Is that why the tribe was picked? Did the masked man bring them to the island?" Neiva asked as she paced back and forth across the room. All her intuition about Darius being connected to the island was just confirmed with Breezy's story. She knew the masked man had to be Darius.

"The island was not protected. There is a mist surrounding the island and it keeps anyone from finding it, but sometimes someone gets through. So, there was a need for a local tribe to inhabit the island, to create diversions to lead people away and to guard the doorway. That's why outsiders never knew of the island's existence."

"But the tribe just left their home? How could everyone agree to that?" Neiva asked in wonder. She couldn't imagine leaving her home and trusting a complete stranger. But she had met Darius. He was very captivating and he instantly stole her heart. She would do anything he asked.

Breezy smiled. "When the tribe had no food to survive, it was easy for the chief to convince them to leave. He was looking out for his clan, all twenty-five of them. Some were scared, but once they got to the island, their fear melted away. They were provided with homes, livestock, and crops. Everything they needed."

"The masked man made the animals disappear in the first place, didn't he? He knew the chief wouldn't have a problem with getting the tribe to leave if their only other option was starvation?" Neiva felt as if a little lightbulb had switched on. "What is this 'Spirit World' that the tribe was protecting?"

"Well . . . it contains all the mystical creatures found in stories or dreams. The town of Spirit was created to protect the Spirit World, to guard its doorway." Breezy paused to watch Neiva nestle into the couch across from her.

"Are you a fairy?" Neiva asked. Her eyes raked over Breezy's body, trying to soak in every detail. She squinted her eyes trying to make Breezy's true form appear.

"No!" Breezy exclaimed. "Fairy tales were created as a diversion. Some of the stories may be based on reality, but they were originally created to mislead the public from our realm."

"So, what about the Fairy Kingdom in Ireland? That's not real?"

Breezy stared at Neiva. That one look told Neiva everything she needed to know. There wasn't a Fairy Kingdom in Ireland. It was just another distraction. For some reason this saddened Neiva. She loved hearing about fairy folklore, and when she was younger, she believed it was real. At least she could say that she was half right. There *was* a magical realm out there full of mystical creatures.

Still staring at Neiva, Breezy spoke softly, "Spirit World was once governed by one ruler. She was a powerful queen, but fair and equal. She loved her family and subjects with all her heart. She ruled her kingdom with her people at her side, and she only thought of their well-being. But there was a dark prophecy preventing the queen from being truly happy. This prophecy kept her on edge because it predicted that the Spirit World would come to an end if royal blood was not shed when the sky bled. Every night the queen would stare out at the sky, watching and waiting for the sign that her kingdom was in danger.

"One night while her two sons and her kingdom slept, the queen was on her balcony gazing up at the stars. She sensed a darkness seeping into her kingdom through her power to feel the environment around her. That power alerted her senses that the kingdom was in danger. But she did not know how to stop it. Just when the queen was about to go inside, the sky split open. Beautiful lights burst out in all different colors— green, white, blue, any pretty color you can imagine. It was so beautiful that it brought tears to the queen's eyes. The following nights, the queen went to her balcony, hoping the strange lights would return. And for two nights, they did. But on the third night, the colors suddenly changed. Red dominated the other colors, swallowing them all up in one instant. It seemed as if the sky was bleeding and an evil presence leaked out of its wound. The queen knew that the prophecy was coming true. Her kingdom was in trouble."

Breezy's voice slowly faded. A roar began to fill Neiva's head. Her vision was sparkling on the edges as if she were going to pass out. The sound intensified, causing her vision to crack and exploded like lightning. A blinding light snaked across her sight. One minute she was in the cabin's family room and the next minute she was transported to another place.

Neiva was standing in a clearing surrounded by trees. It was dark out, yet there was a reddish glow coming from the sky, illuminating the shadows. Neiva raised her eyes and gasped. The sky looked as if someone had slashed it open with a knife. All shades of red leaked out, running like a river across the sky. It was the northern lights, but it felt evil and powerful at the same time. Neiva knew she'd somehow been transported into Breezy's story.

Anguished cries from far off grabbed Neiva's attention. She glanced in the direction where the noise had originated. There was a castle nestled on top of a small hill. Lights flickered on throughout the castle as it came alive with activity. Shouts filled the night, calling out someone's name. It seemed the people of the castle were searching for someone.

A figure suddenly burst out of the tree line. Her hair flowed behind her like a wedding train, and her skin glowed in the red light giving her an eerie silhouette as she ran. Graceful and lean, she moved with the speed of a predator. Before Neiva knew it, the woman was right in front of her, causing Neiva to try to step back, but she couldn't move. She was paralyzed, almost as if she'd taken root in the ground. She could only stare at the beautiful woman, who stood just several feet from Neiva, barely breathing.

The woman's eyes glowed a deep blue with yellow swirling around the center of her irises. Deep auburn hair fell in soft curls down her back. Her skin was flawless, casting a golden glow around her. She wore a white shift that flowed down to her ankles, pooling at her feet. On her forehead was a crown with diamond-shape jewels shining brightly under the red sky.

The woman stared right through Neiva, not seeing her at all. Reaching into the tunic tied around her slim waist, she brought out a knife that gleamed with radiance and power. The knife was about eight inches long with a hilt made of solid ivory. It looked beautiful, but very deadly.

Thrusting the tip of the spear toward the bleeding sky, the woman started to sing in a language that Neiva didn't recognize. The song was full of strength and sorrow. Neiva could feel the woman's song seeping into every living thing, even her own soul. She could feel its power vibrate up toward the strange phenomenon in the sky.

When the woman finished her song, tears slowly trickled down her cheeks leaving a trail of glitter in their wake. Sadness seeped into her face as she closed her eyes. She was quiet for only a moment, as if she were lost in her own thoughts. Then her eyes snapped open as though she was in a trance. "To the earth and sky, I give you my life. Take freely what is mine so that others may live. Let my spirit force give strength to the spirit realm and act as Guardian to all."

With her final words, the woman plunged the knife into her heart.

Neiva didn't realize she was screaming until her legs could move and she was halfway to the woman. Blood oozed out of her wound and fell to the ground like a flood on a stormy night. It pooled beneath the woman's feet as she slowly slouched over. She was still breathing, but her respiration was getting slower and shallower. She put one hand on the ground as she lowered her face to the dirt. With her last breath, she kissed the ground and whispered, "It is done."

The woman fell over lifelessly as Neiva dropped to her knees beside her. Neiva's hands hovered over the woman's body, hesitant as to what to do. She reached down to check the woman's pulse, but she couldn't touch her. It was like she was a ghost or just a transparent image. Neiva's hand went right through her. There was nothing she could do but watch the earth soak up the woman's blood. It disappeared fast as the ground eagerly drank it in.

Holding her breath, Neiva leaned in to inspect the woman. She looked down at her pale face and stared at her shut eyes and thick lashes, silently hoping those eyes would open. The woman looked so fragile and vulnerable lying there. She was dying, her glow slowly fading like a candle burning the last of its wick. And there was nothing Neiva could do.

The world started to shake, and the ground lifted and dropped beneath her feet. It rolled like waves during a forceful storm, throwing Neiva off her feet. She couldn't regain her balance, so she crawled on her hands and knees back toward the woman, scraping her knees on the jagged rocks.

To her horror, masculine arms made of clay burst through the ground and forcibly grabbed the woman. They embraced her as if she was a lost lover and within a blink of an eye, they pulled her back into the ground until she disappeared. Once she was gone, the ground quickly closed up, leaving no traces of the woman or the masculine arms.

Neiva sat up. The cries were getting closer. They would reach the clearing in several minutes. She pushed herself to her feet and glanced toward the stone castle. Out of the corner of her eye something twinkled, catching her attention. She shifted her eyes to see a large ruby lying where the woman's body had disappeared. It was beautiful, about the size of a golf ball. It was rich in color, but that was not the strangest part. There was a stream of white energy bouncing around inside the ruby, as if it were alive.

"Where is she?" a strong voice shouted from the tree line.

Neiva turned to look at the figure within the shadows. Darkness surrounded him. She could only see his outline and, judging by the height of the trees, he was tall. Another figure appeared beside him, also cloaked in the shadows. He was the same height as the other, but the shadows engulfed him more as the other figure started to glow amidst his dark surroundings.

Holding her breath, she moved closer to get a better view of the two strangers. Feeling like she was moving in slow motion, Neiva stretched her hand out, reaching for the figures hiding in the shadows. She didn't get a chance to investigate further. The world split open again and a pain crackled through her like a whip, bringing Neiva to her knees. Her head felt like it was about to explode. Her vision blurred as her breathing became labored. Just when the two figures were about to step out of the shadows, Neiva's vision wavered and everything went dark.

NEIVA SLOWLY OPENED HER EYES. She was in a huge and magnificent room. It was filled with books lining every wall from floor to ceiling. Chairs with arched backs and mahogany tables were scattered around the room. It looked like something out of a museum. The bookshelves were a rich cherry color lined with bright gold metal that shone like the sun. Adjacent to the entrance of the library was a balcony with two French doors, slightly opened. Two voices seemed to be arguing with each other.

She had to steady herself against one of the bookcases before she could move any farther. The room was spinning, making her feel nauseous. Taking slow and deep breaths, Neiva stood straining her ears. The voices were getting louder.

"I don't care. She's gone, so what now? Just share the kingdom? You obviously know that we don't see eye to eye on virtually every subject, including politics." The voice was strong and pure. When the next person spoke Neiva's heart instantly stopped. She knew that voice.

"Darius," Neiva whispered helplessly.

"We have to try to work together, Gabriel. That's what she would have wanted." There was a hint of begging in his voice that pulled at Neiva's heart. She quickly moved toward the balcony. She felt like she had to see him, but with every step she took closer to him, time seemed to slow. Her body felt weighted down, like it was lined with lead.

"Look Darius, there is no other way. I can't rule with you," Gabriel said with force.

Neiva could hear someone walk across the balcony and pick something up. There was a loud noise, like metal hitting metal. A red eerie glow slowly started to flash from the balcony. Neiva was about to reach her destination when a sudden blast threw her across the room. She landed against one of the bookcases, tumbling to the floor in a pile of books. Exhaustion overtook her body. Blackness engulfed her once again. That last thing she heard was Darius's voice whispering in the dark, "Gabriel, what have you done?"

Chapter 6

VOICES DREW NEIVA OUT of the darkness. She could tell by their urgency they were worried about her. She tried to open her eyes, but little shock waves of pain forced them shut.

"She's coming out of it," the soft voice whispered. It sounded like Breezy.

"Why is that thing on her forehead glowing?" That was Nate's voice. He sounded worried but curious at the same time.

I must be sick, Neiva thought. *Why else would I have fainted and had those crazy dreams? It could be the only explanation for the way I'm feeling.* Her head was throbbing and her skin was on fire.

"I think I'm going to try to tap it and see what happens," Nate added.

As he bent down, Neiva could feel his breath on her face and his hand grazing her hair. Before Nate's hand reached her forehead, Neiva shot up like a rocket and collided with his head. Pain streaked across the area behind her eyes. Her head throbbed even harder. It took a tremendous effort to open her eyes. After three attempts, Neiva slowly opened her eyes to see a pair of luscious lips within inches of her face.

It was Nate. He was looking down at her lips. Puzzlement and awe crossed his face. Something flickered in his caramel-colored eyes and before she knew it, Nate leaned in and kissed her.

The kiss was tender and his lips were soft. In that instant all coherent thoughts were lost. Her brain was on autopilot. She couldn't think. What was happening? Nate was kissing her. What the heck was he doing? She inhaled, and her eyes grew wide as she pulled back. Nate stared blankly at her, not knowing what to say. He brought his hand to his lips as if to make sure they were still there.

Neiva was dizzy and confused. Her muscles were clenched tight like steel.

"I don't know why I did that! I didn't mean to." Nate exclaimed, his cheeks turning bright red. "Forget it ever happened!"

"Wow. Can we say awkward?" Viv said sitting next to Neiva. She gave Nate a viscous stare before turning to Neiva. Just for the briefest moment, Neiva saw a hint of jealousy in Viv's amber-colored eyes, but it disappeared as a questioning look materialized.

Gently brushing Neiva's bangs away from her forehead, Viv's fingertips briefly touched the stone. It sent a jolting wave throughout Viv's body, causing her to yelp and jump off the couch.

"What did you do, Viv?" Breezy asked, turning from Neiva to Viv. Nate's kiss was long forgotten as everyone stared at Viv.

Viv was back in her spirit form. Her long tail swished back and forth behind her while her yellow eyes glowed like headlights on a dark road. The tribal tattoos on her arms lit up like flares. Agitation coursed throughout her body, making her muscles shake and her claws extend. There was an odd look in her eyes.

Rainbow light spilled out of the stone on Neiva's forehead, intensifying the light in the room. Anyone standing near her could feel the remnants of the power left behind.

"I hardly touched her forehead. I didn't mean too. I just wanted to comfort Neiva." Viv paused and looked thoughtfully at Neiva. She licked her black lips with her forked tongue.

"Did I make you change, Viv?" Neiva asked intrigued.

"It seems that you have the power to bring down our spirit shields, which protect our true form." Viv said. Her body briefly shimmered as a wave of energy rippled down her limbs. Within seconds she was back to her human form, but like a bungee cord, the energy shot back up from the ground and she transformed back into her spirit form.

"Wow, that was epic," Neiva whispered. She couldn't believe it took just seconds to go from one form to another.

"Yeah, I'm pretty epic." Viv winked at Neiva.

"Ha, ha," Neiva smiled, thanking Viv silently for managing to make her feel relaxed.

So many bizarre things had happened since she came to Spirit. Considering anyone else in her position, Neiva thought she was taking this very well. She couldn't explain what was happening to her, but she needed to hear the rest of Breezy's story. "How long was I out?"

"For a couple hours. I thought you had fallen asleep but when we couldn't wake you up I got nervous," Breezy said. She looked at Viv. "We all got nervous."

"I'm feeling so overwhelmed right now. Breezy could you finish telling me everything about the Spirit World? I want to know everything," Neiva demanded.

The silence that followed was long and awkward. Viv and Breezy were staring at each other, seeming to have some unspoken conversation between them. It was easy to see the stress on Neiva's face. "Okay, hon. I will finish telling you everything. How far into the story did you hear before you passed out?"

Neiva took a deep breath; her voice began to quiver. "The crazy thing is that I didn't pass out. Somehow I was transported into the story. I saw everything that happened, from the queen sacrificing herself to her two sons fighting over the kingdom. It was so intense. . . . I don't know what happened or how it happened."

Breezy was staring at Neiva, her emerald eyes searching. "You had a vision of the past?"

"No, I was actually there. I saw everything as if I was witnessing it happening firsthand, like I was a ghost watching everyone. No one could see me and I couldn't touch anything."

"Hmm." Breezy scratched her chin and looked thoughtfully at the ceiling. "It seems you might have the power of visions. I'm not sure since this is the first time you had one though. Let me know if you have another one."

"I will." Neiva placed a hand on her forehead. Her throat felt dry and her body was aching all over. "I feel really weak right now actually. Kind of drained."

"Nate, could you please grab a blanket for Neiva and then make us some hot chocolate?" Breezy said sternly, giving Nate a glare. "It will make Neiva feel better."

Neiva had a feeling Breezy and Viv didn't approve of the kiss Nate gave her. She wasn't even sure how she felt about it. The timing was way off, and she was a little bit embarrassed. She was attracted to Nate, but the kiss made her think of Darius and how it would be to kiss him instead.

Nate quickly grabbed a blanket off the opposite couch and handed it to Neiva, then headed off into the kitchen muttering to himself.

"So, you said that you saw the queen's two sons, Gabriel and Darius, fighting over the kingdom?" Breezy asked with curiosity.

"Not exactly. I was in a library. I couldn't see them because they were on a balcony, out of my range of vision, but I could hear them arguing. Gabriel wanted nothing to do with Darius. They kept arguing, then there was this sound, like something was split in half, similar to swords clashing. That's when the red glow started and everything just blew up."

"Wow. You witnessed—well I shouldn't say exactly witnessed—but you were in the presence of the splitting of the Spirit World. Legend said that the princes could not come to terms with their mother's death and could not rule the kingdom together. So, in the struggle for power, somehow the brothers split the realm into two halves: one light and one dark, with Darius ruling the dark spirits and Gabriel ruling the light spirits."

"Does that mean the light is good and the dark is evil?" Neiva asked nervously.

She was hardly breathing. Her heart felt like it was going to burst out of her chest. Just the mention of Darius's name sent her hormones skyrocketing. She still couldn't understand her feelings. When she was with him it was like time stood still and they were the only two people left on the planet. *When would she see him again?* she wondered as her mind continued to wander.

"Neither realm is good or bad." Breezy watched Neiva intently. She didn't miss a beat. She saw Neiva's eyes light up and her breath quicken every time Darius's name was mentioned. "Neiva? Have you met King Darius?"

Neiva raised her gray eyes to the group. She didn't know what to say. Darius never said anything about keeping his identity a secret; and with the stern look on Breezy's face, Neiva felt that she had to tell someone. He did say trust your friends.

"Yes, he visited me the night of my birthday and another time after that." Neiva quickly got up and sat next to Breezy. "Breezy, I don't know what's going on, but I feel safe with him. He's kind and very helpful. He let me know that things were going to change but to keep hope. Somehow I feel drawn to him, connected."

Viv came over and sat on the floor in front of Neiva, her tail whipping behind her as her yellow eyes glowed brightly, showing her excitement. "You've actually talked to King Darius? Wow! There must be something more to you than we know if you caught his interest."

"What do you mean?"

Viv nervously played with her black claws. "Well, for years he has never shown interest in anything but politics and his kingdom. He literally kept himself in the shadows and out of the spotlight. That is, until now," she said looking at Neiva with interest.

"Viv is from the Dark Kingdom," Breezy said, smiling at Viv. "Her father is one of Darius's Dark Knights, or as most call them, the Shadow Guards. Viv knows everything there is to know about King Darius and has every intention of becoming a Dark Knight herself. So, anything that interests King Darius interests Viv. Plus, you're our friend, and we want to know what's going on."

"Thanks, Breezy." Neiva paused for a couple of seconds then looked at Breezy with a quizzical glimmer. "Then are you from the Light Kingdom? You're a light spirit?"

Breezy smiled warmly at Neiva. "Yes. I am a wood spirit from the Light Kingdom."

"What's the difference between the two kingdoms?" Excitement bubbled within Neiva's belly. She was fascinated despite the dramatic turn of events.

"Well, you now know the Spirit World was split into two kingdoms; with King Darius ruling the Dark Kingdom and King Gabriel ruling the Light Kingdom. Each brother ruling their separate land." Breezy paused before continuing. "Just as a dark spirit's power is stronger during the night, a light spirit's power is stronger during the day. You can think of it as a shifting of powers when the sun sets and rises. In your world, the Light Kingdom watches over us during the day while the Dark Kingdom watches over us during the night."

"And the two kingdoms? What do they look like?" Neiva urged Breezy on.

"In the Light Kingdom, the sun never sets. Colors of silver, gold, and bronze shine throughout the valleys and hills. Light spirits are usually bright in color with wings, small horns, or any other beautiful characteristics." Breezy looked over at Viv. "The Dark Kingdom is full of the creatures that hide in the shadows. Dark spirits don't usually come out during the day because their powers are stronger at night. Most dark spirits wear masks to hide their faces. Giant horns, claws, sharp teeth, or leathery wings are some of their characteristics."

"Hey, not all dark spirits are ugly, but by law we must wear a mask. When dark spirits turn eighteen they receive their first mask, marking their transition to adulthood. I'll get my mask next year!" Viv growled.

"Do you have powers?" Neiva asked cautiously.

"All dark spirits do! You should see some of Viv's powers!" Nate exclaimed as he entered the living room. He passed out the hot chocolate to each girl, avoiding any eye contact with Neiva.

Neiva looked at Breezy and Viv perplexed. Breezy just shook her head. "This isn't about us. It's about Neiva."

"What? You have to show her!" he exclaimed, looking at Breezy, then back at Viv.

"Okay, real quickly, then back to the story," Breezy held out her hand.

In her palm rested a single seed. A green glow emanated from the seed as it started to levitate above Breezy's palm. It began to spin faster and faster until the seed exploded in a shower of glitter. When the glitter disappeared, the seed was gone and in its place was a beautiful pink flower.

"Wow!" Neiva exclaimed as she leaned closer to the flower. She brought her finger up to touch the flower, but it began to wilt and fade until it was gone.

"I have the power to control plants," Breezy said with excitement.

"Yeah, she's like Poison Ivy from Batman," Nate laughed.

"I guess you can compare me to her," Breezy blushed, batting her eyes at Nate.

Neiva quickly looked at Viv with excitement and anticipation.

Viv raised an eyebrow, and a sly smile formed on her face. With a flick of her fingers, bright yellow flames engulfed her hands and arms. "I have the power of fire."

Neiva gasped. The flames danced up and down Viv's arm, giving Neiva the sense that they were alive. With a snap of her fingers, the flames faded back into her skin.

"See! I told you! Awesomeness!" Nate bounced on the couch.

"How do spirits get their powers? Do new powers develop sporadically throughout their life?" Neiva was puzzled.

"When spirits hit the age of seventeen, they start coming into their own powers," Breezy explained. "This gives spirits the chance to strengthen and harness their gifts before they turn eighteen. Once spirits turns eighteen, they gain access to their full powers, becoming stronger and more adept at manipulating their energy. This is the beginning of the full transformation into adulthood, the awakening."

Breezy clapped her hands together to get everyone's attention. "Okay, okay. Let's finish telling Neiva the history of the Spirit World."

Nate took a deep breath and started to talk very fast. "To sum it all up, there was a kingdom ruled by a queen, who sacrificed herself to save her kingdom. After her death, her sons could not see eye to eye, so they divided the kingdom into two realms—one dark, the other light. But they didn't feel safe, so they came together and agreed on two terms. One: There would be one gate to reach both of their kingdoms and it would be heavily guarded. Two: They would create diversions so no outsider would ever know of their existence. So, the Guardians like me were created from the tribal community that moved in after their food sources ran dry," Nate said pointing to himself. "Then fairy tales were created and a security spell blanketed the island so no one would leave with the knowledge of Spirit. They would simply forget the moment they left."

Neiva blinked a couple of times at Nate.

"See? Short and simple, Breezy. We don't have to spend

an hour telling her about Spirit when we could just sum it all up in one sweet description," he rolled his eyes while taking a sip of hot chocolate.

Neiva took a long sip from her cup as she thought over everything that had happened to her in the past twenty-four hours. It oddly all made sense. But there was one thing that bugged her. She remembered seeing all the Eskimo kids at school with tattoos like the one on Nate's neck. Neiva took one last sip before setting her cup down. She felt warm and renewed.

"What about the tattoos on everyone's neck? Are they all Guardians?" Neiva asked as she pointed to Nate's neck.

Nate brushed his fingers over his tattoo. "Yes, every Guardian has a tattoo of their spirit guide. Mine is a fox. I can call on her in a time of need or she appears when she feels I need help."

"How did you get them? I mean, how did this idea of a spirit guide come to be? Was it created to help the Guardians?" Neiva leaned forward, intently waiting for Nate's answer.

"When the tribe first came to Spirit to guard the doorway to the Spirit World, King Darius knew the Guardians would need more than weapons to fight off intruders. So, he gave each Guardian a gift, a tattoo of their totem. When they received their totem on their seventeenth birthday, he would bring that totem to life to help guide them and protect them. Guardians never have the same totem. Each one is different. Like mine is the fox and yours is the raven," Nate explained.

Neiva played with her necklace. She didn't have a tattoo like Nate and the other Eskimos, but she did have a giant bird following her around. Maybe that was her spirit guide, but somehow she felt the bird was more. She could feel its presence outside right now, a strong force of protection. She didn't know how but she knew the bird was watching the perimeter of the house, guarding them.

"I don't have a tattoo but what about a giant bird that's

following me?" Neiva asked, intrigued by what the answer might be.

"The raven is your totem, so maybe the bird can feel your power. I've heard that some Guardians can talk to animals. Maybe down the road you will be able to communicate with ravens," Nate answered.

"Maybe," Neiva bit her lip and nodded in agreement. She was overwhelmed with all this new information and everything was hard to process. Her brain could only take in so much information at one time.

Concern climbed back into Breezy's eyes. She got up and reached her hand out to pull Neiva off the couch. "We'll figure it out, Neiva."

When Neiva's hand touched Breezy's, a slight shock surged up Breezy's body. In a flash, she was in her spirit form. Emerald cat eyes stared back at Neiva as her wings fluttered behind her.

"Well, I guess Neiva wanted all of us to be in our true form," proclaimed Viv slyly, smiling at Breezy with her hands on her hips. Her tail whipped back and forth playfully.

Neiva swallowed a couple of times and licked her lips; she could feel her palms getting sweaty and her left eye starting to twitch. She didn't know how it happened, but when Breezy touched her, she had the urge to see Breezy in her spirit form. Then poof there she was, in her birthday suit.

A loud sigh shattered the silence.

Viv caught Neiva's eye, and her smile grew large like the Cheshire cat. Laughing, she said, "Breezy doesn't like the fact that she can't control her spirit shield around you," Viv remarked.

Fixing her gaze on Viv, Breezy's eyes narrowed in anger. "A spirit shield is essential to every spirit. It hides our true form from any non-spirit or spirit alike. It guards who we are!"

"I'm sorry, Breezy. I just had this urge to see you in your spirit form. I didn't know I was actually going to change you!" Neiva replied in defeat. Shaking her head, Neiva breathed in deeply, hoping she could calm the emotional bubble that was ready to bust and stop the tears threatening to spill out. Everything had changed and nothing would be the same. She got what she wanted, the answers that unlocked the secret to the island, but it didn't make her feel happy. Instead, she felt sad. Her whole life was a lie, and the people she loved the most kept the truth from her.

The tears burst like water through a broken dam. This was all too much. She wanted everything to go back to the way it used to be.

"Oh, it's okay, honey. Don't worry about it. We will figure out how to deal with this. Don't get me wrong; it's a great power and it will be useful in the future. We just have to figure out how you can control it to where it doesn't bring our spirit shields down," Breezy gave her a reassuring hug.

"Well, enough of all this spirit mumbo-jumbo. Let's give Neiva her gifts." Nate said, distracting Neiva from her thoughts.

He ran to a set of luggage by the front door. He rummaged through the black bag sitting on top of the pile. When he found what he was looking for, he turned around quickly with excitement, but stumbled and lost his balance. He fell back onto the luggage, sending everything flying in all directions.

"Jeez! Nate, what did you bring? Neiva's closet? I told you to just grab a couple of things for her," Viv said while helping Nate up.

With a quick flick of her tail, Viv grabbed the object from Nate's hand that was the cause of all of his excitement. It was long, about twelve inches in length, and was wrapped in a black cloth.

"Hey! That's a gift for Neiva from my dad!" Nate yelled in defense. He tried to grab the item from Viv, but she was too quick. The object was flying through the air. With precise accuracy it landed in Neiva's lap, leaving shocked expressions on both Neiva's and Nate's faces.

"Viv! What if you missed my lap?" Neiva exclaimed as

she eyed the gift. It was long, not too heavy, but not too light either. She slowly unwound it from the cloth.

"That's the tusk from the walrus that we found on the beach," Nate said.

It was larger and longer than she remembered. Beautiful drawings were etched onto its glossy surface. It showed a raven in flight over the town of Spirit. Behind the raven were the northern lights, taking up most of the sky. The detail was incredible. It almost looked like a real black-and-white picture.

"It's beautiful," Neiva whispered.

Nate pointed to the tusk. "It's called scrimshaw. It is elaborate carving or engraving in the form of pictures and lettering on the surface of the ivory. Most scrimshaw artists highlight the engravings using a pigment of black ink."

"Interesting," Neiva stated as she scanned the smooth surface of the ivory. She could not see the engravings. It looked as though it was just drawn onto the surface. She glided her thumb over the ink and, sure enough, she felt the engravings.

"Yeah, Dad wanted to give this to you himself, but he had to work at the shop."

"Oh, well I will have to thank him when we get back. This is so special." Neiva said as she gently put it onto the side table next to the couch. She knew exactly where she was going to put it in her room. She had a shelf next to her desk and she could use one of her small easels to prop it up.

"Here, I also got you something," Nate said shyly, digging in his pocket.

He handed a small object to Neiva. It was made from ivory and about the size of her pinky finger. To Neiva the object kind of looked like a Buddha figurine with its huge belly and wide smile. But this figurine had a pointy head and its eyes were more slanted, drawn in a black line forming two upside-down smiles. Black eyebrows marked its forehead, giving it a wicked yet funny look. A nose was carved onto its face, with black dots marking its nostrils. Underneath the nose was its mouth, drawn into a huge smile, taking up half its face. Just like the Buddha, it had a round belly, but feet were carved in front. Its arms lay straight down at its side with giant hands taking up a position by its feet.

"Now that is a billiken. It's Alaska's good-luck charm. You're supposed to keep it in your pocket so you can carry the good luck around with you."

"Wow! Thanks, Nate," Neiva replied as she rolled it around in her hands.

"You know Nate made that Neiva," Breezy added.

"You did?" Neiva's eyes grew large with surprise.

"Yeah, it was nothing. I took the other broken ivory from the walrus and carved the billiken out of it. It only took a couple of hours." Nate shrugged as he walked back to the pile of suitcases.

"Sure it did, Nate," Viv said sarcastically. She pointed a claw finger at the billiken in Neiva's hand. "It took him all night to get that baby done. After you fainted, he began working on it nonstop, whereas it only took his dad several hours to scrimshaw that beautiful imagery onto the tusk."

Nate whipped his head around to glare at Viv. "Whatever. That was my first carving and semi-scrimshaw. My dad is a pro and can do scrimshaw in his sleep. I wanted Neiva to have it and to always carry good luck with her. What's wrong with that, *Viv?*"

Viv caught Nate's tone. A rasping growl rose from her chest, threatening to escape. Her eyes and tattoos flared up in anger as she stood up, her tail whipping behind her in agitation. She took a step forward, lowered her shoulders, and then took a second step and jumped.

She was halfway through the air before Breezy caught Viv's tail, causing Viv to fall like a penny from the Empire State Building. She landed right on the coffee table between the two couches, hitting the table with such force that thunder echoed around the cabin. Silence quickly followed as everyone waited for Viv's next move.

"Thanks, Breezy," Viv said as she pushed herself off the

trunk. She looked down at her chest to find crushed pieces from the chess set stuck to her white tank top. She quickly brushed them off and looked at the rest of the set once she got up. There was nothing left; even the board itself was cracked.

"Sorry," she muttered, mortified.

"It's okay, Viv. We're used to your short temper." Breezy smiled. Her wings beating slowly behind her, she helped Viv clean up the mess she had made and tried to calm her down.

"I hope Grams won't be mad," Viv said looking at Neiva with huge, yellow eyes.

"Don't worry about it. We just got the set last summer. It was cheap and on sale. It doesn't mean anything," Neiva said with a laugh as she hugged Viv.

"I'll get dinner ready," Nate said.

"I better go help him. He might catch something on fire," Breezy ran after Nate.

Viv smiled, showing her sharp teeth. Her tail curled around Neiva's hand as she led her into the kitchen. Before they entered, a thought crossed Neiva's mind and she stopped Viv.

"Viv? What does Darius look like under his mask?" She was hoping Viv would know since her father was one of Darius's Shadow Guards.

Viv turned around. She had a puzzled look on her face. "Why?"

"I was just curious. I know they say looks shouldn't matter, but I'm just trying to imagine what he looks like. He's a mystery that I want to solve."

Viv let out a long sigh. She put her clawed hands on Neiva's shoulders and looked her right in the eye. "The truth is that no one knows. Some say he is so hideous that the mask hides his deformities; while others say he is made up of shadows, that the mask holds his body together. He never takes the mask off, Neiva. It's his crown. I don't even think his brother knows what he looks like anymore."

"Oh," Neiva replied. It was hard for Neiva because she

was a visual person. She always wanted to see what she was dealing with.

"Thanks, Viv," Neiva said, forcing a smile. Neiva tried not to think of what sinister things could lurk behind Darius's mask, but the thoughts quickly disappeared. He was protective toward her. She felt connected to his soul, and deep down inside she knew he was beautiful. She could feel it within her heart.

As Neiva entered the kitchen, her nose was engulfed with the sweet aromas of chocolate and sugar. She glanced at the kitchen table where a feast of sweets lay out before them. A huge chocolate cake was placed in the center of the table surrounded by her grandmother's cupcakes. A blueberry pie with chocolate-covered blueberries surrounding it sat steaming in the far corner of the table. Huge glass bowls were full of chocolate-covered strawberries and bananas, Neiva's favorite. Fresh banana bread and pumpkin bread filled up the rest of the table.

"Wow, Nate. This isn't dinner. This is a sweet tooth's fantasy!" Neiva exclaimed, trying not to drool all over herself.

Nate looked at the girls smugly. Puffing his chest out, he smiled and gestured toward the table. "It's Neiva's birthday celebration! I thought we could use a sugar rush after today's events!"

Both Neiva and Viv smiled at each other as they grabbed the chairs across from Nate and Breezy. They all grabbed a plate and started digging in. Everyone ate in silence at first, but soon they started talking about school and their teachers. Once they had their fill of food, the girls cleared the table and bagged up all the sweets for later. They cleaned the kitchen, closing the cabinets and making sure the burners on the old wood stove were off. They then headed into the family room, where Nate was starting a fire in the fireplace.

To the girls' surprise, Nate had folded out the bed from one of the couches, which fit perfectly over the coffee table, landing just an inch shy of the other couch. Pillows, sheets, and covers were strewn all over, making it look like a fluffy dream.

"Okay," Nate turned around to look at the girls, "game time."

The group picked the game Clue. As Breezy and Neiva set up the game, Viv and Nate fought over which side of the board they wanted to be on and who would be on each team.

"It's a love/hate relationship between those two," Breezy mumbled.

"Is that healthy?" Neiva asked glancing at Viv and Nate, who were having a stare down. So far it looked like Viv was winning. Steam was rolling out of her nostrils and her tail was in a striking pose that would intimidate any grown man.

Breezy let out a long sigh and set the cards on the center of the board. "From experience I can say no, and no I am not talking about myself personally. I am talking about my parents. Theirs has been a love/hate relationship since before I was born. My mother is a wood spirit and my father a cat spirit. Wood spirits are very beautiful and flirtatious, while cat spirits tend to be very possessive and territorial. My mother is very friendly and uses her flirtation to get what she wants. My father, on the other hand, is always following my mother in his jaguar form to make sure she doesn't get into trouble. Don't get me wrong, my parents love each other, but they love to argue as well."

Neiva didn't know what to say. "Oh," was all she could manage. A tinge of jealously crept through her veins. She casually glanced at Viv and Nate, who were arguing over which color they wanted to be.

A thought struck Neiva, "Can you turn into a jaguar?"

"No, I mostly take after my mother. I did inherit some of my father's characteristics though. Hence the cat-like eyes, pointed ears, tail, and the jaguar spots on my wings," Breezy pointed to her wings, which stilled for a second so Neiva could inspect them. They were jaguar spots instead of regular circular spots. Neiva hadn't noticed before.

A couple hours had passed when the game ended. Neiva and Viv lost to Breezy and Nate, who were gloating as they put the game away. Neiva got up and headed to the door. She had an urge to write in her journal. She grabbed her coat and the flashlight hanging by the door, and then she grabbed her journal from her backpack.

She stepped outside, quietly shutting the door behind her. The night air was fresh and cold. A slight breeze came out of the east, sending a chill down her spine. She couldn't see anything past the porch, but looks could be deceiving. There could be a bear lurking around the corner, and she wouldn't even know it.

Sitting in the swing to the left of the door, Neiva turned her flashlight on. She opened the journal and let her feelings flow onto the blank pages.

September 4 (Second Entry)
Wow. Now I know how Alice felt when she found Wonderland. Lost. Crazy. Excited. A big ball of emotional stress. I still can't believe what I've learned. It's so much to take in, and I swear my head is going to explode. Maybe that's why I have these headaches. Oh, wait. . . . No. It's actually from the crystal that's sticking out of my forehead!!!!

Unicorn? No, I wish. I don't know what it is. The gang doesn't even know what it is. I'm hoping my grandmother will know. I knew she was hiding things from me, but this? This new world, why didn't my parents tell me about this? Why hide it? I'm going to talk to Grams about all of this. She can't hide anything anymore. When we get back from camp, I am going to make her tell me.

Oh! And WOW! Nate KISSED me!!! Why? It was so awkward. The timing was bad and it just didn't feel right, like it wasn't meant to be. I can't explain it, it just felt off.

Anyway, I've learned there's a dark world and a light world. Kind of reminds me of heaven and hell, good versus evil. But Breezy said both worlds are neither good nor bad. They used to be one world, but when the brothers couldn't agree with each other, it was split into two. Isn't that what happened between Satan and God?

Darius is the king of the dark spirits. I know he isn't evil. He's helped me this far. Plus, I wouldn't fall for someone evil, would I? And how can I explain the feelings I have for him? I've known him before. In another life. I wish I could know all of his secrets. Well, I was determined to find the island's secrets. How hard would it be to find out Darius's secrets?!

A NOISE BROUGHT Neiva's attention back to the present. She sprang out of her chair, pointing her flashlight around the deck. Sweat trickled down her neck as fear crept into her belly. She swallowed hard when the beam from her flashlight caught the silhouette of the raven.

"You're not getting this journal," Neiva grunted, tucking it into her jacket.

The raven was perched on the porch railing, obsidian eyes staring back at her. It let out a loud caw, throwing its head in the direction of the outhouse.

"What do you see?" Neiva asked nervously. She was still slightly scared of the raven, but maybe the bird would answer her. Nate said she might have the power to communicate with animals. She had seen Viv and Breezy perform their magic; maybe she could too.

"Do you always talk to birds?" a strong voice asked from the shadows.

Neiva gasped. She jumped back when a figure materialized out of the shadows. He was tall and lean, just like Darius, but where Darius's hair was black, this stranger's hair was pure white. It flowed past his shoulders, disappearing down his back. The front of his hair was braided into tiny braids flowing along his face. A mask covered most of his face from his forehead to just above his upper lip. The mask was black, which formed to his face, almost like it was molded to him. Holes in the mask marked the area of his eyes, which were like nothing Neiva had ever seen before. The whites of his eyes were actually black, while his irises were white and his pupils, red.

The area of skin showing through the mask was a soft pale-gray color, almost white. His lips were dark gray; and when he smiled at Neiva, she could see sharp incisors graced his mouth. He was dressed in a black, long-sleeved shirt covered by a dark gray vest. A black belt with a silver skull on the front held up his tight-fitting suede pants. Long pirate boots landed just above his knees.

"My name is Sasha," he said holding out a black, clawed hand.

Neiva backed away until she hit the cabin wall. Her eyes were wide, and she began to shake. A panic attack was about to set in, something that had been happening quite frequently. Just thinking about it made her shake inside. She almost felt like she was going to hyperventilate. At the brink of screaming or kicking the stranger below the waist, she heard Darius's velvety voice in her head.

"Don't worry, Neiva. Sasha is my right-hand man, and I trust him with my life. I am dealing with kingdom matters at the moment, so I couldn't get away. I sent Sasha in my place. He has brought you a gift from me. Please accept it."

Neiva's lips opened and closed silently. She was dismayed, confused, and exhausted. The nerves and panic dissolved into curiosity. She didn't know how Darius did it, but he always made her feel better. She was sad Darius wasn't able to make it himself, but when he said Sasha brought a gift for her, Sasha suddenly had Neiva's full attention.

"Enjoy, my sweet. I will see you in your dreams tonight," Darius's voice sent a light caress throughout her mind and then slowly disappeared. With the last of Darius's voice echoing in her mind, she stuck her hand out to shake Sasha's clawed hand.

"It's nice to finally meet you," Sasha said, bringing his hand back. "I would like to say I have heard a lot about you, but that would be a lie. Darius is a very secretive man."

Neiva could detect an unknown accent, possibly Russian. It wasn't thick, but it was apparent to anyone listening closely.

She stared at Sasha's mouth. "Can I ask you a question?"

"Go ahead. You may ask anything, my dear."

"Are you a vampire?" Neiva quickly let the question slip from her lips.

Another laugh escaped from him. "Ah, a good question. No, I am not a vampire, but I could see where you got the idea. I'm actually a shadow spirit. The legend of the vampire was born from my species' existence."

"So you thirst for blood?" Neiva slouched down into her coat, making sure her neck was hidden.

"Ah, that's a fairy tale made up by humans." He paused. "No, I do not thirst for blood. My kind only takes the blood from our enemies to steal their powers or to enter their thoughts. It's a way to gain information and knowledge from our enemies. For your information, I like to eat meat and my favorite food is actually Mexican food," he added with a smile.

"What about the sun?"

"Another myth, but partly true. Like any dark spirit, we can go into the sunlight, but we find it very annoying. We prefer to stay within the shadows. As for the other questions that I know you're going to ask, those are mostly true. I can't turn into a bat, but I can turn into a wolf. I can't fly, but I can teleport from one area to the next. I do have super-strength, but my vision is average unless I am in wolf form. I don't need to be invited into a house, but I do like sleeping underground. It's so much cooler and it's great for your skin."

Neiva studied Sasha. He was handsome in a haunting, almost nightmarish way. His eyes were the creepiest-looking characteristic of all. They would send anyone running in the opposite direction; in fact, they made her want to run screaming off the porch into the tundra.

"Anyway, enough about me. Darius sent me here to give you your birthday gift. He couldn't make it because he was dealing with matters of the court, political matters with the king of the light spirits—and it will probably take days for them to agree on one thing." Sasha said the last line under his breath.

Neiva looked at Sasha questioning what he just said, but he simply ignored it. He reached into his gray vest and pulled out a purple velvet box. He slowly handed it to Neiva, who took it out of Sasha's clawed hand.

The box was small and square. It looked like one of those ring boxes from a jewelry store. Neiva's heart quickened as she opened it. She was shocked; it wasn't a ring, but a beautiful bracelet curled up inside of the box. Neiva delicately took the bracelet out and held it up so she could see it in the moonlight. It was a silver or platinum chain with red rubies nestled between each link, sparkling brightly at Neiva. At the end of the chain was a raven's head with its beak open so it could clasp onto the other end of the bracelet.

"It's so beautiful," Neiva whispered in awe.

"Here, let me help you put it on," Sasha took the bracelet out of Neiva's hand. He wrapped the bracelet around her right wrist and clasped it together. It fit perfectly, neither too big nor too small. It sparkled under the moonlight, reminding Neiva of a lost treasure.

"The jewels on the bracelet are some of the rarest rubies in the world. They're called star rubies. These gems get their name from the six-spoke star that seems to travel over them when they're moved," he said as he pointed to the rays sliding across the bracelet's surface.

Neiva could tell they looked like stars, but they almost

looked like silk as well. Neiva stood amazed as she gazed at the fiery gift.

"Rubies are always associated with blood and fire. The Eskimos believe that rubies are a source of warmth and life for mankind. They believe rubies are a sign of passion and love." Sasha gave Neiva a wink as he said the last line. "Anyway, rubies were brought to Alaska by Chinese trading ships long ago. The townsfolk of Spirit would trade ivory for rubies every once in a while."

Neiva wasn't paying attention to the rest of Sasha's story. Her mind was reeling in all directions. Was Darius saying he loved her? But they hardly knew each other. Why did she feel this way? Could people fall in love that fast? Was it all about passion? The biggest question of all was, what did Darius look like underneath his mask? She could not get that question out of her head.

"I know you have many questions about Darius, but they're not for me to answer. I'm sure you have heard this saying before, but secrets are always revealed in the end," Sasha said with a slight smirk on his face. It was as if he was reading Neiva's mind.

The raven let out a loud caw, catching both Neiva's and Sasha's attention. The raven was staring out across the porch with his feathers puffed out. He let out another loud caw, shaking his head toward the sky. Stepping out from under the porch overhang, Neiva gazed at up the sky and gasped.

"What's the rat with wings cawing at?" Sasha asked as he stepped up to Neiva's side. His eyes turned to the sky. "Oh, damn."

The northern lights were flowing across the sky. Deep reds overpowered the usual colors of blue, green, and yellow, giving the sky a menacing appearance. It looked exactly like the colors from Neiva's vision except these seemed more threatening, more real.

Sasha quickly put his hand on Neiva's shoulder. He glanced at the horizon just below the northern lights. A thick fog was forming and creeping across the tundra. The cloud was heading toward the cabin. As it grew thicker, lights started to glow inside the mist, blinking on and off. It almost reminded Neiva of the old 1980s movie *The Fog*.

"Quickly get inside. You will be safe there. I have to go warn King Darius," Sasha said as he pushed Neiva toward the cabin and dissolved into the shadows.

Without hesitation, Neiva listened to Sasha's warning. She quickly ran to the cabin door and opened it. She looked at the raven. "Do you want to come in?"

The raven opened his wings and cawed loudly. With the quickness of lightning, it flew into the house, becoming a blur of black feathers. Neiva scanned the porch. Who knew birds could fly that fast? But then again this was no ordinary bird she was dealing with. Slamming the door behind her, she rushed into the living room and began waving her hands frantically toward the window.

"Hey, what took you so long?" Nate popped his head up from the couch. His expression changed as he saw the look on Neiva's face. He quickly sat up. "What's wrong?"

"Trouble's coming," Neiva replied pointing out the window.

Viv, Breezy, and Nate all ran to the window. They were in such a rush, Nate's face smushed against the glass, while Viv and Breezy looked out toward the horizon.

Viv turned to Nate, her eyes now glowing yellow. "It's fog and it's getting closer."

"Uh, oh," Nate replied, peeling his face away from the window.

"Please tell me what's wrong, and why is the fog glowing? It suddenly appeared when the northern lights turned red," Neiva's voice quivered.

"Did you say the northern lights are now red?" Nate asked. His eyes grew huge when he saw Neiva nod her head. "It's a bad omen. It means something evil is coming our way, and we must be prepared."

"Neiva, you remember your vision, the one were the queen sacrifices herself to save the kingdom?" Breezy asked and stepped closer to Neiva.

"Yes. It looks exactly the same as the one in my vision," Neiva said with a shaky voice.

"This means another sacrifice must be made," Breezy said with her eyes fixed on Neiva. "The prophecy said to appease the earth, the life of a royal must end."

Chapter 7

A TIDAL WAVE OF EMOTIONS crashed within Neiva. She immediately thought of Darius. Did this mean he was next? She would not let Darius sacrifice himself. No. They had just discovered each other, and Neiva still had so much to learn about him.

"The fog is almost to the porch!" Breezy called out.

"Wait. It stopped," Viv said incredulously.

Neiva turned to the window. Viv was right. The fog, or whatever it was, was just five feet from the house. Thick and pulsating, as if manipulated by an unknown entity, it surrounded the house in a perfect circle. It did not seem to be moving any closer to the cabin.

"It's the Ishegocks," Nate explained, suddenly sure.

"What?" Neiva asked. "What is Nate talking about?"

"Ishegocks are an Eskimo legend," Nate didn't finish his sentence. His eyes rolled up into his head as his body hit the floor with a thud.

"Nate!" the girls screamed in unison. They rushed to his side trying to assess the damage. He looked okay. His face was pale and occasionally his eye would twitch, but other than that he looked like he was just sleeping.

Viv tried to move him onto his back, but he wouldn't budge. It was like he was glued to the floor. The girls tried everything, but Nate would not move. Viv was getting ready to smack his face when the lights blinked out, leaving the fireplace casting an eerie glow around the room.

"What's going on?" Neiva asked as the girls got up to form a protective circle around Nate.

"Whatever it is, it has upset Nate's spirit guide," Breezy pointed to Nate's neck.

It was true. Nate's tattoo was swirling to life, as if something was alive and moving underneath his skin. The swirling became faster and faster until the tattoo suddenly vanished from Nate's neck.

"Where did it go?" Viv asked, glancing around the room.

Her question was answered by a low growl coming from behind her. Viv slowly turned around to see a massive fox about the size of a large wolf standing just a couple feet away. It was impressive in size and weight. It had black fur over most of its body and gray fur gracing its legs, the tip of its tail, and around its eyes. The eyes themselves were white with no pupils. They glowed like small orbs that could stare deep into your soul. The beast's teeth were bared, showing its long, lethal incisors. It had sharp claws that looked like they belonged to a bear. They clicked on the floor as the fox stalked closer to Nate's body.

"Easy boy," Viv whispered as she brought her hands up to ward off the fox. "What should we do?"

Neiva turned to look at the fox. Its eyes locked onto hers. They pulled Neiva into them. She could feel the spirit guide's emotions and she caught some of its thoughts—correction *her* thoughts. Neiva could feel the fox was female, but the strangest thing was that the fox did not seem upset about the fog outside.

The words "protected" and "safe" popped into Neiva's head. From what she could gather from the fox's thoughts, the fog was protecting them, and, as long as they stayed inside, they were safe.

"I'm not sure, Viv. But I'm getting a strong feeling that we're okay for now. I think it's best to let Nate explain everything when he wakes up," Neiva replied. "He seems to know about this."

"How do you know this?" Viv asked while she slowly crept closer to Neiva, as if Neiva would protect her from the fox.

"I don't know how. I am catching little bits of her thoughts and feelings. Not whole sentences but just words and fragments of thoughts," Neiva said as she looked at the fox, who was circling around Viv to inspect Nate.

The fox laid her forehead against Nate's before turning quickly to let out a long growl at Viv. The furry fox flicked her tail up, and then within the blink of an eye, she disappeared and was back on Nate's neck as his tattoo.

Viv let out a long, exaggerated breath, as if she had been holding it the whole time. She slowly sat herself on the floor, and then looked intently at Neiva. "Now please explain to me how you knew Nate's spirit guide's thoughts. I thought that only the Guardians could talk to their own spirit guides. And how can you know it's female?"

Neiva was still looking at Nate's tattoo. She still felt a small connection with the fox. Faint, but it was still there. A sense of contentment hummed through the back corner of Neiva's mind. She turned to look at Viv, but was distracted as a moan came from the direction where Nate lay.

"Oh, I feel like I have been hit by a bus," Nate moaned as he slowly sat up. He blinked a couple of times before he could focus on the girls.

Breezy, who stood still as a statue by the window during the encounter with Nate's spirit guide, moved to check on Nate. Viv just sat in the same spot on the floor, still staring at Neiva with daggers in her eyes. She wanted answers and probably was not going to give up until she got them. Neiva moved to sit down beside Nate.

"What's the last thing that you remember?" Breezy asked as she inspected Nate's head for any cuts or bruises.

"Well," Nate scratched his head while looking around the cabin. "I just remember that I was going to tell you about the legend of the Ishegocks. Then everything went blank."

"Just to let you know, when you blacked out, your spirit guide decided to make an appearance," Viv added dryly, whipping her tail back and forth in irritation.

Nate's eyes grew large as he looked from Viv to Breezy then to Neiva. "Is that true?"

"Yes, it's true Nate," Viv hissed. "Why don't you just ask Neiva? She kind of bonded with her."

"Huh? Really?" Nate asked as he turned to look at Neiva. "I've never heard of anyone talking to another Guardian's spirit guide."

Neiva quickly glanced at Nate's neck again. She still felt the slight hum from the fox. She wondered if it was a short-time deal or if it was going to last. Suddenly she received her answer. The word "family" and the feeling of protection emanated from the fox. Neiva now knew it was for the long term.

"I don't know how it happened, but suddenly I could feel the emotions from your, um, fox friend and could make out some words from her too. She wanted to let us know she was not a threat," Neiva said.

"You knew Roxy was a female?" Nate asked puzzled.

Viv smirked, rolling her eyes at Nate. "You named your spirit guide Roxy?"

"You wouldn't understand. It's a connection between Guardians and their spirit guides. You feel it deep inside," Nate pointed to his chest and then he looked at Neiva. "Spirits can't connect with a spirit guide because they don't have one. Only Natives have spirit guides, but they can only connect with their own. I wonder what other powers you have. You're Eskimo, Neiva, but with special powers. This has never happened before."

"Well, we know she has the ability to bring our spirit shields down. But I want to know what an Ishegock is and why that fog has circled around the house. Is it evil? I don't like it one bit," Breezy said abruptly, which usually wasn't like her. She was always the calm one in the group, who never showed any annoyance toward anyone.

Nate got up to check outside, then walked over to the couch at the end of the bed and sat down. He patted the spot next to him, indicating for the girls to come over to sit by him. The girls crawled into the bed, snuggling under the covers. Neiva was in the middle with Breezy closest to the fireplace. Each girl stared at Nate urging him to go on with the story.

Nate wrapped a blanket around himself and he stared at the flames within the fireplace. The wood crackled like popcorn as the flames intensified with the start of Nate's story.

"Our culture believes that when a soul leaves the body, it goes to a place beyond the northern lights. Legend says that the soul is escorted by the raven, the only known animal able to cross to the other side. Without the raven's guidance, souls would not be able to make this journey. They would become lost among the marshes, left to wander for eternity.

"Well, over the years these lost souls have adapted to their situation, or you can say 'evolved.' They've become something more, new beings that travel within a thick cloud of fog. They can travel at any time, sweeping over the land to take the bad children from each village, according to my parents. Kind of like the boogeyman, but no one knows where the children go. Some believe the children's souls are taken and become lost souls themselves, but there are others who believe the children are eaten by these new beings, which in return gives them more power and strength. But no one knows for sure. The only way to escape their grasp is to be a good child or whenever you see the fog rolling in, just stand still and listen. If you don't see or hear anything within the fog, you're safe. But if you see any lights within the fog or hear any high-pitch whistling, then run the other way because the Ishegocks are coming to get you." Nate finished his last line with a dramatic whistle and jumped on top of the girls who all screamed in unison.

"That wasn't funny!" grumbled Viv, who clung to Neiva.

Breezy just laughed at Nate, while Neiva peeked her head out of the covers. "What do they look like, Nate?"

"I'm not sure, but my dad swears he caught a glimpse of one on a camping trip with his friends. The fog came in during the night while my dad's friends were sleeping. It came in really fast, so he wasn't prepared for it. It infused their entire campsite to where he couldn't even see his tent. He tried to get to his tent, but something huge got in his way. He said it had to be seven feet tall with green hair over all of its body. It had glowing yellow eyes like the sun and sharp teeth. My dad barely saw it before he blacked out. He woke up in the morning in his tent. When he went outside to check on his buddies, that's where he saw the footprints in the sand."

"Of the Ishegocks?" Breezy asked, giving Nate a skeptical look.

"Actually, no, Breezy. The prints in the sand were very large and had little prints around them. My father thought it was a sow with her two cubs. So, he and his friends decided to pack up and head out. When they were driving out of their camping area, the truck was suddenly plowed from the side by something very large and strong. It ended up being the mother bear. He saw the cubs playing in the bushes as they booked it out of there."

"Wow. Your father was lucky. A mother bear is really aggressive and is known to attack when she has cubs," Breezy stated as she looked at Viv and Neiva.

"Do you think the Ishegocks saved him?" Neiva asked.

"That's what my dad believes. Why else would it not let him go to his tent?" Nate replied with a serious look. "If the Ishegocks didn't show up, he would have been bear meat."

"Nice pun, Nate," Viv said sarcastically, her amber eyes glowing. "Tell us more about the raven. Word throughout the Spirit World is that the raven is a powerful totem, only meant for powerful souls." She glanced at Neiva, giving her a knowing smile. "What do you think it means?"

Before Nate could even open his mouth in reply, a loud

cry boomed from the kitchen. It echoed around the room, causing Viv to jump out of bed with her stinger ready to strike. Breezy sat up with her eyes locked toward the kitchen, her hands slowly opening and closing in front of her. Nate stood there still as a statue, staring into the kitchen with his mouth slightly opened.

"Oh!" Neiva exclaimed as she jumped off the couch. "I totally forgot!"

How could she have forgotten about the giant bird in their kitchen? So many things were happening that it was almost too much to take in. It's like her memory could only absorb so much information at once.

Neiva ran to the kitchen and suddenly stopped short. The raven was perched on one of the kitchen chairs. It looked slightly annoyed, but that all changed when its eyes met Neiva's. It was as if a door had opened, releasing all of the raven's emotions and thoughts. They slammed into Neiva, knocking the breath out of her. As with Nate's spirit guide, Neiva was in tune with the raven; the only difference was she felt a deeper connection. It was strange. She felt a link between herself and the raven before, but it didn't feel this strong.

She could feel the raven's agitation and his yearning to go outside. He wanted to fly. Neiva was certain of that, but she did not understand why he wanted to go outside with the fog still surrounding the cabin.

A smooth voice suddenly filled Neiva's mind: *To protect you, Neiva.*

Neiva's eyes widened as she looked at the raven. "You can talk?" she asked out loud.

Yes, I can speak to you telepathically, just as you can speak to me telepathically, he replied, emphasizing the word telepathic.

Dumbfounded, Neiva scratched her head. She knew the raven was different . . . but a raven who could communicate telepathically was totally preposterous. But as Neiva thought about it, she wondered what had been normal in her life anyway? So far, the world that she knew was changing right in front of her. What difference would it make that she could talk to a raven or that it was her totem? Was this raven really a raven, or could it be from the Spirit World?

I know you feel confused, the raven pleaded. *In time I will explain things to you, but first I need to go outside.*

Dry-mouthed, Neiva stared at the bird. All her senses were fixed on the oddly beautiful fowl. She could hear the flutter of his wings and the fear in his mind's voice. Agitation radiated from it like a talon pushing its way into her chest. The need to be outside became stronger and overwhelming. It engulfed her and without thinking, she ran to the cabin door and opened it.

Chapter 8

"NEIVA! What are you doing?" shouted Breezy from the living room.

She jumped off the couch and ran toward Neiva. But before she could get to the door, the raven flew in from the kitchen. With one flap of his wings, he hovered for a split second, giving Neiva a nod of approval before flying out the door with the speed of Superman.

Breezy stopped and stared at Neiva. She blinked a couple of times, slightly shocked. "Was there a giant bird in our kitchen?"

Neiva closed the door and laid her check against the cold wood doorjamb. She could feel the raven circling the perimeter. He was relaxed and at ease now, circling high in the sky. She could almost feel the beat of his wings and the intake of his breath as he swooped around the cabin.

The feeling of falling made Neiva grip the door. Her vision began to shimmer, causing everything around her to blend together like watercolors running together on canvas. Within a blink of an eye Neiva was outside, but she could still feel her body on the ground, inside the cabin.

Excitement and wonder bubbled through her veins. She

was flying. Through the raven's sharp eyes, she could see they were high above the cabin, drifting on the wind that blew in from the east. She could see the fog; it went on for miles with no end in sight. The lights still pulsed within it, giving Neiva an overwhelming sense of dread.

Don't be afraid. Think of it as your curtain of protection. I wanted you to see how far it went and how protected you are, the raven replied to Neiva's unease.

Neiva felt herself being pulled backward. The vision was receding faster and faster until darkness surrounded her. Suddenly, as quickly as it had come, the darkness was gone and she found herself back in the cabin. Still dizzy, she blinked and shook her head, trying to wrench her mind back.

"Hell! Earth to Neiva!" Breezy said as she shook Neiva's head.

Breezy looked like a rumpled, angry kitten. Her hair was puffed out in all directions and her cat eyes were dilated with fear. Both of her hands tightly gripped Neiva's head, shaking her. Sharp claws burrowed into Neiva's skull causing Neiva to hiss.

"Breezy, your claws are hurting me. Please let go," Neiva stated as she tried to pry Breezy's claws away from her head.

Breezy paused for the briefest moment, not realizing she grabbed Neiva's head so tightly. She blinked a couple of times, then slowly let go, giving Neiva a concerned stare.

Checking her head for cuts, Neiva eyed Breezy suspiciously. She couldn't find any traces of blood, which was good. But she swore she could feel little indentations where Breezy's claws had been. "Jeez, Breezy."

"I'm sorry. I'm a little bit frazzled right now." Breezy said embarrassed as she retracted her claws. "Everything that is happening is so strange. I don't know what to think."

"So, what's the deal with the giant bird? Was it a raven?" Viv asked as she glided over to stand next to Breezy. She put her hand on Breezy's shoulder to give her a little comfort. Even Viv noticed Breezy's sudden change in attitude.

Speechless, Neiva didn't know what to say. She was still trying to wrap her mind around the raven and what their connection could mean. He was more than just a bird. Power and intelligence glittered behind those obsidian eyes. Looking out the window, Neiva reached her mind out to see if she could connect with the raven.

It did not even take a second before she felt the flap of wings at the center of her mind. *Yes*, replied the raven.

Neiva could feel him perched on top of the northeast corner of the roof. He was watching the horizon, not the fog. He swiveled his head back and forth so he wouldn't miss anything that could attack them from the sky.

What should I say to my friends? They want to know why a giant bird was in our kitchen. I don't think the answer "I don't know" will suffice. But first off, I want to know what's going on and what you are and why you attacked me on the boat. Neiva urgently asked telepathically.

Just tell them I'm your spirit guide. If they ask why you don't have a tattoo, tell them you're different and you don't need one. Ask them if it would make a difference if you had one. That should satisfy them for now. As for your questions, they will all be explained in time. But I will tell you this, I did not attack you. I was trying to grab your journal and accidently cut your hand. I was obeying strict orders. Now go get some sleep, for I believe you have a date with His Darkness tonight, the raven responded with slight amusement in his voice.

The air exploded from her lungs as if a balloon were pricked. She forgot. How could she have forgotten that she would see him tonight? Would it be like their first meeting on the beach? Would she be wearing the same black dress again or could she somehow manifest a different outfit? She didn't know what to think.

A loud laugh erupted inside her head and amusement bounced off her skull like a dodgeball. *Only girls would ponder about what to wear in a dream. Just go into it with an open mind. Now, I must go patrol the area for anything lingering in the skies.*

You're safe on the ground. The Ishegocks will protect you.

"Thanks," Neiva managed to muster out. Her thoughts were still on Darius. Neiva had a feeling the raven knew more than he was letting on, which seemed to be the standard way of handling things in Spirit.

By the way, Neiva, my name is Riley. You don't have to think of me as "The Raven" anymore. She felt a brush of his wings and a gust of wind as he exited her mind.

Oops. Neiva had totally forgotten to ask. That's the first thing she should have asked or even thought of. It was the polite thing to do but she had other things on her mind. *Oh well,* she thought as she turned her attention to Viv and Breezy. They were both giving her concerned looks. Nate was now by their side, standing with his arms crossed.

"What?" she asked them.

"Where did you go? You had this faraway look in your eyes as if you were seeing something else," Breezy asked crisply.

"Yeah," Nate grumbled. "What was with the bird too?"

Neiva took a quick breath, "First off, the raven is my spirit guide, and second, I was talking to him just a minute ago. He was showing me how far the fog went."

"Wait, the raven is your spirit guide? How is that possible?!" Nate demanded. He quickly walked behind Neiva and firmly pulled her hair back to get a good look at her neck. "Nothing."

"Would it help if I had a tattoo? Would that make a difference?" Neiva asked defensively, turning around to look at Nate.

"Yeah, it would!" Nate yelled crossing his arms. "This goes against every rule we know."

Neiva let out a mental grunt, hoping Riley would hear her.

"What rules, Nate?" Viv stared back arrogantly and poked him with her claw. "There are no rules when it comes to King Darius. He can do whatever he wants. If he wants Neiva to have a spirit guide, then she will have one. No ifs, ands, or buts about it."

"But—" Nate was swiftly cut off by Breezy.

"Enough! This night has taken a downhill spiral. It's turning into total chaos instead of a celebration of Neiva's birthday. We wanted to slowly integrate her into the Spirit World and explain everything to her, but we keep interrogating her about things she doesn't have a clue about," Breezy firmly said while frowning at Viv and Nate. "Eventually the truth will be revealed. It always is. Just like the Ishegocks, nothing to worry about right?"

It almost sounded like Breezy was trying to tell herself everything was all right, as if she really didn't believe everything was okay. Something was different with Breezy. Neiva couldn't put her finger on it, but something was bothering her.

"You're right, Breezy," Neiva calmly stated.

The night had turned into something out of *The Twilight Zone*. She didn't know what to expect next, but she knew that they were safe. The Ishegocks stayed within the fog, but were protecting them, and Riley was watching the skies for any enemies. Plus, Darius wouldn't let anything happen to them. It was probably why he hadn't shown up, because they were safe, Neiva kept telling herself.

"Ah, you're right," Nate grumbled as he stuck his hands in his pockets in surrender. He slowly shuffled to the couch where he dramatically fell onto it with a thud, making weird noises into his pillow.

"Yeah, I guess when dealing with the Spirit World you can always expect the unexpected," Viv said while still glaring at Nate as he sat up to look at Neiva.

"We'll do whatever you want to do, Neiva. This night hasn't turned out like we planned," Nate grumbled as he watched Breezy walk over to hug Neiva.

"Are you okay, Breezy?" Neiva asked as she let go to give Breezy a closer look.

Breezy shuttered violently and shut her eyes. Her ears were twitching, as if she was listening for any movement that was not theirs. Her wings beat faster than a hummingbird's, almost as if she were going to take off right before their eyes.

Her hands were shaking, curled into fists at her sides.

"I'm okay. I just get scared and stressed out too easily. I think it has to do with being part cat spirit. And it's hard not knowing what's going on. But it has to be harder for you, Neiva. Your world is drastically changing and it makes me feel bad for having an anxiety attack over the fact that I don't know what's going on either," Breezy replied with her hand on her heart. Tears came to her eyes.

Stress can sneak up on anyone like an ugly snake. Breezy was the one person in the group that everyone came to for advice. Breezy always had the answers; except now she was clueless about what was going on.

"Yeah, it's a lot to take in," Neiva told Breezy, turning to look out the window. The fog seemed thicker now.

"I think it's time for bed," Breezy said, leading Neiva back to the couch. Viv joined them. As soon as they got to the bed, all three girls jumped under the covers to snuggle into their pillows. They silently stared at the ceiling for several long minutes before Nate spoke up.

"I didn't realize how tired I was," he declared, barely getting the sentence out as sleep overwhelmed him. He curled into a little ball on the floor and was out like a light, soon mumbling about Ishegocks and ravens in his sleep.

Neiva couldn't keep her eyes open either. It took a lot of her willpower just to tell everyone good night. Viv was the only one who responded to her. She let out a small grunt before turning onto her side. Neiva could sense Breezy was hidden underneath the blanket, snoring ever so slightly. As Neiva settled into her pillow, one thought entered her mind just before she slipped into sleep. How could they sleep after everything that had happened today? It was almost as if they were getting a little push from somewhere.

Chapter 9

NEIVA BLINKED A COUPLE OF TIMES before her mind could register what she saw before her. She didn't know if it was her eyesight that was off or maybe she was going crazy again, but she was seeing everything in black and white. Well, almost everything.

White trees with thick, black trunks surrounded her. The trees' leaves looked as if someone had used a purple highlighter to outline the edges, causing them to give off a slight glow. The grass was a light gray color, but dark purple flowers sporadically popped up through the ground, giving the vista some life and character. Neiva felt an urge to pick one of the flowers. From the obstructed view of the sky through the trees, Neiva could see light pinkish-purple clouds slowly floating overhead, giving Neiva a calm feeling.

Glancing down at the flowers near her feet, she noticed she was no longer in her pajamas. Instead she was wearing a short violet dress that ended at the middle of her thighs. Black lace trimmed the dress, causing it to ruffle out at the end. A black belt was tied around her waist with a diamond-incrusted raven for a belt buckle. The top of the dress was almost like a corset tied up in the back. It was very tight-fitting, but surprisingly it didn't show off any cleavage, which Neiva preferred. It left her shoulders and arms bare except for the black fishnet gloves on both of her hands. Black stockings with horizontal purple stripes started just below her knees leading down into black lace pumps with purple bow ties that completed the outfit. Her hair was tied back into a high ponytail. Thick strands of her hair were left out to fall down around her face. The black ribbon was tied neatly around the right strand, weaving in and out of her hair. Neiva could feel that she was wearing lipstick. She brought her finger to her lips. When she pulled her finger back, a metallic purple color was left smudged on her fingertip.

She knew that she was dreaming and somewhere in the middle of a gray forest. The trees seemed to go on forever as she slowly turned around to see if there was any sign of Darius. Where was he?

Suddenly, Neiva saw a white object bouncing toward her. It was zigzagging throughout the trees at a fast pace. Within a blink of an eye the object was right before her feet, grunting at her.

As Neiva peered down at the creature, she noticed it was a little white ball of fur with two beady purple eyes peeking out of its fur. It sat on two purple feet that kind of looked like Barney the dinosaur's feet. The strange thing about the creature wasn't the big smiling mouth full of sharp teeth, located just below its eyes, but the giant clock, which sat where its round stomach should have been. The hands on the clock were spinning in all directions, almost as if it didn't know what time it was.

The creature squeaked at Neiva and bounced around her feet all the while staring at her with its beady eyes. It started to hop off, then bounced back toward Neiva just to stare at her again. She had the feeling the creature wanted her to follow it somewhere. It was probably sent from Darius. Who else would be in her dreams asking for her audience but Darius?

The creature suddenly bopped its head into Neiva's leg then ran off before she could even react.

"Hey, what was that for?" she asked rubbing her leg.

The creature turned and stared up at Neiva, blinking its eyes several times. It looked innocently at her before opening its mouth.

"Must follow," the creature replied in a high-pitched voice while bouncing around. "It's Durby's job."

"Durby?" Neiva asked squatting down to look at the little creature. "Did Darius send you?"

"Yes! Yes! His Darkness sent me to you! Now you must follow!" he said as he ran around Neiva before bouncing off. He stopped several yards away before running back to Neiva to stare at her again.

"Follow?" Neiva asked while pointing in the direction Durby kept running to.

Durby gave Neiva a look that she could have sworn had the word "duh" behind it. He shuffled back and forth from foot to foot before bouncing off; this time he didn't wait for her. So, Neiva did the only thing she could do, follow Durby deeper into the gray forest.

IT SEEMED LIKE HOURS before Durby stopped. Neiva's feet hurt from the four-inch heels she was wearing, and she felt tired. *If this was a dream, than why was she so tired?* she wondered.

"Durby got you here," he squeaked as he finally stopped before a beautiful gate.

The gate was about twelve feet high and fifteen feet wide. It fit perfectly between two huge trees that sat on either side of it. The weird part about the gate was not the fact that it was in the middle of the forest but that Neiva couldn't see around the trees. It was as if they grew in width every time she tried to peek around them.

"Knock. You must knock," Durby said as he ran around Neiva's legs.

He paused for the briefest moment to rub his cheek

against her leg before he bounced off into the gray woods. He disappeared before Neiva could even get her thoughts together.

Turning to the gate, Neiva marveled at its wonder. It was breathtaking. There was nothing she could compare it to and there was no way she could have dreamt this into her subconscious. It was simply beautiful.

The gate was made out of some kind of metal that had a hint of purple flecks in it, making it sparkle like the stars in the midnight sky. Twisted metal bars wrapped around each other to form a dramatic scene before her. The design was of a raven in flight with its wings stretched out to the sky. Long, scary hands with claws seemed to be reaching out toward the raven, as if they were trying to keep it from escaping. The lock on the gate was in the shape of a heart, but there was no keyhole. Instead there was a symbol on it. It looked like a symbol of a black castle, but on closer inspection, Neiva could tell it was a dragon instead. Its wings looked like two castle towers, while its open jaw was a drawbridge. *It was different and would make a cool tattoo*, Neiva thought as she stepped back.

"Here we go," Neiva whispered excitedly as she knocked on the lock.

She ran back a few steps not knowing what to expect. There was a loud click and the lock suddenly vanished as the gate slowly swung open to reveal a beautiful garden. Rose bushes with vivid purple roses lined a stoned wall that surrounded the garden. Neon-purple vines crawled up the stones to disappear over the other side. In the middle of the garden sat a long black table with a dark violet tablecloth covering it. Teacups, doughnuts, and muffins covered the table, while a giant teapot sat at its very center.

Neiva didn't notice the four strangers occupying the chairs until she brushed up against one of them. She was too caught up in her surroundings to notice at first, but once her arm brushed up against something prickly, it had her full attention.

At first Neiva didn't know what it was. It looked like

a pincushion that was somehow attached to the chair until Neiva noticed it was an armful of long spines. It ran into a purple velvet jacket only to sprout out at the neckline into the face of something in a horror movie.

"No," cried Neiva. She backed away, trying not to see the ghastly creature's face. Was this a nightmare? Was she wrong about Darius? She stepped back and her feet got tangled together causing Neiva to lose her balance and fall back into the arms of Darius.

"Whoa. It's okay, Neiva," Darius's smooth voice whispered across her skin. He pulled her in close until her head was resting against his chest. The steady beat of his heart caused Neiva to calm down and relax slightly.

"What is that thing?" she mumbled into Darius's chest.

Neiva felt a rumble deep within his chest. She didn't know what it was until she glanced up at Darius only to hear laughter escape out of his mask.

Bewildered, Neiva looked up at Darius. How could he find her question so amusing, she asked herself as she quickly turned back to look at the prickly pear man. He looked very intimidating to Neiva, but the longer she stared at him, the blurrier his image appeared. Once she put all of her concentration into seeing what was really before her, the air seemed to shimmer around him giving Neiva the answer as to why Darius had laughed at her.

The scary image before her melted away to reveal a small porcupine wearing a purple bow tie. Cute and playful-looking, he was only three feet tall with big brown eyes and a little pointed nose surrounded by whiskers. Neiva wanted to run up to him and pinch his cheeks. Only the thought of being stabbed by his long quills stopped her from doing it.

"Remember, Neiva, looks can be deceiving to the eye and mind. You have to look beyond one's spirit shield to see the true creature behind the power," Darius said as the porcupine disappeared before her eyes.

With his hand on the small of her back, Darius slowly

guided Neiva around the table to the next chair.

A woman occupied the next chair. She was an elegant lady in her late twenties with bright blue eyes that were so enchanting they seemed to draw Neiva into them. Pink-blossom lips pouted underneath an elfish nose. Her black hair was braided up into a crown with white flowers intertwined with the plaits. She wore a black dress with a weird design on the front. It was in the shape of a gray diamond located just below her chest.

Weird fashion, Neiva thought as she glanced back to the lady's face. Her eyes suddenly snared Neiva into them and she couldn't look away.

"What do you see, Neiva?" Darius asked as he gently laid his hand on her shoulder.

"She's normal," Neiva replied robotically, as if she were in a trance.

"Are you sure?"

Neiva continued to stare at the woman. She couldn't take her eyes off of her. The woman didn't move or even blink. She was still as a statue, just as the porcupine had been. She didn't seem to change as Neiva willed herself to see her true from. The longer Neiva stared at her, the more enchanting and beautiful the lady became, leaving Neiva more perplexed and confused.

"Pretend you're a dancer on stage, Neiva. It's almost showtime and you're prepared to go on, but before you do, you just want to get a sneak peek at the audience that you're performing for—to assess the mood and atmosphere. The problem is that you don't want the audience to notice your presence. In order to do that, you must open the curtain ever so slightly, just enough to give you a small, quick look without it rippling, which would then let the audience know you're there," Darius explained as he leaned in to whisper in Neiva's ear.

The action sent a shiver down Neiva's spine, causing her stomach to flutter. It was that moment that Neiva noticed a flaw on the woman's face—a small wrinkle at the corner of her left eye. On closer inspection, the wrinkle was actually a crack. As Neiva stared deeper into the crevice, it started to spread across the woman's face, leaving a fissure in its wake. Charcoal-colored skin was revealed beneath the crack as it spread down the woman's chin, disappearing into her dress.

Neiva blinked a couple of times before the woman's image suddenly shifted. The woman's flawless skin fell into crumbles onto the ground around her. Her glossy black hair unraveled out of its braid and slowly rose above her head, as if pushed by an unseen force. The ends of the hair slowly started to disappear until a short, silky gray mane lay in messy waves upon her head. Her eyes were now red and covered by long, spiky lashes. She still retained her elfish nose, but her mouth had drastically changed. Her lips were blood-red with pinchers bursting out on either side of them, reminding Neiva of an insect. Her slender hands were graced with long black claws, but that's not what had Neiva gasping. It was the sharp blades coming out of her back.

There were a total of four blades, two on each side. They were silver in color and curved up the woman's back, coming to sharp points just above her head. They almost looked like appendages. Then it dawned on Neiva as she looked down at the lady's dress, they weren't blades but legs. The creature was actually a giant spider, not the elegant lady that Neiva had seen before.

"Is she a black widow?" Neiva looked at what she thought was a diamond on the woman's dress. It was bright red now.

In answer to Neiva's question, the woman's body slowly morphed into thousands of tiny black widows, all scurrying across the table to flow smoothly into the teapot that sat in the center.

Neiva's mouth hung slightly open as the last spider entered the teapot. She made a mental note not to have any tea if it was offered to her. She turned to give Darius a puzzled look, but he was already moving Neiva around the table. He positioned her so she could look at the third guest that sat across from where the spider lady once sat.

Surprised, Neiva couldn't believe she had missed seeing this creature. He was huge, reminding Neiva of an ogre. She couldn't believe his massive frame could fit in the small chair. It looked as if the chair was straining under his weight and would give out at any moment. He had a pudgy face with two giant tusks protruding from the bottom of his jaw. His nose was flat and his eyes were black as the night. He seemed to be staring out into space; he wasn't even blinking, just as the other two occupants before him.

The creature wasn't wearing a shirt exposing his fuzzy chest, which had more hair than the top of his head. Small spikes pierced each nipple and his huge stomach was pressed up against the table leaving no room for him to maneuver. Large hands were laid straight out onto the table, thick hair covered his knuckles, and he had black nails that looked like they had been slammed in a door, several times.

Neiva looked back at the ogre's face. He wasn't pleasing to the eyes, which made it even harder for Neiva to stare at him. She took a deep breath, and then tried to gently peek through the ogre's spirit shield. Nothing worked at first, causing Neiva to get agitated. Grinding her teeth together, she gave a little growl, surprising herself in the process. Usually she didn't get this annoyed, but she was with Darius. This made her want to do her best and do everything right. She kind of wanted to show off in front of him, but because that wasn't working, Neiva became more frustrated every second.

Her anger flared through her annoyance, blazing so bright that it fueled her energy to a boiling point. Then a tingling sensation surged throughout Neiva's body. It took away all the frustration and anger, leaving her mind clear. Neiva already knew the source of the power. It was Darius. He had closed in behind her, brushing his chest against her back. The mere contact made Neiva's heart flutter briefly before the calm feeling took over.

"Relax," Darius whispered, as he gently laid his chin down

on the top of her head. Neiva could slightly hear Darius's breathing as he exhaled out of his mask; this made Neiva relax even more, causing her to lean back into Darius.

She imagined a curtain surrounding the ogre. She visualized herself seeing through the curtain with X-ray vision, kind of like Superman. It only took a couple of seconds before Neiva saw the mystical shield surrounding the ogre, which did look like a curtain. It was full of different colors, leaving a rainbow that projected the ogre's current image. The middle of the curtain suddenly folded in to reveal a little elfish boy sitting in the chair. He was nine or ten years old, with spiky brown hair and long pointed ears poking out of the sides of his head. Large blue eyes were surrounded by thick lashes. There was a mischievous smile frozen on his face, as if he knew he was getting into trouble.

"A little boy?" Neiva asked.

With his hands clasped behind his back, Darius walked around the table to stop behind the boy's chair. He cocked his head to the side to stare at Neiva.

"You know the saying, don't judge a book by its cover," Darius stated as the little boy burst into a cloud of smoke and disappeared.

Darius walked over to the last chair that sat to the right of where the boy had just been. Unlike the last three chairs, this one was empty. Neiva raised her eyebrow at Darius. *What test was this?* she wondered.

"What do you see?" he asked while walking back to where Neiva was standing. He stood right next to her, his shoulder lightly against hers, letting her know that he was there to help.

The chair was just like all the other chairs. Swaths of purple fabric covered gold-etched dark wooden chairs. It seemed like a normal empty seat even when she tried to give it her whole concentration. She pushed so hard with her mind that she thought her eyes would pop out of her head. In the end, it just left her with a huge headache.

"Each spirit is different, Neiva. Some are stronger than

others, making their spirit shield harder to penetrate. The weaker spirit's shield falls faster while the stronger spirit's shield needs more power to break through it."

Neiva turned to look at Darius. His mask was darker, almost a black-gray color. The decorative stars that were usually sprinkled on the side had disappeared, leaving the mask bare. He was wearing a dark purple long-sleeved shirt unbuttoned at the neckline, showing that his mask covered his neck and part of his chest as well as his face. His shirt was tucked into a nice-fitting pair of black dress slacks complete with shiny black dress shoes. He looked really good, leaving Neiva faint and dizzy.

She pried her attention away from Darius to look again at the empty chair. It was still unoccupied, but Darius clearly indicated that it was not empty. Having seen through the other shields, she thought it shouldn't be that hard for her to see through this one. The fact that everything was changing around her should have made it easier to believe that what she was seeing was simply a trick of the mind's eye. She had found out that she went to school in a giant tree, her friends weren't human, and Nate was a spirit Guardian. Neiva could do this. She wasn't weak but strong. Granted, sometimes her temper and emotions got the better of her, but she knew she could do this.

As she concentrated harder, an outline of a shape suddenly started to appear, but she could barely see it. It was almost like in the movie *Predator*, where the predator was invisible and the viewer could only see its outline briefly at certain angles. She imagined another colorful curtain around the chair. It took a little bit longer for the curtain to appear this time, but when it did Neiva instantly saw who was behind it. Sasha was sitting in the chair.

He was wearing a pirate hat with his long white hair falling around his face. He wore a white button-up shirt, making his gray skin seem darker. His hands were clasped together in front of him. His expression was blank. Like the others, he didn't move or speak a word. Neiva couldn't see his eyes, but she noticed that Sasha was still wearing the same black mask. *It must be a part of his uniform*, she thought.

"Even a friend's spirit shield is hard to break unless they want you to peek through it." Darius said as Sasha sank back into the shadows to leave the chair empty.

"What about controlling the powers so you don't accidently take down someone's spirit shield?" Neiva asked as she stared at the empty chair.

"You're a freshman when it comes to your powers. You must learn to balance them out in order for you to control them. They are wild now, but with the right training you will be able to harness them," he replied while gesturing for Neiva to sit down.

She glanced at the chair beside her. It was empty, but she didn't know if she wanted to sit where the spider lady had been sitting.

Darius sat down, folding his hands together while waiting for Neiva to make her decision. "The spiders are gone, Neiva. They wouldn't hurt you even if they were still here."

Tingles crawled up her arm. Neiva looked the chair over one more time before she slid into it. She trusted Darius, but her fear of creepy-crawly things made it hard for her to sit still. She tried to calmly place her hands in her lap and turned to focus on Darius. He looked every bit like a king sitting in the chair across from her. His mask was shining brightly, while his hair sparkled like diamonds. The air around him throbbed with power she could feel from across the table. She also could feel him staring at her with intrigue. Neiva knew that he was waiting for her to ask him questions.

"What is this place?" Neiva asked. *Might as well start with something simple*, she thought.

A chuckle escaped Darius's mask. Out of all the questions she could possibly ask, she wanted to know where she was, and he found this quite amusing. To answer Neiva's question, Darius gestured at the environment around them. "This is a collection of your thoughts and dreams. I wanted you to feel comfortable and yet be in a mystical place at the same time."

Neiva glanced around. This place was beautiful even though almost everything was in black and white. She turned back to Darius and raised her eyebrow. "But this doesn't feel familiar to me."

"It's not a place you have physically been too. I took multiple thoughts from your dreams and memories, and then intertwined them. This is actually based off of two of your favorite stories," Darius said while folding his arms together. He didn't give Neiva a clue about what two stories he chose, but he patiently waited for her to figure it out. The surroundings looked sort of familiar to Neiva, as if she had the answer at the back of her mind but couldn't grasp it. It was like chasing a butterfly that was within arm's reach but never being able to catch it.

She turned around to try to see if anything would click. The surrounding plant life was beautiful beyond words and the table setup added more character to everything as well. It reminded Neiva of a party, a tea party in fact.

Everything snapped into place and Neiva instantly knew the answer. She had several favorite stories that she had loved since childhood but her two favorites had to be *Alice's Adventures in Wonderland* and *The Secret Garden.* The long table with all the sweets and tea on top of it (with the mysterious guests around it) were from *Alice's Adventures in Wonderland*, while the garden and the beautiful gate in the woods were from *The Secret Garden.* Neiva couldn't believe that she hadn't recognized it immediately.

She turned to Darius with an excited smile. "You picked my favorite stories. What made you pick them?"

"Most spirits are artistic. When we get the chance to do something creative, we tend to go all out and for you, Neiva, I wanted to do just that." Darius leaned forward, reaching out his hand for hers. Neiva slowly put her hand in his and instantly felt a spark. She swore she would have melted into the chair if not for Darius holding her hand.

Darius reluctantly pulled back from Neiva, once again folding his hands. He waited for her next question. Seconds ticked by before Neiva asked it.

"Why do you wear a mask, Darius?" Neiva let the question slip out. She originally wanted to ask what he looked like but didn't have enough courage to ask the question.

"I've been waiting for you to ask that one. I was so sure it would have been your first question," Darius whispered while he leaned forward.

He maneuvered his head to the side, as if he was glancing off into the distance beyond the garden's wall. "Neiva, when you're alone in the dark what scares you the most? The monster that you know is under your bed or is it the unknown entity lurking about; something that you know exists but you will never see?"

"Probably the unknown entity. A monster under my bed would be scary, but I could see it and I would know it was there unlike the entity. How can you fight against something you can't see?"

"Exactly," Darius replied, lightly clapping his hands. "If people don't know what I look like, then they fear me more because most people fear the unknown more than anything else in the world."

"Except death," Neiva added.

"Yes, death is high on the fear scale as well, but most people fear death because they do not know what will happen next . . . because it is unknown to them." Darius once again stared at Neiva. "Does it bother you that you cannot see my appearance?"

Neiva thought about Darius's question. She could say yes but then she felt that was only partly true. She did want to know what Darius looked like. Then there was that feeling deep down in her soul that told her she didn't care what he looked like. She felt a connection to him beyond anything she had ever felt before.

"I don't know. I really want to see what you look like

underneath that mask," Neiva mumbled, pointing at Darius. She wanted to lie to him, to tell him that it didn't matter but she couldn't lie to him. "Then again, I don't know if I want to know."

"Telling the truth is a great quality, Neiva. A lie might be a good thought at first, as if you were protecting someone's feelings, but the truth is always better in the end, even if it sometimes hurts."

"I didn't mean to hurt you!" Neiva defensively blurted out. She wasn't sure what she wanted. No teenager is ever sure of what they want.

"I know, Neiva. I was just giving you something to think about if you ever come across a similar situation. Just know that some spirits are able to detect lies." He paused for a couple of seconds before adding, "You can say my mask is my crown. It's what holds me to the dark land and dark spirits."

Neiva could see what Darius was saying. The mask did remind Neiva of a crown in a way, how it was always changing colors and seemed different every time she saw him. She also felt the mask had more power than Darius was letting on.

The next question just popped out of Neiva's mouth. "Why me?"

It was the question that she has been asking herself every day.

"Neiva, have you truly looked at yourself lately? You're a beautiful girl who is so talented in every field. You have family and friends who love you, but most of all you give back to others. You're not selfish or ignorant. You love life and everyone around you. You have many doors opening for you now and many obstacles in your way, but you will conquer them all, not just for yourself, but for those you love as well. And I, for one, find you enchanting. I would do anything for you, Neiva."

Neiva's face was flushed. She could feel the heat burning in her cheeks. She had never received so many compliments before. It made her heart flutter. But she still didn't understand what the connection between them was. What was this spark?

Darius stood up and walked around the table. He helped Neiva up then brought her hand up and lightly kissed it with the lips of his mask. "It's time for you to go into a deep sleep and rest, my dear."

"But I have so many more questions," Neiva pleaded as Darius guided her to the gate.

"I will answer two questions after every training session, as an award for your hard work. But understand this; these questions cannot pertain to yourself and some questions I cannot answer. There are many laws in the Spirit World that cannot be broken. One of those laws forbids any spirit from interfering with a new spirit's awakening."

"Awakening?" Neiva was puzzled. Was that what was going on with her?

"Ah, a question that we shall postpone until next time," Darius stated as he opened the gate with a flick of his hand. He turned to face Neiva, bringing her in close to him. He brought his face down to her ear and started whispering.

"Many people go through life meeting friends and spouses along the way, but few have truly met their soul mate, Neiva. In the Spirit World, we believe each spirit has a destined spirit mate—someone to spend the rest of their life with in this world and beyond." He said the last sentence as he leaned back, slowly bringing Neiva's hand up to his mask, lightly brushing it against his cheek.

Neiva's heart fluttered as Darius escorted her beyond the gate. "Until next time, princess."

As soon as Neiva let go of his hand, it slowly started to get dark. The deeper she went into the forest, the darker it became until suddenly everything was black, and she sunk into a deep sleep.

DARIUS STOOD AT THE ENTRANCE to the cabin. The girls were sleeping quietly while Nate's snores sounded like a foghorn occasionally breaking the silence.

Darius glanced out the windows to see the fog still engulfing the cabin. They were safe.

With a long sigh, Darius called upon the shadows. He didn't want to leave her. He wanted to protect her and never leave her side again. She was his world now and the feelings running deep in his heart would never fade. When his mother killed herself to save their kingdom, his heart had died that day. But now, it was alive again. He would protect her even if it cost his life. He not only wanted to keep her safe, he had to, for one day she would save them all.

Darius cast one last look at Neiva before the shadows engulfed him and welcomed him home.

Chapter 10

SUNLIGHT LEAKED THROUGH the cabin's windows causing Neiva to stir. She slowly opened her eyes to focus on the room. She felt so refreshed; it felt like she slept twelve hours instead of five. She heard the others stirring as she sat up in bed. Breezy poked her head out of the covers to wish Neiva a good morning. Viv growled in response.

Neiva was shocked to see Breezy back in her human form. She turned to look at Viv, who sat up with a scowl on her face. She was back in her human form too. Was it because of the sleep or was it Darius? The last time the girls changed back into their human forms, Neiva had seen Darius before the transformation had occurred.

"You're human again," Nate grumbled from his nest of blankets. Sometime in the middle of the night Nate had stolen the top blanket from the girls and thrown it onto himself.

Breezy sat up with a start. She glanced down at her arms and hands and inspected her face and ears before replying, "Thank goodness! Try to concentrate on not taking down our spirit shields, Neiva. For some reason, we're powerless when it comes to your abilities."

Viv slowly looked at her pale skin and tattoos. She glanced

up at Neiva and gave a shrug. "We'll see how long it lasts."

Neiva frowned. She had a feeling she would be able to control her abilities or feelings to see the girls in their true form. She felt she had more confidence now thanks to Darius's training.

"I'm hungry," Nate mumbled. He let out a giant yawn at the same time he was talking, so his words came out really slow and mumbled.

"Cereal?" Neiva suggested.

"Sounds good to me," Viv replied jumping up and out of bed. "I'll get the bowls."

Nate slowly removed himself from his hoard of covers. "I call the last of the Cinnamon Toast Crunch."

"Well, you better come and get it before I shove it into my mouth!" yelled Viv from the kitchen.

Nate was off the floor within seconds. When he reached the kitchen, he ended up mumbling something to Viv. Neiva heard the pouring of cereal and milk before Nate sat down at the table.

"There's plenty of Cinnamon Toast Crunch. Whenever you're ready, go ahead and pour yourself a bowl," Viv called out to Breezy and Neiva.

"Very funny, ha, ha," Nate said sarcastically while gulping down the cereal.

"Nate, I didn't mean for you to think that there wasn't enough cereal left. I just meant that for you there would be no cereal left if you didn't grab a bowl ASAP," Viv snickered as she sat next to Nate with two giant bowls of Froot Loops.

"Guess we should eat breakfast before we go fishing. We need to get our energy up! I'll make the hot cocoa!" Breezy stated as she shuffled into the kitchen.

Usually, local Alaskans didn't fish during this time of year. Winter was approaching and the spawning season was over. In Spirit, though, things were very different. Any local in Spirit could go fishing any time of the year, even in the depths of winter. Neiva had always thought it was because of some form of luck, but now she knew it had to do with the Spirit World and the pact her ancestors made with Darius.

"Hey, Breezy?" Neiva tried to quickly ask her question before Breezy disappeared into the kitchen.

"Yes?" Breezy turned around to look at Neiva. Her eyes sparkled with knowledge, as if she knew Neiva was going to ask her a question.

"The reason we can fish all year round is because of the Spirit World, right?"

Breezy pursed her lips together into a small smile. "Yes, you are correct. It was one of the bargains for the tribe to guard the island. They would have access to food year-round, regardless of the elements."

Neiva nodded her head. She watched Breezy go into the kitchen with her hair bouncing behind her. Neiva wondered why she had never thought it was weird when Nate would e-mail her about his huge catches during the winter season. She guessed it had never occurred to her to even ask anyone why the rivers in Spirit were always full of fish instead of being frozen solid.

Neiva slowly got out of bed. She walked to the window to assess the weather for the day. It looked partly cloudy with a slight breeze blowing in from the west. It didn't look too cold out but that could change. It was a sweater and light jacket kind of day. Hopefully Nate and Viv packed one for her.

"You coming, Neiva?" Viv asked from the kitchen.

"Coming," she said as she jogged into the kitchen. She stopped to smile at her friends. They were quite the group. Nate was shoving spoonfuls of Cinnamon Toast Crunch into his mouth and Viv was flicking Froot Loops into Nate's bowl. Breezy was humming to herself while looking out the window. Neiva's heart warmed. She felt so blessed to have them in her life. She didn't know what she would do if she had to go through all these changes without them.

Neiva went to the kitchen counter and grabbed a steaming mug of hot chocolate sitting next to the sink. Breezy had already made it for her, as Neiva knew she would have. She brought the mug to her lips to take a small sip. It was still hot, but it smelled so good that Neiva had to take a gulp. Marshmallows graced her cheek as she swallowed. She could taste chocolate chunks as well. Breezy always made the best hot chocolate. Her ingredients included chunks of milk chocolate and one teaspoon of honey mixed in with hot milk. She always topped the hot chocolate with marshmallows and colorful sprinkles. It was something to look forward to on a cold winter's day.

As Neiva turned to thank Breezy, a sudden feeling of dread overtook her emotions. Her body began to shake while her vision waivered for a second. She looked up to see if anyone had noticed her change. For the briefest moment her friends were not at the table, but then suddenly there was a flash of light, and they were back.

Her throat closed and her mind collapsed. The mug flew from her fingertips, falling to the floor where it shattered into several pieces. Her hands shook at her side as she stared at the scene before her and screamed.

Nate, Viv, and Breezy were all dead. One of Breezy's wings was ripped off her body, the remaining wing only attached by a thin ligament. Her antennas were tied in knots and blood streamed from a head wound on her right temple, the rest of her face lay flat on the table caked in blood.

Viv's lifeless body was positioned upright in her chair, her head thrown back at an odd angle. Her horns were broken into pieces and looked like dust covering the table. Long slashes disfigured her arms and chest, destroying her beautiful tattoos. Nate looked the worst of the bunch. He was lying on his stomach on the floor. His arms were tied behind him with some kind of leather cord. Deep marks penetrated his back leaving a puddle of blood around his body. The skin on the back of his neck had been stripped off. His legs were a jumbled mess, as if someone had put them in a cage with a ravenous lion. They were shredded to the bone.

Neiva let out a strangled cry. She quickly backed into the cabinets, squeezing her eyes shut, telling herself over and over again that it was just a dream. It wasn't real. She just wanted it to go away. Make it disappear.

It will be all right, Neiva, Riley's smooth voice broke the spell.

Neiva felt a slight flutter of wings in her mind. She had a sudden vision of Riley's wings surrounding her, as if he were encasing her in an armor of feathers.

Unseen forces are at work now, Neiva. I can feel it directed toward you. Whatever it is, it's trying to scare you. Believe that it is not real, Neiva. I am here with you. King Darius would never leave you unprotected.

At the end of Riley's sentence, Neiva could feel a slight brush on her check, almost as if Riley rubbed his feathered face against her. That calmed her, enabling Neiva to open her eyes.

Everything was back to the way it was before. There were no traces of the horrible scene she had just witnessed. Everything was calm and normal. Nate was still inhaling his cereal, while Viv slurped down the milk from her bowl. Breezy was singing to herself as she stared out the window. No one noticed anything was wrong. Neiva had imagined the whole thing. Tears blurred her vision as she ran outside to seek out the comfort of the one being who knew what she had just seen.

"Riley!" Neiva yelled as she jerked open the cabin's door.

She glanced around, looking for the giant bird. She didn't need to look very far because Riley had just landed on the railing to Neiva's right. Within a couple steps, Neiva slammed into Riley, wrapping her arms around his massive form. Burying her face in the feathers on his chest, she let the tears flow down her cheeks.

"I can't lose them, Riley," she said between her tears that soaked his feathers.

She felt Riley lay his head down on top of hers. *It was just an illusion. Someone is trying to scare you, Neiva. Nothing is going to happen to your friends. You are more powerful when you're together, and your friendship is strong. No one can break that.*

"Why didn't Darius come when I needed him, Riley?" It

had bothered her that he wasn't there. She expected him to show up like the other times and make the nightmare go away.

He can't be here all the time, as much as he wants too, Neiva. Sometime you have to battle your own demons and not rely on others. Don't get me wrong. He has many dark spirits watching over you, like me for example. But he knows you can handle yourself. You just have to believe.

Riley was right. What she saw was just an illusion, not a vision. She just needed to think of it as a nightmare and put it out of her mind. But that was hard because it had left her shaking in her boots. She just had to remember that Darius had faith in her and so did Riley. It was comforting to have Riley there for her but she needed to be strong. Someone was trying to scare her and she felt her friends were the bait. She had a feeling that whatever sent the illusion wasn't going to back down.

"What's after me, Riley, . . . and why?" Neiva asked, afraid of the answer.

I don't know. Whatever it wants, it has your attention now. His Darkness would know more than I do, but we just have to be on our toes for whatever comes next. I don't think this is the last we've seen of whatever it is that's after you."

Neiva could feel a sudden rage overtake her. It was like a beast rising out of the depths of her soul, ready to strike out at whatever had tried to scare her. Her head started pounding, causing her to grind her teeth. She almost wanted the thing to come back so she could pulverize it into a bloody pulp. Her temper was red-hot at the moment.

Ride your anger and let it take away the fear and nervousness that the illusion has left behind with you. You're the only person who can control how you feel; don't let others force you to feel anything else.

Neiva could feel Riley smile. She knew that birds didn't smile, but she could feel it within him—a warm light that projected happiness into Neiva's mind, forcing her to smile as well.

"Why is Neiva hugging a giant bird?" Nate's voice squeaked from behind Viv. "Is that her raven?"

Neiva slowly brought her face out of Riley's chest to glance behind her. She saw Nate peeking his head around Viv, who was leaning against the door frame with her arms crossed. One eyebrow was raised up in a questioning look. Breezy was standing a couple of inches from the door. Her head was tilted to the side and her eyes were dilated. She wasn't looking at Neiva but at Riley.

One of Breezy's stronger powers is to communicate with animals. It's a part of the cat spirit in her. She has been trying to communicate with me ever since she saw me in the kitchen. So, I thought this was a good time to start communicating with her. I told her about what happened with the illusion. She will bring everyone up to speed.

"Hey guys. Let's go inside and leave Neiva alone for a bit," Breezy said, ushering Viv and Nate back inside.

Neiva could hear Nate arguing all the way inside until the door shut behind them.

Backing up so she could look at Riley in the eyes, Neiva took in the sight before her. His eyes weren't black but an intense blue, glowing like dark sapphire jewels. There was power and knowledge swirling in those eyes. Like Darius, there was more to Riley.

Riley puffed out his chest and shook himself, reviving the flat feathers from where Neiva had cried. He spread out his wings, causing Neiva to gasp. His wingspan had to be at least six feet in length. His feathers weren't just black but an iridescent blue, glowing in the sunlight. They cast a rainbow glow onto the porch around him. His beak and talons were obsidian black, shining like a polished stone. He was absolutely stunning. Neiva couldn't believe she had never noticed it before. Maybe because the first time they met was when he was attacking her.

I must go and let King Darius know what has just happened. He felt the disturbance and sent me to you. But don't worry. You will be safe with your friends. Plus, if something does happen, just let out the anger you felt earlier." He said this with a laugh as he launched into the air. Neiva knew he was referring to her temper, which had been lying dormant until then.

She watched him disappear before entering the cabin. Breezy was talking to Viv and Nate by the fireplace. She walked over to them catching the tail end of Breezy lecturing Nate to behave and not act up. Nate gave Neiva a quizzical look before Breezy turned around to grab Neiva's arm, leading her to the couch.

"Okay. Riley told me what happened. I related what he told me to Viv and Nate. We have your back, Neiva; remember you can tell us anything. We're here for you. We would never abandon you or think you're crazy." Breezy's eyes glistened with tears. Her smile waivered just slightly as a tremor quivered in her bottom lip.

"Thanks guys." Neiva was a heartbeat away from crying herself. She loved her friends so much and she still was shaken from the illusion earlier. She felt like she was an emotional mess, as parents would say, "a typical teenager."

"I swear! The three of you have to be the most emotional group of girls in Spirit, crying one minute and angry the next. No wonder men don't understand women! I think it's contagious too. It's affecting me, just like a virus," Nate blurted out, trying to hide the sniffle from his runny nose brought on by the tears welling up in his eyes.

"Well, I'm satisfied," Viv calmly stated as she walked over to the pile of suitcases still by the door. She grabbed a large box sitting at the side of the pile. It had a large red bow wrapped around it with balloon wrapping paper covering it. Viv brought it over to Neiva and set it on her lap.

Neiva gave Viv a confused look. What was she so self-satisfied about? That Neiva knew not to keep any secrets from them?

"I'm satisfied that Nate finally admitted he has some emotions and is not just a block of uncaring testosterone," Viv replied to Neiva's look.

"What? I didn't say that! I said you girls are crazy!" Nate yelled defensively.

He tried to sit up while he wiped the tears that were leaking down his face. "Just because I care about all of you doesn't mean I'm a sap. Neiva's my friend. I would be lost without her." Nate paused for a second before adding in a whisper, "Plus Breezy and even Viv. Life would be boring without Viv."

Viv's head whipped around in response to Nate's statement. Her eyes were as large as saucers, while her mouth was slightly opened, forming an O shape. She reminded Neiva of a deer caught in the headlights of a car—shocked and still as a statue, not knowing what to do.

Breezy saved the day with her reply. "We love you too, Nate. We've all been through a lot in the last couple of days."

This caused Nate's demeanor to change. He sat up straight, not glancing in Viv's direction, and turned to Neiva. Calmly he told her the gift was from both Viv and Breezy.

Not knowing what to say, Neiva unwrapped the gift and opened the box. Neiva pulled the tissue paper out and giggled with excitement at what she saw. The girls had bought her a pair of rain boots, and Neiva instantly fell in love with them. They were black with pink skulls and silver stars on them. They came up to Neiva's knees and were perfect for the rainy weather Alaska unleashed on Spirit. She didn't just like them because of the design; she liked them because they could be used for just about anything. She could hike in them because of the sturdy soles on the bottom, she could wear them to school on rainy days, and she could fish in them.

"Thank you, Viv and Breezy! I love them. They are perfect for fishing today." Neiva jumped off the couch to give them a hug.

She grabbed Viv, giving her a giant bear hug. This snapped Viv out of the trance she was in. She blinked a couple of times when Neiva tried to pick her up. A sly smile formed on Viv's face. In one swift motion, Viv was out of Neiva's arms. She picked Neiva up, put her over her back in a firefighter hold, ran to the couch that still had the bed folded out, and threw Neiva onto it.

"Body slam!" Viv shouted as she jumped on top of Neiva. WWE wrestling was one of the group's favorite things to watch on TV. They all loved mimicking the wrestlers' moves, but the girls were especially fond of ganging up on Nate.

"Dog pile!" Nate shouted as he jumped on top of Viv, causing her to grunt in protest. Breezy was next, but her body weight was like adding a feather to the pile.

"Jeez, Nate. How much weight did you gain over the summer?" Viv asked as she pretended to suffocate under his weight.

"Whatever, Viv. This is all muscle weight from the gym," Nate said as he moved Breezy to the side and jumped off. He proceeded to flex his arms. "Welcome to the gun show ladies!"

The girls stopped moving around to stare at Nate. He had nice muscle definition and looked like he could hold his own. Neiva instantly felt it when Viv realized the same thing because her body went still. She wasn't breathing or moving one bit.

"Okay. That's enough, showoff. Let's get ready for fishing! Whoever catches the largest fish gets to pick who does the dishes tonight," Breezy stated as she bounded into the kitchen to finish cleaning up breakfast.

"Ah, that's not fair, Breezy. It always ends up being me." Nate quickly followed Breezy into the kitchen trying to persuade her to change the rules.

Viv slowly climbed off of Neiva to sit back against the couch. She looked at Neiva with a confused look. "Hormones suck," she hissed.

Neiva laughed at Viv. Her face was still in shock. It was as if Viv couldn't understand why she felt this way.

"You can't pick who you have feelings for," Neiva whispered as she placed her hand on Viv's knee.

Neiva slowly took her hand away. She could tell Viv's temper was beginning to surface. Her eyes began to glow a bright yellow, as if a fire had ignited deep within them. Smoke slowly escaped her nose while her teeth grew in length. A growl started to rumble deep in her throat.

"Hey! Are you girls getting ready?" Nate came around the corner. One glance from Viv had him yelping back into the kitchen.

"Yeah, we'll be ready shortly." Neiva responded.

Staring with intense rage at the spot where Nate had just stood, Viv kept her mouth shut. She turned her demon eyes back to Neiva. Something caught her eye, bringing her attention to Neiva's wrist. The bracelet Darius had given Neiva was still clasped around her wrist, sparkling brightly in the morning sunlight. Its bright rubies sparkled like little stars, as if telling everyone around *I'm here. Look at me!*

"Beautiful," Viv whispered as she brought Neiva's wrist up for closer inspection. She turned Neiva's hand back and forth while making little comments to herself.

"It was a birthday gift from Darius," Neiva told Viv once Viv let go of her wrist.

"Wow. He even put your totem on it. That's special," Viv said as she sat back. Her eyes slowly transformed back into her human features while her sharp incisors receded into flat surfaces again.

"It is," Neiva replied, smiling at the bracelet. It meant a lot to her, not just because it was from Darius, but also because it was her first gift from someone of the opposite sex for whom she had strong feelings. It also made her feel like Darius was always with her. She swore she smelled forest and lavender every once in a while.

Viv slowly got up. "We better get ready. I packed some long-sleeved shirts and a sweater for you." Viv stood up. She grabbed Neiva's arm, helping her stand. She brought Neiva's arm closer to look at the bracelet again, so she could inspect the rubies.

"King Darius got the rubies from one of our mines."

"Your mines?" Neiva blinked a couple of times. She wondered

what Viv meant. Did her father own a mine, a ruby mine?

"Demon spirits don't exactly live in the Dark Kingdom, Neiva. We have a doorway or you could say a fissure that cracks open. It's our connection into the Spirit World." Viv's eyes seemed to glass over as she thought about her home. "In our realm we have a variety of mines with different gemstones, such as diamonds, tanzanite, and even rubies. They make our world sparkle like a treasure hidden deep within the earth."

"So, you're not an actual spirit?" Neiva stepped back from Viv. She inspected her from head to toe. She could see the shimmer of Viv's spirit shield draped over her. There wasn't any sign that she was something different. If she wasn't a spirit, than why did she have a shield?

"Yes and no. Our commander made a pact with King Darius. If we could have access to the Spirit World, then the demons would do whatever he wanted. Most kings or people in authority would take advantage of this vow, but King Darius did not. The only condition he asked for was that the demons interact with the spirits. He wanted the demons to go to school, get jobs, or become friends with the townsfolk and spirits, even join his army if they wished too. So, the commander agreed and a blood treaty was signed, leaving Darius access to our mines as well. But at the last minute, just as our commander was leaving, King Darius told him that any demon who wanted to venture out into town or go to school would have a spirit shield.

"Our commander was briefly put off by this, because it was a great honor for demons to show themselves to other beings. We don't hide from anything. But King Darius explained how important it was that the town of Spirit and the Spirit World stay a secret. It would become complete chaos if the world knew that they existed. Our commander understood King Darius was protecting his own people, a great sign of loyalty and trust. He trusted the demons to stay hidden, not ordering them too. Our commander gained great respect for the Dark King and agreed. So, demons were allowed out into the world.

Some started straying, but there were others there to make sure they didn't stray too far. And when we are in our true form, we must wear masks in the Dark Kingdom." Viv looked at Neiva to see if she understood what she was being told.

"So, the demons that children see or the people possessed by demons are actually strays from the Spirit World?" Neiva asked, lifting her eyebrows.

"Yes, they became too power hungry. They, like some spirits, believe humans are weak and that demons should be in power." Viv shrugged. "It's happening more and more now though."

"Oh. How do you protect yourself from a demon?" Neiva rubbed her hands over her arms. She suddenly had a chill run up her spine, giving her goose bumps all over her body.

"Oh, a cross will do. The cross is a symbol of life and rebirth. When a demon goes stray, they lose the life within them, becoming a dark force bent on conquering, becoming something evil."

"Could a demon be after me?" Neiva couldn't think of any other reason why someone would be after her, other than something demonic and evil.

"No, demons become evil, but they don't have enough power to make people hallucinate or turn the northern lights red. It has to be something ancient, something supernatural." Viv looked out the window imagining what could be after Neiva. "Demons only have the power to possess people and scare them."

"Well, I wish I knew, but it seems I have a lot of people looking out for me, which makes me feel a little bit safer." Neiva smiled. She was trying to tell herself that no one would let her get hurt, but like Darius stated in her dream, something unseen is scarier than anything else, and she was scared beyond words.

Neiva looked at her bracelet again. The rubies were shining like fire. Neiva swore she could feel them heating up, sending a calm and warm feeling throughout her body. She headed over to the pile of suitcases to grab her clothes for the day when Viv caught her attention.

"One last thing before we go, Neiva." Viv's face became serious as she walked over to Neiva. "Those rubies are from our deepest mine and are considered our prized possession. Anyone who wears one within the Spirit World is considered noble—someone of high rank."

"What do you mean, Viv?" Neiva's heart started to beat faster while her hands started to shake. Was this heading where she thought it was?

"Neiva, I believe King Darius has just made you a princess."

Chapter 11

SHOCK PULSATED THROUGH Neiva's nerves. Her heart fell into the pit of her stomach and her jaw hung slightly open, as if it were unconnected. She couldn't breathe or even swallow. So many thoughts were running through her mind. Why would rubies make her royalty?

"Those aren't just any rubies, Neiva. Those are blood rubies," Viv declared while pointing at Neiva's wrist.

"I thought they were star rubies. Well, that was according to Sasha," Neiva stammered out.

"He is correct. They are a relative to the star ruby, but only in appearance." Viv walked to the window by the front door. She crossed her arms and leaned against its frame. "Where do you think all the blood in the world goes once it's spilled onto the ground?"

"Into the earth?" Neiva asked. She walked over to Viv and stood by the window next to her.

Viv let out a giant sigh, and then took a deep breath before answering Neiva's question.

"The earth soaks up all the blood that has spilled on her land, and in her oceans, lakes, and rivers. It gets pulled into the very center of her being, to the heat that makes her live. The blood warms up, mixing in with her life force, and then it is suddenly expelled into her veins, traveling to the very heart of our mines. These rubies are only found in our deepest mines where they are cared for. We only extract them when someone of royal blood can pay for them. They are worth more than gold or any gem in the world." Viv paused to glance down at Neiva's wrist. "If you look closely Neiva, you will see the earth's life force flowing within it."

Neiva brought the bracelet up to her face. The rubies stopped glowing, allowing the light in the room to turn them iridescent. She would be able to see right through them if it weren't for the white substance floating around inside of them. To Neiva, it looked like tiny crystals bouncing around the center of each ruby. They swirled as if they were dancing, giving Neiva the feeling that they were alive.

"It's alive, Neiva. Both the earth and an injured person gave a part of their life force to help create them. It's a precious gift. They're only given to royalty." Viv held up Neiva's wrist again. "This is a crown jewel. Only demons would know this, so you should have no worries about anyone else knowing about your status now."

"Status?" Neiva gulped.

"That you're a royal princess." Viv smiled at Neiva as she let her arm go.

Nate walked in with a frown on his face. "You're not ready? It's been an hour! Breezy and I cleaned the whole kitchen. I even mopped the floors." Nate crossed his arms, tapping his foot impatiently.

"Oh yeah, we were just grabbing our clothes. We will be ready in five minutes, Nate," Neiva said as she bent down and grabbed her pink sweatshirt, worn jeans, and some clean underwear and socks. Turning around, she saw Nate walking back into the kitchen, while Viv started to change into her clothes.

Neiva had just finished pulling up her rain boots when both Nate and Breezy bounded into the living room. Breezy had her pink rain boots on over her black jeans. She wore a gray wool sweater and a gray hat with a pink stripe on the side. Nate had a pair of hiking boots on with a pair of green cargo pants and a black sweater. His hair was a mess, spiked out in every direction, making him look like he just crawled out of bed. He had four fishing poles in his hand and seemed anxious to go.

"All right, let's go," Viv said as she finished tying her hiking boots. She had a pair of skinny denim jeans on with a pink hoodie. She grabbed Neiva to help her up off the floor and headed out the door.

It only took them fifteen minutes to walk down to the river. It was just north of the cabin, through the bushes and trees.

"Looks like the river is high today, which means good fishing." Nate smiled as he handed out the fishing poles to each girl.

Higher than normal, the river flowed forcefully, making Neiva a little bit nervous about wading into it. Only Neiva and Breezy would be going into the river. Viv was going to stay on shore with Nate because he was deathly afraid of the water. He lost his older brother when he was just six years old to this very river. His brother had fallen in while trying to make it back to shore. The water instantly filled his boots up and he was swept away by the current. His shoes were like weights keeping him from reaching the surface. He didn't last five minutes. Mike didn't find his body until an hour later. It was devastating to the family, but this accident wasn't the first time a local drowned in the river. It happened a lot. The river was known to sweep locals away, so anyone fishing had to be extra careful.

"Are you sure it's safe?" Neiva asked, glancing back and forth at the rough current. It made her a little bit nervous.

"Yeah, it will be fine. We'll just wade out a couple feet from shore and we will be safe." Breezy grabbed her pole. She walked into the river several feet before stopping. She glanced back at Neiva with a big smile on her face. "See, nothing's going to happen."

Halfway across the river, Neiva heard Viv whooping loudly. Neiva stopped to glance over in Viv's direction. Viv and Nate were at the edge of the river, and Viv's line had just caught a fish. She was working furiously to bring the line in, while Nate was jumping around in excitement. Neiva could hear him yelling to pull the line in faster, while Viv just bared her teeth at him.

Neiva laughed to herself as she made it to where Breezy was standing. She was a little jealous of how close Nate and Viv were getting, but Neiva's infatuation with Nate was slowly fading with each contact and visit from Darius.

"Why don't you go about fifteen feet upstream? Then we will have more coverage and won't get our lines tangled." Breezy pointed to her left. Neiva stopped about fifteen feet from Breezy. Casting her line out, it swooped like an arch landing halfway to the other side. She began to reel it in, hoping she would tempt a fish swimming by, but it didn't seem like luck was on her side. She tried several more times before she let a huff out in frustration. She looked over to Breezy. It didn't look like she was having any luck either. Breezy had a scowl on her face, and she was squeezing her pole with so much force, Neiva thought it was going to break.

Another yell came from the area where Viv and Nate stood. This time, it was Nate who had caught something, and Viv was yelling at him to reel the fish in before it escaped.

"I guess we will have better luck on shore," Breezy said as she looked back at Viv and Nate.

"Yeah, let's go." Neiva started to follow Breezy into shore. Neiva glanced back at the spot where she had just been. The water was frothing with more force now, so much more that it was creating a giant wave, which seemed to be heading right for Neiva, growing steadily larger as it approached her. Neiva was momentarily shocked, but snapped out of it when the water started rising around her.

"Swim, Breezy!" Neiva yelled, trying to head toward shore. Breezy turned to see what Neiva was yelling about and her perplexed look quickly melted away into fear. Her eyes filled with panic as she screamed for Neiva to swim faster. Breezy's spirit shield dropped to reveal her true form. Her lion tail swished back and forth as her wings began to beat faster and faster. With a powerful burst from her wings, Breezy was up and out of the water. She flew straight for Neiva, with every intention of saving her.

Breezy was within inches of reaching Neiva when suddenly a wall of water slammed into her body, flinging her over thirty feet into the air. Her limp body fell onto the beach, landing in front of a shocked Nate and Viv. She wasn't moving.

"Breezy!" Neiva called out as she tried to fight the current and swim to shore. But it was too strong. Her boots were filling up with water, making it harder for her to move. Her arms felt like lead as she pushed against the current. She didn't know what to do; her body was tiring from the extreme exertion. Her stomach was starting to cramp up and she could barely keep her head above the water.

A shadow passed over Neiva followed by a loud screech echoing throughout the sky. Neiva glanced up to see Riley circling above her. She instantly felt relief wash away any doubts about getting out of this predicament.

Neiva searched her mind for Riley but she couldn't feel him. She felt empty and alone, like something was missing. She shouted his name while stretching her arms toward the sky. Within seconds she felt his talons grab her arms and slowly lift her out of the water. But she slipped out of his grip, splashing back into the dangerous river.

Neiva coughed out the water she had accidently inhaled as she looked for Riley. He was banking back around to grab her again. Neiva's heart raced as she threw her arms up in the air again, hoping Riley would snag her this time. Just as he was reaching out to her with his talons, Neiva was suddenly pulled under water. She didn't even have time to grab a breath of air before she was tumbling around like she was trapped inside of a washing machine. She didn't know which way was up or down. Neither the surface nor the riverbed was visible as the water churned around her, but it felt like she was being dragged deeper, beyond where a normal river bottom should be.

Neiva tried to use her arms to maneuver her body around, but it didn't work. She looked around to see if she could catch any light from the surface, but it looked all the same to her: dark.

Panic surged through her. She needed to get to the surface. Her lungs were burning and it took every ounce of her strength not to gulp in any water. Neiva tried to swim in the direction she thought was up but her body wouldn't move. It was as if a force field kept her in place. Her boots weren't helping either. They felt like blocks of cement holding her down in the dark. She couldn't take them off. Her feet were trapped inside.

Neiva's body started to shake. She tried to reach out to Darius with her mind but she couldn't feel him. The connection to both Riley and Darius was severed. They weren't there. She was alone.

"You're alone, Neiva. You'll always be alone," an insidious voice whispered in the dark.

The voice had come from a black substance materializing in front of Neiva. It was thick and oily and its surface undulated, as if someone was trapped inside. A face formed into that of a woman with red hair. Her features seemed to be intertwined with the oily substance giving her an evil and scary appearance. She smiled demonically at Neiva, like a shark grinning at its prey, as she moved her head back and forth like a snake. After stopping to stare at Neiva for a second, the creature launched herself at Neiva.

"You're mine!" the woman shouted as her face transformed into a hideous monster. Her teeth became elongated as her jaw stretched wide like a snake ready to eat its prey. She came at Neiva as if she would swallow her whole.

Neiva screamed as water filled her mouth and poured into her lungs. She couldn't get away as darkness surrounded her.

Chapter 12

DARIUS ALMOST KEELED OVER. His head ached and his heart felt empty. Something was wrong. He couldn't connect with Neiva or Riley. He knew there was trouble, but he couldn't teleport to her. The white light that held them together was being blocked by something. He didn't know what it was, but his heart was racing and panic started to overtake him. The darkness that surrounded him whispered for blood. He needed to find Neiva.

"BLAKE!" Darius's voice boomed off the walls and echoed throughout the kingdom.

Within seconds, one of his Shadow Guards was bowing before him.

"Yes, Your Darkness?" his servant asked. He kept his head low in a submissive pose.

Darius turned to his warrior. "Go to Neiva. She's in trouble." His voice conveyed the urgency of the situation so Blake would know the importance of his mission. If anything happened to Neiva, all would be lost, including Darius's very soul.

THROUGH THE DARKNESS Neiva saw a light. It had a beautiful face as if it were carved out of marble. It was very masculine with piercing, aqua-colored eyes that broke through the emptiness. The eyes caused the evil creature to retreat into the dark depths of the river, leaving only calm waters around Neiva. The beautiful light grabbed Neiva's hand. Her heart slowed and she felt light as a feather as strong arms encircled her. Soon she broke through to the surface and could breathe again.

Neiva could feel herself being carried out of the water. Strong arms held her firmly against a muscular chest. She could hear the slosh of water as they reached the beach. There was a shift in weight, and she was gently laid down onto the shore with care.

When she was released, Neiva finally was able to focus her eyes. She blinked a couple of times to find Viv's worried face hovering over her. She was asking a lot questions, but Neiva couldn't hear her. Her attention was turned to the stranger standing behind Viv.

He was six foot four and gorgeous. Fine navy blue hair fell in curls around a well-sculpted face. An orange coral mask covered his nose and eyes, stopping just above where his eyebrows should be. His blue lips smiled at Neiva, showing sharp white teeth. His skin glowed like pearls, like an abalone shell was trapped underneath his skin and was trying to get to the surface. He wore gray leather pants with a gray leather vest that covered his well-defined chest. A black belt held a mysterious bag and a knife around his waist. His feet and hands were webbed with long blue claws jutting out of his fingers. Small gills protruded from his neck.

"My name is Blake. King Darius sent me to rescue you." He introduced himself with his fist over his heart, giving a slight bow to Neiva.

Neiva brushed her hair out of her face and breathed slowly, trying to think. Was their connection still broken? She reached her mind out but she could only feel emptiness. She then tried to reach out for Riley, but felt nothing.

She eagerly searched the skies for Riley, but there was no sign of the giant bird. She glanced down the beach to see Breezy standing up with Nate's help and heading toward Neiva.

"What happened to me?" she asked Blake, hoping he would give her answers.

"You were attacked. I'm not sure what it was, but it put a kink in your connection with King Darius and your spirit guide," Blake said as he knelt in front of Neiva. He lightly grabbed Neiva's chin to turn her face back and forth, inspecting her for wounds. Moving his eyes up, he stared at the crystal in the middle of her forehead. His gaze lasted for several seconds before he stood up.

Neiva instantly got to her feet. "When will the connection be fixed?"

"Neiva, it's not like an electronic device. It can't easily be fixed," Viv said. She walked over to put an arm around her. "Something strong messed with your connections and the fact that it did it to your connection with King Darius tells us that it's something very powerful."

What was so strong that it could mess up the connection between her and Darius? It made all the feelings of dread resurface. What was after her? How could it be stopped?

"Nothing is indestructible, Neiva. Everything has its weakness," Blake said as he walked toward the river. His back was to Neiva, showing a well-defined ass. Neiva blushed. Was everyone this beautiful in the Spirit World?

Blake briefly looked over his shoulder. His eyes glowed as he smiled at her. "Things always work out in the end. The universe has a way of realigning itself."

Blake merged with the water and was gone, leaving Neiva standing on the pebbled beach staring at the spot where he had just been. Nate and Breezy came up behind Neiva asking if she was okay.

"Physically I am, but mentally I can't take anymore," Neiva gasped as she turned to look at the group.

Breezy was hanging onto Nate. Her golden glow was dim. Neiva could hear her wheezing, indicating she had bruised her ribs. Nate's eyes were red from crying as he laid his head onto Breezy's shoulder. Viv was standing straight as an arrow. Her spirit shield was down, revealing her true form. Her tail was swishing back and forth. She was on edge, her claws were out, and her eyes were blazing.

"We will find out what's going on. Nothing will stop us. I will talk to my father. He is King Darius's confidant. He will tell me what King Darius thinks is happening and why it's separating you from him," Viv stated as she hugged Neiva. She turned to give Breezy and Nate a nod.

A loud crack made Neiva and Nate jump as the earth opened up around Viv. Red flames escaped the massive crevice as a staircase formed, leading down into a fiery pit. Viv's eyes glowed yellow as she winked at Neiva.

"I'll get some answers, Neiva. Don't worry. I will meet you back at the cabin." She turned to Nate and Breezy. "Be aware of your surroundings. Protect Neiva at all times. I won't be long."

Viv descended the rocky staircase. The flames engulfed her as if they were welcoming her home. They danced around her, becoming brighter as they touched her skin. The ground closed up above her head as she disappeared deep within the earth's core. There was no trace of the fissure or Viv. It was like they had never even been there.

"Wow. That's a great exit," Nate exclaimed as he pulled Breezy closer to him.

Neiva noticed his eye twitch. Was he nervous about Viv leaving or was it the cavernous earth that upset him? Neiva made a mental note to ask him later. The first thing she wanted to do was get back to the cabin and go over the dramatic events that had unfolded today. Most of all she wanted to find a way to reach Darius.

"Let's head back to the cabin." Breezy whispered, reading Neiva's mind. Her eyes were small slits, barely open, and her wings laid against her back while her tail was tucked under her legs.

Neiva knew she needed some hot chocolate to rejuvenate her, but most of all she needed some sleep and so did Neiva. She was hoping to see Darius in her dreams, maybe the kink in their connection didn't affect them meeting there. She could only hope.

"Okay." Neiva grabbed Breezy's other side as they trudged back to the cabin. It was hard for her to help carry Breezy. Neiva was still trying to get her bearings straight. Her lungs still hurt and her legs felt like Jell-O.

The return trip took longer than expected. By the end of the trek, Nate was practically carrying both Breezy and Neiva up to the house's steps. He set both of the girls down and backed up a few paces to look them over. Breezy's face was white as snow. Her golden glow had disappeared and was replaced by dull, waxy skin. She could barely move her wings or even keep her head up. Neiva didn't look any better. Her eyes were glassy, as if she was on some kind of medication. Her breathing was ragged and shallow.

"I better get you girls into the house and get some hot chocolate in you." Nate climbed the steps and passed the girls. He tried the knob to the door, but it was locked. He didn't remember anyone locking it before they left. Usually when locals were out at camp, they didn't lock their doors. It was easier to have it open in case a bear was around. Nate tried the windows too, but they were locked as well.

"Nate!" Neiva tried to yell his name, but only a hoarse whisper escaped. She tried to position her body so that she could grab him, but she was too weak. It felt as if all her energy was sucked out of her, leaving her stuck in a lifeless body.

"Nate!" Breezy screeched louder. She could barely keep

her eyes open but during the brief time they were open, she saw a large object looming in front of them.

"What?" Nate asked annoyed. He was trying to jimmy the door open with his driver's license. His wallet was lying on the deck by his feet. He never went anywhere without it. "I think I almost have it!"

"Nate!" the girls screamed in unison.

"Okay, I know you both don't feel well, but I am seriously trying here." He turned around with a big scowl on his face and tapped his foot impatiently.

Breezy rolled her eyes to the area in front of her. Nate was puzzled at first, but when he caught sight of the huge object standing a few feet from the cabin, he could see what the problem was.

"Holy giant bear," he exclaimed as he stared at the huge beast standing before them.

It was enormous, bigger than Breezy's Volkswagen Beetle. Bulging muscles covered its body. Huge paws held up its massive form with lethal six-inch claws embedded in the ground. Its huge mouth hung open, showing very long and sharp teeth. The eyes of the bear were not the usual honey color that grizzlies normally possess; instead the whole eye was black, reminding Neiva of a great white shark. There was a substance around the bear, black ooze flowing in and out of the bear's fur. The hairs on the back of Neiva's neck stood on end. The ooze reminded her of the woman in the river. It felt evil.

"I don't like this," Neiva grunted. She couldn't move. Nate was going to have to protect them.

Sensing Neiva's unease, Nate instantly jumped off the porch to land in front of the girls. Slightly crouched, he brought his arms out at his sides and stared at the bear. Neiva could see the tattoo on the back of Nate's neck coming to life. The ink shimmered and swirled around until Roxy stood next to Nate. She was in a defensive pose, ready to strike. Her tail flipped back and forth in agitation. She glanced back at Neiva, to make sure she was okay, then quickly turned her attention back to the bear and growled.

Nate let his hand fall against Roxy. His fingers lightly brushed the top of her head as he said, "Let the spirit guide and Guardian fight as one. Let our souls merge and our strength give power to the other. So let it be."

Once he finished his sentence, Roxy bit Nate's hand. Blood welled up in the freshly made wound and slowly dripped down Nate's hand. It fell onto the ground with a loud boom, surprising Breezy, Neiva, and even the bear.

A mystical light escaped from the ground where Nate's blood had marked it. The light twirled around him like a ribbon burning brightly until it disappeared, leaving Nate transformed.

Neiva's eyes grew large as the creature turned around to look at her. He was the same Nate with his wild hair and tanned skin, but now he had long gray claws that clicked together as he opened and closed his hands. His white teeth were sharp as glass as he smiled at her through gray lips, and pointed ears broke through his messy hair. But the most shocking transformation was his eyes. They had become white orbs just like Roxy's, glowing as brightly as the sun. The skin around his eyes was gray, almost like a striped mask.

Roxy stood next to Nate during the transformation, protecting him in case the bear chose to attack.

"Don't worry, we have this," Nate growled as he turned to leap onto the bear.

The bear swiped its massive paws at Nate, barely missing his sleek form. In a kung fu–type maneuver, Nate somersaulted over the bear while raking his claws down its back. The bear screamed out in rage causing the hairs on Neiva's arms to rise.

Quickly turning on Nate, the bear charged forward but was instantly cut off by Roxy. She bared her teeth, then jumped onto the bear's back, sinking her incisors into its neck and holding on for dear life as the bear furiously swung its head back and forth. Feverishly trying to release Roxy's grip, the bear threw its body into the closest tree. Its full body weight slammed into Roxy, sandwiching her between the tree and the bear. When the bear moved, Roxy fell to the ground in a whimper.

"Roxy!" Nate roared.

With his claws out, he ran with inhuman speed toward the bear, swiping the bear's snout and digging through its jaws. The bear roared with such force it threw Nate back several feet. Once Nate hit the ground, the bear was on top of him. He tried to use all his strength to keep the bear's teeth from piercing his skin. Nate's hands surrounded its neck, trying to choke the bear, but it was like squeezing metal. The bear wouldn't bend.

Nate's strength was wavering. It only took a brief slip before the bear's teeth clamped down onto his shoulder, causing Nate to scream. He felt his power escaping through the punctures where the bear's teeth were now embedded. Black ooze dripped down the bear's teeth into the wounds, blackening and poisoning the area around them.

Neiva couldn't watch anymore. Someone had to help him. She tried to move toward Nate but all of her energy was gone, drained to exhaustion. There was no way she could help him.

"You should be more careful," an angelic voice firmly told her.

A golden globe appeared before Neiva. It slowly formed into a human figure, about six feet tall. The light quickly faded into his body, leaving him with glowing golden skin. He had short blond hair with bangs falling just above his forest green eyes. A ring of gold surrounded his pupil causing his eyes to shine like the sun. Straight white teeth shone brightly as he smiled at her through pink lips.

"Don't worry, Neiva. I will help your friend. He seems to be in quite the predicament," he teased her as he turned around.

Neiva gaped at the giant wings folded against his back. The feathers looked like spun gold, as if they were made of silk. They sparkled, making Neiva wonder if he was an angel.

Neiva watched the golden angel spread out his wings. They gleamed in the sunlight, blinding her. With a forceful flap, he rose into the air, and then dove at the bear. Waiting until the last second, he grabbed the bear's neck, jerking the beast off of Nate. He slammed the bear into the ground, resting most of his body weight on it. He brought his now-glowing golden eyes up to the bear's face.

"Old Ben, what has gotten into you?" he asked the bear as he closely inspected its eyes. He instantly saw the oil-like substance oozing out of the bear's fur and mouth. The ooze lashed out at the angel but he zapped it with a streak of light from his right index finger. It vaporized in a poof of smoke.

"Looks like I have to surround you with my light. You're not going to like this, old pal." The angel became a burning ball of light, causing the bear to scream in pain. There was a demonic scream intertwined with the bear's, but it only lasted several seconds before it was only the bear left groaning. The light was suddenly cut off as if a switch had been flipped. The angel was now standing and smiling at the exhausted bear. Gentle, honey-colored eyes stared back at the angel.

"You know what you have to do, Ben," the angel said, pointing to Roxy and then Nate. "I gave you some of my healing power. You must distribute it between the Guardian and his spirit guide."

The bear grunted in protest as he got up and glanced at both Nate and Roxy. He walked to stand several feet from Roxy and turned his head around to whine at the angel.

"Hey, it's not their fault. They were only trying to protect their friends." The angel shrugged at the bear.

The bear slowly trotted over to Roxy. He let out a small huff before quickly licking her backside in one fluid sweep. He backed away while Roxy's back began to glow. Golden vines were reaching out of Roxy's body. They surrounded her, giving off a pulsating glow. Roxy stirred, slowly flipping her tail back and forth. When she opened her eyes, the golden light disappeared, leaving Roxy rejuvenated and able to get to her feet.

Next came Nate. The bear gently pushed Nate with his giant paw to see if he was awake. Nate didn't move. The bear bent down to lick the wounds on Nate's shoulder where it had bitten him earlier. Nate's wounds were deeper and some of the oily ooze had receded into his bloodstream, so it took longer for him to heal. For well over five minutes, his body glowed, like hundreds of flashlights were illuminating his skin. Finally, Nate began to stir. As the light faded, Nate sat up. His animal features had disappeared and not one single mark was left on his body. The blood on his torn shirt was the only evidence that he had been hurt or that anything had happened.

"I feel all funny inside," Nate said as he opened his eyes to find himself staring straight into the eyes of the bear. He let out a horrific scream before backpedaling as far as he could go. A tree blocked his path, causing him to kick up dirt. He tried with all his might to climb up the tree but failed miserably. With his back to the tree, his arms had a hard time gripping the trunk behind him.

The angel stepped forward to help Nate to his feet. "Oh, control yourself, soldier. Old Ben won't hurt you. Whatever parasite latched onto him is gone now."

"Who are you?" Nate asked as the angel turned to walk back to the cabin.

"Oh, no one important. Just your average king of the light spirits," he said with a flick of his hand, as if he was brushing away the idea his status was important.

"Eek. I've been touched by the Light King," Nate squeaked as he tried to brush away the king's touch from his hands. Without thinking, he ran over and brushed his hand up against the bear's back, which growled in response to Nate's touch.

"Gabriel?" Neiva asked, barely getting her voice out. She was about to fall sleep. Her lids felt heavy and everyone's voices sounded muffled and far away.

"Ah, you know my name," he whispered as he bent down to inspect her.

Neiva's skin was turning the same color as Breezy's, a waxy gray. She couldn't keep her eyes open, but what she could see through the small slits in her eyes was that he looked very angelic standing in front of her, wearing a white button-down shirt and white beach pants held up by a gold cord. He had golden leather sandals, which looked very masculine. He looked like he could be seventeen or eighteen years old, but Neiva couldn't tell for sure.

"Hang on for a couple more minutes. You'll be okay. I need to help my fellow light spirit out," he stated with concern as he turned to inspect Breezy.

"Oh my, what has caused your powers to drain so drastically that you're on the brink of fading, my little wood spirit?" His voice was soothing as he asked Breezy.

He gently stroked her hair out of her face and then brought his hand to Breezy's forehead. A bright light shone beneath his hand and then there was a loud poof as the light disappeared into a cloud of sparkles.

Gabriel turned to Neiva. He moved over to her and placed his hand on her forehead. A jumble of unrecognizable words escaped his mouth. She was lulled by the beautiful sound of his voice, until she felt the searing pain in her forehead. It intensified with each word Gabriel pronounced, causing Neiva to scream and recoil from his touch. She lashed out with her right hand, sending a ball of silver energy straight into Gabriel's stomach, flinging him into the air. With quick reflexes, he unfurled his wings, landing on one of his knees with grace. As he looked up at Neiva, his eyes glowed like liquid gold.

"So, it seems my brother has been keeping secrets," he hissed as he stood up, his wings extended at his sides. He narrowed his eyes at Neiva.

"I'm sorry. You were hurting me and I don't have control of my powers. Darius is teaching me," Neiva pleaded as she stood up. She didn't mean to hurt him or anger him.

"Ah, it's not your fault but my brother's. He always likes to best me," he growled as he looked down at Neiva's bracelet. The center of his body started to glow. It burned bright with intensity. "This will make the games between us even more interesting. Until next time, my dear princess."

In a flash of blinding light he was gone, leaving trails of golden dust behind. For a moment it was hard for her to see. She had to blink a couple of times before she could focus on Breezy, who was sitting up. Her golden glow was back and her emerald eyes shone brightly.

"What happened?" she asked Neiva expectantly, turning to look at Nate who was still standing next to the bear, too afraid to move.

"Well, uh," Neiva paused for a second before continuing on, "we were saved by Gabriel. He saved Nate and Roxy and healed the bear. Something possessed it and it looked a lot like the thing in the river."

"Oh," Breezy pursed her lips, "I thought I felt His Lightness."

"His Lightness?" Neiva raised her eyebrow at Breezy.

"It's like saying His Highness, except in the spirit realm, dark spirits call the Dark King, His Darkness, while the light spirits call the Light King, His Lightness," she explained as she started to walk over to where Nate was continuing to glare at the bear.

"What is Gabriel like?" Neiva asked. She wondered if he was similar to Darius.

"Well, he is a king who cares about his kingdom but nothing outside of it. He constantly works against his brother and will do anything to seize an advantage. They're very competitive." Breezy looked at Neiva and gave her a shrug. "Just like King Darius, King Gabriel is full of secrets."

"So, do you think Darius sent him to help me?"

"I'm sure that's what happened. Gabriel loathes his brother, but deep down he won't let anything hurt him. If

Darius asked for help, then Gabriel would do it, but he would expect something in return. It's a strange relationship." Breezy explained, then quickly added, "Do you know they're twins?"

A new shock rocked Neiva. "Twins?"

"Hello! A little help over here!" Nate yelled at Breezy and Neiva, trying to get their attention. He was still standing across from the bear, not knowing what to do. The bear let out a grunt as if he was just as confused as Nate. Roxy stood staring at the two of them with her tail wagging.

"Oh, Nate. He's not going to hurt you," Breezy said as she walked over to the bear and gave him a giant hug.

The bear rubbed his head against hers. If bears could purr, Neiva swore he was doing it. When Breezy let go of the bear, he playfully knocked her legs out from under her and gave her a great push, causing her to fly onto his back.

"Oh Ben, you're still young at heart!" Breezy exclaimed as she landed on the bear's back. She laid her head in his soft fur, smelling traces of dirt and pine.

"Are you sure he's safe for us to be around?" Nate squeaked as he ran to Roxy's side. Roxy's tail was still wagging, indicating she wasn't worried about anything.

"Yes, Nate. He is fine. Something was controlling him before." Breezy turned her head toward Nate. "Why don't you come over here and introduce yourself, and tell him you're sorry for hurting him?"

"What?!" Nate yelled as he pointed at the bear. "He was the one who hurt me. Remember? Giant jaws embedded into my shoulder? Pain. Lots of pain!"

Breezy sighed. She narrowed her eyes at Nate. It had a great effect on him. Each of the girls knew that if they showed a little hint of anger toward him he would cave.

"Fine," Nate breathed out. He kicked the ground in frustration before scurrying toward the bear. He gulped loudly before sticking his hand out.

"My name is Nate," was his only response.

Breezy slowly cleared her throat.

"Uh, uh . . . ah, jeez. I'm sorry I hurt you. I was just defending my friends," Nate croaked as he brought his hand back to run it through his unruly hair. Then he suddenly brought his hand down to his side while his eyes glazed over.

"You know, it's hard watching over three girls, and it's especially hard understanding them. You think you are doing the right thing and suddenly you find out you're doing the wrong thing. You even get yelled at for looking at them the wrong way. Then one minute you like one girl and the next you like another. I just don't understand," Nate looked at the bear with big, earnest eyes.

The bear stared at Nate for several seconds before responding in deep grunts. Nate couldn't understand what the bear was saying, but he was just happy it was not trying to eat him again.

"Hmm. Well, males are the same in any species," Breezy muttered as she slid off the side of the bear, dropping to the ground to slowly turn to Nate. "He wants you to call him Ben, and sadly he agrees with everything you said. Apparently he had triplets with a sow and they were all girls, which may I say is rare."

Usually local bears had between one or two bears. So, it was very unusual when a sow had three cubs. It was unbelievable if they all survived to adulthood.

"Really?" Nate excitedly jumped to the bear's side to give him a big pat. "We should talk more then old pal!"

Nate guided the bear away from the girls. The bear was grunting in response to Nate's comments. They looked like two peas in a pod, inseparable. Roxy did not like the sudden connection between them and ran to Nate's side.

"No, Roxy. You stay with the girls. We need some man time," he replied, shooing her way as he sat down next to Ben.

Roxy ran to be near Neiva, who was standing and staring at the bear. Neiva could almost make out what he was saying but his words seemed to be mumbled, like static. Neiva peered down at Roxy. She felt her distress about the bear and Nate's sudden closeness.

"Don't worry. Nate just made a new friend. He is not replacing you with a bear. I guess he just needs to be with another male sometimes." Neiva patted Roxy's head. She could understand Nate's clinginess to another male, even though it was a bear. He was always surrounded by females.

"Hey, Roxy? Is there a chance you can get into the house? For some reason it is locked," Neiva asked as she turned to look at the house.

Roxy responded with a huff. She barked once at Neiva before running full speed at the cabin door. Neiva thought Roxy was going to collide with the door, but instead she glided right through it. Within a couple seconds the door opened revealing Roxy wagging her tail excitedly.

"Good job, Roxy!" Breezy exclaimed with excitement as she walked up to Neiva. "Let's make some hot chocolate, and then I need a nap to recharge."

"I need a nap too." Neiva was tired but she wanted to try and see if she could connect with Darius. She was going to get answers, even if she had to threaten the King of Darkness with blasting his mask off. She didn't know if she could do it, but she would try. She was determined to get some answers.

The girls quickly got into their pajamas, while Roxy stayed outside to keep an eye on Nate and Ben. Breezy made some hot chocolate, while Neiva got the bed ready. Once she was done straightening the covers, she joined Breezy in the kitchen.

"Are you feeling better?" Neiva asked as she took a mug of hot chocolate from Breezy and sat down. She took a sip and was pleased to taste mint and white chocolate, a pleasant combination.

"Yeah. I feel better now. Just tired." Breezy set her mug down. She turned her head slightly to the side, scrunching up her eyebrows at the same time, giving Neiva a puzzled look.

"What?" Neiva asked.

"It was strange. When the water hit me, it felt like it was draining all of my powers. I kept getting weaker and weaker." Breezy brought her arms up to rest her chin in her hands.

I felt the same when we got back to the cabin, like my strength was drained," Neiva replied. It was as if she couldn't control her body at the time, like she was fading.

"Breezy, Gabriel mentioned that you were beginning to fade. What does that mean?" Neiva asked. Then she looked at Breezy, whose face was losing all of its color.

"He said that?" Breezy asked as she brought her hands down. They were shaking, making it hard for Breezy to grab her coffee mug.

"Yes, he did," Neiva replied. She tried to steady Breezy's hands with her own, but Neiva could still feel Breezy quaking inside.

"Fading is death, Neiva. It's when a spirit fades out of this world and ceases to exist. Their life force doesn't join with the earth or go beyond the northern lights, they simply fade into nothing. It's feared by all spirits," she said simply. "It means someone was stealing my powers and draining my life force dry."

"I thought spirits were immortal?" Neiva wondered aloud.

"No, everything dies and nothing is immortal. We just stop aging at eighteen, but we still can die, Neiva," Breezy stammered. "Even kings die."

Neiva's heart stopped. Darius wasn't immortal, which meant he was at least eighteen and he could die. Would he die for her?

"But what could be so powerful that it was draining both of our powers?" Neiva muttered the question while bumping her head on the table. Great, Neiva thought, one more thing to add to the growing list of dangers.

"It has to be something ancient," Breezy replied, blowing out some air. She still was in shock. She couldn't believe she had almost faded. Breezy didn't even want to think about what could have happened if the king hadn't shown up when he did.

"Yeah, we figured that out already," Neiva mumbled, her face still down on the table. "We just need to figure out how to defend ourselves."

"Stick together, that's what we have to do," Breezy stated. She tapped her nails onto the table. "Hopefully Viv will get some information and you will hear from King Darius soon."

Neiva brought her head up from the table to focus on Breezy, who looked like she was staring into space, lost in thought. Neiva could tell her friend was tired by the circles underneath her eyes. So, Neiva suggested they get some sleep and talk about it more after their nap. Neiva was hoping she would see Darius and that Viv would be back by then too.

She quickly grabbed her journal.

September 5

I almost died today. Some crazy lady came for me in the river. If it weren't for one of Darius's guards, I would be fish food and floating at the bottom of the ocean.

> *My savior's name was Blake, who reminds me of Aquaman from DC Comics. He was very good-looking. He was very nice and proper, a true knight in shining armor. But he wasn't Darius or Riley. Where were they? I lost my link with them today. Will I get it back? I don't know! But I do know that Gabriel and Darius are twins and they're both eighteen. Well, that's the age spirits stop aging, kind of like Edward in* Twilight. *Edward was hundreds of years old. So, what's wrong with my feelings for Darius? Gabriel was like any other eighteen-year-old boy . . . well except for his wings and gorgeous features and the fact he's a king. The big question is: Are they identical? Thank goodness there won't be a craggy old man or corpse behind Darius's mask. But if there was, would I still have feelings for him? YES!*

Neiva threw the journal on the floor and snuggled into the bed. It didn't take Breezy long to fall asleep, but it was harder for Neiva. She kept seeing the woman's evil face every time she shut her eyes. It was as if the woman's image was burned into her retinas. She tossed and turned, but sleep finally found her as her eyes became heavy and her dream began.

Chapter 13

NEIVA FOUND HERSELF running barefoot down a long hallway. She could feel the cold, black tiled floor beneath her feet. As Neiva glanced down, she could see that she was wearing a long white skirt that flowed around her as she ran. A black satin belt was tied around her waist with a lacy black tank top completing her outfit. Neiva brought her hand up to her head as she ran. She could feel that her hair was up in a tight ballerina's bun, while her bangs were pinned back, leaving the crystal on her forehead exposed.

Neiva glanced at her surroundings. Dark concrete bricks lined a wall to her left. Every fifteen feet there were dome-shaped windows that revealed nothing but blackness. Purple curtains hung loosely around each window, flaring out from a light breeze. To her right was only darkness.

Neiva turned her attention back in front of her to see where she was running to. She couldn't see anything. It was as if the hallway just kept going on and on, stretching out into infinity. She ran a couple more paces before stopping to look around. Everything looked exactly the same except Neiva noticed a single mirror that sat between two windows. It was square-shaped with silver designs carved into its black frame.

Neiva went over to examine the mirror. It reminded her of the mirror in her first dream, the one where she met Darius for the first time. The only difference was this one was smaller.

Black eyeliner swept out in long strokes at the corners of her eyes. She had silver eye shadow on with spiky black lashes. Her lips sparkled like silver crystals. As Neiva glanced at her forehead, she could see the crystal glowing silver, as if it were trying to match her outfit. The ribbon that was usually intertwined with her hair was now holding her hair up in the ballerina bun.

Eyeing herself in the mirror, Neiva tried to determine whether she liked her appearance or not when her reflection suddenly rippled. It began to change, and, to her surprise, Neiva found herself staring into the face of Darius, except he looked very different. His mask was so dark that it was almost black. It jutted out in the front, ending in a point at his nose, reminding Neiva of a knight's helmet. His hair was braided all around his head. The slits in the mask curved up, giving him an evil appearance.

"Darius?" Neiva asked, her voice trembling.

"Yes. I am here," he replied.

"What's going on and why is something after me?" Neiva slowly brought her right hand up to the mirror. She rested it on the side of mirror, close to Darius's face.

"I am trying to figure that out. Something old and ancient is trying to get to you, Neiva. You're coming into your full powers and it wants to control you. You are special. Your blood sings of pure magic, which has only been seen once or twice throughout all of time. On your birthday, it was like a beacon was turned on as soon as you gained some of your powers. You must be careful," Darius replied earnestly. He brought his hand up to place it near hers, as if he was going to hold her hand. But his touch never reached Neiva because the mirror blocked it.

"How is it that I can't feel you or Riley anymore?" She whispered her question because she was afraid of the answer.

"It will be fixed, Neiva. The fact is that this creature is very powerful. It can interfere with the bonds between spirits, but it can't destroy them, only block them briefly," he calmly told her, keeping his voice smooth and low so he could keep Neiva calm.

"But you know what it is, and what was the black oily-looking substance?" she asked him.

"I have an idea, but it will take more investigative work. As for the oily substance, it is known as a Soul Eater. It's similar to a black hole, draining the power from its host or target." He stopped Neiva from asking another question. "I think you would be safer if you were kept in the dark for now."

"But I am sick of being kept in the dark. I want to know everything now," Neiva demanded. She was sick of all these secrets. If it was after her powers than what were her powers? How come no one knows what she is?

"I understand how you feel, Neiva, but just trust me. You are rare and I am trying to get to the bottom of this. But our ancestor foretold a being of great power would come into our house. That it would awaken evil from our past. We don't yet know who or what it is, but my brother and I are working on it," Darius said as he took his hand away from the mirror.

"Did you send Gabriel out to help us?" Neiva asked, bringing her hand down to her side.

Darius vanished from the mirror. Neiva's heart ached. She did not want him to go. She started to feel anger and resentment toward him. Why won't he tell her? Neiva was ready to hit the mirror when someone grabbed her hand. She quickly turned around only to be staring straight into Darius's mask. The anger melted away as Neiva jumped into his arms.

Darius wrapped his arms around her. He didn't know how long their connection would hold but he had to see her, to be close to her. He felt her heart calm and her breathing slow. The white light was back, wrapping itself around them. Darius brought his hands up to cradle Neiva's face in them and brought his head down so he could rest his mask against her cheek.

"I sent one of my Dark Knights and Gabriel to help you since I couldn't reach you," he replied as he slowly faded. "You are my first priority. I will keep you safe, Neiva. Just know you will always have someone helping you even when I am unable to."

"It's true, Neiva. You are never without protection," an accented voice replied from behind her.

Neiva tried to hold onto the last remnants of Darius, but he was gone. She turned around to look off into the darkness. She instantly noticed a pair of red eyes staring at her. She knew right away that it was Sasha, but she couldn't see anything except for his glowing eyes.

Darius's voice filled her head. "Sasha will continue your training tonight while I attend a meeting with my brother. You did well with your training in the garden. You should be able to control spirit shields and bring them down at will. After tonight you will be visited by my other two guards."

"Wow. Sounds kind of like *A Christmas Carol* except it's September, and instead of ghosts, magical beings are visiting me," Neiva smiled to herself, thinking her joke was really funny.

Darius was silent.

Maybe spirits have never heard of the three ghosts of Christmas, she thought. "Never mind, Darius," Neiva said, waving her hand. "I was making a joke about a story where three ghosts visit a greedy, selfish man on Christmas Eve. I was just comparing the story with what you said. It doesn't matter." Neiva shrugged her shoulders.

"Ah, I see. You know there is more to that story. It is based off of several spirits." Darius could feel Neiva's curiosity was piqued. He quickly replied, "I will wait until it gets closer to Christmas to tell you."

"Figures," she replied in defeat.

"I must go now. The meeting with my brother and his government officials is about to get underway. Sasha will take care of you tonight. Listen to him and do pay attention, for what he teaches you will come in handy in more ways than you know. So now I must say goodnight, my dear. But know this, you are always in my thoughts and I am only a heartbeat away. I shall see you in three nights and there shall be a quiz," Darius playfully said as his connection faded from her mind.

Every time she saw Darius, Neiva's feelings grew stronger and more intense. She felt as if she was born to be with him.

"So, Neiva, are you ready to begin tonight's lesson?" Sasha asked.

Neiva looked behind her in the mirror. She could see Sasha's eyes glowing brightly as he got closer. When he fully materialized out of the shadows, Neiva was shocked to see his attire. He was dressed formally. He wore a black suit with shiny black dress shoes. His coat fell down in a long tail behind him. He wore a red shirt with the top two buttons undone, showing part of his gray chest. The color brought out the intensity of his eyes. His white hair was tied in a low ponytail that fell down his back. He was still wearing his black mask, adding a more dashing and mysterious demeanor to his appearance.

"Speechless, I see. I have that effect on all women." He laughed as he walked up behind Neiva.

"Is every dark spirit so beautiful?" Neiva stuttered as she gazed at Sasha.

"Ah my sweet, it pleases me to hear that. Most female spirits wouldn't even glance at me," he replied as he folded his hands behind his back to stare into the mirror.

"But Sasha, you're so . . . you're so dashing!" Smiling, Neiva turned around to look at Sasha head-on. She could see the seriousness masked behind the playfulness in his eyes. He wasn't joking, but he was trying to make light of his situation.

"Ah, a bad rap for my species. We weren't ones to follow the rules in the beginning—lots of bloodshed and carnage. That was the time when the legend of the vampire was born."

"Oh." Neiva didn't know what to say. "Aren't there any female Shadow Spirits, Sasha?"

Sadness creased Sasha's eyes as his smile faded. "Only a few exist. We are mostly a male species. Our mortality rate is very low. Some think we can live forever. But everything dies, Neiva, even my species."

"Can't you make more?" Neiva wondered why he just didn't make a Shadow Spirit like a vampire can make another vampire.

"We can't. We can only possess the knowledge from the subject we take blood from. It leaves them dazed and sick-looking for several days, causing everyone to believe they are dead or undead," Sasha said as he moved closer to Neiva.

"Enough of this sour talk. Let's get your lesson under way so you can go into a deeper sleep and get some rest," he continued while he grabbed Neiva's waist with his right hand. He picked up Neiva's right hand with his left hand and folded his fingers in between hers, holding their hands up near their heads.

"Are we dancing?" Neiva squealed as she rested her left hand on Sasha's shoulder. She wasn't the best dancer. In fact, she had two left feet when it came to dancing.

"Yes we are, my pretty ballerina. You wouldn't believe how dancing can transform your body and change the way you look at things." Sasha guided Neiva around the room.

"What about my shoes?" Neiva asked as her bare feet tried to follow Sasha's.

"Oh, that can be easily fixed," Sasha replied as he nodded his head at Neiva. In a blink of an eye, black glittery dancing shoes were on Neiva's feet. They felt comfortable and flexible. She could tell all of her weight was on the balls of her feet, making her movements smoother and her balance steadier as Sasha guided them into the darkness beyond the pillars.

As they swept past the black pillars there was a loud boom. A flash of light chased away the darkness. It lit up the whole room, making Neiva stare in wonderment at her new surroundings. An enormous room illuminated, revealing a high black ceiling that had deep arches grooved into it. The arches looked as if they were made of silver. A huge diamond chandelier hung from the middle of the ceiling; it sparkled like twinkling stars. The walls around the room were painted silver with blue metallic borders. The floor was a dizzying mix of black, white, green, yellow, orange, red, and blue. As Sasha swept Neiva around the room, Neiva noticed the floor wasn't just a mixture of colors, it was a picture of outer space. She could see several galaxies rotating around them, so it was as if she was dancing in outer space.

"Now, I know the floor is engrossing, but please keep your eyes up here on me, Neiva. It doesn't help your feet or your balance when your head is down," Sasha instructed. He sighed as he guided Neiva around the room. Within two minutes he knew it wasn't going to be easy teaching Neiva how to dance. It was as if she was made of lead. She wasn't flexible and she was stiff as a board.

"Is the floor a picture?" Neiva asked as she tried to glance down without moving her head. It was hard to be sneaky about it because Sasha was looking directly into her eyes.

He smiled and nodded at Neiva, causing her to blush again. "Magic, my dear Neiva."

"Now just count one, two, and three. One, two, and three. Quick, quick, slow," Sasha said as he straightened Neiva's posture, positioning her head to the side.

"Is this ballroom dancing?" Neiva asked as she tried to rearrange her weight to match the position of her head. She could feel the difference.

"Okay, let me lead and just follow. All you have to do is trust me, Neiva. It's just like going into war. Trust your fellow fighters at your side. Trust their instincts and follow," Sasha stated as he twirled Neiva around.

Neiva laughed as her body spun around. She felt free and at ease. She knew Sasha would make sure she wouldn't fall. True to his statement, Sasha caught Neiva, guiding her back into his arms.

"What kind of dance is this?" Neiva looked into Sasha's eyes. They seemed to be sparkling with mischief.

"It is a dark spirit dance called the Dark Waltz. It's similar to a traditional waltz, but some of the moves are very different," Sasha replied. A smile slowly spread across his face. "I think it's time to add the music."

A single note emanated from the ceiling. As more notes were added, the whole room began to resonate. The next thing Neiva knew, a magical chorus of violins, flutes, and other instruments meshed together to form a beautiful melody. It was fast-paced, but not too fast. Neiva could feel the beat and see how their movements blended in with the music.

"Remember to listen to the beat. You want your body and senses accustomed to hearing every sound. This can help you in battle. If you listen to your surroundings, you can hear the slightest breath from an enemy or the break of a twig. There could be a shift in the air leading you to make your next move."

With that information, Sasha led Neiva into more steps and moves for the next couple of hours. He fixed her posture, made sure her eyes were not on her feet, and even counted out every step for the first hour, so Neiva would feel it more. By the second hour, Neiva could do the steps herself and she even felt relaxed.

"I think you're ready," Sasha said as he came to a stop.

He slowly let go of Neiva's waist and hand. He stepped back several steps to casually glance down at her feet, making Neiva curious as to what he was looking at. She brought her right foot out from underneath her skirt. Nothing looked different. She was still wearing the sparkly dance shoes that Sasha had magically put on her feet earlier. So, what was he looking at?

"What?" Neiva asked.

She looked over her foot one more time before she brought her eyes up to meet Sasha's, giving him a puzzled look. He was now looking at her with a smile slowly creeping over his face. It reminded Neiva of the sun rising at dawn, how everything lightened up at its touch.

"Do you like the shoes? They are comfortable, correct?" Sasha asked Neiva as he started to walk around her. He folded his hands behind his back as he observed his student.

"Yes, they fit perfectly. It's almost as if they were worn by someone else, like they had already been broken in," Neiva replied as she pointed her foot out.

"All dancing shoes are flexible and ready for wear. It's so the dancer can start right away and not worry about getting sore feet from breaking the shoes in." He stopped in front of Neiva, his smile getting wider.

"Why are you smiling?" Neiva asked, now annoyed.

Sasha was about to reply to Neiva's question, but Neiva quickly cut him off with her own punchline, making sure lots of sarcasm was added to it. "Oh, wait. Let me guess. I have to wait because the truth will eventually be revealed."

Neiva brought her hands up in the air with frustration. "You know I am so sick of hearing that. If one more person tells me that, I am going to explode."

"Ah, that's nice to know, but I was going to say they would be perfect for the upcoming Halloween party on All Hallows' Eve, but please continue. You have my full attention," Sasha calmly said, his eyes glowing with laughter.

Slamming her arms down at her side in anger, Neiva let out a frustrated grunt. She looked at Sasha with narrowed eyes and crossed her arms, a frown slowly forming on her face. Tamping down her temper, Neiva asked Sasha about the dance.

"Ah, in due time Neiva, in due time," Sasha whispered as the shadows started to blend in with him.

"Sasha!" Neiva yelled, trying to grab his arm before it disappeared into the shadows. She was too late and her hand passed right through him. The only thing that remained of Sasha was his evil eyes and a giant fanged smile. It seemed to get bigger as he bid her good night with a humorous laugh.

"Until next time, poppet," he said before he completely vanished; and suddenly everything went dark.

Chapter 14

"AH!" NEIVA SCREAMED as she opened her eyes.

She quickly sat up trying to figure out where she was. For a second she thought she was still dreaming, but as she looked around the room she realized that she was back in her grandmother's cabin. It was still Saturday, she figured, but she assumed it was past dinnertime because it was almost dark outside.

The sun was slowly setting in the western sky, causing shadows to creep along the room and over toward Nate, who was sprawled out on the floor snoring lightly. A small puddle of drool rested near his face causing Neiva to let out a silent giggle. She glanced near the door. There was no sign of Viv yet. Neiva figured she was talking to her father about the events that had transpired earlier in the day. She turned to see if Breezy was still sleeping, only to find her staring at Neiva through one open eye.

"You okay? Bad dream?" Breezy asked softly. She was back in her human form.

Neiva felt bad. She must have woken Breezy up when she had yelled out earlier. "Oh, no. I was just frustrated because I had a lesson with Sasha and he was very secretive. It's like he was trying to egg me on."

Breezy opened her other eye. She stretched her body out just like a cat. "The whole Spirit World is a mystery Neiva, especially its men."

"Men," Neiva muttered as she stared at Nate on the floor, who had his butt in the air with his arm twisted at an odd angle.

"So, what did he teach you?"

"He gave me dance lessons." Neiva paused briefly as she scrunched her nose up in thought. "I didn't understand it at first, but once he took me through the steps and explained the similarities between battling and dancing, I started to understand. But now that I'm awake, it feels like it is second nature to me. Like I could hop up now and do a performance in front of everyone."

Breezy sat up with a smile. "Every spirit learns a kingdom's dance, Neiva. The dark spirits learn the Dark Waltz and the light spirits learn the Dance of Light. The only way it's done is through the spirit's dreams. Deep down in the subconscious is a place that we are able to imbed a memory, so it's like we have had it with us since birth." Breezy paused for a brief second so that Neiva could process the information before continuing on. "You can compare it to a photographic memory. You will never forget it and it will always be there. The only ones that have access to this place are the Dream Wielders, and in this place they teach us about our heritage and our culture. Every lesson is ended with the homeland dance. It's important that each kingdom performs these dances at major events. No kingdom is allowed to have a party or celebration without inviting the other kingdom. King Darius mandated it many years ago."

"Okay, so if I was taught the Dark Waltz than that must mean that I am a dark spirit? Right?" Neiva asked, confusing herself at the same time.

"Basically, Neiva, I have no clue what you are or which

spirit realm you belong to. But you're Eskimo and that makes it even stranger." Breezy shrugged her shoulders.

"Dancing is like war. You fight with your partner until the bitter end. It's for the victory of the competition or battle. I think Darius is teaching you how to survive, so that you realize what your body is capable of doing. Dancing is art, and it's big in the Spirit World. Who's to say that King Gabriel won't be teaching you next?"

"True," Neiva replied as she stretched her hands over her head. It was impossible to predict or assume what was going on. Secrets were supposedly being kept for her safety. She wanted to know everything, but that might be an overload of information and too much for her to handle at one time. She suddenly had an image of her head exploding with all of the information she couldn't hold.

"I wonder what's taking Viv so long?" Neiva asked, changing the subject with a shudder. She turned to look out the window again. The sun was sinking faster and it had to be almost dinnertime. She could feel her stomach growling, letting her know that she needed food.

Hearing Neiva's stomach, Breezy instantly got up and headed to the kitchen. There was some clanging around followed by silence. Neiva was going to ask if Breezy was okay, but before she could, Breezy walked back into the living room.

"I put the pizzas in. They should be ready in twenty minutes," Breezy said, walking over to help Neiva off the bed with a smile. She slowly bowed. "May I have this dance, my lady?"

Neiva raised an eyebrow. "You may indeed, sir."

Breezy led Neiva around the room in the exact same steps that Sasha had shown her earlier. This puzzled Neiva. "I thought the Dark Waltz was only for dark spirits to dance to?"

"Oh, no. Each kingdom learns the other kingdom's dance as well. You know, in case someone from the other courts asks them to dance?" Breezy smiled and winked at Neiva.

As the girls made their way around the room, Neiva found

it was as easy to dance with Breezy as it had been with Sasha. She didn't even have to think about it. It was second nature to her and this led her to feel comfortable in asking her next questions.

"So, what are the Dream Wielders and how come I didn't see one in my dreams?" Neiva asked as Breezy twirled her around in a spin causing Neiva to giggle.

"Oh, you will never see a Dream Wielder's true form. They are one of the few creatures of the Spirit World that pledge their alliance to both the Light and Dark Kingdoms. They stay invisible or in disguise, only showing themselves to the kings when called. They make sure no one invades each other's minds and that sleep comes to those who need rest. They are also known as the protectors of children's dreams."

"They sound sort of like the sheriffs of dreams," Neiva stated as she quickly outmaneuvered Breezy, spinning her into a double twirl.

"Yes, exactly!" Breezy exclaimed, laughing as she was caught by Neiva. "Very good! I can see that you retained the memory of the Dark Waltz very well. I can't wait until you learn the Dance of Light. It will be interesting to see you perform it."

Neiva stopped herself to ask Breezy about the Dance of Light, but she never got the chance. A scream cut through the air like a knife, causing both of the girls to quickly turn their heads toward the front door. There was a couple seconds of silence before another scream erupted.

"Bear! Why is there a huge bear on the porch?" Viv's yell drifted through the house, waking Nate out of his slumber.

"Oh, it's just Viv." Neiva relaxed. Nothing dangerous, but as Neiva thought about it, she was suddenly second-guessing herself. She turned back to Breezy, "She wouldn't hurt Ben, would she?"

Breezy's eyes became wide as she pushed Neiva out of the way so she could get to the door, but she wasn't fast enough. Nate was already off the floor and two steps ahead of her.

"Benny!" he shouted as he burst through the open door. There was a bright light and a loud whoosh followed by the smell of burning tires. Smoke slowly drifted through the front door. Neiva was afraid to peek outside. She didn't know what Viv's powers were, but she hoped the result wasn't a burnt bear on their porch.

As both Breezy and Neiva slowly peeked their heads outside, their jaws dropped at the sight that stood before them. Viv was back in her human form with her long black braid falling down her back. She stood still as a statue. Her right hand was thrown out in front of her while her face was frozen in shock. To the girls' left sat Old Ben. If bears could be shocked then Old Ben looked like one shocked bear. His lip was curled up and his eyes were wide with surprise. He wasn't looking at Viv. Instead, he was looking at Nate. In fact, everyone's attention was on Nate. It was hard not to stare. He was covered in soot from head to toe. Smoke billowed off of his burnt hair while some flames still lingered at the tips of his hair.

"I guess Nate's gel is not flame-resistant," Neiva whispered.

At the sound of Neiva's voice, Viv suddenly sprung to life. She lowered her arm and pounced up the steps to stand in front of Nate. "I am so sorry. I didn't mean to set your hair on fire. I saw the bear and got defensive. You just got in the way."

Nate had a huge scowl on his face as he stared at Viv. He coughed right into her face, releasing ash from his mouth that fell in thick clouds around Viv. "Ben wouldn't hurt you. He was just protecting us while we napped."

Viv blinked a couple of times while the cloud of ash settled onto her face. "Okay, I deserved that. I am sorry. How was I supposed to know he wasn't rabid or possessed by something?"

"Because he already was possessed before, that is until the King of Light saved him and us," Nate stammered as he narrowed his eyes at Viv.

"What? What happened? What did I miss?" Viv asked as she looked at Breezy then Neiva, urging them for answers.

"It's true. His Lightness was here and saved Ben from killing Nate," Breezy said as she watched Viv suck in a breath and her eyes widen in surprise. "Everyone is fine now, Viv. His Lightness healed everyone and we took naps to recharge. But if he hadn't shown up . . ."

Breezy let her sentence drop without even finishing. Nothing needed to be said because she understood the power of evil, but Viv felt badly. "I should have been here to help."

"It wouldn't have mattered even if you were here. We were all weak and you wouldn't have been able to fight a possessed bear by yourself, Viv," Breezy explained.

Viv frowned. "You never know."

Nate puffed more ash into Viv's face. "Okay, okay. You're right. Who knows what would have happened?" she replied.

Ben grunted. Neiva could feel that he was anxious to leave. Her connection with him was slowly getting stronger, making Neiva wonder if she was developing the power to communicate or connect with animals.

"Ben wants to leave," Neiva stated, receiving a curious look from Breezy.

"He says there will be others to protect us soon," Breezy added as she continued to stare at Neiva.

Nate tried to brush the ash off of his shirt. To his dismay, it was not working. "I bet it will be the Ishegocks."

"Oh, let me help you," Breezy said as she guided Nate off the porch. She positioned him with his hands out at his side. Stepping back, she raised her arms into the air. "Wind, chase the dust and ash from Nate's body, leaving him clean and free."

Breezy brought both of her hands down, thrusting them in Nate's direction causing a stream of wind to blow all around Nate. The wind whipped his hair up in a frenzy, blasting the ash off his body—and his clothes.

"Oops. Too strong," Breezy said as she shoved her hands into her pockets. Nate's eyes were wide open, his hair had been blown back straight as an arrow, and he was standing on the porch in just his underwear.

"Very funny," Nate screeched as he ran into the house.

The girls stared at him. Every muscle was so well-defined he looked like he had popped out of a muscle magazine. Breezy and Neiva were in shock, but Viv was fighting back a smile as she said, "Well, at least Nate is clean now!"

Both Neiva and Viv laughed, causing Breezy to scrunch her mouth to the side in an awkward smile. "Next time I will be more careful."

"Wow. So you can call upon the wind, Breezy? You have another power besides controlling plants?" Neiva asked, staring from one girl to the next.

"Well, I'm just learning how to harness the wind. It's obviously kind of new to me," Breezy replied, as her smile intensified.

Viv smiled at Neiva. "Fire is second nature to me. I was born in it. Demons are born with their powers; we don't have to wait like you spirits do."

"I can't wait to harness my powers," Neiva said with excitement. "What else happens when a spirit turns seventeen?"

"Well, it is a time when a spirit could find his or her spirit mate," Viv said while looking at Breezy. She turned back to Neiva. "It's different for me because I am a demon and I was not born a part of the spirit realm. We aren't bonded pairs like spirits. We are more like humans, choosing who we want to be with."

"What do you mean? I can't choose who I want to love?" Neiva asked. Her family taught her to love freely and to choose whomever she wanted to spend the rest of her life with. But what about Darius? He had her heart. She crossed her arms and stared at Viv. "Well, rules are meant to broken."

"It's not a rule, Neiva," Breezy stated sadly. She looked off into the distance. "Spirits can have many partners if they wish, bouncing from one relationship to the next, but they never will be truly happy or feel complete until they are bonded with their spirit mate."

Neiva's forehead creased up in frustration. She didn't

understand the Spirit World at all. Now that she was a part of it, she was being told she couldn't choose whom she wanted to be with or that she wouldn't be truly happy or complete without him.

Breezy let out a sigh. "Spirits don't always find their mates right away. It could take them years before they do, but when they do, they will know."

"How?" Neiva grumbled. Could the electric shock and white light between her and Darius be a sign? She had a year until her eighteenth birthday, but she was different. Maybe the spirit mate was different for her.

"It's different for each person." Breezy responded. She turned her attention back to Neiva. "I turn eighteen in five months."

Breezy's birthday was just around the corner. So, that would mean she could possibly find her destined mate next year, if she was lucky.

"Aren't you scared, Breezy?" Neiva asked. Just thinking about it made Neiva's stomach turn in knots.

"No. What's meant to be is meant to be. Things happen for a reason, Neiva. I am just going to continue on the path that I am leading and hope to find my spirit mate on the way." Breezy shrugged. She was having a positive attitude about the whole situation.

"What if it's someone you loathe or despise?" Neiva asked.

"We don't have a choice on who we pick, Neiva. It's our destiny," Breezy stated as she glanced into the house.

Viv's eyes narrowed and her voice became lethal. "What? Do you think Nate might be your spirit mate?"

"I'm not suggesting that Viv. I am just saying it could be any spirit including Guardians," Breezy replied in defense.

"Guardians are included?" Neiva wondered aloud. She wasn't sure if it only pertained to spirits.

Viv answered Neiva's question while still giving Breezy the evil eye. "Yes, it has been known for Guardians and spirits to become spirit mates or, as the humans say, soul mates."

"So, humans can have soul mates *or* spirit mates?" Neiva asked. Things just kept getting more complicated. It was making Neiva's head spin.

"Yes, the select few humans who find their soul mates actually are bonded with their companion spirits. Those spirits choose love over their true form and stay hidden within their spirit shield for the remainder of their lives. They leave the Spirit World behind. Eventually their spirit form dissolves and they age just like their human mate," Breezy said, looking right at Viv.

"True, Breezy, but Guardians are in a different category than humans. They know about the Spirit World and can live within it," Viv shot back, practically spitting her remark out.

"Yes, Guardians are given the gift of a spirit mate if it is destined. They are a part of the Spirit World as much as you or me! Without them, we wouldn't be protected or have the safety of this island," Breezy fired back, balling her fists at her side. "I'm keeping an open mind to a Guardian as a spirit mate. Because you never know who it will be, Viv."

Viv's eyes began to flame when Breezy's statement sunk in.

"Okay, okay. I get it." Neiva brought her hands up to break Viv and Breezy's stare down. *Who knew that all the girls would be infatuated with Nate?* Neiva thought.

"Pizza's ready!" Nate said as he poked his head out the front door. His mouth scrunched up to the side when he saw the intense expression on Viv's face. He slowly walked out as if he was afraid one of them would leap on him in anger. "What's going on?"

"Just more spirit mumbo-jumbo," Viv growled as she stomped past him and entered the cabin. She jerked her rain boots off, throwing each one into the kitchen. They bounced across the floor, landing underneath the table.

"Uh, do I even want to ask?" Nate raised his eyebrow as he looked at Breezy then Neiva.

They both shook their heads no and headed into the cabin.

"Girls," Nate muttered as he shut the door and locked it.

He walked back into the kitchen to see the group devouring the pizzas. Both the pizzas were disappearing before his eyes.

"Hogs! Save some for me!" Nate shouted as he rescued two slices from being devoured by Viv, who in response whipped a forked tongue out at him. Nate ignored her and sat down in front of Viv, quickly inhaling the pizza.

Within minutes, the pizza was gone. There was not a morsel left on the table, not even a crumb. Everyone sat back with their hands on their bellies, content. Nate glanced out the window. "It's getting really dark outside."

Neiva looked out the window. He was right. The sky had darkened dramatically with only a trace of light left, which meant that the Ishegocks would probably be on their way soon to watch over them.

"I'm going to use the bathroom before it's completely dark." Neiva got up and quickly rushed to the door.

"Good idea!" Breezy said as she ran past Neiva. She opened the door and ran out to the outhouse.

Neiva turned to look at Viv then Nate.

Viv waived Neiva off. "I'm fine. I used the bathroom back at home."

"If I really have to go I can just go off the porch," Nate said with a shrug.

"Okay, if you guys say so," Neiva said as she headed out the door. She barely heard Viv mention to Nate something about losing body parts when she felt a wind rush past her. It was Nate. He was in such a hurry that he bumped into Breezy when she was exiting the outhouse.

"Hey!" Breezy shouted as Nate pushed her out of the way and slammed the door behind him.

Breezy had a scowl on her face as she walked past Neiva. "I guess he really had to go."

Neiva laughed as Breezy walked up the steps to enter the cabin. If only she knew what Neiva was thinking as she looked at her surroundings. The bushes were casting shadows onto the ground. The trees seemed darker, making it easy for something to hide in them. Neiva didn't see any sign of Riley. In fact, she didn't see any birds or wildlife around, which was strange. Usually the cabin was never quiet. There were always birds singing or squirrels darting around that livened the place up, but before Neiva could delve deeper into the thought, Nate suddenly rushed past her.

"All yours!" Nate said as he bounded toward the cabin.

Neiva quickly grabbed the outhouse door before it slammed shut and stepped inside. She was suddenly engulfed with a wicked smell, causing Neiva's eyes to water. She covered her mouth and nose while she grabbed the air freshener that sat to the side of the toilet. She sprayed the freshener all around the outhouse, not stopping until every inch was covered. When she thought it was safe, she brought her hand away from her mouth to take in a small breath. She didn't even get half a breath in before she started coughing. She had sprayed too much; the freshener was overpowering. It took a couple minutes for it to dissipate, but once her cough settled down, Neiva quickly used the toilet.

When Neiva was done slathering her hands with disinfecting gel, she made sure to put the spray back in its original place. She glanced at the toilet paper, checking to see if it was stocked up as well. There were two full rolls. Neiva could remember several times when she had used the outhouse only to find that there was no toilet paper on hand.

Neiva was about to open the door when a sudden rush of goose bumps broke out over her arms. The hair on the back of her neck stood on end; her smile disappeared. A feeling deep in her gut told her not to open the door. Something dangerous was just outside.

Alert, she drew her eyes above the door. There was a small window toward the top of the outhouse, just above the door. It was positioned there to let the sunlight in during the day, and in the summer that is until two o'clock in the morning. But the sun doesn't really set. It rolls just under the horizon, still producing a faint light for the three hours it's out of sight. This was great if you had to use the bathroom at night. It was also the perfect opportunity to look out and see what was lurking near the outhouse.

Making sure the door was latched shut, Neiva grabbed the stool that sat in the left corner of the outhouse, near the door. She placed the stool just under the middle of the window. She took a deep breath before she stepped onto the stool to look out the window. Neiva noticed right away that it was darker out, much darker than before she went into the outhouse. The shadows seemed thicker and slimier. It almost looked like they were alive, slithering toward her. Darius had told her the shadows would help her, but she had a funny feeling that these shadows were not shadows at all and that they were not here to help her. It looked like the same substance that had attacked them before. This sent chills down her spine. Soul Eaters.

Neiva glanced at the cabin to make sure everyone was inside. It seemed like everyone was safe until Nate walked out to see what was taking Neiva so long.

"What, did you fall in?" Nate cupped his hands around his mouth to yell across the yard.

"Shh. Be quiet, Nate," Neiva whispered urgently.

She didn't want him to gain the attention of whatever was out there. Her silent prayer went unanswered; it was too late. One of the creatures turned toward Nate and slowly started creeping across the ground in his direction. Nate didn't notice it at first. It wasn't until it was almost to the porch steps that he finally saw it.

"Holy crap, a Soul Eater," Nate gasped as he saw the Soul Eater creep up the steps toward him. Nate turned to run back into the house but only took two steps before falling face first onto the porch with a thud. He wasn't moving. Neiva screamed as the creature crept over him.

Chapter 15

THE SOUL EATER started to rise up. It was about six feet in height, looking like a giant compared to Nate's small lifeless form. A gaping hole appeared where its face should have been. Large teeth shielded the entrance to its mouth. It was the only distinct feature on its body because it didn't have any feet or legs. To Neiva, it looked like a giant black blob with teeth.

"Nate!" Neiva screamed as she banged on the window. Her efforts did not have any effect on Nate, but it did provoke the other Soul Eaters to quicken their pace toward her. Neiva glanced back at Nate and suddenly saw Roxy appear at his side. Her white eyes glowed with intensity as she stared at the creature, which was mere inches from Nate's fallen form, making the hairs on Roxy's back stand up.

Anger surged out of Roxy and her need to protect Nate shook her body. She bent low and gave a fierce growl that echoed around the cabin. Both Breezy and Viv gasped when they saw the creature so close to Nate. But the strange thing was that the creature suddenly stopped moving, which caused Roxy to stop growling. She cocked her head to the side befuddled.

The other Soul Eaters were almost to the outhouse. They were halfway across the yard before they stopped moving as well. *What were they up to?* Neiva wondered. She glanced back at Roxy, who was now sniffing at the creature. Neiva didn't understand what was going on until the fog appeared. It came out from behind the outhouse, slowly encircling it like long arms reaching out to grab something. It thickened as it surrounded the oily Soul Eaters. Lights began blinking on and off throughout the fog. Neiva thought she saw dark shapes moving within it.

The fog engulfed the area, swallowing up the Soul Eaters. Nothing could be seen, only thick whiteness and the sporadic glowing lights. They reminded Neiva of a lantern that someone was holding while making their way through the dense fog, except Neiva knew that whatever was in the fog was not human.

There was a sudden forceful knock on the door, causing Neiva to lose her balance and fall off the stool. She tumbled to the floor, banging her head against the wall on her way down. Neiva was momentarily stunned. She had hit the crystal in the middle of her forehead and it sent a shock wave throughout her head. She sat on the floor trying to get her bearings and to ease the ache that had just started in her head.

After a moment, Neiva stood up. Feeling slightly dizzy, she steadied herself against the door, taking in deep breaths to calm herself down. For a second she thought she imagined the knock, but that was until another knock pounded at the door.

"Who's there?" Neiva shouted through the thick wood. She double-checked the latch to make sure it was locked. To Neiva's satisfaction, it was.

Another knock pounded at the door, but lighter. Neiva glanced down at the handle. To her horror, the latch suddenly unlocked and the door burst open. Neiva cringed and covered her head defensively while she waited for something to grab her. It took her several seconds to realize there was nothing there, only the fog.

Neiva tried to shut the door, but it wouldn't budge. An invisible force was holding it open. Feeling vulnerable and open to attack, she realized she wasn't safe. She had to get back to the cabin. The Ishegocks wouldn't let anything happen to her. At least she hoped they wouldn't. She tried to contact Darius but she didn't feel anything, so that left her with no other option but to run.

Neiva slowly scanned the area to see if there were any sightings of the oily creatures or the Ishegocks. She didn't see anything, not even the glowing lights. She took this as her cue. With a deep breath she ran full speed in the direction that she thought was the cabin. It should have been easy. The cabin's back door was just twenty-five feet from the outhouse. She should have reached it within seconds, but she didn't. It seemed like several minutes went by before she stopped. She should have been there by now. Where was it? What was going on?

Turning in circles, her heart beat fast and she didn't know where she was. Everything looked the same, just white fog everywhere. She couldn't tell which direction she had originally started in. Was it behind her? She glanced over her shoulder only to see a shadow approaching. Her heart jumped into her stomach. Was it a Soul Eater? She didn't want to find out, so she ran in the opposite direction. She got a couple of feet before slamming into a solid object.

Dazed, Neiva blinked a couple of times. Her head was starting to throb again. She glanced up at the tree she had collided with. It was about eight feet tall. Green moss covered its trunk, and flowers sporadically popped up through the moss. There didn't seem to be any leaves on the tree, only four branches. *Strange*, Neiva thought. The tree's limbs almost looked like arms and legs. Neiva brought her attention to the top of the tree. It seemed normal except for the two fireflies floating around the top of the tree. They were staying in one spot blinking on and off. It almost felt like the fireflies were watching her. It took her a couple seconds for her brain to process what was in front of her. Suddenly the truth slammed into her. It was too cold for fireflies and this wasn't a tree. Trees don't have yellow eyes staring back at you.

The fog dissolved around Neiva, leaving her able to see the full extent of the thing that stood before her. It was definitely not a tree. It had to be an Ishegock, and it was huge. It had a human form with powerful arms and legs. Giant hands were closed in fists at its side. Its chest was so well-defined that it would make any art student happy to sketch it. As Neiva looked up at its face, she saw something partly resembling a human. The Ishegock was entirely covered in moss so it was hard to distinguish the human features, but she could make out an elflike nose and a mouth surrounded by green lips. Its eyes were all yellow, almost as if the creature had some kind of light glowing within it.

The Ishegock opened its mouth to reveal sharp serrated teeth, reminding Neiva of a large piranha. It started speaking in another language that Neiva didn't understand. She thought she caught several words that sounded almost like the language the Eskimos used.

Neiva wasn't scared of the Ishegock. She felt it wasn't evil, but she couldn't understand it. Neiva put her hands out in front of her, as if she was warding off the creature. "I don't understand what you're saying."

The forest creature stopped. It glanced in the direction behind Neiva then back at her again. It brought up one of its massive arms to point back in that direction. Neiva turned around to see the fog clear a path all the way up to the cabin. She was just ten feet away. She had been running in the wrong direction. If the creature hadn't shown up, she probably would have been running in circles around the cabin all night.

Neiva brought her arms down and turned back to the creature. "You're an Ishegock?"

The Ishegock stared at Neiva for several seconds before it nodded in response. It brought its hand back up, making a strange motion, as if it was waving her toward the cabin.

Responding to its gesture, Neiva backed up a couple of steps. The fog started surrounding the Ishegock the more steps she took back. Once she reached the porch, Neiva could only see the outline of the Ishegock, but soon it quickly blended in as well. All that was left of the Ishegock were its eyes, glowing brighter and brighter until the light resembled lanterns within the fog.

"So, that's what the lights are," Neiva whispered as she watched the Ishegock disappear as it went farther into the fog. A loud bark caught Neiva's attention. She turned around to see Roxy's head poking through the door with her head cocked to the side. Neiva could feel her worry. Roxy had been wondering where Neiva had been this whole time.

Neiva was about to tell Roxy what had happened but she didn't get the chance. The door burst open with such force that Neiva thought it was going to come off its hinges.

"Are you all right? Where were you? I thought those freaky shadow things got you." Nate bombarded Neiva with questions. He swept Roxy to the side so he could get closer to Neiva. He was close enough to where Neiva could see his left eye twitching.

"I'm fine. If the Ishegocks hadn't shown up, I think I wouldn't be here right now." Neiva responded, trying to persuade Nate that she was okay.

"We were worried," Viv said as she appeared in the doorway. She was back in her true form. Her tattoos were glowing like lava and her tail was whipping back and forth assertively.

Breezy poked her head around Viv's body. Her catlike eyes stared at Neiva. "We couldn't get the door open after we dragged Nate in. It shut as soon as he crossed the threshold."

Roxy barked in response. Neiva could feel her frustration. "Roxy couldn't get out either?"

"No," Nate hissed, crossing his arms. "Roxy was going to help you, but she couldn't go through the door once she came inside. It was like an invisible force field kept us all trapped inside."

"How did you manage to get back to the cabin once the fog came in?" Breezy asked Neiva, who stepped outside. Breezy's wings were fluttering behind her. She was slightly shaken up. Neiva knew Breezy didn't like anything pertaining to the Ishegocks.

"I had a little help." Neiva looked back into the fog, briefly seeing the lights blinking in the distance. She felt safe in the vicinity of the fog.

"So, it really was an Ishegock?" Breezy quietly asked while ushering everyone inside. She shut the door behind her and followed everyone to the bed and couch. They all sat down, feeling exhausted from the day's events.

"Yes," Neiva replied, looking at Nate.

His eyes widened and she could see a trace of excitement behind them.

"Did you see it? What did it look like?" his voice squeaked. He was bouncing up and down on the bed reminding Neiva of a three-year-old.

Neiva nodded her head. She was trying to figure out the best way to describe the creature when Nate cleared his voice to get her attention.

Neiva stared at Nate for a couple of seconds, and then replied, "Like a piece of marsh with teeth."

Nate's face fell flat. He suddenly had the image of a little piece of marshland running around with giant teeth, nipping at people's ankles.

Neiva saw the disappointment on Nate's face. This was a legend among the Eskimos, and only a select few Eskimos have ever seen them and lived to talk about it. Neiva didn't want to leave him hanging. So, she took a deep breath and added excitement to her voice as she told them what it looked like in detail.

"It was huge, at least eight feet tall with huge arms and legs. It was green and covered in the marshland. It had a mouthful of teeth and yellow, glowing eyes. It reminded me of the swamp man." Neiva turned to look at Breezy. "So, the lights blinking in the fog are their eyes looking around, watching us."

Neiva whispered the last part to add a dramatic effect. She instantly saw Nate's demeanor change. The excitement was back in his eyes. He slowly leaned back against the couch and turned to look out the window, lost in thought.

"I knew they were impressive," Nate said under his breath. His eyes were glazed over.

Neiva had a question of her own. "Nate? Why do you pass out every time the Ishegocks show up? It's happened the last two times they were here."

Nate's eyes focused back on Neiva. He twisted his mouth to the side, knotting his eyebrows in thought. "Huh. I've never thought about it, but you're right. It does seem like every time they show up, I lose consciousness."

"I wonder if it has to do with your Eskimo heritage," Breezy added, tapping her chin. "But then why is Neiva immune to them?"

Nate looked back outside. The fog still surrounded the cabin, protecting it from further intruders. The glow that kept the fog visible was slowly dimming, causing Nate's eyes to become heavy.

Viv let out a loud yawn, showing off her sharp teeth and forked tongue. She slowly crawled under the covers, pushing Nate's feet off the end of the bed and back onto the couch.

"I guess the Ishegocks want us to go to bed too," Nate mumbled as he piled the blankets around himself.

"Probably so we don't get into any more trouble and to keep our energy charged," Breezy replied. She was trying to keep her eyes open, but it was very difficult for her. Her wings slowly folded behind her as she swayed back and forth. She rocked a total of four times before falling onto her pillow fast asleep.

Neiva looked around at everyone sleeping. No one moved. They were out like a light. She then glanced out the window to see two lanterns staring in at her. They were so bright that

Neiva thought she would be able to see the Ishegock's appearance but she couldn't. The eyes were hypnotizing. She could feel herself relaxing and her eyes slowly shutting. She leaned back against her pillow that was between Viv and Breezy, and moved down. She used her feet to bring up the covers so she could grab them and then snuggled up to her pillow.

Breezy was probably right, she thought. The Ishegocks probably thought they were a handful, which was true. They were. Neiva smiled as sleep surrounded her again.

Chapter 16

THE SOUND OF WAVES CRASHING instantly woke Neiva up from a deep slumber. She found herself on a beach. It was not the same beach where she had first met Darius. This beach was different in appearance and atmosphere. The sand was white as snow and soft to the touch. It almost didn't feel like real sand.

The waves lapping at the shoreline were a lime-green color that blended out into the ocean to meet with a deep forest green, revealing the ocean's depth. Behind Neiva was a forest full of aqua-colored trees with orange trunks. They stretched out into the night sky, reaching up as far as Neiva could see. The sky itself was a dark purple with a thousand stars twinkling throughout it. A giant moon sat in the center of the sky, shining brightly down on Neiva, making it brighter than the night normally should have been. Behind the moon was a rainbow of colors, such as pink, white, and gold flowing like a curtain across the sky. It moved up and down like a wave, reminding Neiva of the northern lights.

Neiva suddenly felt something bang into her left leg. As she looked down, she wasn't surprised to see Durby staring up at her. His purple eyes were wide as baseballs. He had a huge smile on his face showing his sharp teeth. The clock on his chest wasn't moving as fast as the last time Neiva saw him. It seemed to be at a slow pace this time.

"What are you doing here, Durby?" Neiva bent down to give him a small pat on the head, which he seemed to enjoy. His eyes briefly shut as he purred softly for a couple of minutes while Neiva scratched his head.

Durby quickly opened his eyes to stare at Neiva. "Must come with Durby again. Show you to Blake." Durby turned around and scampered off toward a peninsula of gray rocks that the green waves were crashing upon below them. Neiva guessed that's where she was going for tonight's lesson, so she started to head in the direction Durby was leading her.

As Neiva walked, she glanced down to see what she was wearing. Every time she opened her eyes in a dream, she was wearing something new, not her pajamas. This time she wasn't wearing a dress. Instead she was wearing a black wet suit that stopped at her wrists and ankles. She had water socks on her feet and gloves on her hands. She reached behind her to feel that her hair was braided down her back. Sitting on her head was a pair of goggles. Neiva was briefly puzzled. Was she having swimming lessons tonight?

Neiva glanced around and her breath caught when she saw Darius standing before her. He was wearing his silver mask with the black stars. He had a black coat on that flapped in the wind like a cape. He reached her within two strides.

Darius gently grabbed her hand and brought it to his heart. "Another training lesson tonight. I believe you will find this one very exciting. The Soul Eaters will not get you, Neiva. I am trying with all my power to keep you safe."

He kissed Neiva's hand before the shadows on the ground wrapped around him. "Have fun, my dear."

He was gone, but the brief encounter made her happy. She was lost in thought when Durby ran up to her. "Blake is coming. Durby must go. Hate water."

Durby bobbed past Neiva on his two dinosaur feet. He

jumped off the rocks, disappearing somewhere on the sandy beach. Neiva turned back to the edge of the peninsula. The drop-off was about twenty feet and reminded Neiva of the cliffs in Mexico. Her parents had taken her there on vacation when she was younger to get away from the cold. She had easily jumped off those cliffs with them, but there was something about this jump that made her stay away from the edge.

"The water won't hurt you, Neiva," a husky voice whispered into her ear. Neiva was startled at the sound of the voice being so close. She turned to find Blake smiling at her with a twinkle in his eye. His curly hair was pulled back into a ponytail, revealing pointy ears with earrings covering the top of each ear. He was wearing a similar suit to Neiva's except his was only shorts, stopping at his knees. Blake was bare from the waist up showing off his sculpted chest and well-defined abs. He had a tattoo along his right side. It was indigo blue in stark contrast to his pearly gray skin. Neiva couldn't tell what that tattoo was. It looked like a design wrapping around the right side of his chest, creeping down his arm, and stopping just above the tips of his claws.

Neiva tried to respond to Blake, but her reply just came out in stutters that didn't make any sense. She was caught off guard by his appearance. He was like a piece of beautiful art that she couldn't stop staring at. Even with the coral mask on she could tell his face was beautiful. Was every spirit this beautiful and if so, did that mean Darius was as well? She really wanted to find out.

"Cat got your tongue?" Blake teased with a smile. When he saw the blush start to creep up Neiva's cheeks, he decided to quickly change the subject and move on with tonight's lesson.

Blake walked toward the end of the peninsula. He looked over his shoulder at Neiva. "Water is one of the greatest elements. It's everywhere and it comes in many forms. It gives life to all of us. Without it, we would die."

Neiva looked out beyond Blake and stared out into the water. It looked very mystical. There was a glow to it, making

Neiva wonder what lived underneath its surface.

"Every body of water holds a mystery," Blake said as he picked up a rock and threw it into the water. The rock bounced several times on the surface before disappearing. To Neiva's amazement, the water glowed wherever the rock touched it. It was like a million stars had suddenly appeared. They sparkled like white diamonds, spreading out until they slowly disappeared as the water's surface became smooth again.

"What is it?" Neiva asked in awe.

"They are tiny organisms that live on the surface. Any disturbance causes them to flare up." Blake turned to Neiva with a mischievous smile. He walked to the very edge of the peninsula and jumped off. He gracefully dove into the water, not even making a splash. Several seconds passed before he surfaced with a giant grin on his face. The water around him glowed with every movement he made. It was very magical and made Blake look even more stunning.

"Well, what are you waiting for? Jump in!" Blake shouted to Neiva.

She walked to the edge. The drop looked higher then it was, making her think it might sting a little when she hit the water. After taking a deep breath, she leapt off, hitting the water feet first. She sunk several feet before opening her eyes. The water was glowing with thousands of the organisms swimming around her. They looked like shooting stars streaking across the sky. She stayed under as long as she could until her lungs started to burn. As she was making her way to the surface, she felt something glide past her. She briefly saw a large object swimming off in the other direction. Not knowing what was in the water caused Neiva to shoot to the surface in a panic.

"Shark!" Neiva gulped in water as she screamed at Blake. She coughed several times before she could focus on him. To her surprise he was just staring at her.

What was his problem? Didn't he feel threatened?

Neiva quickly looked around to see if she could see the shark.

"Don't worry, Neiva. It's not a shark and it's not going to hurt you," Blake stated as he raised his hand out of the water. Within seconds a dolphin appeared. It touched Blake's hand with its nose before disappearing beneath the surface again.

Neiva whipped her head around to see if she could see where it had gone. She didn't have to look very long before it suddenly appeared in front of her. It turned on its side so its gray eye could focus on her.

It was a dolphin, but on closer expectation Neiva saw that it didn't look like a normal dolphin. Instead of gray skin, the dolphin's skin was a light purple speckled with pink spots. It had dark green scales on the side running up and down the length of its body. Large spikes graced its dorsal fin and flippers. There were strange black markings around its eyes, almost like tattoos that decorated its face. The dolphin didn't look menacing at all, but instead, sweet and innocent.

"What do you feel?" Blake asked as he swam closer to Neiva.

The dolphin continued to stare at her as she tried to feel what it was thinking. She didn't sense anything at first, but slowly she felt his playfulness. The dolphin was wondering what Neiva was as much as Neiva was wondering what it was. As she felt more connected to the dolphin, she realized it was a female.

"Her name is Astrid," Blake told Neiva as he swam next to her. He gave Astrid a little pat on her back. "She is young like you, just learning her way in the world."

"I'm not that young. I'm almost an adult," Neiva muttered as she slowly reached her hand out to touch Astrid. In response to Neiva's need to touch, Astrid brought her nose up to meet Neiva's hand. Once Neiva's hand touched Astrid, images suddenly flashed before Neiva's eyes. She saw a beautiful city deep down in the depths of the ocean. It was made out of coral and pearls. It glowed with such brilliance that it illuminated its surroundings. Dolphins just like Astrid circled the palace in playful pods. Jellyfish lined the castle, slowly bobbing up and down illuminating a path to its entrance.

Suddenly the image started to change. It was like she was watching a projector, going from one picture to the next. Neiva now could see the inside of the palace. A large throne sat at the very end of a long hallway. It was made out of gold with white coral wrapping around its arms and legs. Sitting on the throne was a powerful-looking man. He had a long white beard with a mustache. His hair fell in long white strands around his face. Blue markings ran down the side of his cheeks, the same color as his blue lips. A huge crown made of pearls and gold sat on top of his head. It matched the shiny armor that he was currently wearing. He held a huge trident in his right hand that was made out of different colors of coral with gold at the tips. What caught Neiva's attention wasn't the beautiful trident but the man's eyes. They were a very intense aqua, the same color as Blake's. And they had the same twinkle of mischief in them.

The images suddenly faded as quickly as they came. Neiva found that she had let go of Astrid. She turned to look at Blake, suddenly thinking of one of her favorite Disney movies, *The Little Mermaid*. "Your father is King Triton?"

"Ah, you saw the palace and my father through Astrid's memory," Blake said with a chuckle. "My father's name is Goliath and he is king of all waters in the spirit and human realms. King Triton is loosely based off of him."

"So, that makes you a prince?" Neiva asked dumbfounded.

With a sigh Blake nodded his head, but he didn't explain further. Instead he told Neiva what she would be practicing this lesson. "Communicating with animals is a great power. They are an early-warning system. They can tell you what is lurking ahead or what's about to attack."

Neiva glanced at Astrid, who had started to swim in circles while keeping eye contact. Two words kept echoing inside Neiva's head: "coming" and "huge." Astrid was warning her that something big was heading their way. Neiva had a sudden feeling of uneasiness.

She glanced around and didn't see anything at first. The water looked calm and relaxing. But as she looked farther out into the ocean, something seemed off. It looked like the horizon had shrunk in size and the water had risen. Suddenly Neiva could tell it was a wall of water that was heading their way. It was moving fast and gaining speed as it rapidly approached them.

Neiva pointed to the giant wall of water. "Uh, should we be worried?"

"What do you feel, Neiva?" Blake asked calmly.

The wall of water was almost upon them. Neiva felt the panic start to rise deep within her. She couldn't understand why Blake was so calm. There had to be more to this. Like everything else, it had to be a test.

Neiva glanced at Astrid. She was still circling Neiva, but there was no fear or terror emanating from her, just the sense of unease.

"Okay. The giant wave isn't something evil. But the question is, is it a wave at all?" Neiva turned to Blake.

"You're getting close." Blake's voice urged her on.

Neiva closed her eyes and reached her mind out, "I feel something gigantic with lots of determination behind it, and it's very old . . . almost ancient. It feels like something from legends."

Neiva opened her eyes. The wave slowed down once it reached them. A giant green head suddenly appeared out of the green water. It was the size of a house with giant yellow horns embedded on top of its head. Huge red eyes stared at Neiva as the water dripped down its face. The creature opened its mouth to reveal huge teeth and a long tongue. A loud roar erupted as its head rose all the way out of the water to reveal a long neck, reminding Neiva of a brontosaurus.

Blake laughed as he swam toward the creature. "He's just saying hi."

Neiva didn't feel any aggression from the dinosaur. Instead, strangely, she sensed playfulness. "He wants to play?"

"Ah, you are manifesting your powers. Excellent!" Blake replied as he climbed onto the massive body that had just surfaced out of the water.

Blake didn't give Neiva the dinosaur's name, which led Neiva to believe she was still being tested. She looked up to see if she could find out its name. When she reached out her mind, she was bombarded with so many emotions that she couldn't grasp it at first. But once she could sort out the different feelings, she saw a single word: Phil.

"His name is Phil? Where did he get his name from?" Neiva laughed. She couldn't believe a dinosaur had a regular human name. She thought it would be something like Giganto or something along that line. Something ancient like the creature itself.

"He chose his own name. You will have to ask him how he came up with that name." Blake gave Phil a big pat on his back.

Neiva didn't even need to ask Phil. Pictures of a fishing captain with a short white beard flashed throughout her mind. "He named himself after a captain?"

"Yes, he did," Blake stated. "Phil met his captain by luck and destiny; their two paths were meant to cross each other."

"What happened?" Neiva asked in awe.

"Well, the captain saved Phil from a hunting expedition. The captain saw Phil was in trouble so he maneuvered his ship to protect the sea creature, blocking the oncoming harpoon that would have pierced Phil's thick skin. He saved Phil but damaged his own ship in the process."

"Wow." Neiva looked back up at Phil. She caught Phil's memories as they flashed before him. She felt his emotions for the captain. They were honor and love.

"Yes, he was young. Just a hatchling when the hunters were chasing him. He followed the captain around for several months, helping him catch large quantities of fish. But when it was the captain's time to go back into port, they had to say good-bye. Phil chose the captain's name to honor him. He always checked in on the captain and his family, making sure they were all right. He did this for generations until the captain's line died out."

"Ah, that's sad. Where did the captain live?" Neiva saw the sadness in Phil's eyes. He was old but time hadn't erased his memories.

"Scotland," Blake said with a smile.

"You mean?" Neiva pointed at Phil. She looked at Blake with awe as he nodded his head at her. "But that means he's the Loch Ness monster? But how? Loch means lake. How would he gain access to it?"

"Underground caves and tunnels, Neiva. There are many that connect from the ocean to lakes or underground systems." Blake paused briefly, and then quickly changed the subject. "I don't think Phil wants to reminisce about the past. Why don't we take his mind off the matter?"

The gleam in Blake's eye was back, making Neiva believe something was about to happen. "What do you have in mind?" she asked.

Blake jumped off of Phil's back, making a giant splash as he cannonballed into the water next to Neiva. He surfaced quickly, flinging back his hair that was now out of its ponytail. He looked like a model striking a pose for a photo shoot, leaving Neiva briefly flustered again. She was not use to the beautiful men of the Spirit World. She didn't think she would ever get used to them.

Suddenly, Neiva got the sensation of overwhelming happiness from Phil. He let out a giant roar of excitement before diving into the water. There wasn't much force behind his dive, but it still caused a giant wave to splash around Neiva and Blake.

Within seconds, Phil's giant head rose around them. One of his giant horns appeared in front of Neiva, slowly rising to the starry sky. It caught Neiva off guard. Her reaction was to grab onto the horn as the rest of Phil's head ascended out of the water, bringing her high above the water. Neiva turned to look at Blake. He had grabbed onto the giant horn in front of him, and then nestled himself in a little pocket located at its base.

"Grab the hairs located in front of the horn," Blake said, pointing to the area in front of the horn that Neiva held onto. "Then tuck yourself inside. Once you're settled, let go and the membrane will keep you secure."

Neiva did as she was told, letting go of the hairs once she found a comfortable position. The skin stuck to Neiva right away, making her feel secure. It was like a seat belt keeping her safely nestled in the passenger seat, leaving her arms free.

"Take this," Blake quickly told Neiva as he threw something at her.

Neiva caught the object in both of her hands. It was a seashell about the size of her hand. She turned it over to see a large opening, reminding her of a conch shell, except this shell had a snail the size of a pickle peeking out at her, which caused Neiva to scream.

The creature screamed back at her. Its high-pitch scream startled Neiva, prompting her to shut her mouth and simply stare at the creature, which stopped screaming once she was quiet. Its antennalike eyes looked at Neiva with fright.

"Put the shell over your mouth, Neiva," Blake sternly instructed.

"What?" Neiva screamed. "I am not putting that thing in my mouth! It could choke me or I might even swallow it."

With a heavy sigh, Blake replied, "He is an oxygenator and he will help you breathe, Neiva. He funnels the water into oxygen, helping you breath underwater. Put it on. We are about to go below."

Neiva looked at the pink snail's huge mouth. Its beady eyes stared up at Neiva with concern. It gave her a squeak before quickly disappearing into the shell's depths. Neiva got the feeling from the snail that it wouldn't be anywhere near her mouth and not to worry. So, she secured the shell over her mouth and pulled her goggles over her eyes. Suddenly there was a loud sucking noise as the shell sealed over her face—just in time, too, because water immediately surrounded her as Phil's head dove beneath the surface.

The water felt refreshing against Neiva's face. All her fears had washed away from her previous water experience, leaving her relaxed and content. The water wasn't too cold or too hot; it was just perfect.

When Neiva opened her eyes, she was greeted with a breathtaking sight. Everything was glowing. The rocks, coral, and plant life were illuminated with lights, in all different colors and shades.

Coral stretched out on the ocean's floor in reds, blues, oranges, and greens. The rocks were purple with a thin gray film stretched over them. Different types of fish swam past as Phil descended farther down into the ocean's depths. They weren't like any fish Neiva had ever seen. One fish was long and very snakelike in appearance. Its body was iridescent, allowing Neiva to see the fish's inner workings. Another fish swam by them. It was huge, about the size of a sofa. It was so fat, it looked like it could hardly swim; its fins worked vigorously to keep it afloat.

"Neiva, I want you to try to connect with the wildlife around you," Blake suggested. His voice sounded exactly the same as above water—not muffled at all. She could understand him. Neiva assumed she could speak underwater just like Blake. So she reached for the shell around her mouth and was about to pull it off, but before she got a chance, she had an image of the snail screaming at her again while throwing its body onto her, sucking her face back into the shell. This made Neiva forget about any idea of trying to talk to Blake.

"Just reach your mind out to any animal that passes by or that is hiding around us." Blake gestured to the scenery around them.

Neiva nodded her head up and down in response. To her right, she saw a pair of seahorses, or creatures resembling seahorses, swimming toward her. They were bright orange with blue scales lining their stomachs. They were bigger than normal seahorses, about two feet in height. Piercing blue eyes stared at Neiva as they swam around her head. She reached her mind out to the pair, instantly getting the same feelings from both of them.

Curious and confused, the seahorses didn't know what to make of Neiva. They thought she resembled Blake, but to them Neiva didn't look like she belonged underwater. They didn't know what to make of the thing on the middle of her forehead either. It was glowing in multiple colors, becoming a bright beacon in the dark ocean depths, and drawing them to it.

A weird sensation vibrated throughout Neiva's body. She glanced past the pair of seahorses to see a massive school of fish swimming toward them. They were in all different shapes and sizes, and they seemed to all be staring at Neiva's forehead with dilated eyes. She suddenly had a bad feeling. She quickly turned back to Blake, trying to get his attention. She waved her hands back and forth, finally catching Blake's eye. Once he turned his head toward Neiva, she quickly pointed to her forehead, and then pointed at the massive group of fish converging in on them.

Blake's eyes grew wide as he glanced over Neiva's head. He quickly said something to Phil, causing them to speed up to the surface. Within seconds Phil's head broke the surface, surging upward until they were fifty feet above the ocean's surface. Neiva quickly took the goggles off, then the shell. She glanced inside the shell to see the snail poke one eye out to look at Neiva.

"Thank you," Neiva whispered as she set the shell onto her lap then quickly added, "You know, I wasn't going to take the shell off. It was just an idea."

The snail brought its other eye out, staring at Neiva for several seconds before squeaking in its shrill voice, "I don't believe you."

It narrowed its eyes then dove back into the shell.

Neiva's laughed. The snail clearly told her that it didn't believe her but it welcomed her gratitude. Neiva gently patted the shell, and then turned to Blake.

"The crystal was glowing. I could tell that it was attracting all the fish," Neiva told Blake as she pointed to her forehead.

Blake narrowed his eyes at Neiva's forehead. "It's not glowing now. Maybe it flares up in dark places. Have you ever noticed it flare up when you've tried to use your powers before?"

Neiva thought about Blake's question. She had never noticed it flare up before, but then again she had never paid any attention to it. She would have to ask the girls and Nate when she woke up. They would have to keep an eye on the crystal to see if it was true. Neiva turned back to Blake, shaking her head no.

"Ah, well make sure to pay attention the next time you use your powers. I will have to let His Darkness know when we figure out this enigma," Blake stated as he turned his head to peer out across the ocean.

Neiva turned her eyes in the direction Blake was staring. Her jaw dropped as her eyes grew large. Above the tree line, high on a cliff stood a magnificent castle. It was huge and looked as if it were made out of some sort of black jewel. It sparkled as if silver dust was trapped within its walls. The silver dust twirled around the castle along its sharp curves and sleek designs. Sharp spires topped two towers, pointing at the distant stars above. A flag flew above the highest tower. It had the same symbol—a dragon in the shape of a castle—that appeared on the lock that led to the garden in one of her earliest dream encounters with Darius. Down the slope of the cliff to the right of the castle was an open fissure. It looked like it was on fire as lava coursed through it.

"Is that . . . ?" Neiva couldn't finish her sentence. Her heart was stuck in her throat as she stared at the castle.

"Yes, Castle Blackness. Home to King Darius," Blake whispered.

Neiva's heart dropped down into her stomach. She could not believe how close she was to Darius's home. She could almost smell the scent of lavender and pine as they came closer to shore.

"Can you take me to the castle? Please?" Neiva tried to keep the begging out of her voice but it didn't work. The desperation seeped through, causing Blake to blink at her several times.

"We will end tonight's lessons and continue where we left off next time. You need to go into a deeper sleep and rest." Blake did not answer Neiva's question as Phil set his head down onto the beach. Blake tucked the conch shell into the bag on his hip as he pulled himself out of the membrane. He helped Neiva get out of hers, and then escorted her off of Phil and onto the beach.

"Keep practicing your techniques. There are animals everywhere; just reach your mind out to them. It will make you stronger," he said as he stepped back onto Phil, who raised his head up to his full height and slowly backed himself out to sea. Blake grasped one of Phil's horns with a tight grip as he stared down at Neiva with bemusement. Such love and devotion was in her voice as she begged him to take her to see King Darius. She hardly knew the king. Was she his spirit mate? He didn't understand, but he couldn't leave her like that seeing the sadness in her eyes when he didn't answer her question.

"You will see His Darkness again soon, Neiva. He wouldn't leave you alone in the dark," his voice whispered around Neiva, warming up her damp heart.

Blake gave Neiva a slight bow before the waves welcomed him back under the ocean's surface. Water surrounded him in a flurry of motion, becoming smooth as silk once he was submerged. The water suddenly seemed brighter, as if his presence brought light and calmness into the underwater world.

Neiva gazed at the spot where he had disappeared beneath the waves for a while, slowly going over the night's training.

Blake was a beauty to behold; and though he was a tease, he also had a gentleness to him. She knew she could count on him as a friend, just like Sasha. She was making friends fast and was really starting to enjoy the Spirit World, its scenery, and especially its men.

She turned away from the ocean and headed down the beach to the spot where she had first appeared in the dream. The closer she got, the more her surroundings started to fade away, giving her a sense of tunnel vision. One thought entered her mind before she gave into the sleep. She knew she would see Darius soon, but her patience was wearing thin. How long would she be able to hold herself together before she broke all the rules and did something crazy? *The end results wouldn't be good*, she thought as she opened her arms to welcome a peaceful, dreamless sleep.

"YOUR DARKNESS, you summoned me?" Blake asked as he bowed before Darius, making a fist near his heart.

Darius glanced over his shoulder to acknowledge his Dark Knight, and then returned his gaze deep into the waters before him. He stood near a fountain in the center of the room with his black-gloved hands clasped behind him. He wore a long black robe etched with silver trim that fell to the floor around him. His long hair flowed around his mask, covering it from Blake's sight. Glowing brightly in the center of a flourishing greenhouse, the fountain before Darius was made out of jade. There were a variety of plants, both from the human world and the Spirit World, adding to the exotic flare of the environment that surrounded them. Bright silver water sprouted out of the fountain, making it look mystical and eerie at the same time.

There was a great legend behind the fountain that whoever obtained the fountain would gain the power to predict the future. But the fountain encased a creature so powerful, that to let it loose would destroy the world. Blake didn't know if those legends were true, but he did know that the water was of its own element. He couldn't connect with it or control it in any way. His power, like his father's, was to wield water however he desired, but this water did not speak to him. It was silent.

"How was Neiva's training?" Darius asked with his back still toward Blake. Normally Darius would never turn his back upon anyone, but he trusted his Dark Knight with his life.

"She is mastering her telepathic powers. I don't think she knows just how strong she is." Blake paused before adding, "She is very self-conscious. If she can overcome this, she can connect with all of her powers and strengthen them in no time."

"Yes, she will overcome it. She just needs a little push." Darius continued to stare into the fountain's water for several more seconds before waving Blake off. "Thank you for teaching Neiva. Visit her every other day. Sasha will be visiting her on the days you don't."

"What about Spike?" Blake asked.

"Neiva is not ready to train with Spike. She needs a little more time." Darius bent his head down farther, his hair falling all around him. "Have a good night, Blake. Give your father my greetings."

Blake bowed again before exiting the room. Once the doors were shut, Darius took off his mask and laid it on the fountain in front of him. He soon resumed his trance, staring into the waters of the fountain, once again becoming lost in his thoughts.

Chapter 17

NEIVA'S EYES FLUTTERED OPEN. She didn't want to get up, but she could hear someone clanging around in the kitchen. The smell of bacon penetrated the air while gentle laughter echoed around the cabin. Neiva tried to move, but she felt something slightly heavy draped over her. She cast her eyes down to see Viv's tattooed arm resting on her stomach, Viv's human hand clutching the blanket beside Neiva.

"Viv," Neiva whispered, trying not to scare her. She didn't want Viv to violently jerk awake. That could result in a black eye or split lip.

"Huh?" Viv grumbled.

"Can you lift your arm up so I can get out of bed?"

"Oh. Sorry," Viv growled as she rolled over onto her other side. She burrowed herself beneath the covers; the only things showing were her feet sticking out at the end of the bed.

Neiva stretched her back as she got up. She felt sore, as if she had been lying stiffly on her back all night. She hoped she could get the kinks out before the long trip home or it was going to be a rough car ride back into town, she thought as she walked over to the end of the bed. She reached down to pick up a pair of socks only to discover Nate crouched on the floor behind the couch.

"What are you doing?" Neiva screeched, frowning at Nate.

"Shh! Be quiet," Nate said with a giggle. His eyes filled up with tears from silent laughter. He was trying to hold it in, but Neiva could see he was having a difficult time.

"This can't be good," Neiva said with a sigh as she saw the feather in one of his hands and whipped cream in the other.

"I tried to warn him," Breezy replied with her arms crossed over her chest. She was back in her human form with a huge scowl on her face. "Nate. Are you crazy? You shouldn't wake a demon from slumber. That's a bad idea."

"I agree with Breezy," Neiva chimed in. "Think, Nate. Viv's already mad at you. This would be like adding fuel to the fire." Neiva knew it was no use. She could see the determination in Nate's eyes.

What Nate didn't know was that Viv was slowly creeping toward the end of the couch with a smelly sock in her right hand. Neiva and Breezy did try to warn him. Whatever happened next was his fault. They knew it wasn't going to be good.

Nate popped his head over the couch, opening his mouth into a wide smile. He momentarily had a gleam of happiness in his eyes, but that changed as soon as he saw Viv's glowing red eyes.

"Uh," Nate began to explain, telling Viv that he was only joking around. But he didn't get the chance, because Viv shoved the sock right into his open mouth, then jumped off the bed and strolled into the kitchen.

"See, Nate? We tried to warn you," Breezy stated as she shook her head back and forth. She turned around and followed Viv into the kitchen.

Nate spit the sock out with disgust. He dropped the bottle of whipped cream and the feather before running into the kitchen. He grabbed the mouthwash stashed underneath the sink and gargled for several minutes before spitting into the sink.

"That was . . . dis . . . dis . . . disgusting, Viv," Nate stuttered while wiping his face with the back of his right hand.

Viv stared at Nate, her eyes flashing red again. "Don't mess with me, Nate." She turned back to pouring her cereal into her bowl. She sprinkled a little bit of sugar on top, and then sat down at the kitchen table to eat her breakfast.

Nate didn't respond. Instead he walked out of the kitchen muttering to himself. The girls heard the back door open and quickly slam shut seconds later. Neiva glanced at Viv as she walked into the kitchen. She didn't look mad, just annoyed as she munched on her cereal.

Neiva grabbed a banana and headed back into the living room to start packing. Once Breezy and Viv were done with their cereal, they washed all the dishes then cleaned the kitchen, making it spotless for whoever visited the cabin next time. When they were done cleaning the kitchen, Neiva took the covers off the bed, and then folded the couch back into its original position. She picked up anything that was left on the floor, including some broken chess pieces they had overlooked earlier. Neiva glanced around the room, making sure she did not miss anything. Once she was satisfied, she put the dirty sheets and any towels that they had used in a garbage bag, and then set it by the door.

"Okay, the kitchen is cleaned," Breezy announced as she walked into the living room.

"I just finished up in here. So, I guess all that is left is the outhouse," Neiva told the girls as she headed out the door. "If anyone has to use it, now would be the best time."

Once everyone had finished using the outhouse, Neiva made sure the lid was down on the toilet, and then locked the door from the outside. She headed back to the front of the cabin only to find Nate loading Viv's Jeep Wrangler with Neiva's stuff.

"I'm going to ride home with Breezy. I thought you could use the time with Viv," Nate said to Neiva as he shut the back of the Wrangler.

"Yeah, that's fine." Neiva glanced at Viv, who was helping Breezy load up her car. "I can't believe it's Sunday already."

"I know. Bummer the weekend went by so fast. By the way, I grabbed all the trash and tied it to the Jeep's roof." Nate pointed to the bag of trash that was tied so tightly that it looked like it was going to burst. It was better than sitting in the back, stinking up the Jeep. They couldn't leave the trash at camp. It would just attract the local wildlife and stink up the cabin. They didn't want any uninvited guests lurking in their grandmother's cabin.

"Thanks, Nate. Let me grab the keys from Breezy and lock the doors to the cabin. Then we can head out."

Neiva ran to Breezy, who tossed her the keys. Neiva went around to the back to lock the door. She double-checked the door to make sure it was locked before heading to the front door. On her way to the front, she made sure all the windows were locked and pulled the shutters over them. Once the front door was locked, Neiva tucked the keys into her jeans pocket and headed over to Viv, who was waiting for her in the Jeep.

Before Neiva opened the passenger door, she heard a rustle in the bushes several yards away from the Jeep. Scared, she paused for a second, because she didn't know what was lurking in the bushes. But then she suddenly could hear Blake telling her to use the surrounding wildlife to her advantage, so she could see what was in the bushes. Neiva reached her mind out and instantly felt the brush of Ben's mind.

"Oh, Ben! You scared me," Neiva said as the giant old bear trotted out of the bushes.

He grunted in response to Neiva. She could feel his apology, but he wanted to say good-bye before the group left.

Neiva waited for Ben to walk up to her. Once he reached her, Neiva patted him on the head. She didn't feel nervous at all. She could feel Ben's emotions and thoughts, so she knew he wouldn't hurt them.

"You better make sure Nate gets his good-bye," Neiva said

as she brought her hand back. "Please keep an eye on the cabin for us."

Ben nodded his head. She could feel his determination that he would guard the cabin until hibernation. Except for polar bears, most bears in Alaska hibernate throughout the winter season. The bears have to gain a lot of weight in the upcoming months so they have enough fat stored for the winter season. Judging by Old Ben's massive form, Neiva could tell he was prepared for winter to arrive.

"Benny!" Nate yelled as he ran up to the bear and gave him a giant hug. Nate bent his head, giving Neiva a glimpse of his tattoo. It briefly swirled to life for a couple of seconds before suddenly becoming still. Neiva could feel Roxy's agitation. Neiva knew it was Roxy's jealousy over Nate and Ben's growing friendship.

"See you later, Nate. Don't forget we open The Magic Pot tomorrow." With that, Neiva waved good-bye to Ben and climbed into the Jeep.

"Nate has a thing for that bear," Viv stated as she watched him shake Old Ben's paw.

"It's just a new, budding friendship," Neiva replied as they passed Breezy in the Jeep. Neiva waved at her, making Breezy respond with a smile. She waved at Neiva before she walked over to say good-bye to Ben.

Viv looked at Neiva, giving her a gentle smile. "It was a very interesting weekend if I do say so."

"Yes indeed it was." Neiva watched the cabin grow smaller in the rearview mirror, slowly disappearing as they turned onto the main road back into Spirit.

"So, are you up for some fun?" Viv asked with a wicked grin on her face.

"What do you have in mind?" Neiva asked as she raised an eyebrow at Viv.

"A little off-road driving will help keep our minds off this weekend's events and add a little excitement to our drive home," Viv replied as she veered off the main road.

Neiva yelped as the Jeep bounced over the rough terrain. It wasn't like the marshland near Spirit. The terrain near camp was sturdier.

The girls spent a good portion of the trip home off-roading until the land slowly morphed into soft marshland, forcing Viv to stay on the main road the rest of the way home. The girls talked about school, boys, and movies to pass the remaining time.

"We should do a movie night at the end of the month," Viv suggested as she pulled into Neiva's grandmother's driveway.

"Yeah, that's a great idea. We just need to check on which two movies are coming to town," Neiva said sarcastically as she unbuckled her seat belt. Spirit had one theater that housed only two screens. Every month there would be only two movies showing. They weren't new movies but whatever had been released already in the lower states. It didn't matter to the locals, though. It was a great way to escape the harsh winter days, especially with sixteen to twenty hours of darkness. It could make anyone depressed.

Neiva opened the door and jumped out, while Viv grabbed Neiva's bags from the back and handed them to her.

"Thanks," Neiva said as Viv got back into her Jeep.

"See you tomorrow. Breezy and I will meet you at The Magic Pot at 7:00 a.m., before school." Viv shut her door and waved at Neiva as she drove off.

Neiva grabbed her keys out of her pocket to unlock the front door. Once she was inside, she set her things down at the foot of the stairs.

"Grams, I'm home!" Neiva called out, glancing around. She waited a couple more seconds before calling out for her grandmother again. There was still no response. Neiva walked to the kitchen table to see a note neatly folded next to a plate of brownies.

Neiva,
I had to help Mike out at the store. I should be back

around dinnertime. If by chance I am not back in time, I made some Muskox chili that is cooking in the slow cooker. It should be ready. Just help yourself. I hope you had a great time at the cabin. I can't wait to hear all about it.

Love you,
Grams

P.S. Your parents called. They will call you back before you go to bed, so listen for the phone! ☺

Neiva smiled at her grandmother's note. She was always helping Nate's dad out, but she never complained about it. Grams knew it was his dream to run a restaurant and she was very determined to keep his dream alive, even if it meant she had to work a couple shifts to help out.

Neiva grabbed her bags and headed upstairs. She unpacked all of her stuff, putting her dirty clothes in the hamper and placing her new rain boots in the closet. She placed her ivory tusk on the shelf above her desk, and then placed her billiken next to it. She was about to get undressed when a muffled noise caught her attention. It came from somewhere near her bed. She turned around and slowly scanned the area around her bed. She didn't notice anything unusual so she proceeded to unbutton her pants. With her shirt halfway above her head, a loud yelp stopped her.

At first Neiva didn't see anything, but when her eyes focused on the wall above her bed, she noticed a large wooden mask hanging several feet above her headboard. The mask was about four feet long and one foot wide. It had two eyeholes carved into it with a flat nose and an open mouth. The face rested two feet down from the top of the mask, just under a raven that was carved in intricate designs. The designs were very tribal-looking with splashes of red and black throughout it.

"Where did you come from?" Neiva asked as she walked over to her bed. She wasn't expecting an answer.

"Well, from the Spirit World of course," the mask responded in a deep booming voice, its eyes and mouth glowing blue when it spoke. "Where else would I be from?"

Neiva screamed and ran back toward her closet. She hadn't expected a response. She grabbed the closest thing on her desk—a pair of scissors—and held them out in self-defense.

"Whoa there," the mask said, "I am not going to hurt you. Besides I am stuck to this wall, so there is no possible way for me to hurt you. Well, unless something tries to hurt you that is, then I can pop right off."

"Who sent you?" Neiva gulped as she slowly crept closer to the mask.

"Why King Darius, of course. He wanted you to have extra protection." The mask paused for a second, scrunching up an eye as if in thought. "Just think of me like a dream catcher hanging above your bed."

"Sure . . . except you're a mask that can talk," Neiva's voice wavered slightly as she took another step toward the mask. She held the scissors out in front of her just in case. She wasn't the violent type, but with the weekend's events, she knew things could change in an instant.

Neiva was almost to the foot of her bed. She didn't get any evil feelings or vibes from the mask, but she did get the whiff of lavender and pine telling her that Darius had been there. With a great sigh of relief, Neiva lowered her hand. She set the scissors on her nightstand, and then crossed her arms to stare at the strange thing on her wall.

Neiva narrowed her eyes at the mask. "Why do I need a dream catcher when Darius, Sasha, and Blake have access to my dreams?"

"Oh, you're right there. How about you consider me like a gargoyle. I will watch over you during the night and sleep during the day. Well, except if you need me, you can contact me during the day; but at night I will watch over you like a pirate guarding his treasure!" the mask exclaimed with a gigantic smile, showing no teeth or throat, only the white wall behind it.

The mask's remark did not make Neiva feel any better. She didn't like the idea of something staring at her while she slept. It was too spooky. She crossed her arms tighter around herself and frowned.

"Okay, okay. I was joking," the mask replied defensively to Neiva's stare. "I'm similar to a force field. If anything enters the house uninvited, I will sense the activity and alert King Darius or one of his Dark Knights. I'm also able to defend you if anything does break through that would try to harm you."

Neiva's frown disappeared as she uncrossed her arms. She sat on the bed, centering herself in front of the mask. She felt better now that she knew the mask wasn't going to watch her 24/7. But it was hard to imagine that the mask would be able to defend her. A picture of the mask jumping off the wall with little arms and legs, running around the room flailing its arms around popped into her head.

"I'm more menacing than you think," the mask said, as if reading her mind.

"Uh, what's your name?" Neiva didn't think the mask would like her calling it "the mask" all the time. She wouldn't like being called "girl" all the time either.

"Paulo, after the famous Eskimo who fought off a dreaded one-eyed polar bear. With just his bare hands, may I add! He defended his tribe with honor!" Paulo's voice boomed with pride.

Neiva was impressed. Polar bears were very aggressive and dangerous in nature. They were known to hunt men once they smelled their scent, even stalking them for miles. The villagers took every precaution they could as a defense against these animals. During the winter months, the locals would leave their doors unlocked in case someone needed to seek shelter when a polar bear trekked into town. It happened quite frequently when the ice formed. There were a lot of bears on the island.

"I'm sorry about disturbing you. I wanted to introduce myself to you before anything else," Paulo's voice became softer, the blue glow dimming slightly.

Neiva smiled. "That's okay. I've had a rough weekend that's made me a little bit jumpy." She started to feel sorry for Paulo. He was just trying to be friendly. Plus, she should have known that Darius wouldn't let anything dangerous in her house. He sent Paulo for extra protection. Better safe than sorry, Neiva figured.

"I will let you get back to your daily activities. Just call my name if you need anything. I can sense you around the house and when you come into the room, I will come to life. It's just a warning," Paulo said with a slight smile before the blue light disappeared altogether.

Neiva waited for a few more minutes before making sure he was gone. She wasn't satisfied until she waved her hands several times in front of him with no response. She jumped off the bed and headed into the bathroom.

She took a long, hot shower making sure her hair was washed twice, feeling that it was slightly dirty from the weekend at camp. While she rinsed her hair out, she thought of the events that had unfolded during the week. It was a lot to take in. She was a part of a whole new world and was becoming a whole new person. Just the thought of her training and new powers made her giddy with excitement. It was so unreal because she had always felt different, and part of her felt like a piece was missing from her life. Not because her looks differed from the natives, but because she had also felt as if she weren't in her own skin. It had always been like she was a robot controlling a body that wasn't hers, but now those feelings made sense. It wasn't just the feelings of being an awkward teenager, like most of the adults had told her, but because she wasn't being her authentic self. She was someone else.

Neiva let out a gasp. The hot water was turning cold, very fast. She must have lost track of time. She quickly rinsed off before turning the shower knob. She grabbed a towel to dry off. Once she was dry, Neiva put on her pink-and-green-starred pajamas, then slipped her feet into her green bunny slippers near the bathroom door. When she opened the door all of the hot air rushed out into her bedroom, colliding with the cool air that felt reviving against her warm skin.

Quickly glancing at Paulo, Neiva walked over to her desk and grabbed her robe from the back of the chair. As she was putting her robe on, she heard a clanging noise coming from downstairs. Neiva looked back at Paulo to see what his reaction would be. He wasn't moving or making any noise. There was no sign of the blue light either. It could only mean one thing: Grams was home.

Neiva rushed out of her room, flew down the stairs, and ran into the kitchen so fast she scared her grandmother when she went to hug her. Grams was so startled that she nearly knocked over the chili pot.

"Neiva!" Grams said, grabbing her chest. I didn't hear you come downstairs. I thought you were still in the shower." She stifled a laugh, then smiled at Neiva, giving her a small pat on her back.

"Sorry, Grams," Neiva said, putting her head on her grandmother's shoulder. "I heard you come in and couldn't wait to see you."

"Well, I am glad to see you too and I really want to hear about your weekend." Grams's eyes turned serious as she picked up two bowls and scooped chili into each one.

"Yeah, I have a lot to tell you," Neiva muttered, grabbing a spoon and one of the bowls of chili. She walked to the kitchen table to sit down. Right away she noticed a tray of freshly baked cornbread sitting in the center of the table. Her grandmother must have baked it when she got home and placed the brownies in the fridge for later. The cornbread smelled sweet and delicious. Neiva grabbed a piece of cornbread, and then dunked it into her chili. She took a large bite, slowly chewing the morsels so she could savor the taste of the spicy muskox chili and sweet cornbread.

Grams sat down next to her. She folded her napkin in her lap, straightening it out until it lay straight across her lap. She looked up at Neiva with earnest eyes.

"So, I bet you have a lot of questions, my Tanaraq?" she asked Neiva.

Neiva fiddled with her food, moving her chili back and forth in her bowl. She thought about what she should ask her grandmother. Most of the basic questions were answered by Breezy, Viv, or Nate. She knew a lot of questions wouldn't be answered right away and that no one had all the answers, so she didn't know where to start.

"I know it's hard to think of what to ask, but let me tell you something. We kept the Spirit World hidden from you for your protection. We didn't know if or how you would fit into this world. We had to wait until now—your seventeenth birthday—to find out." Grams placed her hand on Neiva's shoulder. She gave her a tight squeeze before letting go.

Neiva frowned as she looked at her grandmother. "It's just so much to take in. There are so many legends and rules to the Spirit World. I can't wrap my mind around it."

"Okay, let's start by you telling me about your weekend and everything that has happened." Grams leaned back, giving Neiva her full attention.

Neiva told her everything, starting from when she met Darius and the crystal appearing on her forehead to the Ishegocks and Roxy, and then ending with Paulo, the giant mask in her room. Throughout her story, Grams nodded her head several times to let Neiva know she understood what she was talking about. When Neiva was finished, Grams sat back with her arms crossed. She looked as if she were staring off into space for several minutes before her eyes focused back in on Neiva.

"The Ishegocks are protectors of the innocent and the Eskimos. They come sweeping in with the fog to fight off whatever evil lurks around where it should not be. Their origin is a mystery. Some elders say they are the spirits of the Eskimos that have passed on from this life to the next, but no one knows for sure. When you see one, it is a sign you are protected and being watched by your ancestors," she finished with a smile while she took Neiva's hand to hold it in her own.

"Then why does Nate pass out every time they appear?" Neiva asked, scrunching up her forehead.

"Guardians are already protected by their spirit guides. When the Ishegocks first appear to the Guardian, Guardians lose consciousness so the Ishegocks can communicate directly with the Guardian's spirit guides. Spirit guides are able to warn Ishegocks about the possible dangers that threaten them. The Ishegocks know where the Guardians are at all times and make sure the Guardian doesn't leave the safety of the Ishegock's fog. Most young Guardians, like Nate, will not know this until their spirit guide feels the need to tell them."

Neiva could understand why Roxy would not tell Nate everything about the Ishegocks. What had Neiva perplexed was why Roxy didn't tell her the truth about Nate passing out.

"Grams? Why didn't Roxy tell me about Nate and the Ishegocks? It would have calmed everyone down faster than learning about them on our own." Neiva picked at her nails while she waited for her grandmother's reply.

Her grandmother raised an eyebrow at her. "Well, I think the main reason is because it's very rare for another individual to talk to someone else's spirit guide. In fact, I don't think I have ever heard of someone doing that."

"Oh," Neiva replied. That explained it then. Roxy probably was taken off guard by Neiva's thoughts entering her mind, but Roxy knew she was Nate's friend. So that made her trust Neiva, but not enough to tell her about the Ishegocks. She was still new to Roxy.

"Then is Riley my spirit guide?" Neiva had never received an answer to that question. She had never thought to ask Darius because she was always preoccupied when he was around, lost in her thoughts and feelings for him.

"I am not sure, honey. That is something you will have to ask the Dark King about." She stared at Neiva with concern etched on her face. "I don't know what his motives are in all of this, but I am thankful he is having his guards train you and that most of all you are being protected."

"Yeah, I think I would be lost without them," and Darius, she thought. She felt blessed that she could unload her burdens to her grandmother, but Neiva could tell her grandmother was worried about her.

"Do you think I will connect with Darius and Riley soon?" Neiva asked. She felt empty without the brush of their minds. She hadn't known them very long, but she had a strong connection with both of them, especially Darius.

"I'm sorry, Neiva. That is another question that I cannot answer. But I am sure King Darius will answer that question. It sounds like he knows more than he is leading on. But let's get this kitchen cleaned. Then we can move into the family room to continue our conversation over brownies and hot chocolate."

Neiva got up from the kitchen table and picked up the dishes. She began rinsing them off while her grandmother packaged up the cornbread and the rest of the chili. Neiva cleaned out the crockpot, washed it until it sparkled, then dried it off and put it away. She then wiped the counters and tables off, while her grandmother made the hot chocolate and warmed up the brownies.

Neiva's parents called when her grandmother had just finished making the hot chocolate. She was so excited to talk to them that an hour didn't feel long enough. Her parents were in Germany. They were exploring the country, which her mother absolutely loved.

Neiva told them about everything going on with her life at the moment. Her parents weren't shocked or surprised about everything that was happening to Neiva. They had a feeling that Neiva was special. Neiva talked about school and her classes before saying good-bye. Her parents told her they would call back in a couple of days and they were glad that she had a great birthday, even with everything going on.

Neiva hung up the phone feeling deflated and sad. She

missed them so much. With a loud sigh Neiva shuffled into the family room, grabbing a blanket to drape over their legs as she sat on the couch next to her grandmother.

"Do you have any more questions?" Grams asked before slowly sipping her cup of hot chocolate.

"Hmmm. Can I see the tattoo of your spirit guide?" Neiva asked as she tried to peek around Grams's shoulder.

She didn't see anything at first but when her grandmother turned her head to the side Neiva instantly saw it. It was the same size as Nate's. It had the same tribal patterns and was in the same spot as Nate's tattoo, but where Nate's was a fox, her grandmother's was a bear.

"His name is Bruno. We have been partners for a long time." She smiled at Neiva when she turned back around. Her right hand went up to rub the tattoo. "Like the spirits, Guardians can hide their tattoos through a spirit shield."

"Cool," Neiva replied. "So, what happens when a Guardian gets older?"

"Well, the spirit guide stays with the Guardian until death. Then the spirit guide can choose to cross on with his or her Guardian, or stay behind and become a guide for a new Guardian. Your grandfather's spirit guide passed on with him." Sadness crept into her face. It always appeared when she talked about Neiva's grandfather. Neiva was just six years old when her grandfather died in a plane crash. The weather had changed in an instant, causing the pilot to lose his bearings just outside of Nome, Alaska. Plane crashes were very common in Alaska because of the unrelenting and unpredictable weather.

"What animal was his spirit guide?" Neiva was betting it was something magnificent to match her grandfather. He had been a great person and friend to the entire townsfolk. He was also very loyal to his family and had loved Neiva unconditionally.

"His spirit guide was a white wolf, which was very rare considering all spirit guides are black. His name was Scotty.

He was very loyal to your grandfather even after death." Grams got misty-eyed.

"But how did you know his spirit guide followed him into the afterlife?" Neiva asked as she rubbed her grandmother's arm. She didn't know if there was some sign or it was because no one saw the white wolf again.

"You know how at the age of seventeen a young Guardian receives his spirit guide and a tattoo magically appears on his neck? Well, when a Guardian dies, the tattoo will either disappear or stay on the Guardian even after death. If the tattoo is still present after death, then it means the guide has chosen to continue on with its Guardian; it will no longer help guard the Spirit World. If the tattoo disappears, it means the guide will soon reappear on another young Guardian.

"Once a guide crosses over in death, its form is reborn into a totally new guide. It will have the same features and visual characteristics as the last guide, but it will not be the same on the inside. The tattoo will look different as well." With her hands folded around her, her grandmother tried to casually glance at Neiva's neck.

"Grams, I don't have a tattoo. But I believe my spirit guide is Riley. How else do you explain his presence?" Neiva was flustered. She didn't know what to think of Riley. She would have to remember to ask Darius when she saw him, but she knew it would be hard. Her brain seemed to turn to mush every time she was near him.

"I believe you are right. I can see your explanation of his connection to you as the most logical reason. I can't think of any other." Her grandmother turned toward the closest window near her. The sun had set before dinner, meaning it was getting closer to winter. The sky was overcast with clouds, covering the moon and stars, making it even darker outside than normal.

"Grams, what's this Eskimo prophecy? I heard Nate mention it once."

Her grandmother stared at her, then nodded, "There is

a prophecy of a savior, of someone who will save our tribe from an ancient evil. The tribal leaders believe he will be a descendant of the Great White Bear. He will become one with the darkness, and his soul will be old as time itself."

"Could that prophecy be about me, Grams?" Neiva was staring in amazement at her grandmother. Is this why she had powers and why she was connected to the Spirit World?

Her grandmother shot Neiva a shrewd, amused glance. "Do you know what the Eskimos called your great-great-grandfather?" She paused for suspense, "White Bear. His name was White Bear, my Tanaraq."

"Oh," Neiva croaked. It was true. She was the prophesied savior. This explained everything. Why she suddenly had these powers, why she felt she had lived past lives, and why she felt drawn to Darius. He was the darkness she was to become one with.

"We knew you were special," her grandmother whispered.

They both stared out the window lost in their own thoughts. Neiva didn't have any more questions at the moment, so she asked Grams if she wanted to watch a movie. She agreed, and they ate their brownies while watching a couple of girl movies. Somewhere in between the two movies Neiva had fallen asleep. She vaguely remembered how she got upstairs and into bed. She woke up briefly on the back of a mass of fur, then heard her grandmother tell someone to carefully put her down on her bed once they were in her room. Neiva heard a grunt from something as she slid off the furry blanket, her head landing on her soft pillows. Grams pulled the sheets over her, and then gave her a kiss on the cheek. When she was leaving, Neiva opened one eye to see her grandmother's right hand resting on the massive back of a giant black grizzly bear. It was the same colors as Roxy, including the gray stripe over its glowing white eyes.

"Thanks, old friend. Now let's go finish our movie," Grams said as she patted the bear on the back. They headed out the door, closing it behind them. Neiva rolled over onto her side, thankful she was in her bed. She was going to have to get up in several hours to open the store. She couldn't remember if Nate was picking her up or not as she closed her eyes, unable to think of anything else but sleep.

Chapter 18

BEEP. BEEP. BEEP.

Neiva's alarm woke her from a deep, dreamless sleep. She groggily reached over to her nightstand and pressed the snooze button. She dove deeper into her covers, snuggling closer to her pillow. She was about to doze off again when a rumbling noise made her quickly sit up in bed.

"I would get up if I were you," Paulo's deep voice echoed around the room, causing Neiva to jump out of bed. She landed on her feet in a defensive pose with her hands out in front of her.

"Oh jeepers. It's you," Neiva grumpily replied. She walked over to the mask and blew a raspberry at him, then she walked into the bathroom slamming the door behind her.

"You're welcome!" Paulo's voice bounced around Neiva as she washed her face and brushed her teeth, ignoring him.

Today was going to be a casual, makeup-free day. Neiva didn't feel like spending time on her eyes or even washing her hair again. She sprayed a couple of spritzes from a bottle of dry shampoo onto her hair and quickly rebraided it, tying it with Darius's black ribbon. She put her uniform on, which was a white button-up long-sleeved shirt with The Magic Pot logo on the right side and a pair of black jeans. She chose her skinny Miss Me jeans to go with her knee-high leather dress boots. She grabbed her black leather belt to finish off her outfit. It had a white, jeweled heart on the front that always made Neiva smile. She made sure her bracelet was still on before running out of the bathroom to grab her black winter coat from the closet. As she was picking up her backpack from the bed, she happened to glance up at Paulo, who was staring right at her with glowing blue eyes and a freakish smile on his face.

"Uh, thanks," Neiva muttered as she walked out of the room.

"See you later, alligator," Paulo laughed.

Neiva ran into the kitchen to find Nate eating waffles at the kitchen table. Her grandmother was making some coffee and packing Neiva's lunch for school.

"Morning! Your plate is on the kitchen table. Better hurry so you and Nate aren't late," Grams said as she handed Neiva a cup of coffee.

Neiva sat down next to Nate and quickly ate her waffles. She gulped down the sweetened coffee in three swallows. She finished her breakfast within minutes and was ready to leave. Neiva glanced over at Nate to see how far along he was with his breakfast. Nate's eyes were only halfway open while his mouth was wide open. He groaned several times before taking a shot of his coffee. He kind of resembled a zombie. If Nate wasn't able to wake up by the time they got to the store, it meant Neiva was probably going to be the one doing all the work.

"C'mon, finish your coffee, Nate. We have to go!" Neiva gathered their plates and handed them to her grandmother, who placed them in the sink.

"I loaded all the dough for the baked goods into Nate's truck. Don't forget your lunch." Her grandmother handed Neiva her lunch while Neiva pulled Nate out of his chair.

"Thanks, Grams. What did you make for the shop this morning?" Neiva asked. Mike was like a son to her grandmother, so she got up every morning to make the shop's baked goods for the day. It varied every day from different types of muffins, to scones, breads, pies, cookies, or any other baked goods she felt like making.

"Oh, just some raspberry-orange and blueberry muffins, vanilla scones, banana bread, oatmeal and chocolate chip cookies, some fruit cobbler, and a blueberry pie. The fresh fruit is also in the truck from yesterday's delivery. Mike should be in at 7:00 a.m. Don't be late for school," she said as she pushed both Neiva and Nate out the door. She briefly waved at them as they got into Nate's truck. She blew a kiss at Neiva before shutting the front door.

It only took them three minutes to get to the store. It was nestled at the corner where Main Street began. The outside of the store resembled the front of a house. There were shutters on the windows and a screen over the front door. A "welcome" rug laid on the entryway, giving a warm feeling to anyone who entered.

Nate and Neiva pulled around back to unload their grandmother's baked goods. Nate turned the engine off and got out of the truck. He ran to the back door to unlock it. It took Nate several minutes to fiddle with the lock, but once he had the door open, he ran inside to turn the alarm off. Neiva got out of the truck and quickly noticed how cold it was outside. The wind was whipping around her in a frenzy, sending chills throughout her body. Winter was definitely around the corner.

Neiva grabbed the first box full of dough from the floor underneath the passenger seat. She ran through the open door. To the right was a small kitchen with a fridge, freezer, sink, and dishwasher. To the left was a small baker's area with two ovens and a baker's table, then toward the back was a small office. Neiva put the dough on the baker's table. She quickly went outside to grab the rest of her grandmother's baked goods. Once she was back inside, she found Nate unloading all the dough and putting it in the oven.

Neiva turned around and shut the door, securely locking it to make sure the wind didn't blow it open. She took her coat off, and then shoved it into one of the lockers next to the office. She grabbed a black apron for herself and Nate then got to work helping Nate open the store. It took them an hour to get all the dough for the baked goods cooked and put out on display. They straightened the chairs, and made sure the coffee was brewing, the espresso machine was clean, and the steam wands were working. Neiva grabbed the money drawer from the office and placed it in the cash register. It looked like they were ready to open for business.

Glancing around the store, Neiva made sure she hadn't missed anything. The inside of The Magic Pot had a homey feeling to it. There were black booths attached to the outer walls with tables made out of red pine. The windows lining the front of the store had red curtains hanging down the sides, tied back to allow the light in. Several more tables were placed throughout the store, leaving walkways for the customers. On each table rested fake flowers in a decorative red vase. They looked so real that sometimes Neiva would forget that they weren't and would water them by accident.

To the right of the door, along one wall was the condiment stand. It had all the necessities for drinks and food. The display case was parallel to the door, allowing the customer to see the stores goodies right away when they entered. Behind the display case was the menu board with all of the store's items and specials. The cash register sat in between the display case and a countertop that resembled a bar. It allowed customers to sit down and enjoy their food while they waited for their drinks.

Nate ran from the back to the front door. He looked at his watch, then looked at Neiva. "Are you ready?"

Neiva nodded her head as Nate flipped the closed sign to open. He unlocked the door, then hurried back to Neiva, who was standing behind the register ready for their first customer. It didn't take long before the first morning customers came in. Usually when the store opened at 6 a.m., it was the dockworkers, airport personnel, and post office employees that were the first customers of the day. Then it was the rest of the townsfolk followed by the students toward 7 a.m.

Within an hour, The Magic Pot's seats were almost full with customers enjoying their morning coffee and breakfast. Neiva tried to use the time in between customers—when she wasn't busy—to practice sharpening her skills of peeking through some customers' spirit shields. She glanced at the older Eskimo at the last table near the condiment stand. He was one of the dockworkers. Neiva forgot his name but knew that he came in every morning for her grandmother's muffins. She glanced at his neck, instantly seeing a shimmer of movement before she saw the tattoo. It was the exact same design and size of her grandmother's and Nate's. It looked like an orca whale, making Neiva wonder how that could protect the dockworker from harm.

The door opened sending a chill of icy wind around Neiva. Without even looking up, she knew the icy wind had nothing to do with the weather outside but with the person standing at the door. It was Miranda and she did not look pleased to see Neiva. She had a scowl on her face and her eyes narrowed at Neiva when their eyes met. She quickly strolled up to the counter to order a cup of hot chocolate from Nate, completely ignoring Neiva in the process.

Nate acted professional and courteous toward Miranda, which Neiva gave him props for. He smiled politely at her comments and pretended to be enamored with her every word, which had Miranda fooled, but not Neiva. Once Nate handed over her hot chocolate, with extra caramel on top, she thanked him with a sickening sweet smile before turning to Neiva with daggers in her eyes.

"I don't know what's going on, but I am going to find out," she whispered to Neiva. She flipped her long hair into Neiva's face and slowly walked away. She stopped halfway to her table before turning around to look back at Neiva. She pointed to her eyes then to Neiva, mouthing the sentence, "I am watching you," before she joined her friends at a table in the corner.

"Wow. I have no clue what spell she put on me before, but apparently it's broken. She really is an icy . . . witch," Nate declared, trying to avoid the word Neiva knew he really wanted to say. She patted him on the back with a smile. She was glad he wasn't enamored of the ice princess anymore. She never liked the zombie look he got every time she was nearby.

"Hello, can I please get a honey hot chocolate with sprinkles on top?" a friendly voice asked.

Neiva turned around to see Austin Brooks standing at the cash register. He was staring right at her, causing Neiva's cheeks to turn pink. His green eyes sparkled with excitement and his lip formed into a crooked smile.

"Sure, man," Nate said as he rung him up. "Neiva will make that for you."

Nate quickly looked at Neiva to see if she had heard the order. She nodded once, and then turned to make the hot chocolate. She made the honey hot chocolate exactly the same way Breezy made it, with the chunks of chocolate and honey mixed in with hot steamed milk poured over it. She added several more chunks of chocolate on top, then added the sprinkles with honey drizzled over the top.

"Looks delicious! Thank you, Neiva," Austin said with a smile when she turned around to hand him the cup of hot chocolate. He carefully took the cup from her hand, briefly brushing his fingers slightly over her hand as she took it away.

Neiva slightly frowned at him when he turned away. She didn't like the brief contact he had made with her. It didn't feel right and was uninvited. Frowning even more at Austin, Neiva had an idea. She would use her powers and try to peek through his spirit shield.

With a deep breath, Neiva imagined herself peering through a curtain, slightly moving a small area aside that would allow her to see what lay behind the curtain. Within seconds the curtain briefly shimmered, then parted, revealing a stunning sight; no longer stood the tall boy with spiky blond hair, in his place was a warrior with bronzed skin. Giant black wings dipped in copper were folded behind his back. His hair was now black, and two giant horns protruded out of his head. His ears were pointed with black feathers lining the tops of them. When he turned back to look at Neiva, his eyes glowed like emeralds. Thick black lashes graced his eyelids, while dark black lips smiled at Neiva, showing glowing white teeth.

Neiva was momentarily shocked as Austin thanked her again before sitting down next to Miranda. She didn't expect him to look so angelic. Now she could see why Breezy and Viv liked him so much. Just like his human form, his true form was very pleasing to the eye.

"Hello? Earth to Neiva?" Nate snapped his fingers in front of Neiva's face several times before she suddenly knew he was there. This slight distraction caused the curtain to fold in, leaving Austin back in his human form.

"Is every spirit so beautiful?" Neiva stammered as she tried to ask Nate.

"You looked through someone's spirit shield, didn't you? Isn't that a crime or something?" Nate looked around the room to see if he could guess who it was. He turned back to Neiva in defeat. "Who was it?"

"Darius trained me and I was just trying to practice it out on Austin, but you didn't answer my question, Nate." Neiva poked him in the chest. There were no customers waiting at the moment; the store was in tiptop shape and ready for Mike to take over. Neiva knew Nate didn't have an excuse not to tell her.

"Austin Brooks? Blah," he exclaimed. He glanced back at Neiva only to see anger creeping into her eyes. She wanted answers. Nate knew she would bug him all day until he told her.

"Yes, even the scariest dark spirits are beautiful, but don't get the idea in your head that every spirit is perfect, Neiva. Just like humans, they have their shortcomings. The difference is, they accept it and make it beautiful in their own way, unlike humans who point out the flaws in others."

"Oh." Neiva knew how high school was. At her school in Anchorage, students tended to shun the other students who were different, especially in looks. It was very different in Spirit though. There was the occasional competitiveness or the ones who wanted to know everything that was happening all the time, like Miranda. Miranda was the only one who made Neiva feel different, but Neiva had a feeling it was more curiosity than anything else. Plus, Miranda was cold as ice— literally. That had to explain a lot, Neiva figured.

"Hey, Neiva," squeaked a nasal voice.

Turning her eyes up, she saw Chad standing awkwardly in front of her. He looked different. His face was deathly pale, bringing out the scar above his lip. His hair was shaggy and a shadow of a beard was forming on his face. His honey colored eyes seemed far off. They looked darker than normal, especially around the edges. Was he wearing mascara?

"Just wanted to tell you that I can't wait to see you later." He was staring at her, those strange eyes raking hers. A cruel smile twisted his face and then he walked out the door.

Neiva flushed, but didn't have time to think about it as a couple more students entered the store and ordered hot chocolate. When Neiva had first started working at The Magic Pot, she couldn't understand why the students of Spirit chose hot chocolate over coffee, but now she understood. The hot chocolate revitalized and awakened the spirits, giving them a recharge for the day.

"Come on, Neiva. Dad is here. Breezy and Viv are out back by the truck." Nate tugged on Neiva's sleeve.

Mike's huge form appeared next to Neiva. He smiled at her while he nudged her to the back. "Thanks for opening the store. Take whatever you want for school. Now don't be late."

"Thanks, Mike." Neiva reached into the display case for a muffin, and then made a large hot chocolate for her to split with Breezy and Viv. Once she was done, she waved good-bye to him and ran into the back. She quickly put on her coat and grabbed her bag out of the lockers all the while trying to hold her hot chocolate and muffin.

Nate opened the back door for Neiva. "Come on, Neiva!"

Breezy and Viv were huddled by the truck. They both were in their winter jackets and Mukluk boots. Neiva handed over the hot chocolate so she could open the door. She lifted the passenger seat and right away Breezy bolted into the back of the truck, her teeth chattering. Viv climbed in next while sipping on the hot chocolate.

Neiva slammed the seat down, quickly got into the truck, and shut the door. It was cold outside. Neiva glanced out the window. The sun wasn't fully up yet, keeping the weather bitter cold. Once winter set in, the town of Spirit would only see the sun for four to five hours a day, leaving darkness to settle over the land. It was a harsh time of year.

"Nate? Can you please put the heater on?" Breezy asked while she huddled closer to Viv, who was radiating heat like a furnace.

"Yup." Nate started the truck, instantly cranking the heat up all the way.

"So, how was work?" Viv asked, passing the hot chocolate to Breezy.

"Good." Neiva told Viv and Breezy about practicing peeking through spirit shields and how she saw Austin's true form. With dreamy looks in their eyes, both girls sighed in unison. Neiva rolled her eyes. Austin was good-looking, but Neiva's thoughts and heart always turned to Darius. Plus, she had a strange feeling toward Austin, which wasn't a good feeling either.

They reached school within minutes. Everyone got out of the truck and started walking up to the entrance. Viv and Breezy were leading the way, excitedly giggling to each other about Austin.

Nate trailed behind with a scowl on his face, mimicking

the girls. Neiva stayed back, casually glancing at the school's surroundings. Nothing was unusual, but Neiva knew that her school was a giant tree with its branches reaching toward the sky.

Right away, Neiva noticed a group of students suddenly appear off to the right of the school, just where the football field ended. There was nothing but marshland and forest beyond the football field, so Neiva instantly figured out where they had come from.

"Ah, guys?" Neiva waited for the group to turn around and acknowledge her before she asked her question. She pointed off in the direction the students were walking from. "Where did they come from?"

Viv glanced in the direction Neiva was pointing to. She raised an eyebrow, and then turned to Breezy. Breezy glanced back at Neiva, then to Nate, who shrugged his shoulders in response.

"Well, she will eventually find out," Viv stated as she played with her long braid, her eyes flashing with fire.

"It's the entrance to the Spirit World," Breezy said, looking straight at Neiva, as if she were daring her to try and get by her. Breezy wasn't far off. As soon as Breezy confirmed to Neiva that it was the entrance to the Spirit World, Neiva had every intention of making a break for it. She didn't have to think twice about it, but now was not the time. She would have to wait for the right moment and try to figure out how to get by the cameras—that was her biggest problem.

"Is it an entrance to both the Light and Dark Lands?" Neiva tried to ask the question calmly, trying to not alert Breezy or Viv to her future plans.

"Yes, it will take the traveler to whichever land their heart desires." Breezy continued to stare hard at Neiva, making Neiva feel that Breezy knew what she was thinking.

"Come on, guys, we're going to be late," Nate whined. He quickened his pace to reach the front doors, jerked them open, and turned to the girls frowning, waiting for them to follow.

"Thanks for the info, Breezy," Neiva slyly smiled as she walked by.

"Don't get any ideas in your head, Neiva. King Darius will see you when he can and the raven will eventually come around. You don't need to get into any more trouble." Breezy lifted her eyebrow, waiting for Neiva to get defensive with her.

Neiva wasn't going to take the bait. She needed to let Breezy believe that she wasn't desperate to see Darius, that she could wait, which was the total opposite of how she really felt. Tingles of excitement coursed through her body. She was so close and she was tired of waiting. As they entered the school, she decided she would make her move sometime later in the day.

Chapter 19

DARIUS STOOD ON THE VERY EDGE of a mountaintop overlooking the valley. The wind rushed around him, sending his hair up in a flurry of movement. His gloved hands were clenched at his side. With great relief, he let out a long sigh as he watched Neiva safely enter the school building. His urge to be with her made it hard to keep his emotions in check. He didn't want to change her daily activities, not until it was necessary. Most of all, he had to make sure she was safe. He wasn't able to fully connect with her mind yet. She still was only a slight buzz at the corner of his thoughts, which infuriated him, knowing he still could not reach her. He needed to figure out what was causing the interference. He was using every resource possible and still he was getting nowhere.

A golden gleam in the sky caught Darius's attention. He didn't need to glance up to see who it was. He already knew that it was his brother, Gabriel. He had called upon his brother to meet him at this very spot and Gabriel never missed an opportunity to puff out his feathers. Gabriel would take any chance he had to confront Darius, without thinking twice.

Gabriel circled Darius several times before making a

dramatic landing. On the descent, Gabriel banked up at the last minute causing him to slam into the ground with such a force that it sounded like thunder, sending a shock wave toward Darius.

Darius tilted his head, turning his attention briefly to Gabriel. He was kneeling on the ground with his golden wings outstretched to their full tip-to-tip twelve-foot length. His eyes were glowing an intense gold and looked as if they were on fire. When he stood up, Darius tried to choke back a laugh but didn't succeed in hiding it from Gabriel.

"What are you laughing at?" Gabriel narrowed his eyes at Darius. His brother was very secretive, one trait that Gabriel loathed, because he could never tell what Darius was thinking. He was always one step ahead of Gabriel.

"When did you start requiring uniforms for flying?" Darius pointed to Gabriel's attire.

Gabriel glanced down at his outfit with confusion. He was wearing a brown bomber jacket that was unzipped, revealing a white T-shirt that stuck to Gabriel's body like a second skin. He wore brown khaki pants tucked into knee-high black combat boots. Silver aviator sunglasses rested on top of his golden hair, finishing off his look.

Gabriel laughed a little as he folded his wings. "I forgot to change after flying lessons." The hard look on his face suddenly melted into a goofy smile, shocking Darius for a second. Darius hadn't heard his brother laugh in years; it warmed his heart just to hear the genuine sound escape his brother's mouth and to see the goofy smile back on his face.

"Training a new flock?" Darius tried to keep his questions simple. He didn't want to ruin his brother's mood.

"Yes, new wings to take to the sky," Gabriel said, playing with the aviator glasses on his head as his eyes narrowed. "I forgot how stubborn young swans are, especially the teenagers."

Gabriel's royal guards were known as Swannards. They were able to take the shape of a swan as a second form. When they weren't in their swan forms, their true forms were known for their metallic skin and giant wings. Gabriel had two males and one female for his royal guards. He called them his Sun's Flock. They would do anything for him and were loyal to the end. In return, Gabriel would train their cygnets and teach them all the skills of aviation and defensive flying.

"So why did you call me here, brother?" Gabriel asked, looking at Darius with curiosity.

Darius had turned back to stare down into the valley and was wearing his standard mask; the silver one with the black stars alighting the sides. Gabriel knew Darius's mask changed colors and shapes. He also knew that it did not come off. Gabriel had tried to rip the mask off several times over the years, but he had never succeeded. It stuck to Darius like glue, making Gabriel believe the mask had become a part of his brother.

"I need your help in keeping an eye on Neiva," Darius stated, a hint of pleading behind it. Darius would never ask Gabriel for help if it wasn't important and there were no other options left.

"Your connection is still broken?" Gabriel asked with surprise in his voice.

"It's slowly coming back, but not fast enough," Darius replied.

"Have you come any closer to finding the source of the problem?" Gabriel sent his flock to search throughout his own land, but there were no signs of disturbances, everything was peaceful in his kingdom. For now it seemed only the Dark Land and human world were threatened by this ominous foe.

"Nothing of dire importance, but I do know it is way before our time." Darius turned toward Gabriel. "I believe it has to center around the time of the dragon."

Gabriel was shocked. The time of the dragon was in the ancient times when dragons and unicorns freely roamed both the earth and Spirit World, before they were killed for their horns and hides. It was a time of pure magic long forgotten.

Gabriel stared at Darius for several minutes, processing

the information before replying, "The time of our grandfather?"

"Yes, but I have to do a little more research before I can decipher the connection. In the meantime, I need some extra eyes to watch over Neiva." Darius didn't move as he stared at Gabriel.

"You already have someone from my court, Breezy, who is Neiva's friend and also a great light spirit. She wouldn't let anything happen to Neiva." Gabriel couldn't see Darius's eyes, but he could feel the weight of his stare. It caused small goose bumps to form along his arms. Gabriel would never admit it out loud, but he knew his brother was very powerful. The scary thing was he had a feeling Darius was even more powerful than Gabriel himself.

"Yes, and I am thankful for Breezy's presence in Neiva's life. But things are changing, Gabriel. Neiva was attacked several times at camp. You saved her once. If you hadn't been there . . . ," Darius's voice trailed off for a brief moment before he could compose himself once more. "This entity or whatever it is, is getting stronger by the minute and it is after Neiva. It sent Soul Eaters after her."

Gabriel walked over to stand beside Darius. He looked out over the valley and the town of Spirit. There were many times his brother infuriated Gabriel, but Darius was still blood and he was all that Gabriel had left. He would never let anything happen to Darius.

"Have you told Neiva yet?" Gabriel knew that answer even before Darius answered. Darius liked to play by the rules, unlike Gabriel who didn't follow them very well.

"No, you know the rules for an awakening. She must find out on her eighteenth birthday on her own accord, with no persuasion from me," Darius stated as he started to fiddle with something in his right hand.

"I know, but I thought I would ask." Gabriel paused for several seconds as he crossed his arms before turning to face Darius. "You know I don't give my help freely, brother?"

"Yes, an eye for an eye," Darius said as he slid a large

ring from his middle finger. He placed it in the palm of his outstretched hand, raising the ring so Gabriel could see it. The ring was light black, almost gray in color against Darius's black leather glove. It was in the shape of a raven with its wings tucked behind its body, its claws stretched out as if it would land at the tip of his finger. Ruby-red eyes glittered in the sunlight giving Gabriel an eerie feeling.

Gabriel gave Darius a puzzled look. The ring flew out of Darius's palm and into the air. It flapped its metal wings in swift motions as it circled around Gabriel.

"Hold out your right hand," Darius instructed Gabriel.

Gabriel kept his eye on the flying ring as he reluctantly held out his hand. The ring stopped in front of Gabriel's outstretched hand, hovering briefly before it dove onto his middle finger. It wrapped its metal wings around the bottom of Gabriel's finger while its head lined itself up with his nail, the beak curving around the tip of his finger. The ring's color suddenly changed from black to a brilliant gold, while its ruby eyes transformed into diamonds. It was no longer a raven but now an eagle, Gabriel's bird to call.

Momentarily shocked, Gabriel stared at his new ring. It was stunning and very much something he would wear. Darius knew Gabriel well.

"When you are in need of my help or ask for my debt to be paid, just take the ring off. It will fly back to me and I will come to your aide." Darius knew his brother would call upon him when he needed his help. He wasn't sure what Gabriel's request would be or if it would be similar to Darius's own circumstances with Neiva, which he hoped for Gabriel's sake, it would be.

Gabriel stared at his brother in wonderment. He was always one step ahead, thinking about others instead of himself, which Gabriel considered Darius's major flaw. It was bound to get him hurt or even killed one day. This thought frustrated Gabriel, because Darius never thought about his own safety.

"Oh, I will call upon you brother. Be sure of that," Gabriel growled as he stepped away from Darius to unfurl his wings. Just as Gabriel was about to step off the cliff, he paused for a split second as if he just thought of something important. He grunted before brushing one of his wing tips lightly on Darius's shoulder then took off in a blur.

Darius watched Gabriel fly for several seconds before he disappeared in a flash of light. He envied Gabriel and the freedom that flight allowed. How he wished he could fly alongside Gabriel like in their younger days. Darius knew Gabriel probably would have allowed it. Gabriel could be cold and downright mean to his brother. But in Gabriel's own way, he showed him love … even if Gabriel fought his inner demons to do so, Darius thought as he noticed a trail of golden dust left behind from Gabriel's wing tip, sparkling like pixie dust.

A warm feeling slowly filled Darius's heart as he continued to stare at his shoulder. Hope for his brother hadn't died yet. The anger in Gabriel's heart was waning. Darius knew this because in Gabriel's flock, Swannards brushed their wings against each other as a form of affection and trust. It was a sign telling Darius that his brother was slowly becoming his old self again and that the hatred in Gabriel's heart would melt someday. But how long would the block of hatred imprison Gabriel's heart? How long would he mourn their mother's death? He didn't know, but hoped to see it one day. Darius glanced at the high school one more time before the shadows sprang up from the ground and surrounded him.

TIME SEEMED TO MOVE SLOWER every second as Neiva stared at the clock behind Mr. Perry's desk. The class was watching *Romeo + Juliet*. Neiva loved that movie and could watch it over and over again when given the chance. Maybe because she loved Leonardo DiCaprio and Claire Danes. She also adored how it dealt with a timeless love, where two individuals fight to the bitter end to be with each other. Unfortunately, she couldn't concentrate on the movie with her own feelings at war. She was on edge and couldn't wait any longer to see Darius. She had to make her move.

Neiva quietly maneuvered out of her desk. She tiptoed up to Mr. Perry, who was intently grading papers at his desk. Neiva asked if she could use the bathroom. She tried to keep her voice low enough so she wouldn't disturb the students who were actually paying attention to the movie.

Mr. Perry looked up, his reading glasses slowly falling down his pointed nose. "Be quick, Miss Ellis. You don't want to miss the best part of the movie."

"Yes, sir. I will try to be quick," Neiva replied as Mr. Perry handed her a hall pass. She swiped the pass out of his hand before bolting to the door. She glanced over her shoulder and saw Breezy and Viv both staring at her, wondering what was going on. Neiva responded with a smile, then mouthed bathroom before she opened the door and entered the hallway.

The hallway was deserted as Neiva walked past several classrooms to reach the girls' bathroom. Once inside, Neiva ran over to the mirror to check her reflection. She looked exactly as she had this morning; her hair was still tightly braided and she still wore her uniform from The Magic Pot. Neiva didn't look that bad, but she decided she should wear her hair down.

She quickly unbound her hair to let the loose curls fall down her back. She tied the black ribbon around a strand of hair then added some lip gloss while she used her other hand to fix her shirt. Lastly, Neiva made sure the raven bracelet was visible for Darius to see. It fit her so perfectly that she always forgot it was on her wrist.

With some final touches, Neiva stepped back from the mirror with a smile of satisfaction on her face. She was ready to go, but there was one problem. She didn't have her jacket and it was very cold outside. The jacket was in her locker in the other direction. The girls' bathroom was near the entrance to the south doors that faced the football field. If Neiva went back to retrieve her jacket, than she would waste valuable time. She only wanted to be gone no more the twenty minutes, using her stomach as an excuse if Mr. Perry asked. There was no other time to go but now. She couldn't escape at lunch because there would be students roaming around the halls on their lunch break. Students were not allowed to leave the school grounds during lunch. As of right then, the cameras were down for their yearly maintenance update but there was no telling when they would be back up. It was now or never.

Neiva stepped into the hallway, instantly noticing the lights were now off and it was unusually dark. Looking in both directions, Neiva slowly walked toward the exit doors. With every step she took, she got a stronger and stronger feeling something was wrong. Darius had told her not to be scared of the dark, that it would protect her. But the shadows surrounding the hall didn't feel right, like ones at the cabin. They gave Neiva an evil feeling that made her stop walking after only taking a few steps. As she looked toward the exit she noticed something was blocking the doors. Neiva couldn't tell what it was, but it was slowly shuffling toward her. Her instincts told her to run, but when she turned around she slammed right into Breezy.

"Whoa. What's wrong, Neiva?" Breezy asked as she steadied Neiva to keep her from falling over.

Neiva looked back toward the hall. "There's something at the end of the hallway."

"Huh?" Viv asked, appearing at Neiva's side. She squinted her yellow eyes toward the exit. "What's that?"

The thing blocking the doors had stopped two classrooms down from the group. One of the lights above the figure slowly turned on, illuminating its characteristics. It was a boy, but he was standing very strangely. His arms looked heavy at his sides, while his head hung at an odd angle. When he started walking toward them, his feet dragged as if something invisible was pulling them.

"We know him," Viv stated with a worried look on her face.

"Who is it?" Neiva whispered. The crystal on her forehead was starting to tingle, as if it was warning Neiva to get the hell out of there.

"It's Austin Brooks." Viv's eyes started to glow a bright yellow as her spirit shield dropped. Within seconds she was in her true form, her tribal tattoos shining brightly like a beacon in the dark. Her tail flipped back and forth as she clicked her black claws together.

"What's wrong?" Breezy asked. She was in her true form, her green eyes wide with fear as she unsheathed her claws.

"He was just in the coffee shop this morning, flirting with me," Neiva gulped as Austin drew closer.

Austin slowed to a stop. He turned to face them, his lackluster eyes on Neiva, and opened his mouth menacingly at her. Black oil oozed over his pale skin and covered his eyes. It was the same stuff from the lake and the cabin. He was infected by a Soul Eater. Neiva turned to look at Breezy and Viv, who both had noticed the oil at the same time as she did.

"Uh, I am afraid to ask, but what is his power?" Breezy took a step in front of Neiva, making sure Neiva was behind her and Viv.

"Spirits of the dead," Viv said as flames ignited on her hands, slow creeping up her arms.

Breezy and Neiva didn't have time to react. Skeletal arms broke through the tiled floor grabbing the girls' legs. One latched onto Neiva's ankle, pulling her toward itself. Its head emerged from the ground causing Neiva to gasp. Maggots were eating away at the rotting flesh on one side of its face while the other side showed an empty eye socket and very lethal teeth. Slime dripped out of its mouth as its tongue fell past its jaw. It snapped at Neiva's leg, missing by just inches.

Neiva reached her hand out, concentrating on pushing it away. Centered on the palm of her outstretched hand, a slight tingle sparked to life. Light flashed and the dead spirit's head was incinerated, leaving the arms and chest behind. Neiva threw the arm off and quickly stood up.

She looked to her right to see Breezy fighting a dead spirit with half of its head missing. It tried to swipe Breezy with its fingernails, but she was too fast. Breezy snapped a foot toward the dead spirit, catching it under the jaw, and sent it flying. It hit the wall opposite the girls.

"How do we kill them?" Viv yelled as she threw flames at the dead spirit attacking her. Half of the dead spirit's body was on fire. The flames ate through the rotting flesh like acid eating through cement. Its neck was partially burned off, held together by a few strings of muscle. Only a couple more inches before the head would be free. With a growl Viv whipped her tail around, sending the tip of her stinger into the skeleton's neck. She jerked her tail, propelling the dead spirit's head down the hall, landing just a few feet in front of Austin.

Breezy quickly finished her opponent off with an upper cut from her claws, tearing the dead spirit's head right off its neck. She brought her hand down to her side, letting the dead head slowly slide down her claws, dropping to the floor with a thud. She folded her wings behind her back, while her tail whipped back and forth. Her green eyes glowed with anger as she snarled at Austin. It was a side of Breezy Neiva had never seen before, but she welcomed this new transformation. They needed all the aggression they could get.

An evil laughter erupted from Austin. It echoed all around them, sounding like a train rushing through a tunnel. The laughter sent shock waves down the hall making the lockers rattle as the lights on the ceiling blinked on and off. The tiled floor rolled in waves causing the girls to fall like bowling pins. Time stood still. There was an eerie silence before the world erupted into chaos.

Chapter 20

DOZENS OF DEAD SPIRITS burst through the floor in all different states of decay. Some looked as if they had died the day before, while others were nothing but skeletons. Some of the dead spirits had all of their limbs, while others used their arms to drag their legless bodies across the floor. Each one possessed sharp teeth and claws, making them more dangerous than the previous group. Black ooze poured out of their mouths, dripping onto the floor. Their rotting flesh fell off their bodies as they moved closer in on the group.

"We need reinforcements! Where's Nate?!" Viv hissed as she frantically looked around. "Neiva, can you call upon Roxy or at least try?"

Neiva didn't even need to think twice about it. She watched the group of dead spirits creeping closer to them. They were in a nightmare, right in the middle of Raven High.

It was hard, but Neiva tried to focus her attention on Roxy. She pictured her nestled on the back of Nate's neck. She imagined herself lightly brushing her fingertips over the tattoo and asking for help. There was nothing at first, but then Neiva felt a flutter of movement at the back of her mind. She heard a soft bark just before Roxy and Nate materialized beside her.

"What's going on, Neiva?" Nate asked. "Roxy said you were in trouble."

Before Neiva could respond, Nate saw the mass of skeletons converging in on them.

"Didn't you hear all the commotion that was going on out here?" Viv asked as she readied herself for the fight. She posed her tail behind her ready to strike, her teeth were bared, and her claws were drawn in anticipation.

"No one heard a th—ow!!" Nate stood still as blood dripped down his hand from where Roxy just bit him.

Silver ribbons sprang up from the ground, wrapping themselves around Nate's body, transforming him into a true spirit Guardian. The gray stripe was back on Nate's face, like warrior paint crossing over his nose and eyes. His eyes became white orbs, glowing as bright as flashlights. He revealed sharp teeth when he growled at the skeletons. His clawed hands were out in front of him, ready to rip anything that would try to get past him. Roxy crouched at Nate's side. The hair on her back bristled up like quills on a porcupine. Her claws grew several inches in length as she glared with hatred at the skeletons.

"Run, Neiva!" Nate growled. The force of his words slammed into her. She could feel his urgency and desire for her safety. He wanted her to leave.

"I can help!" Neiva exclaimed. She looked from Nate to Breezy then Viv. They all had the same look in their eyes, the same determination radiating off them. They wanted her to leave and they were right. She was a liability. She would only get in the way. With the only thought of her friends' lives at stake, Neiva turned around and ran down the hallway as the first wave of skeletons attacked. She could hear the grunts and growls coming from her friends while they covered her escape.

Neiva ran with all of her might down the hallway. She burst through the double doors leading to the second hallway, never slowing down or even glancing back. She pushed the muscles in her legs to work faster as she focused on the doors that led outside. Neiva had almost reached her destination when something grabbed her from behind.

"I knew you weren't telling the truth from day one," Miranda hissed as she twirled Neiva around to face her. An icy storm was brewing in Miranda's eyes. Her upper lip curved into a smile of satisfaction at the thought of catching Neiva ditching school.

"Miranda, I don't have time for this. We need to get help. My friends are in trouble." Neiva urged. She glanced at the hallway doors behind them.

"Like I'm going to believe whatever comes out of your mouth," Miranda quipped. "Mr. Perry sent me to see if you were all right, but obviously you are. And to top it off, you're trying to leave!"

Neiva was dumbfounded that Miranda did not see the fight raging in the next hallway. Was she so fixated on getting Neiva into trouble that she didn't fully see her surroundings? It was infuriating.

"Miranda," Neiva began, "did you not see what was going on in the hallway just outside of our English class? Are you so high on your pedestal that you can't see anything past your own fake nose?"

Miranda's eyes widened in shock. People didn't normally speak to her like that; first Nate and now Neiva. Something was going on and for the first time since Miranda had grabbed Neiva, she noticed the fear in Neiva's eyes.

"What are you talking about?" Miranda asked, letting go of Neiva and taking several steps back. She inspected Neiva's appearance, instantly noticing the rip on Neiva's right pant leg; and Neiva's white shirt looked as if it had blood splattered all over her left shoulder and sleeve.

Neiva was about to reply to Miranda's question until she was cut off by someone crashing through the hallway doors. The figure hurtled through the doors with so much force that the hinges on the doors broke loose, sending the doors flying in both directions. The doors skidded down the hallway several feet before they were embedded into the lockers lining the walls. The figure that caused the commotion bounced down the hallway like a rag doll until it landed right in front of Miranda and Neiva. Neiva stifled a scream when she saw who it was.

"Viv!" Neiva shouted, running to Viv's still form.

Viv was lying on her back with her limbs twisted at odd angles. One of her four horns was broken, only connected by a strip of skin. Bright red blood dripped out of the corner of her mouth, trickling down her chin and landing in a small pool of blood that had started to form on the floor. Her flat stomach was scraped up with teeth and claw marks, and a large bruise started to form on her chest.

"Is she okay?" Miranda asked in a whisper as she bent down next to Neiva.

"I don't know, but she's breathing," Neiva responded. She put her head down onto Viv's chest.

Suddenly, a scream of rage filled the hallway. Neiva glanced up to see Nate running toward them, his white eyes glowing brightly. He slashed at any dead spirit that got in his way.

Roxy was right at his heals, snapping at the bones that Nate threw behind him. Within seconds, Nate reached the group. He dropped down onto his knees letting out a small whimper as he looked at Viv's mangled form. Nate slowly brought his clawed hand to Viv's face, lightly brushing back the strands of hair that had escaped Viv's braid. He looked up at Neiva with fear in his eyes.

"She saved me," Nate gulped. "I didn't see the dead spirits at my back until Viv pushed me out of the way. That's when Austin blasted Viv out of the hallway."

Roxy was suddenly at Nate's side. She let out a whine and pushed her nose against Viv's face, trying to get Viv to move. Roxy lifted her head to look at Nate and slowly brushed her face up against his.

"RUN!" Breezy screamed.

Everyone glanced up to see Breezy running. Her wings burst out at her sides and began to pump faster and faster until they moved as fast as a hummingbird's wings. She took to the air within seconds, glancing behind her before gaining speed.

"Oh no!" Neiva stood up once she saw what trailed behind Breezy. It looked as if the hallway was being engulfed by total darkness, but this darkness was actually a giant black wave and it was slowly gaining speed and height. Made of Soul Eaters and the black slime they create, the wave was thick and gelatinous. The dead spirits rode the black wave like boogie boarders, snapping their jaws and swiping their claws as they slowly surfaced then fell back into the oily wave.

"Run!" Nate exclaimed. He swiftly picked up Viv.

"I'll take her, Nate!" Breezy cried as she threw a gust of wind at the doors.

The doors flew open. With a surge of speed, Breezy shot toward Nate who held Viv up so Breezy could grab her. Breezy reached Viv within seconds and hoisted her with ease. The extra weight didn't interfere with Breezy's flying as she shot through the doors.

"Come on!" Nate commanded as he followed Breezy through the doors. Roxy trailed not too far behind him.

Neiva saw the wave was almost upon them. She helped Miranda up, trying to push her through the doors, but Miranda wouldn't budge. "Run, Miranda!"

Miranda's eyes were glowing like icicles illuminated by the sun. Her spirit shield suddenly dropped and she pushed Neiva toward the open doors. A blast of arctic air surrounded Miranda, sending her indigo hair flying in all directions. She brought her pale blue hands up and sent blasts of ice toward the oncoming wave. The wave slowed down, but it took several blasts before it finally stopped about eight feet from Miranda, frozen solid.

"Let's go. The ice won't hold it for much longer," Miranda exclaimed, sending another blast of ice before turning around. She grabbed Neiva's hand and bolted out the door as the ice began to crack behind them.

Miranda and Neiva ran to the others, who were standing

in the middle of the football field. Nate was cradling Viv, while Breezy hovered next to him. Roxy had her head down low and her tail curved underneath her body. She swiveled her head from side to side as she let out a subdued growl from her battered body.

"What's wrong? Why aren't we running for the gates into the Spirit World?" Neiva asked glancing around at the group.

"Something feels wrong," Breezy groaned. She slowly set her feet onto the ground, folding her wings behind her as she unsheathed her claws. Her antennas flicked back and forth as if in anticipation, while her tail slowly wrapped around her waist.

Neiva tried to see if she could sense anything that was out of the ordinary while she scanned their surroundings. Nothing seemed off, but a tingling sensation slowly began to form at the center of her forehead, as if the crystal were trying to warn her. That was when Neiva noticed the fog coming in toward them. It was approaching from the west. The Ishegocks were coming to help, but Neiva had a feeling they wouldn't reach her friends in time.

"The ice is about to break," Miranda said as she looked back at the school.

There was a loud crack, then an explosion as pieces of ice blew through the door, quickly followed by the black oily wave of Soul Eaters. The dark mass banked around, heading straight for them. It moved almost as if it were a serpent slithering back and forth as it approached the group. It was about thirty feet away, expanding out to surround the group. The dead spirits were still within the oily substance trying to snatch at whatever came close to them.

"How are we going to get out?" Neiva asked.

The fog finally reached the black wall surrounding them. It slammed into the oily substance, causing it to hiss in protest. The earth shook as the black wall suddenly grew in height, towering twenty feet in the air, blocking the Ishegocks from reaching the group. Neiva instantly noticed puddles of the Soul Eaters forming just a few feet in front of them. They slowly rose into the air. The Soul Eaters' mouths hung open like gaping holes with lethal teeth ready to chomp on any unlucky victim.

Neiva noticed something behind the Soul Eaters. It was a large figure that had magically appeared out of nowhere. A gigantic form slowly solidified. Its face resembled a boar with giant tusks on each side of its mouth; its teeth looked like they could chomp through bone. Thick black hair covered its head, as did large ears that flicked back and forth. Its eyes were full of the oily substance; and it seeped through the boar's skin as well. Huge muscles lined its chest and arms, reminding Neiva of a football player. The boar's hands were huge, about the size of her head.

A deep voice shook from the boar's mouth as oily slime dripped down its jaw. It was infected by a Soul Eater. "Hello, Neiva. My master has called upon me to bring you to her. I cannot disappoint her; the punishment would be too severe."

Nate hissed as he set Viv down, putting himself between Viv and the boar. Roxy instantly stood above Viv, with her feet spread apart so Viv's body lay underneath her belly, safely protected from whatever was about to happen next.

The tingling sensation in Neiva's forehead started to intensify, causing Neiva to throw her head back. The sensation stopped once her eyes locked onto something flying above her. It circled back around the perimeter of the black wall, suddenly diving down toward them at the last second.

"Riley!" Neiva screamed. She watched the raven descend from the sky. His giant wings pushed the air around him as he neared the ground. His speed was increasing the closer he fell toward the earth. Neiva was afraid he was going to collide with the ground, but at the last second Riley changed his form to land gracefully on two feet.

Neiva, stay behind Nate and Breezy! If anything comes near you, use any last defense possible to protect yourself. Riley's voice was filled with both relief and concern. Relief that their connection was back, but concern that Neiva's life was in danger.

Neiva couldn't comprehend what Riley had just telepathically said to her. She was too shocked by his new appearance. Riley was no longer the giant raven. In his spirit form, he stood six feet tall and had giant blue wings spread out behind him, at least ten feet from tip to tip. The spikes on the back of his head at first looked like hair, but they were actually feathers ending in a slight upward curve, like a cardinal's head. His bare chest and brawny arms led to glistening obsidian talons that started at the elbow and ended with rapierlike claws. Riley looked as if he was wearing a pair of jeans; but like his hair, they were feathers, stopping short just above his human-looking feet. When he turned to look at Neiva, his features almost looked Asian, his sharp eyes glowing like blue sapphires. He had a blue mark running down his right cheek, as if someone dipped their fingers in blue paint and spread them down Riley's face stopping just below his chin. Riley's lips were the same obsidian-black color as his beak, slowly forming into a smile at Neiva's shocked expression.

"King Darius is on his way. Be ready," he warned. He turned to his opponent, spreading his wings out farther as he sent a horrifying screech in the boar's direction.

"Ah, a visitor. Welcome. You've managed to arrive just in time, but don't worry. I will fix it so that we don't have any more unexpected guests," the boar laughed. Its eyes began to glow an eerie gray color.

The boar raised its giant hands toward the sky. There was a sudden hiss as electricity shot out of its hands toward the black wall. A pop sounded as the electricity jumped across from one part of the wall to the next, spreading out until it resembled the top of a cage. The group was trapped. The only way out was through the black wall of Soul Eaters or through the electrified fence.

All eyes turned to the boar as it brought its hands down. Electricity crackled throughout its fingers as laughter erupted from its mouth. Before he finished chortling, the swine shot one of its hands up toward Riley, sending a bolt of lightning in his direction.

Riley moved out of the way just in the nick of time, though the bolt singed one of his end feathers. He landed on the ground with a thud, but within seconds, he bounced back up and launched himself into the sky.

"Get ready! The fight is about to begin!" Riley exclaimed. He performed impressive aerial maneuvers as the boar shot more lightning bolts at him. Riley twisted and rolled as he dove at the boar, slashing out his talons and raking them along the boar's back. With a scream, the boar tried to grab Riley's wing, barely missing it by inches as Riley shot up toward the sky with the boar's skin embedded in his talons.

With Riley's warning, the group was ready for the next attack. The Soul Eaters screamed unlike anything Neiva had ever heard. It reminded her of someone scratching their fingernails across a chalkboard—that intense screeching sound that makes anyone cover their ears.

"Here they come!" Breezy shouted, shooting a gust of wind at the closest Soul Eater. The wind only stalled the creature briefly before it pressed on toward Breezy, growing in height.

All of a sudden the dead spirits started to emerge from the oily substance, slowly trudging toward the group. A skeleton threw one of its arms at Nate, who ducked just in time as the arm rushed over his head and ended up landing in the mouth of the Soul Eater in front of Neiva. It sucked the arm down with ease, not even faltering in its steps.

"Protect Viv!" Nate pointed to Roxy as he ran toward the skeletons closest to the group. His speed increased like a predator about to take down his prey. He lashed out at four skeletons, simultaneously slashing off all their heads. Their bodies fell like dominoes, each knocking the other down before landing in a pile of body parts.

Roxy snapped at anything that came near Viv. She leaped onto a skeleton grabbing Viv's leg, viscously ripping off the skeleton's head. It only took Roxy seconds before she was back over Viv's still form, protecting her from any other danger.

Breezy was trying to keep the Soul Eaters at a distance with the wind, but it wasn't working. The wind only stalled the creatures briefly before they continued on toward the group. Riley was still battling with the boar and some of his feathers were smoking from the lightning bolts that had managed to hit him. He landed several strong blows on the boar's thick hide, but it only seemed to agitate the boar more.

Neiva didn't know what to do. She didn't have any weapons to use on the skeletons or Soul Eaters. She didn't even know how she incinerated the skeleton back in the hallway. It was just an urge to push the thing away, it was the same urge she had when she shot Miranda down the hallway last week.

"Watch out, Neiva!" Riley shouted from the air.

A Soul Eater appeared out of nowhere next to Neiva. Its mouth gaped open as it lunged at her. Neiva shot her hand out trying to imagine herself pushing the creature away. Nothing happened as first. She concentrated even harder. Finally a warm sensation tingled in her hands. She pushed her hand out farther, but only a few small sparks hit the Soul Eater. It paused for a second, not knowing what to think of the sparks. Its mouth closed briefly before opening wide to devour Neiva.

Neiva screamed when the creature dove down upon her. She squeezed her eyes shut, waiting for the creature to swallow her whole, but as the seconds ticked by, nothing happened. With great fear Neiva opened her eyes to see Darius standing in front of her. His back was toward her, blocking the Soul Eater from reaching Neiva. His long black hair sparkled in the light as it fell down his back. His right hand rested behind him, inches away from Neiva, ready to grab her at a moment's notice. His left hand was out in front of him with his fingers spread wide. Black shadowy tentacles escaped out of his hand, wrapping themselves around the Soul Eater and making it hiss in protest.

"Sasha! Blake!" Darius shouted.

Like clouds overhead, shadows suddenly appeared and

quickly slipped through the electrical cage, descending upon the group. The shadows separated into two forms taking the shape of Sasha and Blake.

"Thanks for the ride, Sasha." Blake's face had lost all of its pearly color, making his orange coral mask bright against his pale skin. He was wearing armor made out of orange shells, which fit his body perfectly. In his right hand he held a trident, similar to his father's but made out of black pearls instead of coral. He swung the trident in a long arc at the skeleton in front of him. When Blake slammed the trident into the ground, a wave of water appeared out of nowhere and crushed the skeletons against the black wall; their body parts flew in all directions. The wave slowly seeped into the ground, leaving only scattered bones.

"Ah, anytime merman, anytime," Sasha said flashing his sharp teeth and looking around for more skeletons to slay.

Sasha's white hair fell down past his shoulders, his red eyes glowing like lasers through his black mask. His chest was covered in silver armor that outlined every muscle and curve. He wore a black belt with a silver scorpion buckle that held up his black leather pants. Dark gray boots with steel toes completed his outfit. A sword rested at his side as he scanned their surroundings. He instantly saw Neiva behind Darius's protection. In a blink of an eye, Sasha stood several feet away from Neiva, holding his hand out to her.

"What about my friends?" Neiva asked. She turned to look at everyone. Viv was still lying on the ground with Roxy protecting her. Viv's color was slowly changing from marble red to ashen gray. She wasn't looking good.

Nate was trying to keep the perimeter around Viv and Roxy clear of skeletons but had his hands full. Every time he dismembered one skeleton, it would magically put itself back together. The wave from Blake helped, but it didn't stop the marauding skeletons; it only hindered them for several seconds. Both Blake and Nate were having a hard time keeping the skeletons down.

Breezy used the power of wind to keep the Soul Eaters from moving any farther, but it wasn't working either. Neiva finally saw Miranda. She had moved toward the back of the group and was trying to keep some of the wall frozen, but the dead spirits and Soul Eaters kept breaking through.

"The skeletons are getting stronger," Miranda shouted as she tried to ice down two different sections of the wall. The strain was starting to show on her face and sweat trickled down from her forehead, freezing into icicles beneath her chin.

"The Soul Eaters too," Breezy announced, pushing several of them back with the wind. The airstream had only moved them a couple of inches back, but it was keeping them from attacking the group, for now.

"Nothing seems to be working on the boar." Riley swooped down to shout out his observation. He maneuvered himself between two skeletons, shooting in like a torpedo, then slashed out his talons with such speed and precision it took several seconds before the skeleton's heads fell off. He swooped back up into the air to continue his fight with the boar.

Neiva, go with Sasha. He will take you to safety. Your friends can take care of themselves. Darius spoke softly in Neiva's mind. She could feel him as strongly as she had before, but this time she felt more of his feelings. His mind surrounded her with worry and fear. He didn't know what was controlling the skeletons or Soul Eaters. They were getting stronger no matter what the spirits threw at them. He wanted Neiva out of the area and safely hidden away.

Darius ensnared another Soul Eater with his free hand as Neiva ran toward Sasha, who was only standing a couple of feet away. Neiva was about to grab Sasha's hand when a scream erupted from above, shouting her name urgently. Neiva looked up to see Gabriel hovering just above the electric cage, his golden wings slowly flapping.

Neiva didn't have time to react as something embedded itself in her shoulder. There was such great force behind it that it threw Neiva back ten feet, away from Darius and Sasha. She landed on her back when she hit the ground, pushing all the air out of her lungs. Pain laced through her body. Gasping, Neiva glanced at her shoulder to see a large tusk protruding out of it. Oil filled the wound and slowly seeped out onto her. It spread down her arm and around her body, encasing her in an oily shell. Neiva fought to move, but it was useless. The shell had trapped her.

"Neiva!" Riley screamed as he flew toward her. As he was momentarily distracted with his efforts to reach Neiva, he didn't see the bolt of electricity heading for his back. Within seconds, it hit his body, sending him into spasms as he fell to the earth.

Sasha materialized right next to Neiva. His eyes glowed a brilliant red as he reached down to pry the oily substance off of Neiva's body, but he didn't get very far. Austin suddenly materialized through the black wall and was running straight at Sasha. Before Sasha had time to react, Austin's body slammed into him, sending Sasha's sword flying out of his hands.

The ground beneath Neiva began to shake as the oily shell solidified around her. She couldn't move and it was hard for her to breathe. Tears came to her eyes. She felt so helpless, so drained. Panic set in and the pain in her arm was too much, her heart accelerated as she sent a mental cry out to Darius for help. She didn't know if Darius had heard her plea, but it was her last thought as she slowly lost consciousness. An anguished roar erupted around her just before she passed out, and the shell that had formed around her sunk into the ground, disappearing within the earth's depths.

Chapter 21

TERROR GRIPPED DARIUS as he watched the oily shell close in around Neiva. He felt her anguish just before the shell plunged into the ground, their connection abruptly cut off. Rage filled Darius's heart as he let out an agonized roar. He quickly turned his attention back to the Soul Eaters in front of him, only to see them slip through his shadowy grasp, melting back into the earth.

Darius turned back to the boar. It was laughing at them as it continued to send lightning bolts in all directions, but its laughter was suddenly cut short as its body fell like a boulder to the ground, unconscious. The skeletons surrounding the group fell into piles of dust as the black wall of Soul Eaters crashed into the ground, disappearing from sight.

"What just happened?" Sasha pushed Austin's body off of him.

He quickly stood up and glanced around. Nothing was left of the Soul Eaters. The fog seeped in on the group, surrounding them in a protective circle. The Ishegocks' eyes glowed like lanterns watching protectively over the group.

Sasha glanced down at Austin's body to find him back in his light spirit form, his eyes staring lifelessly at the sky. His neck was broken, his legs and arms mangled, and his black wings were gone. The oily substance was nowhere to be seen. Austin's golden copper skin was clear, as were his once bright green eyes that were now clouded over by death.

"Neiva!" Nate screamed, running to where Sasha was standing. The ground where Neiva once laid was singed black and still smoking.

Breezy ran up to stand next to Nate. Tears trickled down her golden cheeks. "How will we find her?"

"His Darkness will find her," Sasha replied solemnly turning to look at his master. There was an aura of rage surrounding Darius. His mask was black, taking on a demonic face. White light glowed out of the eye slits in his mask, casting an eerie shadow around him.

"Gabriel, assess the damage and make sure the wounded are treated. I am going to find Neiva." Darius's voice slightly shuttered, as if he were holding back a monster from rising deep within his soul. His eyes began to glow brightly and shadows began to spin faster and faster around Darius, like a tornado destroying a town. Within seconds the shadows exploded out in all directions in search of Neiva, taking Darius with them.

Riley stood watching his master disappear. He shook out his flattened feathers and stretched his wings to their full length. The electrical bolt from the boar had shocked Riley, but it was the fall that had hurt him. His right shoulder was bruised and he had a busted lip from the impact with the ground.

"Riley, are you okay?" Blake asked as he inspected Riley's right shoulder. It wasn't broken, but Riley's pale skin was starting to bruise along his shoulder and down his chest. It was very painful and Riley knew it was going to be a problem when he tried to fly.

"Yeah, I'm fine," Riley lied. He walked away from Blake, slowly tucking his wings behind his back. In truth, Riley's ego was hurt. He was mad that King Darius wouldn't let him help search for Neiva. He was Neiva's protector after all; it was his job to watch over her and make sure she was safe. He had failed and his punishment was to clean up the aftermath of their battle.

Riley bent down to inspect the unconscious boar. Strangely, the boar's features had shifted slightly to reveal a human appearance. Its nose and ears shrunk down to human size while its body deflated into that of a skinny teenage boy. The boy's hands were still huge and one tusk still protruded out of his mouth.

A golden light shimmered as the King of Light landed next to Riley, with his wings out at his sides. He wore gold-plated armor around his chest and on his legs. His arms were bare, revealing muscular biceps with golden tattoos spiraling around his shoulders. A gold encrusted belt with rubies surrounding its buckle held up his dark brown pants.

"From the air, the boar did not look human at all," Gabriel walked around the body and tried to piece everything together. The tusk had started to shrink, stopping at two inches, while the boy's hands were back to their normal size.

"Chad?" Nate walked up behind Riley. He bent down to check his friend's pulse. It was faint but he was alive.

"You know this human?" Gabriel asked.

Nate glanced behind him to see Roxy and Miranda watching over Viv. Roxy would growl at Miranda whenever she got too close to Viv, in return Miranda would hiss back at Roxy. Nate knew they would protect her, and the Ishegocks wouldn't let anything though the thick fog. Breezy stood several yards back, still staring at the spot where Neiva had disappeared.

"He's a fellow Guardian," Nate replied simply. He took several steps back, and a feeling of horror crept into his chest.

Gabriel sensed the change in Nate as he stepped back from the Guardian's unconscious friend. "What animal is his spirit guide?"

Nate's heart accelerated, his palms began to sweat. "A wild boar."

Riley's eyes widened. He glanced from Nate to the Light King. Shock showed on the king's angelic face while fear spread through Nate's face. Riley stood up, and a feeling of dread coursed throughout his body, causing him to become dizzy. He felt as if he was going to lose consciousness, but a hand on his feathered back steadied him.

"Whoa there, friend," Sasha helped Riley stay up until his dizziness passed.

"I'm fine. Thanks," Riley replied.

Sasha turned toward the young Guardian lying on the ground. Chad's appearance resembled an Alaskan native: dark skin and black hair, with a scar above his mouth, but one tusk was still embedded in the boy's mouth making him something nonhuman.

"Turn him over," Gabriel ordered. He tucked his wings behind him, bending down to inspect the boy.

Riley bent down and slowly turned Chad's body over while Gabriel pushed down the boy's collar. Once Chad's neck was revealed, gasps echoed around the group. Chad's neck was bare. There was no sign of the tattoo, only a white outline where it used to be.

"How did this happen?" Blake asked. His aqua eyes glowed like jewels and anger coursed through his veins. From the way his fists were balled at his side and the grimace on his face, Blake was scared.

Gabriel stood up. He clasped his hands behind his back, becoming lost in thought. He needed to talk to his brother. They needed to pull all of their resources together. He glanced at Riley, who still was standing near the body with Sasha next to him. Nate was shaking as he walked back to Roxy and Miranda to let them know what was happening. Blake was still inspecting Chad's body, hoping to find more clues.

"Riley, take Chad back to his house, then pay a visit to Old Lady Gertrude. See if she knows why this has happened," Gabriel said before quickly adding, "and take Nate with you. He needs to know what's going on as well. His life could be in danger."

Riley bowed slightly before picking up Chad's still form. Riley walked over to Nate, to let him know what was going on, carrying Chad gently with his talons, making sure he didn't accidently scratch the boy's dark skin.

"I'm not leaving, Viv, and I want to find Neiva," Nate growled. His glowing eyes shifted into his human eyes. Pain filled his light brown eyes as tears formed at their corners. His bottom lip started to tremble as he fully transformed back into his human form.

"Sasha will take Viv back to the demon realm. She needs to be laid into the fires that she was born in," Gabriel stated, walking over to Nate. "It's the only way she will get better. Her parents will help her. And my brother will find Neiva."

Nate glanced at Viv's face. Her red marbled skin was gray while her tattoos barely glowed, as if her light was being extinguished. Roxy moved around to stand beside Nate. She gave Viv a quick lick on the cheek before fading out and reappearing as the tattoo on Nate's neck.

Sasha materialized next to Nate. He patted Nate's shoulder before using his powers to levitate Viv's body off the ground. Within seconds Viv was in Sasha's arms, her tail hanging down toward the ground. Nate bent down and delicately placed Viv's tail on her stomach so it wouldn't drag.

"Don't worry, Guardian. Vivian is a fighter, just like her father." Sasha winked at Nate before disappearing in a cloud of shadows, taking Vivian's body with him.

"Come, Nate. We must leave." Riley carried Chad's body with ease. His right shoulder hurt, but he didn't pay attention to the pain. He had a job to do. Neiva would want him to watch over Nate, and Riley would die before he let anything happen to Neiva's friend.

"Can I come with you?" Miranda asked politely. She didn't know what was going on but she wanted to find out.

"No, Ice Princess." Gabriel ordered before Riley could give Miranda a reply. "You need to give your father a message."

Gabriel waited until Miranda's icy eyes focused on his

golden eyes, giving him her full attention. "Tell Old Man Winter that it's time. Winter needs to come in full swing and darkness needs to fall now."

"Yes, Your Lightness," Miranda said with a curtsy. She quickly glanced at Nate, mouthing the word sorry before disappearing in a flurry of snowflakes.

"Come, Nate." Riley started to head into the fog.

"But won't I pass out?" Nate asked. He slowly followed Riley toward the fog.

Riley stopped. He glanced over his shoulder with a small crooked smile on his face. "No, you only pass out when the Ishegocks don't want to have to deal with keeping an eye on you during dangerous times. You tend to wander away."

"What? I can take care of myself." Nate frowned as he looked into the fog. "Did you not see me earlier? I held my own."

Riley laughed before disappearing into the fog. Nate followed as the fog opened a path leading both Riley and Nate into town.

"I will take Breezy home," Blake said with a stern voice. He stared at Gabriel, ready to fight if Gabriel disagreed with his decision.

Gabriel turned to look at Breezy, who was now on the ground, her small hands gliding over the singed grass where Neiva had disappeared. Her wings drooped behind her and her antennas sagged in defeat. Bright blue tears trickled down her cheeks as she tucked her tail underneath her legs.

"Yes, that's fine. Make sure she is cared for," Gabriel said a little numb, but still in control. Blake put his hand over his heart and bowed. He gave Gabriel a hard stare before heading toward Breezy. Gabriel could have sworn he saw something else besides anger floating around in Blake's aqua eyes.

"Come, sweetheart," Blake wrapped his muscular arms around Breezy's tiny form.

"They took her, Blake. Why?" Tears trickled down Breezy's cheeks as she buried her face into his chest.

"It's all right, honey. King Darius will find her." Blake picked Breezy up, cradling her in his arms. Breezy's tail wrapped around Blake's waist as they walked up to the Spirit Gate. Blake's hard eyes locked onto the entrance as he ordered the gate to take them to the Light Land. A shimmer of rainbows appeared before them, revealing the gateway. Blake walked through the gate as he whispered to Breezy that everything would be all right.

Gabriel watched the two disappear into his realm. Blake would take care of Gabriel's subject, but Gabriel had a feeling it was more than a duty for Blake to watch over Breezy. There was something more. Before Gabriel dove deeper into the thought, three forms in the sky caught his attention. It was his sun flock. They had been flying overhead, keeping an eye on the surrounding area, but now one of them broke formation to land in front of Gabriel.

"Your Lightness, the surrounding area is clear and the fog has blanketed the town in safety," Gabriel's first lieutenant reported. His name was Kiya, and he was the leader of the Swannards. He was just as old as Gabriel. Several hundred years ago Kiya struck an alliance with Gabriel to save his species from extinction. The Swannards were once thought of as a weak species, easily killed, but with Gabriel's help the Swannards became very lethal in the ways of combat. They earned a place in his royal court and became known as Gabriel's royal species.

"Good. Fly back to the castle and watch over the land. Let the other Swannards know what has happened and tell them to take to the skies. We are at war." Gabriel watched his first lieutenant's reaction. Kiya's black wings flared back and his bronzed eyes glowed with shock. Kiya was Gabriel's height, but unlike Gabriel's lean form, Kiya's build was very stocky, full of muscles. His black hair was in a Mohawk, the Swannard's standard style. His bronzed skin glowed a metallic silver color against his white armor. Kiya frowned, his black lips twisting into an upside down smile.

"And what about you, Your Lightness?" Kiya wasn't afraid to ask Gabriel of his plans or where Gabriel planned to go. It was Kiya's job to keep the Light King safe.

"I will watch over my brother's kingdom and make sure it is on high alert." Gabriel saw the disapproval on Kiya's face. Kiya was not a fan of the Dark Land and made sure that no Swannard ever entered the dark domain.

Obedient, Kiya nodded his head at Gabriel before taking off to the skies. He joined the other Swannards that were hovering above. Kiya gathered them into formation and then led the way back into Gabriel's realm to watch over the kingdom until his return. They disappeared in a flash of light, leaving Gabriel alone on the football field.

Gabriel let out a long sigh before walking toward the Spirit Gate. He stopped short, just a few feet away. Anxiety started to grow in the pit of his stomach. He did not like going into his brother's land—it was very dark and strange creatures lived within its realm. They did not like Gabriel, a thought that made him slowly smile as his anxiety transformed into a flutter of excitement.

"Take me to the Dark Land," Gabriel said as his smile intensified. Why couldn't he have a little bit of fun while he was seeing to his brother's duties? The dark spirits hated Gabriel, so why not make sure it stayed that way?

Gabriel lit himself up like the burning sun as a black hole appeared before him. Dark spirits hated the sun, so why not bring it to them? Gabriel laughed and walked through the gate. He promised to help his brother out, but he never promised that he would stop causing trouble between the light and dark spirits. He wanted to make sure the dark spirits knew they were beneath the light spirits, as it had always been. Gabriel's laughter was cut short as the gate quickly closed around him, sending him into the Dark Land of his brother's realm.

Chapter 22

NEIVA MOANED as she tried to open her eyes. Pain emanated up through her right arm. It felt like it was on fire. Neiva sat up frantic and opened her eyes to look at her arm. She pulled back her sleeve to reveal a shocking sight. The bracelet that Darius had given her was no longer on her arm. Instead she had a tattoo. It was exactly like the bracelet, a raven twisted around her arm, but instead of metal it was ink. The bright red rubies were transformed into diamonds, embedded in her skin like jewels in a royal necklace. The raven's eyes were the only rubies left, two tiny little jewels staring up at Neiva.

"Impressive," a musical voice sang.

"Who's there?" Neiva asked, her voice quivering with fear. She quickly stood up, whipping her head around to look at her surroundings. She was in a cell. Rusted iron bars lined the front of the cell, while rocks cordoned off the rest of the space. Several lanterns lined the rocky wall, brightening the area around Neiva. She couldn't see anything beyond her prison bars, only blackness.

Neiva backed up against the rocky wall behind her. All of the pain in her arm was forgotten as she tried to see where her captor stood. Her crystal wasn't tingling; in fact, Neiva couldn't feel anything. She was no longer connected to Darius or even Riley. Where was she and who had captured her?

"Ah, so many questions, my dear. Let's solve that problem. What would you like to ask me first?"

A figure materialized out of the wall to Neiva's left. She had a strong shadowy, purple aura of power around her. It was as if it pulsated with life, sucking the air out of the room causing Neiva to gulp in more oxygen to fill her lungs.

The woman's appearance was stunning. She had dark red hair loosely twisted up on the back of her head. Metal spikes sporadically poked out of the woman's hair, resembling knives that were four inches long. Metallic golden eye shadow was artistically drawn around the woman's eyes, which were outlined with thick black liner that curved up and beyond the woman's eye sockets. The golden shadow and black eyeliner brightened the woman's eyes, bringing out her golden irises that held immense knowledge. The whites of her eyes were black, but not the same black as Sasha's eyes. This black was the oily substance like the Soul Eaters that hunted the group. It moved around as if it were alive, living in the woman's eyes. Neiva shuddered at the alien-like creature before her.

A smile formed on the woman's golden lips, revealing sharp incisors both on her top and bottom row of teeth. Golden glitter littered her neck, leaving a sprinkled pathway down her throat and onto her chest. She wore a form-fitting, long-sleeved black dress lined in gold. The neckline was open, revealing cleavage that left Neiva blushing. A large ruby rested on her chest with a thick golden chain wrapped around it. A golden belt hung loosely around her waist with threads of gold hanging off her right hip. The dress fell around the woman's feet in waves with a small train trailing behind her.

Neiva was too shocked to say anything as the woman stopped in front of her. The woman reached her slender arms out revealing delicate hands etched with golden paint. Long fingers with golden claws gently grabbed Neiva's face, turning her head from side to side as if she were inspecting Neiva for purchase.

After scanning Neiva from top to bottom, the woman let go of her. "My, my, you are a pretty little princess, aren't you?"

"Who are you? What do . . . you want . . . from me?" Neiva stammered as she placed her hands on the wall behind her. The woman looked strangely familiar.

A laugh escaped her lips. She slowly turned her back toward Neiva to walk toward the cell door. The woman's dress was backless. The same spikes that were in the woman's hair fell down her back like scales on a dragon. She abruptly turned around with narrowed eyes.

"I am older then the earth itself; I come from a species that was thrust into this prison of despair centuries ago. I am Aria." The woman's voice had suddenly turned dark and threatening. She slowly started walking along the iron bars, raking her claws against them. She stopped just short of the rocky wall to turn her attention back to Neiva.

"What do you want from me?" Neiva mustered the courage to ask Aria again. Intense fear gripped Neiva. She didn't want to make the woman upset.

"Ah, I see Your Darkness has not told you everything." Aria brought her hand to her chin, staring intently at Neiva as if contemplating something. "He likes to follow the rules. How interesting. Well, I guess I can play along with him."

"What do you mean?" Neiva asked, sensing that Aria knew more than she revealed.

"Ah, but what would be the point in telling you everything? Instead I can watch you struggle on your journey to your awakening. You know what the awakening is now, don't you?" Aria raised an eyebrow at Neiva.

"Something to do with my powers?" Neiva wasn't sure. There was so much information given to her at one time that it was hard to assimilate everything.

"Spirits follow a set of rules, and one of those rules is not to interfere with a young spirit's awakening. Initiates must take that journey on their own. The young spirit can seek guidance in training, but only pertaining to their powers." Aria waited for Neiva to ask another question, but when Neiva kept quiet, Aria decided it was time to make her lethal move.

Aria walked over to stand next to Neiva. Aria held up her hand to point her golden claw at the wall out of which she had just materialized. Images started to pop up on its rocky surface, as if it were a high-definition television.

"I know you are wondering why I am after you." Aria turned her alien eyes upon Neiva. Her long, thick eyelashes slowly closed and opened as she paused briefly before continuing her explanation. "Power. It's the ultimate source that any creature is after, and, my dear Neiva, you're one of the most powerful creatures on this planet. You're a part of both cultures, spirit and Eskimo."

"But what am I?" Neiva turned her earnest eyes on Aria, searching Aria's alien eyes for answers, immediately realizing she would get none.

"You see the images on the wall, Neiva? I want you to pay close attention because I don't think you will want to miss this."

Aria turned Neiva to face the rocky wall. An image of two people popped up onto the screen. It was of a man and woman on a small airplane. It looked as if they were sightseeing, because they had their binoculars in their hands as they were excitedly talking to each other. Neiva instantly recognized the couple as sound flooded into the cell.

"I wish Neiva were here." Neiva's mother smiled as she glanced out the window. Her long black hair was pulled back into a ponytail then wrapped into a bun at the top of her head. Her brown eyes sparkled when she looked back at Neiva's father.

"Me too," Neiva's father agreed, his smile brightening up his olive skin.

Her parents laughed and cracked jokes at one another as the pilot pointed out something. The smiles on their faces caused Neiva's chest to hurt. She missed her parents dearly and wished she could be with them.

Suddenly there was a loud bang causing her parents to scream in response. Smoke poured into the cabin as the plane took a nosedive. The pilot was on the radio making a Mayday call back to the control tower. They were going down. Her parents' screams pierced the air as the image switched over to a news anchor.

"Breaking news, a sightseeing airplane just south of Anchorage has been missing for over an hour. A Mayday was received just before the plane disappeared. Search and rescue is still looking for the wreckage and any survivors. We will keep you updated as this story unfolds."

"NOOOOOOO!!!" Neiva screamed as she fell to the floor, her heart breaking, her world falling apart. Tears poured out of her eyes as she turned to hit the mad woman standing next to her. "Why? They did nothing to you!"

"Oh, but they have. They are a distraction and would hinder your growth, my dear. But don't you find it funny that they're still in Alaska and never left for Europe?" Aria paused as she jerked Neiva back to her feet.

"I wanted to show you what I am capable of." The image switched again to reveal Grams lying in a hospital bed. Her head was wrapped in bandages as well as her right arm. She was hooked up to several machines and a breathing tube. Nate sat next to her, his head bent down as he listened to his father, Mike.

"I don't know what happened," Mike began, totally confused. "She was sitting in the office, helping me out with my paperwork and going through the bills. There must have been a leak in the pipes, because the ceiling suddenly caved in on her, destroying the whole office. It took us several minutes to get her out. She was unconscious and suffered a severe head wound." Mike placed his head into his giant hands, as he tried to hold back the tears. "She's always been like a second mother to me. I don't know what I would do without her."

"Grams!" Neiva screamed, almost falling to the floor but Aria kept her up.

"Know this, Neiva: Your loved ones aren't safe. No one is safe."

Aria grabbed Neiva's neck and tilted her head up to watch the next image. The image showed a fiery pit miles below the earth. There was a staircase leading into the pit with several demons of all colors and sizes surrounding it. In the middle of the demons stood a powerful figure that was black as the night. Out of his head curved giant horns, which resembled the horns of a bull. Red eyes glowed bright as the figure carried Viv down the steps. The creature's giant arms had the same tattoos as Viv, glowing like lava.

"Fires of Birth, heal Vivian Blackheart. As her father, I submit her body and powers to the earth. Please bring her back to us," Viv's father asked as he lowered his daughter into the fiery lake. Viv's gray, lifeless body floated across the burning surface for several seconds before slowly sinking into its fiery depths.

A beautiful woman resembling an older version of Viv walked down the stairs to stand next to Viv's father. The woman looked strikingly human. She had tan olive skin with long black hair down to her waist. She wore a white dress that was wrapped around her body like a toga. Bright red tears trickled down her cheeks as she placed a hand on Viv's father's shoulder.

"Will she heal, husband?" Viv's mother laid her head on her husband's shoulder.

"I am not sure, Chloe. Her life force was very low, almost gone," he said sadly as he helped his wife up the stairs and into the darkness.

The picture faded, leaving the wall as it was before—nothing but a rocky surface. Aria let go of Neiva to watch her crumble to the ground. More tears of despair flowed down Neiva's face, and she screamed in agony.

"You're taking everything away from me that I cherish!" Neiva screamed in anguish. The pain was unbearable; she felt like she was dying inside.

"You must be quiet, my dear. You don't want to wake the others." Aria's lips formed into a cruel smile as she glanced out the cell's bars.

Through her own cries, Neiva suddenly heard a whimper coming from somewhere beyond her own cell. Neiva tried to clear her eyes of the relentless tears to see if she could find the source of that whimper. Suddenly a bright red glow appeared in the cell before her, illuminating the bars and part of the hallway. Neiva saw a slender hand with red nails reach through the cell's bars as if asking for help. Strangely, the hand looked similar to Neiva's own hand, but before she could look harder, Aria zapped the hand back into the cell. The light suddenly dimmed and silence reclaimed the air.

"Now see, Neiva? You're being too loud." Aria brought her hand back and smacked Neiva across the cheek, leaving a red handprint.

Neiva's eyes filled back up with more tears. She brought her hand up to her cheek and gave Aria a hard stare. Anger filled Neiva's heart, replacing the pain and loss she had felt only moments before. Heat coursed through her veins, while her ears were filled with a roaring sound. Her eyes lit up like silver flames, casting gray shadows all over Aria's face.

Aria's alien eyes glowed with excitement as she watched Neiva's eyes radiate brighter, resembling a lighthouse on a stormy night. The crystal on Neiva's forehead began to glow in a variety of colors as she stood up. "That's it, Neiva. Feel the anger in your heart. Let the beast of hatred drive out the pain of loss."

Aria got up to stand next to Neiva. "Hatred is all you will know, Neiva. Embrace it."

Silver flames ignited along Neiva's outer arms. The tattoo on her arm started to glow an intense red, the diamonds turning back into their original rubies. The bracelet sent shock waves that pulsated throughout Neiva's body, causing the hate to decrease in volume. A voice filled Neiva's head full of passion and safety.

Neiva, I am coming for you. Darius's voice was very weak, but it broke the trance Neiva was falling under and quelled the hatred brewing in her heart.

The bright lights suddenly extinguished within Neiva's eyes, transforming them back into their normal soft gray color. The flames disappeared along Neiva's arm, leaving the bracelet shining in its aftermath. Neiva blinked several times before focusing her vision on Aria's shocked face.

"No! How did you break the spell?" Aria cried as droplets of oil began to seep out of her eyes. She raised her right index finger to catch the droplets that were now trickling down her pale cheeks. Once Aria had caught a decent amount of droplets on her fingertip, she threw her arm toward the ground, sending the droplets in all directions. When the droplets hit the ground they began to sizzle and boil. The oil slowly began to rise, morphing into Soul Eaters with huge mouths and sharp teeth. When the creatures reached their full height, they began to surround Neiva, cornering her against the rocky wall.

"I'm disappointed in you, Neiva. You were supposed to succumb to your hatred, allowing your powers to intensify. Somehow you broke that spell, and, sadly, I will have to encase you inside one of my minions as punishment." Aria glanced at her subjects, who had just stopped short of Neiva to form a barrier around her.

"Have a nice sleep, dear. I will wake you up in several weeks to see how you're progressing," Aria whispered as she sent a kiss off in Neiva's direction. She gave Neiva a wink before disappearing through the wall, leaving a trail of golden dust and oil behind her.

As the woman disappeared, Neiva suddenly realized who she reminded her of. The red hair and flawless skin. Her features were the same as the woman who had sacrificed herself. Shock filled her soul. The woman was Darius and Gabriel's mother.

Neiva's wide eyes turned to the Soul Eaters. They hissed and their mouths hung open as they slowly drew their bodies together. They merged their forms into one huge Soul Eater, towering over Neiva. The giant had to bend its body so its head wouldn't hit the ceiling. It stooped over Neiva's head, ready to devour her at any second.

Neiva began to scream as the single Soul Eater moved to ensnare her within its jaws. Just when its mouth was a foot away from Neiva's head, black shadowy tentacles burst out of the rocky wall. They slammed into the Soul Eater's oily form, stopping it from swallowing Neiva whole. The shadowy tentacles intertwined themselves around the Soul Eater as it hissed in protest. Muscular arms materialized out of the shadows to wrap themselves protectively around Neiva. Darius's gentle voice whispered in her ear, telling her she was safe and that he had her in his arms and would never let go. The smell of forest and lavender engulfed Neiva as her mind slowly drifted off into sleep and the shadows embraced her, taking Neiva to safety. A powerful scream from Aria shook the cell as the shadows disappeared into the night.

Chapter 23

A CONSTANT BEEPING sound woke Neiva. She was groggy at first, but as she blinked, her eyes opened and she realized she was in a hospital room. She glanced down at her shoulder to see it was wrapped tightly in a white bandage. She had totally forgotten about the tusk that had knocked her down during the fight in the football field. It hadn't hurt when she was captured and it didn't even hurt now.

"It's just bruised," Nate said in a gentle voice that surprised Neiva. He was sitting on the other side of the room, next to a bed where Neiva's grandmother rested. "You heal fast."

Neiva quickly jumped out of bed to rush to her grandmother's side. Dark purple bruises peeked out of the bandage wrapped around her head. Breathing tubes covered her mouth as the machine pumped oxygen into her lungs.

"She hasn't changed in the last twenty-four hours," Nate said as a tear trickled down his cheek. He grabbed Neiva's hand to make sure he wasn't hallucinating. He needed to know that she was there.

"How long have I been gone?" Neiva asked as she squeezed Nate's hand, reassuring him that she was alive.

"Two days, Neiva. Two days, then suddenly you appeared

out of the shadows and dropped into the hospital bed next to your grandmother." Nate let go of Neiva's hand to point at the bed where Neiva had just been.

"My parents . . . ?" Neiva asked, too scared to finish her sentence. She wanted to know if the authorities had found them. Were they alive? Neiva's heart accelerated in pain as she waited for Nate's answer.

Nate's eyes filled with sadness as he looked into Neiva's gray eyes. "They're still missing. I'm so sorry."

A whimper escaped Neiva as she sat down on the armrest of Nate's chair. Tears formed in her eyes as she hyperventilated, trying to breathe but not succeeding.

"Why weren't they in Europe?" Neiva gasped.

"I don't know, Neiva! But they'll be all right. They're Alaskan natives, and you know Grams taught your mom how to live off the land and survive. She's prepared for any situation." Nate paused to rub Neiva's back. "They wouldn't leave you here alone. You know deep down in your heart that they're still alive."

Neiva's breath slowed as her heart lifted in hope. Nate was right. She would know when her parents died. It was an Eskimo legend among the natives. It was said a raven would perch on your windowsill the night a loved one died. The raven would stay there until the departing soul came to bid farewell to his or her family. It was believed that once souls pass, they visit their loved ones one last time before crossing over into the northern lights. Then they would be guided by the raven into the afterlife. Neiva had not been visited by her parents' souls, a sure sign that they were still alive. She had a feeling they would come back to her alive.

"Yes, Mom is always prepared for the worst." Neiva managed a weak smile, silently thanking Nate for his positive thinking.

"I haven't heard anything about Viv." Sadness filled Nate's voice as he stared off into space. "I knew you were going to ask."

"She is strong, stronger than all of us put together, Nate." Neiva ruffled Nate's ungelled hair. The sadness crept back into Neiva's heart as she climbed onto the bed to curl up against her grandmother's sleeping form. Warmth emanated off of her body, causing Neiva to have hope her grandmother would eventually wake up.

A COUPLE OF HOURS LATER, Neiva woke up to find Mike at her grandmother's side. His giant form was hunched over against the chair, his strong hands resting together in his lap. He was staring at the floor, lost in thoughts or memories.

Neiva slowly sat up. She glanced down at her grandmother, hoping to see any change in her, but there was none. With a sigh of regret, Neiva climbed off the bed and landed on the floor next to Mike.

"Feeling better?" Mike's brown eyes were rimmed in red, a sign that he hadn't been sleeping.

"I'm okay." Neiva glanced back at her grandmother and quickly asked, "Any word on my parents?"

"Not yet, but don't give up hope. Your father, my best friend, is very strong-willed. They will come back to you," Mike said. He stood up to give Neiva a hug. His large size swallowed Neiva up. When he let go of her, he inspected Neiva's shoulder.

"It's fine, Mike. It doesn't even hurt." Neiva proved it by moving her shoulder around without even wincing.

"Okay, but take it easy." Mike sat back down in the chair. He turned to look at her grandmother.

"I will. If it's okay with you, I think I will go back to the house and clean up." Neiva wanted a hot shower and nothing more than to curl up in her bed. She felt numb at the moment but knew the feeling of loss would hit her again, and Neiva wanted to be alone when it happened.

"Okay, dear. I will send Nate over once he finishes his shift at the shop. I will call you if I hear anything about your parents or if your grandmother's status changes at all."

Mike watched Neiva nod her head before she shuffled out the door, her form slouching in sadness.

Neiva walked out of the hospital to find her raven waiting for her. His eyes glowed with happiness at the sight of seeing her safe and alive. He cawed once before flying off the railing he was perched on. Riley transformed in a flash, and before Neiva knew it she was in his arms. His talons gently patted her back as the tears started to flow down Neiva's cheek. Riley's wings folded around her, giving her warmth and shelter from the cold. It looked as if winter had finally begun. Small snowflakes drifted down from the sky, slowly blanketing the ground in white powder.

Riley stepped back a few steps, but still kept Neiva shielded from the cold with his giant wings. "Everything will be all right, Neiva. Your family and friends are fighters just like you. We'll get through this."

The only response Neiva could give Riley was a slight nod. The dam that was holding back her emotions was about to break. She didn't know how much longer she could keep it together.

"Can you please take me home, Riley?"

Riley gave Neiva a long look before picking her up. He cradled her in his arms and brought her close to his warm bare chest. His wings burst out behind him, flapping once before he shot into the air. Any normal day, Neiva would have been thrilled to be among the clouds, but not today. She felt lost as she nestled against Riley's chest, ignoring the cold wind that whipped around her body.

Within minutes, Riley landed at the front door of her grandmother's house. He set Neiva down before opening the door for her. Before entering the house, she turned around and jumped back into Riley's arms. She hugged him with all her might, not wanting him to disappear.

"Please be careful. You've become a part of me. I don't want anything to happen to you, Riley," Neiva whispered. She backed up to see Riley's sapphire eyes sparkle with unshed tears.

A smile formed on his face as his heart filled with happiness from Neiva's words. She felt his emotions and the affection he had for her. Whatever worries Riley had about Neiva's feelings toward him disappeared.

"I promise," Riley said. Then he shot up into the air and shifted into the giant raven, circling high above Neiva before landing on top of an electrical pole across the street. He cawed once to let Neiva know he would be watching out for her safety.

Turning around, she walked into the house and slowly shut the door behind her. Leaning against the door, she listened to the eerie silence around her. Her grandmother was always in the kitchen cooking or making some sort of noise. She always welcomed Neiva home with a smile and a hug, always making sure to ask how Neiva's day had been. Not hearing Grams's voice or greeting brought tears back into her eyes.

Her heart became heavy as she ascended the stairs. She walked down the hallway and entered her room, too lost in thought to notice the destruction at first. But when she stepped on a piece of broken wood, Neiva jerked her head up to the shocking sight. Her room had been torn apart. There was nothing left. Her bed had been shredded into pieces, her desk broken in half, the mirror next to her closet was shattered, all of the pictures on her wall lay shredded on the floor, and part of her ceiling was ripped off, leaving a gaping hole open to the dark sky. Snowflakes slowly drifted into the room, sending chills down Neiva's back.

Instantly, Neiva noticed the broken tusk Mike had given her. It lay in three pieces on the ground next to the demolished desk. It was such a beautiful gift and now it was ruined. Neiva tried to maneuver around the wreckage, but stopped when broken pieces of wood stuck to her shoe. When Neiva bent down to throw it out of the way, she recognized the raven carved into the wood.

Neiva gasped as she looked at the wall above her bed. There was nothing left. The wall had a huge hole through it with black singe marks around its edges. Paulo was gone.

"No, not my little dream catcher," Neiva whimpered. She fell back to the floor, frantically searching for the shattered remnants of Paulo's form. She could only find part of his face and the shard of the carved raven she had stepped on. He was gone.

The floodgates broke open. Tears poured out of her eyes and her lip trembled. Her hands tightened around the remainder of Paulo's face, willing him back to life. Another soul lost.

Her family and friends were falling like flies because of her, because someone wanted her powers—powers she hadn't even known existed or cared about less than a week ago. Anger and grief collided as she threw her head back toward the sky and screamed. All of the pain she felt was thrown into the single scream, crying out to the heavens for her loved ones. Her anger subsided as the grief overtook her.

"Why?!" she sobbed uncontrollably, rocking back and forth with Paulo still in her hands. Neiva hadn't known Paulo very long, but he came to her as her protector, to watch over her and guard her. Now, he was gone.

She felt so alone. Her parents had disappeared and her grandmother lay unconscious in a hospital bed, while doctors were uncertain if she would ever wake up. No one knew if Viv would survive her injuries; and the evil witch, who wanted nothing more than Neiva's powers, took Chad's life and Austin's life, two innocent lives. Neiva believed this all happened because of her. The anger surged through her as she screamed again at the heavens, "WHY?!"

Emptiness started to eat its way through her heart. It slowly spread across her chest, making her body heavy and her limbs numb. She bent her head down, her sobs quieted, and her tears slowly dried. She didn't know who or what she was. Her world had suddenly changed in a blink of an eye.

She was no longer the carefree high school girl she once was; instead she was a struggling rookie warrior caught in a battle for power, and it was all over her. No one knew what she was or how she felt.

"I'm alone," Neiva whispered to herself as the last tear lingering on her eyelashes fell to the floor, disappearing into the snow that now formed around her shaking body.

Suddenly the smell of lavender and pine filled the air. Strong arms embraced Neiva, encasing her in warmth and happiness. Darius's voice filled her soul. She could feel his heartbeat when she leaned her head back against his chest. The loneliness was slowly slipping away with each breath Darius took. His words soothed the ache in her heart, making her feelings for him resurface and intensify.

"Neiva, I believe two souls can be destined for each other and they can overcome any obstacle that is standing in their way," Darius exclaimed, slowly letting go of her.

A flutter of butterflies formed in Neiva's stomach as she listened to Darius's words. She was lost in Darius's presence. Overcome with emotions and a strong yearning to kiss him, all other thoughts disappeared. The loneliness and anger seemed as if they had never existed.

Deep in thought, Neiva almost didn't feel Darius take the wooden pieces of Paulo out of her hands. He slowly replaced it with something light and cool to the touch, gently sliding his gloved fingertips against her hand as he slowly let go.

Not knowing what the object was, Neiva slowly looked down to see what lay in her hands. Shock overtook her mind as she stared at the object. Her breath suddenly stopped and her heartbeat accelerated as Neiva held Darius's mask in her hands. Its white surface shone like moonlight. The stars bedecking the side resembled broken glass sparkling fiercely. The mask was breathtaking.

"I want you to see who I am underneath this mask," Darius whispered. Soft lips grazed Neiva's ear, sending shivers up her spine.

Fear soon followed. This was it. This was the moment she had been wishing for. It had all started with the unknown feelings at their first meeting, then transformed into butterflies in her stomach at his presence. Neiva cared for him and wasn't afraid. Her feelings for him swiftly devoured any fear or unease, turning into excitement at what lay ahead. She didn't care what was behind the mask; it was the kind and protective soul she had instantly fallen in love with. He was the soul that would never leave her.

"Look up, Neiva," Darius whispered, sending a shiver of anticipation down Neiva's spine.

Neiva shut her eyes as she slowly lifted her head. The crystal in the middle of her forehead felt warm and soothing, giving Neiva a calm feeling throughout her body. It wasn't warning her but instead urging her on. Still she kept her eyes shut when Darius took her hands into his own.

"You're not alone, Neiva. You never will be," Darius whispered as he leaned forward, his lips meeting hers. The white light connecting them wrapped itself around them, encasing them in magic and love. Binding their hearts together, forever.

When he finally pulled away, the connection was still there, stronger than ever. "Now, please open your eyes, Neiva," he said softly.

Shock waves from the kiss coursed throughout her body, sending shivers of pleasure up her spine. Nothing mattered anymore but this soul that stood before her, this soul that would give up everything for her. He laid his heart out before her and would go to the ends of the earth to find her. He was hers and she was his. Nothing could break their connection or destroy their love.

With a deep breath, Neiva opened her eyes and gasped.

He was young and beautiful. Chiseled yet delicate, clean features formed his face. His sensuous red lips looked innocent, but full of passion and hunger. His skin was the color of moonlight, glowing warm and bright, chasing away the shadows and darkness. His hair was like the night sky sparkling with stars. Strands of black hair hung loosely around his face, framing his elfish cheekbones. His eyes, the color of dawn, stared back at her, full of love and passion. They were surrounded with thick long lashes so heavy they seemed to weigh his eyelids down.

Darius gently cupped Neiva's face, "I love you, Neiva. I will keep you safe. I will fight for you and I will die for you."

His gaze was full of love and promise. And Neiva knew she was safe and everything would be okay.

September 9:
I found my soul mate, my purpose. I've become one with the Darkness, for he has my heart. I was meant to come to this island to find my destiny and save this town. I am the legend the Eskimos prophesied. I am the descendant of the White Bear and an old soul on my final journey. I am the savior, and I am ready to fight. . . . I am the Blonde Eskimo.

"May you have warmth in your igloo,

oil in your lamp, and peace in your heart."

— ESKIMO PROVERB

ACKNOWLEDGEMENTS

This book would not exist without the help of so many people, including friends and family. Big thank you to Crystal Patriarche for believing in me and offering me the chance to bring my story to life. It took almost five years but we did it. Thank you to my editor, Wayne Parrish, for finding my voice and making my words make sense. To the amazing team of BookSparks and SparkPress, thank you for your hard work and for making this story available to all the young readers yearning for something new.

Thank you to my husband who helped me keep my sanity. You pushed me and helped me gain the courage to finish this book, even though there were times I wanted to quit. Without your support, this book wouldn't have been written. Thank you to my parents, who let me be creative and believed in my dreams. You are the best cheerleaders a daughter could ask for; even though at times I didn't want to listen, your wisdom always made sense. Thank you to my other half, my twin, who was my critique partner and flew on this journey with me. I can't wait to see what wonderful stories you have in store for us. Thank you to my family and friends who gave me wonderful support and spread the word about *Blonde Eskimo*.

Lastly, I would like to thank the readers, for giving this book a chance. I hope you enjoyed the story and that you found your spirit guide along the way. May they guide and protect you in this wonderful adventure known as life.

ABOUT SPARKPRESS

SparkPress is an independent boutique publisher delivering high-quality, entertaining, and engaging content that enhances readers' lives, with a special focus on female-driven work. We are proud of our catalog of both fiction and nonfiction titles, featuring authors who represent a wide array of genres, as well as our established, industry-wide reputation for innovative, creative, results-driven success in working with authors. SparkPress, a BookSparks imprint, is a division of SparkPoint Studio, LLC.

To learn more, visit us at gosparkpress.com.

ABOUT THE AUTHOR

DAVE KELLEY

KRISTEN HUNT, known as the desert Eskimo, lives in the sunny state of Arizona with her husband and two cats, Odin and Thor. She doesn't mind the 100-degree weather. Anything below 64 degrees is freezing. It's been years since she's traveled to Nome, Alaska, to visit her family. On her last trip, she was chased by a grizzly bear and never went back. She plans to one day visit, and maybe through her travels another story will be born. The legend of Alaska lives in her soul.

In her spare time, Kristen loves to read graphic novels, paint, watch movies, cosplay, and have tea parties with her friends. She is obsessed with unicorns and feels that everyone has a little magic inside of them.

Kristen's totem is the Raven.

SELECTED TITLES FROM SPARKPRESS

SparkPress is an independent boutique publisher delivering high-quality, entertaining, and engaging content that enhances readers' lives, with a special focus on female-driven work. Visit us at www.gosparkpress.com

The Revealed, by Jessica Hickam. $15, 978-1-94071-600-8. Lily Atwood lives in what used to be Washington, D.C. Her father is one of the most powerful men in the world, having been a vital part of rebuilding and reuniting humanity after the war that killed over five billion people. Now he's running to be one of its leaders.

Serenade, by Emily Kiebel. $15, 978-1-94071-604-6. After moving to Cape Cod after her father's death, Lorelei discovers her great-aunt and nieces are sirens, terrifying mythical creatures responsible for singing doomed sailors to their deaths. When she rescues a handsome sailor who was supposed to die at sea, the sirens vow that she must finish the job or faced grave consequences.

Red Sun, by Alane Adams. $17, 978-1-940716-24-4. Drawing on Norse mythology, The Red Sun follows a boy's journey to uncover the truth about his past in a magical realm called Orkney—a journey during which he has to overcome the simmering anger inside of him, learn to channel his growing magical powers, and find a way to forgive the father who left him behind.

Wendy Darling, by Colleen Oakes. $17, 978-1-94071-6-96-4. From the cobblestone streets of London to the fantastical world of Neverland, readers will love watching Wendy's journey as she grows from a girl into a woman, struggling with her love for two men, and realizes that Neverland, like her heart, is a wild place, teaming with dark secrets and dangerous obsessions.